Eden Lake

Jane Roper

Jane Roper

LAST LIGHT STUDIO

Boston

Last Light Studio
423 Brookline Ave. #324
Boston MA 02215
www.lastlightstudio.com

Printed in the United States of America

FIRST EDITION

Publisher's Cataloging-in-Publication
    Roper, Jane.
        Eden Lake / Jane Roper.
        p. cm.
        LCCN 2011921154
        ISBN-13: 9780982708415
        ISBN-10: 0982708416

    1. Camps--Maine--Fiction. 2. Summer--Maine--Fiction.
    3. Family vacations--Maine--Fiction. 4. Families--
    Fiction. 5. Adultery--Fiction. 6. Maine--Fiction.
    7. Bildungsromans, American.   I. Title.

        PS3618.O74E34 2011   813'.6
                                    QBI11-600036

Interior design by Joel Friedlander
www.TheBookDesigner.com

For my parents

Eric

JUST BEFORE NOON ON the morning after Memorial Day, Eric filled the tank of the John Deere, started the engine and rolled out of the barn into broad sunlight. He'd mowed just a week before, but already the grass was too long again—shaggy and soft and starting to bend under its own weight. He'd never seen it grow this fast, this early. This spring had been the mildest in years. The mud had come and gone sooner, as had the black flies. By the second week of May the oaks along the drive, always the last to bud, were already sprouting tender leaves. Everything was rushing toward summer.

Eric and his father and Gail, plus Doug Kotch, an old friend of his father's from Wesleyan, and the Crary brothers from down the road, had spent the long weekend waking the property up. They dragged the docks back into the lake and pulled the racks of canoes out of the boathouse. They swept the dead leaves and pine needles off the tennis courts and strung up the nets. They tossed all two hundred vinyl-covered foam mattresses down from the loft over the infirmary, loaded them onto the bed of the pickup twenty at a time, and distributed them to each of the cabins.

They worked briskly and took long breaks between jobs, sitting in the sun on the deck behind the dining hall, drinking from pottery mugs of coffee in the mornings and cans of beer in the afternoons. Then, on Monday, after Doug had left and Gail had gone into the office to do paperwork, Eric and his father traded their work boots for sneakers and tried out the brand new climbing wall behind the soccer field, at the base of the meadow that climbed the hill to the property line. Eric went first, and only halfway up the wall; he could tell his father was champing at the bit. Then they switched and Eric belayed his father.

"This is excellent!" Clay said over and over again as he climbed. Each time he attained another few feet of height, got steady on another foothold, he'd pause and grin down at Eric, holding the rope, and say it: "EX-cellent!"

Eric was alone on the property now. His father and Gail had left that morning, headed up to Bar Harbor in the Cessna for a quick, romantic getaway before the work of getting ready for the summer began in earnest. Eric had his own plans. Besides the mowing, which could take a good two hours start to finish, he intended to put a coat of polyurethane on the floor of the rec. hall. He had his evening planned out, too: a pizza and a couple of videos from the General Store. After that, if he wasn't too tired, he'd see if any of his friends—real or virtual—were online and felt like chatting. He kept in touch with a couple of people back at UMass this way.

Officially, he hadn't dropped out of school; he was just taking time off. But in his heart he knew he wasn't going back. Living in a tiny dorm room, sitting in crowded lecture halls where he had to strain to see the professor, eating bad cafeteria food and racking his brain to think about what he'd do after graduation, constantly coming up blank—why would he choose that, when he could choose Eden Lake instead?

He mowed the lawn around the farmhouse first, careful not to get too close to the tiger lilies alongside the house. Next, he went around back and did the main lawn, which stretched from the gravel drive to the west of the farmhouse all the way across to the rec. hall and the arts and crafts buildings nestled in the strip of thinned pine forest that backed up to the lake.

As he was starting toward the soccer field he noticed that the gas gauge was already down to half a tank, which concerned him. He shouldn't be burning fuel that fast. He brought the tractor back around to the barn to take a look. As he was inspecting the tank—sure enough, there was a good-sized leak along the seam—he heard the distant rumble of a car coming down the road.

Even now, after all these years, whenever he heard that sound, his first instinct was to run and dive behind the lilac bushes by the mailbox. It was a pointless game he used to play when he was a kid: he'd stand by the side of the dirt road listening for cars, which were rare, and waiting until the last possible second to get behind the bushes, down on his belly, so he wouldn't be seen. He could do it for hours and never get bored. It was the anticipation—the noise of the car so distant at first that you might mistake it for the wind, growing steadily louder and closer, until you could hear the rubber of the tires peeling up from the dirt and the stones kicking up against the chassis. And then the thrilling, panicked knowledge that you *must not* let the driver see you. Sometimes he imagined the driver (who, in Eric's mind wasn't necessarily *driving,* just *advancing,* fast and

3

ominous) was Darth Vader, other times a Ringwraith or a Nazi. Sometimes it was just a generic, imagined bad guy. In any case, Eric had to hide in time, or he was doomed. *Doomed!*

As he was positioning an old rubber basin under the tank to catch the last of the leaking gas, the approaching car finally turned and crunched up the driveway. Eric saw, to his momentary amusement, that the driver was something like an actual bad guy: a Maine state trooper. His first thought was that he must have forgotten to pay a speeding ticket. He was constantly getting pulled over—one of the drawbacks of being young, long-haired and bearded in rural Maine.

But when the trooper—paunchy, gentle-faced, white-haired—got out of the car, he took his ranger's hat off and held it against his chest, reverent, and Eric knew that this wasn't about a ticket. "Pardon me, sir," the trooper said. "I'm looking for Eric Perry."

"Perryweiss," Eric said, standing. He was used to people getting it wrong, this gryphon-like fusion of his parents' names. "That's me."

The trooper gathered up his breath as if he was about to say something. Then he narrowed his eyes and scanned the farmhouse and its two attached barns. "So this is a summer camp, huh? I expected tents and totem poles and things. Real rustic."

"It used to be a sheep farm," Eric said.

The trooper nodded. "Mr. Perry," he said, and took a step forward.

"Perryweiss." Eric took a step backward.

The trooper clasped his hat to his chest with both hands now. "Were you aware that your father and mother were out in their plane today?" He glanced up at the sky, as if they might

4

be passing overhead at that moment.

Eric nodded, dread creeping into his belly. "Gail's my step-mother, actually."

"Stepmother," the trooper said. "Well, son, I'm real sorry to have to tell you this, but their plane went down, just west of Belfast. Appears to be a mechanical failure of some kind." He took another step forward, and this time Eric didn't move. "I'm afraid they didn't survive."

Eric said nothing. He'd heard the man's words, but they hung in his mind unconnected with any meaning.

"It was instantaneous. They most likely didn't suffer."

Eric looked down at the ground. Blades of cut grass lay like crystal shards, strewn in countless random angles over the shortened lawn. He let his eyes blur, then close, and in his mind he saw his father's face as it had been that morning just before he left, smiling, lifted with almost boyish glee: "Beautiful day to fly away," he'd said, rubbing his hands together in front of him. Then, glancing back at Gail, as if he knew she wouldn't approve of his asking, "You sure you don't want to come?"

Jude

JUDE DRAINED THE LAST of her martini, rolled the olive around in her mouth for a few seconds and spit it back into the glass. She smiled at Mitch, who was watching. "I know. Aren't I charming?"

"You don't like olives?"

"A little. But not enough to actually eat them."

He laughed. "Get yourself another drink. I'm still working on this one." He lifted his glass of whiskey from the bar.

"Are you trying to get me drunk?"

He just smiled down into his glass, and she wondered if she'd gone too far.

Once again, it was just the two of them. Phil, the Technical Director, and his grunts had left almost half an hour ago, Courtney and Jess soon after. Jude wondered if people talked about the fact that she and Mitch always ended up alone together at these outings. It wasn't like they planned it, or talked about it ahead of time. But they both knew. They both made sure to let it happen.

She knew it was stupid. And dangerous. He was married, for one thing. Not particularly happy in his marriage, from what she could tell, but married nonetheless, with a five-year-old son. And he was forty-three, which meant that when she was born, he was a senior in high school. She tried not to think about this too much, lest the whole thing start to seem disgustingly Freudian, which it most definitely wasn't.

The worst thing was the fact that as Executive Director of the theater, Mitch was, technically speaking, her boss. Not that he supervised her directly (that would be Debbie, the Marketing and Fundraising Director) or that she had that much interaction with him on a day-to-day basis. But still.

The whole thing was just wrong. And yet, they'd never actually let that final wall come down. They'd never admitted they were attracted to each other, never kissed. There were times when Jude still wondered if maybe it was all in her head; if he just saw her as a precocious kid and enjoyed spending time with her, but felt nothing more than an innocent, surface-level attraction. Other times, though, like tonight—the way he'd told her to get another drink in that low, authoritative voice, and how he'd smiled at her when he first came into the bar, like she was the one he'd really come to see—she had to wonder.

She ordered another martini.

"With extra olives," Mitch called to the bartender.

"No!"

Mitch laughed. Jude loved the way lines rippled out from around his eyes and mouth when he did, like water hit by raindrops.

"So," he said, "do you actually like martinis, or do you drink them in an ironic, retro sort of way? To go along with the swing dancing and the Sinatra records and whatever else youse kids are into these days?" He liked to poke fun at himself with her, pretending he was ancient and out of touch. But he still went to rock concerts and occasionally smoked pot. He wore black cowboy boots and jeans to work most days. Not exactly hip, but hardly geriatric.

Jude rolled her eyes. "I do not swing dance."

"No?"

"No. I slam dance." This wasn't actually true, but it was fun to say.

"Anika tried to get me to take swing dancing lessons a few months back," Mitch said. "But I said no way. She's actually somewhat graceful. I'm not. It would have been a disaster."

Jude was glad that, just then, the bartender set her drink in front of her, so she had something to react to instead of the mention of Mitch's wife. He rarely brought his family up, but whenever he did, the air seemed to congeal between them and Jude felt a twist of shame. She was never quite sure if he was trying to remind her that he was married or remind himself.

Mitch got up and took a couple of menus from a stack at the end of the bar. "Want to get some dinner?" He offered Jude a menu. "I'm not in any hurry to go if you're not."

Jude hesitated for a moment. Dinner was new territory. They'd ordered appetizers before, but never actual food. She hoped he wouldn't suggest that they move to a table. She hoped he would.

"Maybe I'll just get an appetizer or something." She scanned the menu, seeing but not quite registering the words.

As she was trying for the third or fourth time to read the description of one of the appetizers—something with arti-choke hearts and goat cheese—her cell phone rang in her bag.

She dug for it and glanced at the name on the screen: Eric. She'd left him a message a few days earlier, just calling to say hello. He never took the initiative to call her, but eventually, usually, he called her back when she did.

"Do you need to take that?" Mitch asked.

"No, just my brother." She silenced the ringer and dropped the phone back into her bag.

"The one in Washington or the one on the farm?"

"It's not a farm," Jude said. "It's a summer camp."

"I know, but it's much more fun to picture you as a little Rebecca of Sunnybrook Farm. Feeding chickens. Baking apple pies with your mother. Your hair in pigtails." He made fists at his ears.

"Hardly," Jude said. Though actually, he wasn't that far off. There were chickens, and apple pies. But she never wore pigtails, just braids. And only until she was eight or nine, when her hair started getting too thick and unruly to be tamed into plaits and elastics and she started wearing it loose instead.

Mitch leaned his head against his fist. "Come on, tell me about Jude from Maine. Living off the land. Making daisy chains. Back before New York corrupted you."

Jude could smell the leather of his jacket on the back of his barstool. And something else; something piney and metallic, dulled by a musky sweetness. His skin.

Something was going to happen tonight.

She gripped the edges of her menu. "I don't know what to get. Why do restaurants have to put goat cheese in every fucking thing on the menu these days? I mean, there's goat cheese on the nachos for Christ's sake."

Her phone rang again. She groaned and fumbled to find it

in her bag. "Sorry."

"If he's calling again, maybe there's something wrong. You should answer it."

But a glance at the phone's screen revealed that it wasn't Eric calling again; it was her mother.

"It'll just be a second," Jude said.

"Judie." Her mother's voice was dry and scraped. Jude's first thought was that she must be having an exacerbation of her MS; they made her voice get that way sometimes.

"Are you OK?"

"Yes. I mean, no. No. Listen, Judie. We're all here together in Camden. Eric and me, and Aura."

Aura was Gail's daughter. She was a few years older than Jude, the result of some free-love fling Gail had way back when. Last Jude heard she was living in Boston, working as a secretary at some big financial firm. She couldn't imagine what would bring her to her mother's house.

"What's going on?" Jude asked. "Is something wrong?" She glanced up at Mitch, who nodded in understanding, took his own phone from his jacket pocket and slipped away. "Mom?"

"Oh, baby," her mother began. Her voice was strung with pain.

After Jude had heard all there was to hear, she let the phone drop into her bag and made her way toward the exit, past Mitch on the phone, telling his wife he was working late.

The last cold words she'd ever spoken to her father, three years earlier at her college graduation, thudded back and forth between her ears, pounding harder and louder until she was sure everyone in the restaurant could hear them: "I just don't want you in my life anymore, Dad. Not now and maybe not ever."

Abe

"Hello?"

No answer.

"Hello? Anybody here?"

Abe stood up from his desk, scanning the other cubicles for tops of heads, looking for lights on in the offices around the perimeter. Nothing. Once again, he was the last one out. He looked at his watch: almost seven.

He'd spent the last—was it possible?—two and a half hours in front of his computer, tweaking the program for Friday's awards banquet, making sure everything was just right. The banquet was AfterStart's second biggest event of the year—the biggest being the annual fundraising gala—where they honored the teachers, volunteers and students in their after-school programs throughout the District. And it was Abe's baby: his first major project since he'd come on board two months ago.

"Trial by fire, huh?" everyone had said when he started, knowing he had to start planning the event right away, on top of all his other duties—coordinating volunteers, serving as a liaison between the teachers and the central office, planning inter-school activities. Duties that were completely new to him and that he wasn't completely confident he had the experience or organizational skills to pull off.

But somehow he was managing to do all right. Trial by fire, sure. The job wasn't easy, but he was starting to get the hang of it. And at some point, he wasn't quite sure when, he'd stopped feeling like the new guy. He'd slipped into the comfort of easy banter with his co-workers and no longer felt like he was faking it when he talked to principals or teachers on the phone, or showed up at a program site and joked around with the kids. At one of the programs he'd visited a couple of weeks ago, at a middle school in Marshall Heights, there was a group of seventh-grade girls he'd played a quick, goofy game of basketball with who now apparently asked their counselors every day when "the guy from the office with the crazy name" was coming back.

And he was doing good work. It didn't take a social scientist to see the impact after-school programs could have: reducing crime and truancy rates, building kids' self-esteem, helping them become responsible, motivated young adults. There was nothing complicated or political or paternalistic about it. It was pure.

For the first time in his life, Abe felt like he might have landed somewhere he could stay for more than just a year or two.

The fact that he was starting to get over Jess also contributed to his new and improved state of mind, no doubt. Thinking about her no longer summoned that dull ache of loneliness and regret in his gut. In fact, this morning when he stopped in at the coffee shop for his tall latte, he'd actually flirted with the girl behind the counter—the one with the nose ring and the dark hair piled messily on top of her head, stuck through with chopsticks. "DiDi" her nametag said. She didn't appear to be wearing a bra.

It wasn't like he hadn't noticed anyone of the opposite sex since the breakup. But this was the first time he'd allowed himself to act on it. His self-imposed penance of celibacy had apparently run its course. Tomorrow, maybe, he'd go down for a late morning coffee when the shop wasn't too busy and talk to her again. Find out if she was single.

He saved the program files to disk a final time to be safe, turned off the lights, and headed out. A quick trip back to his desk, to the piece of paper buried in his second desk drawer with the alarm code on it—why couldn't he manage to retain four simple digits?—and he was out of there, trailing his fingertips along the exposed brick in the stairwell, jumping the bottom two steps and pushing against the aluminum bar of the door with two hands: click, clunk, swish.

Outside it was still light, the sky bright blue, the shadows sharp on the sidewalk. The air was cool at the edges, and it felt almost like a summer evening in Maine, except for the tang of asphalt and car exhaust in the air. There wouldn't be many more evenings like this. Soon, humidity would engulf the city and stay put until September, swampy and stagnant. It was the one thing Abe couldn't stand about living in DC.

But right now, even the prospect of the humidity didn't seem so bad. With the summer came barbecues. After work beers. Late-night league soccer games under the lights. Not to mention lots of bare limbs and cleavage on display. The whole city was a little frisky: tales of Oval Office blow jobs dominating the airwaves, baby boomers popping Viagra, everyone feeling irrationally exuberant.

He slowed down as he passed the coffee shop to see if the girl was still there, then remembered the hour and realized that of course she wouldn't be. But tomorrow she would. He'd talk to her. He'd tell her what he did for a living, and she'd melt: *you work for an organization that helps inner city kids? Wow. That's really great.*

"What an asshole I am," he murmured to himself, smiling. A middle aged woman in a sari who happened to be passing him at that moment, walking a pair of Dachshunds, smiled back.

He stopped into Kinko's to drop off the disk and was assured that the programs would be ready—copied, folded, stapled, and ready to go—by Thursday afternoon at the latest. Perfect. His next stop was Rico's Taqueria, just around the corner from his building: one super chicken burrito for himself and one for his roommate, Ben, who never turned down food when it was offered.

He trotted up the two flights to their apartment, the burritos a warm, aromatic bundle under his arm. Ben's keys were on the phone table inside the door, but the apartment was quiet, which was strange. Ben almost always cranked Pearl Jam or Jane's Addiction when he was here. And he almost always toked up after he got home from his job on the hill—he worked for a Democratic congressman from Georgia—fogging the apartment with fine, sweet smoke. But tonight the air was clear.

"Ben?" said Abe. "You here, man?" He went into the kitchen and opened the fridge to see if there was any beer. A lone Corona stood next to the orange juice. As Abe was opening it, Ben shuffled into the kitchen, looking like he'd just woken up. He'd changed out of his work clothes into knee-length shorts, flip-flops and a Phish T-shirt. His hair fanned out behind his head, flattened, like a little halo.

"Good morning, sunshine," said Abe. "I got you a burrito if you want it. Should I go on a beer run? This is the last one."

"Thanks," Ben said, sitting down at the table. "I'm not really hungry."

"So, let's spark one up." Abe didn't smoke nearly as often as he used to, but every once in awhile, when the mood was right and he was feeling good, he indulged. "It's the perfect night for a little doobage."

Ben didn't even crack a smile. "Listen, Abe, man, your mom called a few minutes ago."

"Yeah, OK…" Abe talked to her every couple of weeks, usually on Sunday night, but it wasn't unheard of for her to call during the week.

Ben wagged his hand at Abe like he was missing the point. "You need to call her back, like right away. It's an emergency."

"Is she all right?" Abe's first thought was that she might have had a fall or accident of some sort, connected to her MS. Her symptoms, which consisted primarily of fatigue and trouble walking, came and went. "Relapsing-remitting" they called it, but each time, it seemed, she recovered a little less fully. The last time he'd gone to Maine, over Christmas, he and Eric had helped her move her bed downstairs, to the study off the living room, so she wouldn't have to go up and down the stairs so much.

"She is, yeah," Ben said. "It's—it was something else. You should just call her." His palms rested unnaturally on the kitchen table. He wouldn't make eye contact.

"Jesus, Ben, what is it? Did she tell you?"

Ben's mouth opened, then shut. "She should tell you. Not me."

Abe slammed his beer bottle against the counter and held it there. "For fuck's sake, what's going on?"

After a pause, Ben looked up. His lips were childishly parted. "Your dad was in a plane crash," he said.

"A plane crash."

Ben nodded, too slowly for it to be anything but the worst. "His plane, the Cessna. Him and his wife."

Abe said nothing. The glass of the bottle, where his hand held it, had become the exact same temperature as his skin. It was as if he wasn't holding anything at all.

Ben stood. "If there's anything I can do…"

Abe nodded, but couldn't make himself speak. He let go of the bottle in his hand and stared at it for a few seconds, then swept it onto the kitchen floor with one swift motion. To his disappointment, it didn't break. The linoleum was too forgiving. Instead, it spun around and around, spewing foam in all directions. He watched it until it stopped and coughed out a last little splat of piss-colored liquid.

Then, though he could barely feel his legs beneath him, he made his way to the phone. He meant to call his mother, but instead his fingers found their way to the numbers of his father's cell phone. The call went straight to voicemail, and for a few seconds, Abe's father was alive—how could he be anything but?—his voice bright. "I can't take your call right now, but leave a message and I will get back in touch as soon as is humanly possible. Thanks, and have a great day."

Abe breathed into the silence after the beep.

From the first brochure for Camp Eden Lake, fall 1968

We are thrilled to announce the opening of a new kind of summer camp for children aged 8-14. Noncompetitive, nonsectarian, and nontraditional, Camp Eden Lake is an intentional community: a co-ed, overnight camp where young people can explore themselves and the world in a nurturing, progressive environment. Arts and crafts (including ceramics, candle-making and fabric arts), hiking, swimming and boating, dance, and music are just some of the activities campers at Eden Lake will enjoy. In addition, campers will contribute to the camp community by helping in the kitchen and dining hall, working in our organic vegetable and flower gardens, caring for the camp pets and animals, and helping maintain the trails and grounds. We like to think of Eden Lake as a vision of what the world might be if everyone lived in harmony with each other and with the land.

The camp is located on a former sheep farm in Talbotts Corner, Maine, midway between Augusta and Bangor, just 40 minutes from the coast. A small lake, meadows, forest, and a 19th century farmhouse and outbuildings create a beautiful, pastoral setting.

Meet the owners/directors:

Clay Perry

Clay was born in Concord, Massachusetts — the hometown of Henry David Thoreau. After graduat-

ing from Wesleyan University in 1965 with a degree
in History, Clay taught public school in the Roxbury neighborhood of Boston. He has also worked as
a tutor and a youth counselor for the Greater Boston YMCA. Clay is an avid outdoor enthusiast and has
hiked most of the Appalachian Trail. Camp Eden Lake
combines his heartfelt commitment to education with
his love of the outdoors and his belief in the importance of community.

Carol Weiss

Carol Weiss, originally of Brookline, Mass., graduated from Wellesley College in 1966 with a B.A. in
Sociology and worked for two years with disadvantaged
youth in Boston. During college, she was a counselor
at the highly regarded Shady Falls Camp for Jewish girls. She believes fervently in the potential
and creativity of every child, and looks forward to
helping young people discover the best of themselves
and the human spirit at Eden Lake.

Eric

ERIC HAD TO SIGN his name twelve times in the first six hours after the crash: three times at the morgue of the hospital in Belfast where the bodies were brought, five times at two different police stations, and four more times at the funeral home. Each time his signature looked messier and more childish, as if he was holding the pen in his fist instead of his fingers. He kept thinking: my father should be doing this. Then the memory of what had happened would catch in his throat, and he'd forget to breathe for a few seconds. The next thought was always: Abe should be doing this. He would know what to do, what questions to ask. He wouldn't have felt, as Eric did, like a twig in a stream, powerless and swirling. First to the morgue, son (why did they keep calling him that? Did he seem not twenty-one but twelve?) and then to the Waldo County sheriff's office, then to the state police, then to the funeral home. Sign here if you would, son; date, too, please, if you don't mind. Just one more time, son. Sorry for your loss, son.

It occurred to him that without a father, he wasn't really a son anymore. Wasn't that right? A man whose wife died couldn't say he was married. Could a man whose father had died still consider himself a son?

Eric's heart had pounded when the morgue technician reached to pull back the sheet, but once he saw his father's body a calm settled over him. The coroner had told him that the impact of the crash had killed both his father and Gail instantly, that their bodies were almost unscathed. But perhaps Eric had still expected something horrible—blood, burns, gashes. Or maybe it was just the pallor and swollenness of death he feared.

But, in fact, his father looked strangely like himself. There was still the shadow of color in his cheeks, and his chin was lifted, his square jaw set, as if he was trying to hold in the last little bit of life.

Eric stood looking at his father's face for a few moments before saying "Yeah, that's him."

Gail's body was closer to what Eric had imagined a corpse would be—pale, dull, unnaturally still. But it was still Gail. She looked much the way she did during her sunbathing snoozes on the dock, the corners of her mouth pulled down into a soft frown.

Once the bodies were in the hands of the funeral home, Eric's job was done, to his great relief. Aura, who'd driven up from Boston, put herself in charge of planning the memorial service, and got started immediately on a list of to-do's and invitees. His mother, meanwhile, set about breaking news to the rest of the family, including Grandmother Perry, and long-time friends.

It seemed to make them both feel better, having these jobs to do. It got them to stop crying, anyway. But Eric didn't like thinking about the details of it all, as if this nightmare was just a big project to be managed. When his mother offered to let him spend the night in Camden with her he declined. He wanted to be back at the camp, in the quiet of his small, carpeted apartment, alone.

But being on the property came with its own sort of pain. Every hour or so throughout the night he would wake up and his limbs would fill with dread as he remembered that his father and Gail weren't sleeping next door in the farmhouse, and never would be.

In the morning he walked the property with the gas-powered brush cutter, cutting back the tall grass and tiny saplings at the edges of the lawns and pathways. He liked doing something he would have done anyway. There was plenty else that needed doing, too: repairing window screens and broken steps; bringing down precarious limbs and trees half-felled by winter storms; chain-sawing them into campfire-sized logs. Patching roofs. Checking plumbing. And that was just for starters.

The Crary brothers had left a message the day of the accident asking when they should come by again and Eric still hadn't called back. He planned to wait a few days, in hopes that he wouldn't have to tell them what had happened. They'd see it on the local news, or, more likely, overhear someone talking about it at the General Store. News traveled fast in Talbotts Corner, especially when it concerned the "rich hippies" at Eden Lake.

Eric knew the way the locals talked. Like Pete and Norma Gill at the General Store. They were friendly enough to his face—friendlier to him, it seemed, than they ever were to his father or Gail, or the counselors who bought snacks and beer there in the summer. But still, sometimes an animated conversation at the register between Norma and a customer would cease suddenly when Eric walked in.

After a couple of hours of trimming and cutting, Eric took a break. He was on his way back to his apartment to make himself lunch when he saw that Aura's Saturn was sitting in the driveway and the farmhouse door was ajar.

He approached slowly, pausing for a moment on the granite step. He hadn't been inside the house since it had happened. He didn't want to see Gail and his father's duck boots by the door, or their phone messages and to-do's on the chalkboard in the kitchen. As he entered, he looked only straight ahead, at the coat closet door.

From upstairs, he heard muted footsteps and a choking, gasping sound that could almost have been laughter, but that he knew wasn't.

"Hello? Aura?"

A few seconds later she appeared at the top of the stairs. Her hair was pulled back in a messy ponytail and her face was blotched. A stack of Gail's blouses, on hangers, lay over her arms. "Hi," she said. "I didn't know if anyone was home."

I didn't know if you were home, she should have said, Eric thought. There wasn't anyone else.

"I just thought I'd pack up some of my mom's stuff. Give it to charity. Or see if my aunts want it."

Eric thought it was a little soon to be doing this, but didn't say so. In his experience, there was no arguing with Aura once she'd decided on something.

"Are you going to take care of your dad's stuff or do you want me to?" she asked him.

"I'll do it."

She looked like she expected him to come up the stairs

right then and there.

"When Abe gets here," he said. "I think he'd want to help."

"Yeah, some of your dad's stuff might fit him. They're around the same size. Of course, some of this stuff might fit me, too." She gave her pile of clothes a little hoist and laughed. "But could you just see me, wearing this freakin' hippie-dippy stuff to work?"

Aura was an executive assistant at Fidelity Investments. Eric didn't know how she dressed for work, but whenever he saw her she looked preppy and neat, in solid colored sweaters and t-shirts, jeans or khakis, simple gold jewelry. Gail, on the other hand, had favored filmy tunic-type things, tall boots, scarves. The kinds of things you found in the boutiques in the coastal tourist towns. Not so much hippie-dippy, Eric thought, but arty. Whimsical.

"I should get back to work," he said. "Lot of weed-whacking to do."

"Yeah, we've got a lot of everything to do. Just so you know, my boss is going to let me take a leave of absence. So I'll go back down to Boston tomorrow and get the rest of my stuff, tie up loose ends, then come back up on Monday. Matt's just going to have to deal."

Matt was Aura's boyfriend or possibly her fiancé; Eric had heard her refer to him both ways on different occasions. She didn't wear a ring.

"I already called the papers to put in a classified for an office assistant for the summer," she continued. "Of course, it's way too last minute to find anyone who's any good, but what can we do, right? We'll just have to fly by the seat of our butts, as they say."

"Yeah," said Eric, though she was talking so fast he was having trouble following. "So, who's going to be director, then?"

Aura thrust her chin forward. "Me, of course. Who else?"

"I thought Abe would do it," said Eric. He hadn't talked to his brother yet, but he'd just assumed that he'd step in as director for the summer—and hopefully for good.

"Abe hasn't worked here since he was in college. If anything, you should do it. But I'm guessing you wouldn't want to."

Eric shook his head with vigor. He was good at managing the property, good at teaching the occasional computer class and pitching in wherever else he was needed. But he could never talk on the phone with parents or comfort homesick campers or stand up and talk in front of all-camp meetings. Then, he couldn't picture Aura doing any of that, either. It annoyed him that she seemed to think she was up to the task.

"Listen, Eric," said Aura, "I spent three summers working in the office here. Not to mention that I'm an administrative professional at one of the biggest financial firms in the country." She gave a little laugh. "And of course, you'll be great with all the facilities stuff. If Abe wants to help, fine. But I don't think he'll want to. He's too busy saving the world, right?"

She was always shooting little barbs at Abe like this when he wasn't around. Eric had never quite understood why. She seemed to think he, Eric, felt the same way.

"He's driving up tomorrow," Eric said, "so I guess we'll find out."

≈

In the afternoon, Eric focused on the animal care area: fixing the ramp up into the chicken coop, hosing out the troughs and feeding bowls and going at the thorn bushes along the fence. He was lost in the roar of the brush cutter, enjoying the satisfaction of watching slim, green thorn branches sever and fall to the ground when, in his peripheral vision, he sensed movement near the gate. He turned to see a man scaling the split rail fence and dropping to the ground inside the animal pen, barely managing not to fall. Eric immediately recognized the outdated, saucer-sized lenses of the man's glasses, the worn brown bomber jacket with its fake military patches and the mop of dark brown hair. It was Sergei Dimov.

Sergei, who must have been forty or so now, had come to the camp for the first time back in 1987, as part of the first delegation of Soviet campers and counselors. Carol had dreamed for years of starting a US-Soviet peace exchange, and got it rolling just as the marriage was falling apart. When the cold war ended, so did the ideological point of the exchange. But Eden Lake still prided itself on having international campers. So, every year, a small cadre of the children of *nouveau riche* Russians spent the summer at Eden Lake. Eric, who'd picked up a good amount of Russian over the years and studied it at UMass, helped translate sometimes.

Eight months after Sergei's first summer at Eden Lake he returned on a moped laden with garbage bags full of his belongings. As it turned out, he'd never gone back to Moscow; he'd been living with the camp nurse in New Hampshire. But she kicked him out and he didn't have anywhere else to go. He convinced Clay and Gail to let him stay at Eden Lake in return for doing odd jobs.

Over the next ten years, he continued to disappear and

reappear periodically, moving in with and being dumped by various women up and down the east coast. He made money, he claimed, by playing the accordion or guitar in restaurants and subway stations. But whenever things got too tight, or he feared he was in danger of deportation, he'd show up at Eden Lake with suspicious gifts (A VCR, a cordless phone, a mantel clock) and teary proclamations of gratitude for Clay and Gail's generosity. Clay barely tolerated him, but Gail, whom he flattered and flirted with shamelessly, welcomed him into their life, inviting him to eat his meals with them and join them on weekend trips to Bar Harbor and Sugarloaf. Eric looked forward to Sergei's stays. It was Sergei who gave Eric his first Russian curse words and his first vodka hangover.

Eric cut the engine, leaned the brush cutter against the fence, and waved to Sergei, who broke into a run, arms outstretched. Eric stumbled backward a few steps as Sergei collided with him. He smelled of cigarette smoke and body odor—a distinctly Eastern European bouquet that Eric found strangely comforting.

"How are you, my friend?" Sergei said. From the brightness of his tone, Eric could tell he didn't know about the accident yet.

"Not too good, actually."

As Eric told him what had happened, Sergei's already broad face seemed to broaden further and his mouth stretched into a grimace. He dropped to his knees, put his head on the ground and wept, while Eric stood watching, not knowing quite what to do, wishing he'd stop. When Sergei reached a hand up, Eric took it and started to pull, to help him to his feet, but Sergei pulled back, and Eric ended up kneeling on the ground instead. Sergei threw his arms around his neck and rocked him. "It's not possible," he said. "Not possible, not possible."

Eric went along with the rocking for a little while, but felt too numb to cry. In fact, he hadn't cried at all yet. He'd been on the verge a few times—felt the tugging at the corners of his mouth and the ache in the back of his throat—but had always stopped himself, struck by how pointless it would be. It wouldn't change a thing.

Finally, Sergei let go and sat down on his heels. He took his glasses off, wiped the back of his hand across his eyes, then polished the lenses with a crumpled handkerchief from his jacket pocket before putting them back on. "Your father was a great man," he said, his chin tucked solemnly. "And Gail was a beautiful and great lady. They were your family, yes, but my family also."

"I know," said Eric, standing.

Sergei bent over and started sobbing again. Eric shifted from one foot to the other and looked toward the farmhouse. He wished Aura would come out. She must have heard Sergei drive in.

Sergei sat up suddenly. "The camp will still exist, yes? This summer, the children will come?"

Eric nodded. "Aura's says she's going to run things, but more likely it'll be Abe. I'm not sure yet."

Sergei's lips bent into a frown. "But what about you? You are the one who stayed here all this time. You didn't move away like others. You should run this camp."

"I'll keep doing what I've always done. Manage the property. Drive the buses. Fill in wherever they need me."

Sergei stood. "Eric, I will stay. I was just coming to visit, you know, but now I must stay and help you, yes? For the summer, for as long as you like. Give me machine, I start now." He held out a hand for the brush cutter. His cheeks were still moist with tears.

"Sure, you can stay," said Eric. "I mean it's probably fine." (He felt like he ought to check with someone, but who?) "But you don't have to start working right now."

"No, I do. We go on with life, yes? It is the only way." He picked up the brush cutter and yanked on the starter cord. The engine growled for a few seconds, then died. He repeated the motion several times, nudging Eric away when he tried to help, saying, "I will do it, I will do it." After a minute more of failed attempts, he handed the machine to Eric. "Here. You do it."

Eric yanked the cord and the engine roared to life.

Sergei gave a little whoop and Eric handed the brush cutter to him, surprised to feel himself smiling as he did.

That night, with Sergei on the couch in the living room of the farmhouse and Aura upstairs in Jude's old bedroom, Eric found that he slept a little better.

≈

When Abe arrived at the camp the following evening, he looked terrible, his eyes small and bloodshot, his curls mussed and greasy, his jaw dirty with stubble. He smelled of sweat and the stale air of his car. Eric thought he smelled marijuana, too. It was unnerving to see his brother so disheveled. But he seemed more concerned about Eric. After giving him a swift, hard embrace, he stood back, his hands on Eric's shoulders, and squinted into his eyes. "How are you holding up? Are you OK? Look at me."

Eric told Abe he was fine and met his gaze, but only for a second. Any longer than that and there was the risk that he'd break down and start crying. Or Abe would. It would be too much, too intense. Like so many things with Abe.

Eric wished the two of them were closer. But for the better part of his childhood and adolescence, Abe simply wasn't there. When Eric was seven years old, Abe left for boarding school in New Hampshire (Agnes Harris, the same small, "alternative" school Jude went to, and that Eric could have gone to, too, if he'd wanted). Then he was at Middlebury for four years. And then he was all over the place: Europe, Asia, San Francisco, Africa, Washington. He came back to Maine once or twice a year, but was always more interested in spending time with their father than with him.

Not that Eric went out of his way to engage his brother in conversation. Whenever they did talk, Abe eventually came around to grilling him about his plans. Specifically, when he planned to leave Eden Lake, leave Maine and do something other than whatever he was doing at the time. He didn't understand why Eric had chosen to stay at Eden Lake and go to the regional public high school, and he certainly didn't understand why he'd dropped out of UMass to come back and work at the camp. "Aren't you tired of staying in the same place?" he would ask. "Don't you feel like you need to get out and experience the world, find yourself?"

Eric would shrug and say, "I'm not lost."

And Abe would shake his head and give Eric's shoulder a soft, big-brotherly punch. That part, Eric didn't mind.

Abe was less than thrilled to learn that Sergei had come. Eric suspected he felt about him the same way their father had. "I don't know what we can pay you," he said when Sergei expressed his intention to stay and work for the summer. "I assume all the staff has already been hired and budgeted for. Right, Eric?"

"Aura said it was fine," Eric said. (Aura didn't think too highly of Sergei either—she thought he was a letch, and was the one who insisted that he sleep downstairs on the couch—but she knew that Eric wanted him to stay.) "I guess she's pretty much going to be in charge," he added, and waited for Abe's reaction—a scoff, a laugh, a "the hell she is!"

But all he did was nod distractedly and say, "I'm starving."

After Abe showered, the two of them drove out to the general store for subs and a case of Budweiser. It was Norma at the counter. To Eric's surprise, she came out from behind the register and embraced him, quickly but firmly, her bony fingertips pressing into his shoulders. "We saw it on the news," she said. "I'm so sorry, Eric. Let us know if there's anything we can do." To Abe, she offered only a handshake and her sympathies.

Back at the house, when Eric took the first bite of his sandwich, he discovered that Norma hadn't put any mayonnaise on it.

"Any in the fridge?" Abe asked. "I'd take some, too."

Eric stood staring into the brightness of the refrigerator for a long time. He hadn't opened it since the accident, subsisting instead on the peanut butter, ramen noodles and granola bars he kept in his apartment. There, on the top shelf, was Gail's Lactaid milk and the (second) bottle of pinot grigio from Sunday night's dinner, two thirds empty. On the middle shelf, among other things, a green paper carton of small, dark strawberries about to turn to mush and a swan-shaped tinfoil package of leftovers from the Hunan House in Belfast, where Clay and Eric had gone for lunch the week before after a trip to the John Deere dealer. On the bottom shelf, a bunch of Romaine lettuce and a bag of baby carrots, its zip-lock top gaping open. Gail had lately been trying to lose a few pounds and snacked on them like they were chips.

Eric had never realized before what an intimate thing the inside of a refrigerator was. Or how inextricably linked it was with life. Dead people didn't need food.

"What are you doing?" Sergei said.

"Looking," said Eric.

"For pickles?"

"No."

"I would like a pickle. Are there any pickles, possibly?"

"I think so," Eric said. He found a jar of dill spears and tucked it into his arm with the mayonnaise, then gave the refrigerator door a gentle push. At the end of its arc it hovered open for an instant, the interior light still glowing, before the magnet caught and pulled it shut with a whisper of suction.

At the dining room table, Abe was reading the typed list of invitees to the memorial service that Aura had left. "I don't know who three quarters of these people are. And what's this?" He pointed to the top of the list. "Father Thomas Denehy, officiating? Dad would freak *out* if he knew there was going to be a priest at his memorial service. Who put Aura in charge of planning this thing anyway?"

"She did," Eric said, trying to sound more annoyed than he actually was, hoping it would urge Abe on.

Abe shook his head. "I'll call her tomorrow and we'll have a little talk about this priest thing. We need to cut the guest list down, too. I mean, look at this." He held the pages at their stapled corner and shook. "There've got to be over three hundred people on this list."

"Four hundred and sixty," Eric said. "They're numbered."

"Your father was a great man, Abe," Sergei said as he chased pickles around in the jar with his fingers. "I am surprised it is not four *thousand* and sixty people on list."

Abe sighed, let his head fall back, and covered his face with his hands. "Shit," he said, and was quiet for a moment. "I can't believe I'm going over a fucking guest list for my father's funeral. A few days ago I was going over the guest list for my awards banquet. That's what I'm supposed to be doing right now. That's where I'm supposed to be." He paused, then kicked the leg of the table, hard. The shredded lettuce that had fallen out of Eric's sandwich trembled on the waxed paper.

Nobody said anything for a few moments and then Sergei spoke up. "I know what we should do."

Abe's hands dropped from his face. "Yeah? What should we do, Sergei? Enlighten us, please."

Eric was glad that he'd said "us."

Sergei's hands, one of which held a pickle, parted in front of him. "We should get drunk, of course."

≈

There was hardly any wood in the shed by the campfire ring, just a few rotting splinters and damp curls of bark. Eric and Sergei gathered up sticks and fallen branches from the ground, moving hunched and quiet in the dark, while Abe used a mallet and wedge to break up one of the big stumps that served as a seat in the campfire ring. Cutting wood had always been Abe's favorite chore and Eric thought maybe it would be good for him to do something physical. Maybe he'd stop kicking table legs and slamming doors and jamming the heel of his hand against his forehead.

The kindling was damp, but Eric was able to coax up a good blaze using balled up newspaper (Abe had suggested using the guest list) and blowing on the nascent flames with just the right amount of force. Once it was clear that the fire had taken, Abe slapped Eric on the back and said, "Damn, you're good." It was so like what their father might have done—the words he chose, the gentle firmness of the slap—that for a split second Eric's heart flooded with relief—*he's here! He's alive!*—then ached anew as the hope drained from it.

"Let's get going on this getting drunk thing," Eric said, and held out a hand for Sergei to toss him a beer.

Abe lifted his eyebrows at him. "Well, well, well."

By the time he opened his third can, Eric was starting to feel sufficiently buzzed, but Abe and Sergei were only just getting going. Sergei started in with stories about how Clay had helped him out over the years, which were more or less all the same: Sergei had shown up, unannounced, penniless and miserable, and Clay had found work for him to do, food for him to eat, and a bed for him to sleep in. ("There are more than two hundred beds on this property," Abe finally said after the third or fourth iteration of the story. "What do you expect?")

What Abe wanted to talk about was the accident itself: what had caused it, if it could have been prevented, whether they should sue the manufacturer if the investigation revealed some kind of malfunction, why the distress call came so late—just seconds before the impact, and why the hell did their father have to buy a plane in the first place? Who did he think he was, Howard fucking Hughes?

"You never went up with him," Eric said to this. "It was really beautiful. To fly over the countryside and the coastline. To see the camp from way up there."

Eric had joined his father for his maiden flight in the plane two years earlier. It was during the first week of camp and there were dozens of things they both needed to be doing, but Clay was practically giddy with excitement: After two years of flight school, he'd finally gotten his pilot's license, and the Cessna Skyhawk he'd bought from a repo auction was waiting for him at the airfield in Portland, fueled up and ready to go.

Clay had cried "yeehaw!" as the wheels lifted from the runway, and the whole time they were in the air the grin never left his face. It put Eric at ease; he'd never been in a small plane before. But once they were up in the air, the landscape sliding slowly past beneath them, as vast and majestic as a map of Middle Earth, his fear vanished.

They'd circled over the camp several times on their way to the airfield in Waterville where the plane would live, low enough that they could see the tetherballs whipping around their poles and the tails of the horses flicking. Kids on the soccer field stopped mid-game to look up and jump and wave their arms, and Clay replied by tilting the wings back and forth. Then he told Eric to reach into his knapsack: he'd brought a big bag full of Jolly Ranchers, which he had Eric empty out the window. They missed the soccer field, scattering across the meadow instead. Most of the candies were retrieved that day, but for the rest of the summer, kids waded up into the grass hoping to find one more, hidden among the wildflowers. Eric

even found one the following spring—sour apple green—
while thinning out a copse of milkweed.

"I guess if you have a kingdom, you might as well have
a way to survey it," Abe said. He smiled with one side of his
mouth, shook his head. "Too much to see from the top of the
meadow these days."

"What do you mean?" Eric asked.

"Nothing." He took a long gulp from his beer. "I just remember going up there with him as a kid and we'd look down
at the camp and it all seemed pretty impressive. Before there
was a climbing wall and tennis courts and a gazebo and a computer loft and whatever else he's built."

"It's still the same place. He just made the improvements
he had to in order to stay competitive." Eric had never understood why Abe was so bothered by the way the property had
changed over the years. It was one thing to look wistfully back
on the old days, when the camp was smaller and simpler. But
Abe seemed to take it as some kind of personal affront that
their father had made capital improvements. As far as Eric was
concerned, it made perfect sense. It was a business, after all,
not a museum. And besides, the camp was still beautiful. More
beautiful, he thought, than it looked in those old pictures from
the first years, when the duck pond was overgrown with cat-
tails and brambles and the roof of the barn was bowed. And
he'd helped make it happen.

"Staying competitive didn't used to enter into the equa-
tion," Abe said.

"It's still a great place," Eric said quietly.

"A magnificent place," Sergei agreed. "Your father may be
gone. But you still have this place, and for as long as you do, he

will never really be gone, yes?"

"It's true," Eric said. He looked to Abe, waiting for him to affirm this—to give Eric some assurance that they'd keep Eden Lake in their family, and that he would fill the place their father had vacated.

But Abe just stared into the fire.

Jude

JUDE KNEW EXACTLY WHAT she was doing when she got dressed for the party on Saturday night. There was no use trying to tell herself now that she hadn't intended what had happened to happen. She wore the white go-go boots, after all.

She was no knockout. She had no illusions on that front. Her nose was a touch too wide and her eyes, while sexy (she'd been told), were a fraction too closely set. Her Jewy hair—courtesy of her mother's Jewy genes—had a tendency to frizz, no matter how much product she pumped into it. She could stand to lose five or ten pounds. But she'd never lacked for male attention when she wanted it. And with the boots…well, no one could resist the boots.

She wore them with a mint-green mini dress that wasn't actually vintage, but that suggested it, with a touch—just a touch—of irony. Red lipstick, thick silver hoop earrings. Not exactly what you'd expect someone whose father had just died to wear to a party. Then, people probably hadn't expected her to come to the party at all, just as they hadn't expected her to take just one day off from work after she got the news. That one day, alone in her apartment, nearly ruined her. Sprawled on the couch in her pajamas, staring at the edge of the coffee table, she almost let herself succumb to guilt, regret, self-loathing, and a host of other pointless emotions for having rebuffed her father's attempts at reconciliation. Fuck that. She would not let herself feel guilty. There was nothing to feel guilty about.

So, she went back to work. And to the party. Wearing the boots.

She wasn't one hundred percent certain that Mitch would be there; he didn't always come to the cast parties, especially for the minor productions, like this one—a pair of one-act plays by an actress-turned-playwright named Bernice who was involved with the theater back in the eighties. Both of her plays, *Pestilence* and *The Loop*, were incredibly dull and derivative, and didn't come close to meeting the criteria of the theater's stated mission, which was to mount "startling, thought-provoking works that challenge conventional definitions of theater, art, and the human experience." Then again, lately it seemed to Jude that a lot of what the theater put on didn't. Just because a set was made completely out of PVC piping or because one of the characters randomly got naked didn't make a play startling or thought-provoking.

Jude had never particularly liked her job. She'd taken it in desperation after an exhausting and penurious year of temping, waitressing and painting sets for free or close to it at whatever off-off-off-Broadway theater would let her. She knew that the administrative end of theater wasn't where she wanted to be, but was tired of being broke and thought, naively, that there might be less separation between the back office and backstage at a so-called "innovative and subversive" theater. Her goal—the one she'd left school with, anyway—was to do scenic design. But she'd been at the theater for almost three years now, and the only remotely creative work she'd done was designing a few programs and promotional postcards.

Sometimes she wondered if Mitch was the only reason she stayed.

The cast party was at a lounge-y new restaurant a few blocks up from the theater. When Jude got there, just after ten, people were well on their way to inebriation. She tolerated a few sloppy, sympathetic hugs from co-workers, as well as from a couple of cast members she didn't even know who'd somehow heard about what had happened. That was most likely Courtney's doing. Courtney, the house manager, was unofficial company gossip. She'd already guessed, several months back, that Jude had a crush on Mitch, (which Jude denied) and declared it most definitely mutual, but swore up and down she wouldn't tell anyone.

A quick scan of the room revealed that Mitch wasn't there. For a moment, inexplicably, Jude found herself on the brink of tears. She made her way to the bar for a martini, then headed for the couches in the corner where the people she considered her friends were gathered in a haze of smoke. An hour and two martinis later, she had stopped watching the door for Mitch. And then, suddenly, there he was, standing just a few feet away, talking to the playwright. He must have sensed Jude's eyes on him, because, mid-sentence, he glanced at her and smiled. She gave him a controlled (God, it was hard) smile in return, and a brief, upward nod of her head. Then she went up to the bar to get another drink and give him the opportunity to come find her there, which he did.

"I didn't expect to see you here," she said.

"I hadn't planned to come." He put his empty glass on the bar and asked the bartender for another—Jack Daniels, no ice. "Anika and I met up for drinks with some of her colleagues after the show, and according to her, I behaved like an ass."

"I'm sure you did."

"Probably. Anyway, I was sick of bickering about it, so I said I was going for a walk, and she said fine, and it was so nice out—you know, that beginning of summer in New York smell…"

Jude nodded. She'd noticed it too—warm asphalt, cigarette smoke and women's perfume, basement vents spewing the smell of fresh laundry.

"—that I just kept walking. And now, here I am."

"Here you are," Jude said.

They smiled at each other.

"How are you holding up?"

Jude shrugged.

"Don't want to talk about it?"

"Not really."

"You know, I lost my dad when I was just a few years older than you. How old are you again?"

"Fifteen," Jude said with a smirk.

"Right, right. My memory isn't what it used to be, being eighty-two and all." He took a sip of his drink. "We weren't close either, my dad and me. You'd think that would make it easier, wouldn't you?"

"We used to be close. Too close. That was the problem."

"Oh," Mitch said with quiet surprise.

"No, no. Nothing like *that*. I'm from Maine, not Kentucky, for Christ's sake."

Mitch laughed with evident relief. "Sorry, I always confuse the two."

"Yeah, yeah. Anyway. Moving on."

"Moving on. How'd you like the plays?"

Jude leaned closer to him. "I thought they blew."

Mitch glanced around to make sure Bernice was out of earshot and then leaned closer himself. "Yeah, I kind of did, too."

They sat grinning at each other in conspiratorial agreement for a few seconds. Jude broke their gaze and shifted on her barstool, uncrossing and re-crossing her legs the other way.

"Those are some boots," Mitch said.

Jude fingered the edge of the leather, just below her bare knee. "You don't think they're a little over the top?"

Mitch shook his head. "They look like they were made for walking."

Jude rolled her eyes.

He laughed. "Sorry, that was lame."

"Incredibly."

"Yeah, well." He paused for a moment. "My incredibly lame way of asking if you want to get out of here."

Jude felt herself warm from head to groin. "Sure," she said, and downed the last of her martini. (Was it her third or her fourth? Who cared.) "Why not."

They circled the block a few times, walking close enough that their arms and hips kept bumping. Then, without either of them needing to say a word, they headed for the theater.

≈

They had sex on the worn, brown corduroy sofa in the green room. She had expected Mitch to be a slow, deliberate lover, given his age and the experience that she assumed went with it. Instead, he was eager, fast, and a little bit clumsy—surprisingly like Adam Weaver, the high school boyfriend she'd lost her virginity to at seventeen. If Adam Weaver had had a hairy chest and a slight paunch. Still, the urgency of it was exciting. And besides, they were both pretty blotto; it wasn't fair to expect a virtuoso performance.

Afterward, as they lay together on the couch, rumpled and sweaty, Jude asked him if he'd ever cheated on his wife before.

"No," he said. "Well—yes. Once. But not…it was different. It was just sex. It was meaningless."

"So, then, what was this?"

"This," he said, and kissed the top of her head, "was Jude Perryweiss."

Jude let herself smile; it was dark, he wouldn't see.

But when she woke up at noon the next day, her head throbbing, her tongue thick in her mouth, she felt sick with shame. (Go-go boots. Could she have been any more obvious?) And just plain sick—the scrambled eggs she idiotically attempted to eat came right back up. She checked her work email account compulsively all day, hoping he'd written, but he hadn't. Courtney, however, had. No subject line, and a single sentence in the message body, followed by a winking, semicolon smiley face: Have fun last night?

≈

On Monday morning she boarded an Amtrak train for Boston. She hadn't planned to go up until the weekend, for the memorial service, and even that she hadn't entirely made up her mind about. But the thought of going into work now, trying to act normal around Mitch, trying to figure out who, if anyone, in the office knew, and what they were saying or thinking about her, made her cringe. She'd sent him a brief email saying that she'd decided that she needed some bereavement time after all, adding, "I'm obviously not thinking straight."

He'd replied almost immediately, saying that he understood; she should take as much time as he needed. But he hoped they could talk soon.

In Boston, she switched to a Greyhound bound for Portland, and as it crossed the Pisquataqua River Bridge and passed the "Maine: the way life should be" sign, she felt a wave of something like relief, chased by a vague sense of yearning; an urge to open the window and breathe in the scent of the pine trees that now lined the highway, let it purify her.

As if this place was so pure. As if it wasn't the very place where she'd first learned how fucked up and duplicitous people could be. Maine—the place where her father preached honesty and openness and respect to a fawning congregation of campers and counselors (not to mention his own family) while simultaneously banging another woman behind his wife's back.

Ah yes, Maine. The way life should be.

Abe was waiting for Jude at the depot, looking as reassuringly Abe-ish as ever, in rumpled jeans, Tevas, and a faded Clinton/Gore '96 T-shirt. She hadn't seen him in the flesh since Thanksgiving. He gave her one of his long, almost-too-tight hugs, and she reached up and rumpled his hair.

When they were on their way, heading north on the Maine Turnpike, he asked her why she'd decided to come up earlier than she'd originally planned.

Jude sighed and forked her bangs back with her fingers. "I

43

got drunk and fucked my boss on Saturday night."

Abe gave a short, explosive laugh. "Nice going."

"It's not funny. It's very bad. He's married and has a kid. And I think people know what happened. At least this girl Courtney knows, or suspects, anyway. She knew I had a thing for him, and then I think she saw us leave the party together. Which means that everyone else at the theater will know within the next forty-eight hours because she can't keep her fucking mouth shut. And everyone is going to think I'm some slutty home wrecking…slut."

Abe laughed again, and Jude punched him in the shoulder. "It's not funny!"

"No, I'm sorry. You're right. It's not funny. It runs in the family, I guess. We're a bunch of sluts."

"You're not a slut," she said. "You just have commitment issues that make you act in slutty ways." Abe had recently torpedoed the latest in a long succession of six-month relationships, this time by making out with a woman at a party who turned out to be his girlfriend's co-worker. Classic. "And Mom's not a slut either. Neither is Eric. He's still a virgin, for God's sake."

"No way. You think?" He grimaced dubiously.

"I know. At least, as of Christmas he was. I asked him."

"Really? Shit. I would have thought at least while he was at school…"

"Oh please. His social life consisted of playing computer games and D&D and watching *X-Files* with astrophysics majors."

"But he's not a bad looking guy," Abe said. "There must have been some nerdy chicks who dug him. And those chicks are crazy, you know. They're all into orgies and bondage and stuff."

44

"Ha. At Vassar, you were a loser if you *weren't* into that stuff. If you did freakish things like, you know, sports." She pretended to shudder. "Soccer and skiing and—"

"Yeah, yeah, I got it."

Abe had played soccer and done Nordic skiing at Middlebury, which Jude loved giving him shit for. Secretly, though, she didn't mind having a semi-jock for a big brother. And it wasn't like he'd played football.

"You know, you didn't have to come all the way down here to get me. I could have gotten on the bus."

It was almost three hours from Portland to Camden, with most of the drive along the often-congested coastal route one. Memorial Day marked the beginning of the tourist season, and the roads were clogged with Midwestern retirees in motor homes, Connecticut families in minivans, Manhattan couples in rental cars, all rolling northward in search of lobster and quaint.

"I wanted to make the drive," Abe said. "It was a good excuse to escape for a little while. Aura's turning this memorial service into a huge production. Caterers, flowers, printed programs. We emailed something like eight hundred people yesterday. The entire staff and camper alumni database."

"Wow. It's going to be like the freaking royal wedding."

"Yeah, I just feel sorry for the people who are going to have to work for her this summer," said Abe. "She's a total micromanager."

"Hang on. What do you mean people who're going to work for her? Aren't you running the camp this summer?"

It hadn't even occurred to her that he wouldn't. Eric certainly couldn't do it, and Jude would rather ram a toothpick into her eye. As for Aura, Jude recalled that she'd helped out in the camp office a few times, so she probably knew her way around. But administrative skills weren't what it took to run a camp. Their father had typed with two fingers, for Chrissake. The important thing was that he knew how to wrap people around them—the counselors and staff, the parents, the referral agents. Abe could do the same.

He glanced at her, looking peeved. "How come everyone assumes I'm going to run the place? Just because I'm the oldest? What is this, the middle ages? Why don't you run it?"

"Uh huh."

Abe wagged his head from side to side. "I've got a good job that I practically just started. Anyway, Aura can handle the camp. And maybe Mom will help."

"Yeah, right," said Jude. When their mother had divorced their father after he'd left her for Gail, she'd divorced herself from Eden Lake, too. She wanted nothing to do with it. Though she'd remained on cordial terms with their father since the split—a fact that drove Jude crazy—she'd only been back to the camp a handful of times, and it always dropped her into a melancholy funk. "I feel like a ghost when I'm there," she'd told Jude after a visit a few years earlier, for the wedding of an old friend from the early days. "A ghost of the old me."

"She might do it," Abe said. "She may talk tough, but when you get down to it, she still loves the place. If I don't step up, maybe she will."

"Ah, ha! *If* you don't? I thought you'd made up your mind."

"I promised Mom I'd wait until we read the will tomorrow. I guess she thinks Dad might have put something in there about what should happen."

Jude snorted. "I'm probably not even in his will anymore: 'To my estranged daughter, Jude, I leave nothing.'"

Come to think of it, she hoped that was exactly what he'd done.

"Don't be ridiculous," said Abe. "Of course you are. He didn't hate you back."

"He didn't have any reason to." Jude picked her bag up from the floor. "Do you mind if I smoke?"

"Yes," Abe said, as if the answer was obvious. He smoked pot like a fiend—at least, he used to—but was sanctimonious as hell when it came to tobacco.

"Fine." She dropped her bag back onto the floor and turned her face to the window. They were passing what she and Abe used to call the BFI—Big Fucking Indian. A forty-foot wooden Sioux in a feathered headdress, standing outside a souvenir "trading post" just off the highway.

"The great Plains Indians of coastal Maine," Jude muttered. "Brilliant."

Abe said nothing, just released a breath from his nose. They'd had the geographic-inaccuracy-of-the-BFI conversation dozens of times. "How are you doing with all this?" he said after a few moments.

"With what?"

He gave her a "cut the bullshit" look.

"It hasn't really sunk in. He hasn't exactly been in my life for a while."

Abe nodded, his eyes on the road. "Makes sense." He was silent for a few seconds, his jaw shifting side to side.

"What?" said Jude.

"I don't know. I just don't understand why Eric and I and

even Mom, to some degree, were able to forgive him for the affair, but you still aren't. He's not..." He shook his head quickly, with frustration. "He wasn't a bad person. He was just human. And he loved you. He's—he was always asking me about you."

"I know," Jude said. "But it's more complicated than you think." More complicated than anyone thought. Or would ever know.

"Complicated how?" Abe said. "Try me."

"No, forget it. I'm just a bitch, that's all."

"Jude, come on, you're not—"

"Yes! Yes, I am, OK? I am."

≈

They rolled into Camden just after four, inching through the tiny downtown, past pasty tourists clogging up the sidewalks, licking giant ice cream cones. Their mother's house, a small mansard Victorian, was up the hill past the row of bed and breakfasts overlooking the harbor, out of tourist strolling range. She came outside to greet them when they arrived, and Jude was glad to see that she wasn't using her cane. In April she'd had an exacerbation that was so bad she could barely walk, and Jude had taken a week off from work to come up and stay with her, run errands, cook meals. Looking at her now, the way she moved slowly but steadily down the path through her perennial garden, full hips swaying, long skirt swishing, you'd never guess that a few months earlier she'd been practically crippled. Such a fucked-up, unpredictable disease.

"You look great," Jude said, after a long embrace. "Walking like a pro. You're feeling OK?"

"Oh yes, physically, yes. Very good. But emotionally..." Her voice wavered and her eyelids fluttered. "Judie, it's like losing him all over again."

Jude looked down at the toes of her Fluevogs. Severely scuffed. She could use a new pair. "Yeah," she said, for lack of any better ideas.

When she'd talked to her on the phone the day of the accident, she'd seemed so calm and strong, so serene. Her usual self. But here she was acting like she'd just been widowed.

She cupped Jude's face in her hands and lifted it so their eyes met. "I'm so glad you're here, sweetie."

"I'm still not sure I'm going to stay for the memorial service."

Her mother closed her eyes and nodded once. Serenely. "Whatever you're comfortable with," she said.

"Thanks," said Jude, relieved.

The trunk of the car slammed and Abe, with Jude's suitcase on his shoulder, breezed past them. "She's coming to the service. Is there anything to eat, Mom? I'm starving."

"Everybody has to grieve their own way, Abe," she called to him over her shoulder, but he was already inside. She put her arm around Jude and they walked toward the door together. "You don't smell like cigarettes for once," she said. "Did you quit?"

"I'm trying," Jude lied.

"That's my girl."

≈

Going to her mother's house was the closest thing Jude had to going home. The only times she had actually lived there for significant chunks of time were summers during high school and after her first two years of college. But each time she visited she was comforted anew by the familiarity of the place: the perfumed earthiness of her mother's patchouli incense and the wet, green scent of houseplants. Some of the old furniture and framed artwork that had been in the farmhouse was here, but arranged differently and mixed with her mother's newer acquisitions, many of them brought back from the two years she spent in New Mexico while Jude was in college—Navajo blankets, terra cotta pottery and other things that had nothing to do with New England.

Upstairs, Jude had her own room, where the posters she'd had at Agnes Harris hung on the walls (Che Guevara, the cover of R.E.M.'s *Green*, Klimt's "The Kiss") and some of her childhood books and knickknacks still occupied the shelves. She'd offered numerous times to pack her things away, so her mother could use the space for something else. Or at least have it resemble a normal guest room. But her mother always said she didn't mind, so Jude left it the way it was. It was disorienting, being surrounded by all these relics of who she used to be. She was never quite sure if she liked it or not.

She lay down, planning on just a quick snooze, but woke up over an hour later, to the smell of onions frying. Downstairs in the kitchen, her mother was sitting on a stool in front of the stove stirring vegetables in her wok. Abe, Aura, and Eric sat at the kitchen table with bottles of beer and small piles of blue tortilla chips in front of them.

Eric stood and gave Jude one of his strained smiles that somehow managed to make him look even more serious. "Sleep well?" he asked.

"Yeah," Jude said and went to hug him. "Hi, little brother."

He patted her awkwardly on the back with both hands. "Hi."

Aura stood, then, and she and Jude embraced, sort of; an A-frame hug, as Jude had heard it called once: heads and shoulders close, bodies as far away from each other as possible. So many years they'd known each other, so much shared history, and this was what their relationship had deteriorated to.

Aura and her mother first came to Eden Lake in the summer of 1976. Gail was hired to replace the long-time dance teacher, Mandy Traynor, who'd bagged at the last minute. A young, single mom from a blue-collar family in Salem, Massachusetts, Gail wasn't the typical Eden Lake counselor. But Jude guessed that was part of her appeal—to her mother, anyway. Obviously, Gail had appealed to her father in more ways than one.

Carol had taken Gail under her wing, showed her how to garden and watched five-year-old Aura while Gail taught her dance classes. Jude didn't remember that summer—she was only four at the time—but in an old family album somewhere there was a picture of her mother, baby Eric in a sling, pulling Jude and Aura in a wagon.

Jude did, however, remember the February night six years later when Gail and Aura came back to Eden Lake. That is, she remembered the next morning, when she came downstairs to see two blond strangers at the dining room table, one of them—Gail—with an angry purple bruise under her left eye. Carol explained later that the man Gail lived with had tried to hurt her, and that she and Aura needed somewhere safe to stay for a while, where he couldn't find them. Jude, who had just read *The Diary of Anne Frank*, found this very exciting.

And it was. For the next seven months, Gail and Aura lived upstairs in the infirmary. Aura was home-schooled along with Jude and her brothers, and frequently slept over in Jude's room, the two of them crowded together in the little twin bed. They'd stay up until what then seemed like devilishly late hours—one, two o'clock!—whispering and giggling. To Jude, Aura was worldly in a way that even the campers from Manhattan weren't. She had a Boston accent that made her sound tough (anything she didn't like—disco music, Scott Baio, the Yankees—she proclaimed "wicked retarded"), and was allowed to wear lip-gloss and blue eye shadow. She knew more curse words than anyone Jude had ever met.

Four years later, when Clay left Carol for Gail, Jude's friendship with Aura—which at that point consisted of monthly letters and summers together at the camp—came to an abrupt, un-discussed stop. Aura didn't move up to Eden Lake with Gail, but stayed in Salem with her grandmother and finished high school. The next time Jude saw her, she was a freshman at UNH (tuition courtesy of Clay) and almost unrecognizable. Her hair, once ropy and wild, had been flattened into a pert bob, and instead of blue eye shadow and chipped hot-pink nail polish she wore subtle, neutral makeup and had a French manicure. Her Boston accent had faded almost completely. In fact, everything about her seemed to have had faded. Jude found that they had almost nothing to say to each other.

"I'm really sorry about your mom," Jude said now.

Aura looked peeved. "She was your stepmother, too."

"Sorry, but I never really thought of her that way." By the time the divorce was finalized and Gail and her father were living together at the camp, Jude was a freshman at Agnes Harris.

Gail never had the chance to be a mother figure to her, and Jude didn't feel any need for it, anyway. She had a mother. Besides, there was nothing motherly about Gail, with her girlish laugh and suntanned skin; her loopy Stevie Nicks clothes.

"No, I guess not," Aura said coolly, and sat back down.

Jude looked to Abe, hoping for a sympathetic grimace, but he was suddenly deeply engrossed in picking at the label of his beer.

"Nothing against your mom," Jude said. "It's just a fact."

During dinner, the conversation turned to speculation on who might show up at the memorial service—which long-lost characters from the past. Names Jude hadn't heard or thought about in years wandered forward from the back rooms of her brain, each trailing its own scrap of memory. She pictured Andy Silverman, four-time program director in the early eighties and creator of the "Hi Ho Silverman Comedy Players," with an orange construction cone on his head and a bed sheet tied around his neck as a cape, being chased by another counselor as part of a skit at an all-camp meeting. She recalled Hans Leder, the tall, long-haired Dutchman, with his face painted white and eyes smudged with black, zombie-walking out of the woods on Halloween Night, sending Jude and her bunkmates screaming away.

She didn't have an actual memory to go with Pam and Roger, good friends of her parents who worked at the camp for most of the seventies, just the photograph that had sat in a dusty wooden frame on the bureau in the upstairs hall of the farmhouse: her mother and Pam, long hair streaming out from beneath bandanas, riding piggy-back on her father and Roger on the shore of Eden Lake. They were all in sandals and shorts, looking young and tan and happy. Jude didn't know for sure, but had always imagined that right after the picture was taken the men ran into the lake with the women on their backs, everyone shrieking and laughing. She could almost hear the suck and splash of the water; could almost smell it, earthy and clean at once.

"This funeral's going to turn into a big love-in, isn't it," Jude said. "All the old hippies getting together and talking about the old days. Peace, love and granola."

Carol smiled. "Probably."

"Yeah, and then comparing which tech stocks they're getting rich off," said Abe.

Carol sat up straighter and said, archly, "The only stocks *I* own are in an alternative energy development fund."

"What kind of return you getting on that, Mom?" Jude said.

Jude glanced at Abe, looking for his laugh, but he was somewhere else. "Remember Dad took the whole camp down to New Hampshire to protest the nuclear power plant?"

"Oh, sure," said Carol. "Seabrook. Summer of '77."

Abe shook his head. "How fucking cool is that. To show up at a protest with two busloads full of kids."

"Fucking good publicity for the camp," said Jude. The clipping from the front page of the Boston Globe's regional section used to hang in the dining room of the farmhouse, matted and framed: "Summer Campers Say 'no' to Nuclear Power in New Hampshire."

"He didn't do it for the publicity," said Abe. "Not primarily, anyway."

"Mom?" Jude looked to her mother.

Carol tilted her head from side to side. "I'd say sixty-forty, conviction, publicity."

"I'd say that's generous," Jude said.

"I'd say you don't have to be such a bitch," said Abe.

"Fuck you," she said, and stood.

"Jude, honey," said Carol. "Come on."

"What? Just because Dad's dead we're not allowed to tell the truth about him? See, this is exactly why I don't want to go to the memorial service. It's just going to be one big tribute."

"Yeah, that's generally what memorial services are," Abe snapped.

"You should have some respect for the dead," said Aura.

"He was our father," said Eric, looking down at the tortilla chip he held.

"Call me when the meeting of the Clay Perry fan club is over," Jude said, and headed for the stairs. "I'm not a member."

Abe

ABE WAS TWELVE YEARS old when he decided that he wanted to run Eden Lake when he grew up. He remembered the day he made the decision. It was June, just before staff week, and he'd spent the morning following his father around the property, helping him patch screens on cabin windows, hang fly-paper strips from the rafters of buildings and flush toilets and twist taps to make sure everything worked. Later, he'd tagged along while his father gave a tour of the property to a family from Long Island. Their son was a little younger than Abe, small for his age and painfully shy. Abe tried to draw the boy out, asking him about his hobbies and interests. When the boy revealed that he had a pet hamster, Abe suggested they go to the animal care area. He showed the boy how to feed the goats and the boy grinned as they snuffled feed pellets from his palm. He held the rabbits and cupped a baby chick in his hands, growing all the time more relaxed and talkative. After the family left, Clay had rumpled Abe's hair and praised him for putting the boy at ease. "You're a natural at this, kid. You want to run the place someday?"

Abe took his father's question seriously. He tried to picture himself doing all the things his father did. Though he had trouble imagining what he would look like as an adult—the best he could conjure up was a taller version of his current self, with a mustache—he didn't have trouble *feeling* himself as camp director. The next night at dinner he announced with some solemnity that he wanted to help run the camp when he grew up.

His father was delighted. "You're hired," he said.

His mother's enthusiasm was more tempered, but she agreed that Abe would do a wonderful job. Jude piped in and said that she wanted to be a famous artist. Eric, just four years old at the time, asked if he could be a Jedi. The answer from their father was—as it always was, to everyone—an emphatic yes. Yes, yes, yes. "Follow your bliss," was one of his favorite sayings. To which he would often add a dictum of his own: "Follow it even if you have no idea where it's taking you" or "follow it no matter how fast it runs from you."

By the time he got to college, Abe's bliss had started leading him away from Eden Lake, toward more serious causes: the environment, human rights, women's issues. (That one, admittedly, had something to do with Lucy Fishbein, the beautiful, militant feminist he dated his sophomore year.) He still spent his summers at the camp as a counselor, coaching soccer and leading outdoor trips. One summer he attempted, with middling success, to resuscitate the camp's defunct community service workshop. But try as he might, he couldn't manage to tap into the vein of passion he once felt for the place.

After college he spent nine months traveling, first to Europe and North Africa, then India and finally Thailand. He managed to do the whole thing on just over five thousand dollars—half of his graduation gift from Grandmother Perry—and with the money that remained, plus what he'd saved from his summer paychecks, he moved to San Francisco and got a job as a fundraising grunt for an environmental public interest research group. To make extra cash, he tended bar three nights a week at a place downtown. When he realized he looked forward to that job more than his other one, he knew that he had to make a change. He might not know what he should do with his life, but he was fairly sure it wasn't mixing martinis for ad execs and flirting with editorial assistants. Still, it wasn't until he was voted one of San Francisco's favorite bartenders by a local nightlife rag—an honor he enjoyed far too much—that he took action. Almost on an impulse, he submitted his application to the Peace Corps. Six months later he found himself in rural Nigeria, teaching English to barefoot schoolchildren.

It was good for a while. His pupils adored him, and the community was grateful and hospitable. But after the initial honeymoon phase, he began to doubt that what he was doing really mattered. Then he began to suspect that it might, in fact, be doing harm. English was a ticket out of the village, to jobs in the cities, and that ticket was almost always one-way. There was a chance—a slight one—that a star pupil might actually make it as far as the university level, get a good job in Lagos or Ibadan and send money home to his family. But it wouldn't be enough to immunize all the children in the village or ensure a clean, reliable water source or give local farmers an alternative to slashing and burning tracts of forest for their crops.

As his two-year term of service dragged on, Abe began spending more time drinking beer in the village bar with his fellow teachers and more of his weekends traveling to see other

Corps volunteers. By the time he left he had decided that the more effective way for him to make an actual difference in the world was from within his own culture, within the system. When he got back to the states, he headed for Washington DC, where, through an old classmate from Agnes Harris, he got a job with the fundraising arm of the Clinton/Gore re-election campaign. For eight months, he was high on the excitement of the race, jacked up on the certainty of victory and shimmering in the glow of the president's popularity. And then, all of a sudden, it was over. They'd won—as they knew they would—and it was as if the whole thing had never happened. He hadn't done anything, he realized, but help preserve the status quo. Certainly, it was better than letting Bob Dole take the reins. But what had it accomplished, really?

The next year and a half was a patchwork of false starts: a job at the Department of Education that he left after two months; a temporary gig organizing college volunteers for a human rights organization; a brief period when he considered applying to graduate school; all against the backdrop of bartending three nights a week at Madam's Organ. There, at least, he had the good fortune to meet Jess, another former Peace Corps volunteer. And Peter Waite, the software entrepreneur turned philanthropist who'd taken charge of AfterStart in '96 and transformed it from a perpetually under-funded homework help outfit into a non-profit force to be reckoned with, getting national press for its innovative after-school programs. The more Abe heard about it, the more excited he got. He and Peter started batting programming and fundraising ideas back and forth at the bar. And then, one night, Waite came in with a job description, which he handed to Abe. "I pretty much wrote this for you," he said. "Come in and meet the rest of the team next week, and we'll see if it's a match."

It was. And Abe was determined to make it last.

Which is why, after Charles Dumont, Esquire, read aloud the provisions of Clay's will, the first words out of Abe's mouth were "I can't."

Charles Dumont was short and almost completely bald, with a neatly trimmed white beard that made him look more psychiatrist than lawyer. His office, upstairs from a dermatology practice in a turn-of-the-century house at the edge of downtown Augusta, was too small for the scale of the heavy furniture in it. The dark green walls made it feel even more cramped. Aura, Eric, and Jude sat stiffly on the burgundy leather sofa, while Abe perched on the edge of a very uncomfortable matching wing chair.

To each of them—Eric, Aura, Abe and Jude—Clay had left twenty-five percent of his personal, liquid assets, which amounted to a little over eighty thousand dollars in stocks and cash for each of them. Aura also got the ski condo at Sugarloaf, and Eric and Jude were each to receive half of the Eden Lake property.

"What about Abe?" Jude asked. "Doesn't he get anything?"

Dumont cleared his throat and gave Abe a brief, almost conspiratorial nod, as if Abe knew what was coming. "To my son, Abraham Perryweiss," Dumont read, "'I leave all assets, material and immaterial, of Camp Eden Lake, Incorporated. Abe has many times expressed his wish to assume leadership of the business, and I sincerely hope that he will do so in the event of my demise, if he hasn't already.'"

Abe shook his head, slow at first, then faster. "I can't," he said. His heel jackhammered the floor now. "No way. Not going to happen."

"Well," said Dumont, "I assumed that you…I mean, your father was quite clear that…"

"It's been years since I said I wanted to run the camp. My dad knows—he knew I wasn't interested in taking over the camp anymore."

He knew, but he'd still harbored hope—and never ceased reminding Abe of that fact.

Just a few weeks earlier, Abe had told his father how frustrated he was with a principal who wouldn't let his students participate in a trash sculpture project because he didn't think it was sufficiently educational, and Clay had responded, "That's one of the great things about running a camp. No bureaucracy. No curriculum guidelines. No bullshit. You're in charge. And you're teaching kids how to live life in the fullest."

"Yeah, yeah," Abe had said. "Price: a mere five thousand bucks. I think I'll stick to teaching kids how to not end up on welfare or in jail."

His father had laughed and said "touché," adding, "But if you ever change your mind, just say the word. I can't do this forever."

"Well, there's nothing legally binding here," Dumont said now. "You can sell the business or the land,"—he glanced at Eric and Jude—"or both as you see fit. But for this summer you don't have much of a choice, unless you cancel the session, which I wouldn't advise from a business perspective. In any case," he began thumbing up sheets up paper from various piles on his desk, "there are some things to sign. And then I encourage you to discuss all of this as a family. Communication is of the utmost importance in situations like this."

"Situations like what?" said Jude.

"Complex ones."

After details were discussed and papers signed, the four of them filed silently out of the office, down the dim stairwell and out into the glaring light of noon. They stood on the front walk squinting at each other for a few seconds. Abe soon realized that everyone was looking at him, waiting for him to say something. Was he supposed to apologize for what their father had done? Express his disbelief? Say they'd find a way around it, a way to even things out?

He had never realized what a powerful thing a will could be. Because his father had written that he wanted certain things to go to certain people, it would happen, and all of their lives would change as a result. Abe couldn't just decide—now, to-day—to ignore his father's wishes because they didn't happen to match his own. It wasn't as simple as that.

Everyone was still looking at him.

"I'm starving," he said. "Are you guys starving? I could really go for a Honey Hut cheeseburger."

The Honey Hut was a dairy stand about three miles from the camp, on the road to Waterville. A favorite cabin night activity used to be when Clay would lead a few bunks' worth of kids on an "expedition" there, taking a shortcut through woods and fields, and right across the property of a small dairy farm. That part of the trip was called the "Cow Crawl," and the tradition was for everyone to moo as they walked the length of the pasture, hugging the fence, so as not to spook the cows and tip off the owners (who, unbeknownst to the campers, Clay was friendly with, and who were well aware that herds of moo-ing kids would periodically creep across their property).

One of the camp's school buses would be waiting at the Honey Hut to take everyone back after they'd had their dipped cones and butterscotch sundaes. When the dairy farm changed hands in the mid-eighties the expeditions stopped. Instead, counselors just drove their campers out to the Hut for ice cream once a session. The adventure was gone.

Abe got his cheeseburger, the others got their own greasy sandwiches, and they sat eating them at one of the picnic tables on the grass next to the parking lot.

"I've never understood why it's called the Honey Hut," Abe said, to break the silence. "With the bee on the sign and everything. They don't serve anything with honey."

"They used to," said Eric. "The original owners kept bees, and you could get homemade honey on your ice cream. And honey flavored shortbread."

"Really? How did you know that?"

"Their grandson was in my high school class. Michael Gilcott."

Abe was reminded of how much more rooted to Maine, to Talbotts Corner, to the camp, Eric was than any of them. But if he felt betrayed or envious of the fact that Abe had been chosen as successor, he didn't show it. Then, he never showed much.

"Listen, guys," Abe said. "I don't know why Dad left things the way he did, but what's done is done, right? For now, we should just focus on getting through the summer. I'll act as director, but Aura, of course I'm gonna need your help. And Eric, you know the place better than any of us, really, so thank God you're going to be there. As for what happens next summer and beyond, we'll worry about it later, once the dust settles. It would be crazy to make any kind of major decisions now. We'll have to figure out what we all want, together. As a family. Agreed?"

"It doesn't really matter what I think," Aura said. "I'm just the stepdaughter."

"The stepdaughter with a ski condo worth three hundred grand," Jude said. "Plus you're not tangled up in a big financial mess like the rest of us. I'd trade places with you in a second."

"Jude," Abe began.

"What? I don't want the property. I don't want anything to do with the camp. I just want out. Aura can have my share. Or Eric. I don't even want any money for it. They can just have it."

"You'd be an idiot to give away your share of the property," Aura said. "Don't you know how much it's worth?"

"It can't be worth the stress it's going to cause me."

"Oh, give it a rest," said Abe. "All you have to do is collect rent."

"You know what I'm talking about," Jude said, looking at him pointedly, still expecting him to take her side. "Emotional stress."

"We're all kind of under emotional stress right now," Eric said. "I think Abe's right. We should just pull together and try to get through the summer."

"I agree," Aura said quietly.

Abe looked at Jude. She rolled her eyes. "Yeah, yeah. Fine."

"Good," said Abe, picking up his burger, nodding. "Good."

Suddenly, he was itching to get back to the camp, get into the office, and get to work. The camp's email inbox was filled to capacity, as was the answering machine. He and Aura had sent an email to the parents of all the enrolled campers telling them what had happened, and assuring them that the summer session would go on as planned. But they wanted details: Who, exactly, was going to be in charge? How much experience did they have? Was the price of tuition going to be lowered?

Abe wolfed down the last of his burger and rubbed his paper napkin between his palms, reducing it to a greasy, shredded wad. "We should get going," he said to Aura. "We've got all those parents to get back to."

"*You* got all those parents to get back to," she replied. "I've still got a zillion things to do for the memorial service. Plus there's bills to pay and vendors to call and supplies to order. We also have to get final counts to the food service company this week. Not that you'd know anything about it."

"Well, now I do," Abe said crisply. "Thank you."

"You're welcome."

"Oh boy," said Jude. "Aren't you two going to have fun?"

Eric

THE MORNING OF THE memorial service Eric got up early, brought the tractor with the flatbed trailer over to the rec. hall and started loading up folding chairs. He set them up at the campfire ring to supplement the log benches, which Aura thought older people might find uncomfortable. Abe and Sergei's help would have been nice, but they'd stayed up late the night before, doing vodka shots and swapping guitar tunes. They needed their sleep, and Eric didn't mind having the time alone. Soon the place would be swarming with people, looking at him, pitying him, trying to read his face. He wasn't looking forward to it.

He laid a start for a fire in the pit—a few curls of birch bark and a heap of small twigs and fine pine branches—then went and sat on the sand at the edge of the lake and took from his pocket the photocopied poem he'd dug up from among his college papers and notebooks: *Thanatopsis* by William Cullen Bryant. He'd read it in the English class he took his freshman year.

No one expected him to read or say anything at the service, and he certainly didn't have to. But he'd always liked the poem. It was about the dead being reclaimed by the Earth. But in a gothic, Tolkienesque sort of way; not like the weird Native American poetry his mother used to make them read.

He took the pencil from behind his ear and scanned down the wrinkled sheet, trying to figure out which parts to read. He settled on a chunk from the middle:

Earth, that nourished thee, shall claim
Thy growth, to be resolved to earth again,
And, lost each human trace, surrendering up
Thine individual being, shalt thou go
To mix forever with the elements.

And the last few lines:

So live, that when thy summons comes to join
The innumerable caravan which moves
To that mysterious realm, where each shall take
His chamber in the silent halls of death,
Thou go not, like the quarry-slave at night,
Scourged to his dungeon, but, sustained and soothed
By an unfaltering trust, approach thy grave
Like one who wraps the drapery of his couch
About him, and lies down to pleasant dreams.

He read it through once aloud, softly under his breath. The wind hushed over the lake and somewhere in the trees a squirrel clucked and chirred. When he'd finished reading, he felt a sense of gentle relief. Now, even if he lost his nerve or fumbled at the service, at least he'd said it. He'd read the words aloud while sitting here on the lakefront with the sun warm on the crown of his head, thinking about his father and Gail, alone.

He wrapped his arms around his shins and leaned his forehead against his knees. He found himself thinking—not for the first time since the accident—about what might have happened if he had taken his father up on his invitation to join them on their flight. Would the plane still have gone down, or might the extra weight in the backseat have changed the balance of things, kept whatever had happened from happening? Would the plane have fallen the same way, or might it have landed differently, in a way that might have saved one or all of them?

At close to ten, he heard the first car rolling down the dirt road. Too soon, he thought. He wasn't ready to start greeting people. He didn't want to greet them at all—that was Abe's job. His was to direct traffic.

But to his relief, it was only his mother, along with Jude and Grandmother Perry, and the aide from the nursing home who'd accompanied her. Eric helped his grandmother out of the car and once she was standing firmly on the grass she laid her slight, veined hand on his and said, "Thank you, young man."

"That's Eric, Dorothy," Carol said. "Your grandson."

"Who?" She squinted up at him. One of her blue eyes was fogged over, but the other was clear.

"It's me, Grandmother," Eric said.

Her face softened with what appeared to be pity, and she said, "You must be here to see Clay. I'm sorry, dear, but I don't think he's coming. I'll be glad to tell him you called, though. What did you say your name was?"

"Come on, Dorothy," Carol said. She flashed Eric a sympathetic smile and took Grandmother Perry's arm. "Let's go inside and get you a cup of tea."

As Carol and the nurse guided Grandmother Perry up into the farmhouse Eric heard her ask, "Are we going to see Abe?"

Jude, who'd been standing back by the car this whole time, came closer. "Don't sweat it," she said. "In the car she kept asking when they'd be coming around with the beverage cart."

Eric smiled briefly. "But she remembers who you are, right?"

"Yeah," said Jude. "I guess she does."

From up the road came the hushed rumble of another approaching car, and Jude cupped a hand to her ear. "Here they come," she said. "The grieving masses."

Eric knew she expected him to smile, but he couldn't bring himself to do it. He wished she could stop being so sarcastic, at least for today.

"I'll go park the car," Jude said. "Behind the barn?"

"Yeah," said Eric. "Thanks."

As Jude pulled their mother's car away, a yellow VW bus rolled up the drive to take its place. Seconds later, Abe emerged from the farmhouse, showered and dressed in a white, African-looking tunic over pressed khaki pants. He walked toward the VW bus with outstretched arms as its occupants—a fat, white-bearded man and a witchy-looking woman in a long, patch-work skirt—clambered out. The three of them came together into a tight, tearful embrace.

Eric watched for a moment, not quite sure what to do, then walked down to the end of the drive to wait for the next car.

The stream of traffic was steady for the next few hours. By two o'clock, Eric had counted one hundred and sixty-one people, not including himself, his siblings, his mother, or his grandmother. Most of them he knew—recent staff members, old family friends, a few locals, probably there out of curiosity more than anything else—but many of them, like the people in the yellow van, he didn't. His father would have wanted this: all his friends and associates and acquaintances, coming here to celebrate his life. But Eric found himself feeling envious, even angry with them for descending on his home and trying to get in on his family's grief. They'd taste sorrow for a few hours, maybe even shed a few tears, but then they could leave it behind and get on with their lives. He didn't have that option.

If he'd listened to Abe and his father and everyone else and stayed at school, he wondered, would all this be easier? Maybe his studies, his friends, the idea of a future career would have offered some comfort. Right now, they would be back there waiting for him. Maybe he would have even had a girlfriend by now. Rachel from the computer building or Kathleen from his Russian class, both of whom thought of him as just a friend, might have changed their minds. He would have someone's hand to hold during the service.

He wouldn't feel so utterly and completely alone.

At half past two, Eric left Sergei in charge of greeting and directing cars, and went around back to see if there was anything else Aura needed him to do. On the main lawn and the deck behind the dining hall, guests were milling and talking, paper cups of lemonade in their hands. The atmosphere was almost festive. Abe smiled and nodded as a heavyset woman with a thick braid down her back talked at him, one hand flat to her chest, the other gripping his upper arm. Not far from them, his mother, Grandmother Perry and her nurse, and a few people

Eric didn't recognize sat in a loose circle of folding chairs. Aura and Matt were on the deck, surrounded by Aura's aunts and uncles and cousins. Eric lifted a hand, hoping to catch her attention, but she didn't see him.

At quarter to three, he went up to his apartment and changed into the outfit he'd laid out: a clean, black button-down shirt, black pants, and the black suede Oxfords he'd had since high school. Before he left, he remembered to take *Thanatopsis* out of the pocket of the blue jeans he'd taken off. He held the folded paper between his fingers for a moment, and then tossed it onto his desk.

Jude

SHE THOUGHT SHE LOOKED different enough that people wouldn't recognize her, but they did. One after another, they approached her where she stood, in the corner of the deck next to the double screen doors to the dining hall, and told her how sorry they were for her loss. She recognized some of the people; others she remembered only from pictures, or stories her parents told. But they all remembered her. Little Judie Perryweiss. The middle one—so smart and creative; so mature for her age. Thoughtful, independent. With that cool, curly hair. They all knew she'd have a wonderful life. Growing up in a place like this how could she not? She was strong. She'd get through this.

When they asked her what she was doing (How would they react, she wondered, if she replied, "My boss"?) she answered vaguely that she did this and that for a theater company, and they all said of course; they expected she'd do something *interesting*.

After a solid half hour of this, she made her way through the crowd to the edge of the garden and lit a cigarette. Smoking wasn't allowed on the property except back behind the kitchen—a concession to the kitchen staff and the occasional foreign counselor who couldn't go without—but she didn't care.

Within seconds, Aura was standing in front of her, so close that Jude could see herself reflected in the lenses of Aura's sunglasses, her cigarette distorted to the size of a baguette.

"I know, I know," Jude said. "Cut me some slack, OK? Just for today?"

"I was actually going to ask if I could have one."

Jude smiled. "But of course."

"But let's go around back," Aura said, glancing over her shoulder. "I don't want Matt to see."

"Gotcha," said Jude. Matt had introduced himself to her earlier: a nondescript, former frat-boy type with a receding hairline who worked at the same big corporation Aura did and looked like he spent a lot of time at the gym. Jude instinctively disliked him, and sensed that the feeling was mutual. "You're the actress or something, right?" he'd said.

Jude and Aura walked through the dining hall and kitchen, where the catering staff was assembling platters of hors d'oeuvres, and out the back door to the service area—the one part of the camp that didn't look like it belonged on a brochure. Here there were dumpsters and propane tanks and empty milk crates. She sat on one of these while she smoked. Aura stood.

Neither of them said anything for a while and then, after a particularly vocal exhale, Aura jerked her head toward the caterer's van and said with what sounded like a trace of amusement, "I planned this whole big freakin' thing, and probably three quarters of the people here hate my mother. The blond bimbo who stole your dad away from your mom. Not that she wasn't a bimbo. I mean, Jesus, she was pretty much the definition of a bimbo, right?" She gave a brittle laugh, and Jude was about to protest—Gail had been flighty, maybe a little flaky, but not dumb.

Aura went on. "You probably hated her, too, right? Not that I blame you."

"I never had a problem with your mom," Jude said. "Just my father."

Aura pushed her sunglasses up onto her head. The skin around her eyes was pink and raw. "Do you wish you'd been on better terms with him? Now, I mean?"

Jude shrugged. "I guess. Yeah."

Aura looked away. "I wish I'd been on better terms with my mother."

"I thought you guys got along fine."

"We did. Only fine, though, you know?" She shrugged one shoulder. "I guess I was probably too hard on her."

"For what?"

Aura took a long draw on her cigarette, her mouth pulling down at the corners, carving marionette-like lines around her mouth. She looked suddenly much older than she was. She blew the smoke out fast and hard. "For being a bimbo, I guess. All the men in and out of our life when I was a kid. And then her getting together with Clay. I always really liked your mom, you know. I thought of her as, like, an aunt or something." She glanced at her watch. "We should go. People will wonder where we are."

"Let them," Jude said. It was nice—strange, but nice—to be having something close to a real conversation with Aura. She didn't want it to end quite yet. "We're the grieving children. We can do whatever we want."

"Yeah, *you* can," Aura said. She stood, dropped her cigarette to the dirt, and started grinding it under the toe of her pointy-toed pumps. "Thanks for the cigarette. I hope I didn't just fuck myself over by having one. I forgot how good it feels."

"How long ago did you quit?"

The corner of Aura's mouth twitched upward. "Probably right around the same time you started." She pulled her sunglasses back down. "So, you coming, or what?"

"I don't know."

Aura looked at her for a few seconds, and Jude couldn't tell if her expression was one of disapproval or disbelief or neither. The dark lenses of her glasses obscured her eyes completely and her mouth was set in a soft, straight line. "All right," she finally said, and left.

Jude crushed the stub of her cigarette out against the ground, then found the remains of Aura's and tossed them into the sand-filled plaster bucket by the door. She sat back down on the crate, lit another, and listened to the caterers clanging and chattering inside. One of them had a ridiculous laugh that sounded literally like HA HA HA. Jude wished she could go inside and join them, work with them and be likewise oblivi-ous to the occasion. As far as the caterers were concerned, this might as well be a wedding, a bar mitzvah, a retirement dinner.

Sitting back here, Jude could almost forget she was at the camp. She'd never spent much time in this little corner of the property, even during the year, when there was no kitchen staff, no one smoking. It always felt off-limits, even a little dangerous: the industrial underbelly of the place.

She looked at her watch. Ten minutes to three. The service would be starting soon. People were probably on their way to the campfire ring. Any minute now the hammered dulcimer music would start. Once everyone was settled in around the fire, the priest (she couldn't believe there was a priest) would stand up in front and put on one of those forced, beatific smiles, look up at the pine trees and say something about how wonderful it was to be celebrating two lives in such a beautiful place. Jude had seen her share of weddings and funerals here, and they did it every time. Priests, rabbis, new-age shamans—it didn't matter. They all loved how goddamned beautiful it was, and smiled up at the trees like they were the first to discover them.

A few wise, calming words. Maybe a passage of scripture or two. Then Gail's sister would do a eulogy. (Gail first, no question—the opening act for the real reason most people had come.) There would be crying. Then a song or five; Jude had seen at least three people carrying guitars, not counting her mother, who planned to play *Moonshadow*. A little grizzly considering the circumstances, Jude thought. *If I ever lose my eyes... my legs...my mouth...* Christ.

Next would come the part of the service when people started talking about how incredible her father was. Abe's eulogy wouldn't be too bad. He wouldn't gush. But others would. One after another they'd stand up and read bad poetry and talk about the vision and warmth of Clay Perry; how he'd brought happiness and meaning to so many lives.

Which he had, of course. There was no denying it. But what about what he'd done to his own family? Aura was right; lots of people probably *did* think of Gail as the home-wrecking bimbo. But Clay, they seemed to forgive.

Jude wondered how much people knew about the situation.

Did they know her father had been seeing Gail behind his wife's back for more than three years? Did they even care? It probably just endeared him to them further. Amazing as he was, he was still human.

Of course none of them knew that he'd made his teenage daughter his confidante as he wrestled with whether or not to leave his wife. None of them knew about the letter he'd slid under her pillow the day he left their mother for good, whose words Jude still remembered: *Dear Judie – By the time you read this, I'll be gone. I'm going to tell Mom about Gail, and then I'm going to go to the cottage…*

Gail's aunt's cottage in Orchard Beach—a halfway point between Boston and Talbotts Corner, where the two of them used to rendezvous, just about every month for two years. It was easy enough for him to come up with excuses—camp business, a visit to his parents.

She was thirteen years old, and he'd told her about their love shack.

But no one here would believe it. It would be unthinkable to them that someone who'd devoted his whole life to the happiness and wellbeing of children could do something so inappropriate, so unfair, to one of his own.

"Pardon me."

Jude whipped her head around. A few yards away stood a man with shoulder-length white hair and a handlebar mustache. He wore black leather pants and a leather jacket over a white collared shirt and skinny red leather tie. His hands were behind his back—a subservient sort of pose, weirdly at odds with his tough appearance.

"Sorry if I startled you," he said. "Can you tell me where

I'm supposed to go for the memorial service?"

There was something familiar about this man, though Jude was almost certain she'd never met him before. Maybe it was just the mustache and the hair. He looked a little like a scrawny Hulk Hogan. "And you are?"

He tilted forward from the waist and back up again, Japanese-style. "Dane Walden. I'm a friend of Carol Weiss's." His eyes narrowed. "You're not her daughter, are you?"

"Yeah, I'm Jude. Have we met?"

He smiled in a shy sort of way that made his mustache swallow up his mouth. "Your mom's told me a lot about you. And your brothers. Are they here?"

"Yeah, they're here," Jude said distractedly. She was searching her memory for the name Dane Walden, but coming up blank. "How do you know my mom?"

He looked down at his boots. "Oh, we go way back. Seventy-six, seventy-seven."

"So you knew my dad, then, too."

Dane nodded once. "I'm real sorry about what happened."

"Thanks."

"Isn't the service about to start?"

"I don't know. Probably."

"You're not going?" The man's voice was soft with surprise, and Jude felt suddenly ashamed.

"Just needed to have a smoke." She stood and dropped the remains of her cigarette into the plaster bucket. "I'll walk over with you. Come on, we can cut through the kitchen."

Dane nodded, took a few steps forward, then stopped. "I put my Harley in the barn. That OK? She's pretty new and I'm a little overprotective." His mustache swallowed up his smile again.

"Yeah, it's fine," said Jude. She held open the kitchen door for him. "Coming?"

"You bet," he said, and followed her inside, his leather pants squeaking.

Abe

THE MEMORIAL SERVICE WAS beautiful. That's what everyone said afterward, and Abe agreed. The readings and stories and songs had been heartfelt and bittersweet. He'd gotten almost all the way through his eulogy without crying, and when he did, it was from laughter that turned into tears as he recounted one of his father's kookier camp activities from the early days: he'd bus the whole camp, counselors and all, up to the Bangor airport, where they'd wait at the gates and welcome arriving passengers: "Picture it," Abe told the mourners. "A bunch of random kids and long-haired hippie adults, clapping and jumping up and down and yelling 'Welcome to Bangor!' to total strangers. It was completely absurd and completely magical."

The service lasted almost two hours but Abe felt like it was over far too quickly. As people wandered away from the lakeside after he and Eric had scattered the ashes, Abe had the sensation that the ground was falling away from under him. *That was it?* he kept thinking. That was the extent of the formal grieving, and now he was supposed to move on? He could have done this for hours more. Days. As long as people were gathered together, talking and thinking about his father, it was as if he wasn't gone yet.

To his relief, a fair number of people planned to spend the night, and after dinner was eaten and most of the guests had gone the property took on an almost festive atmosphere. Lanterns glowed inside the tents set up at the base of the meadow and the campfire was rekindled. Flashlight beams bobbled along the ground as people walked, talking softly, laughing. Bottles of wine and cases of beer appeared, as did a few pipes. The air was cool and clear, shot through with the scent of wood smoke.

Abe changed into jeans and a sweatshirt and settled down by the campfire where people were swapping songs. He accepted a few hits off the pipe being passed by group of college-aged, neo-hippie kids who'd been campers in the early nineties, and let the sound of people's voices and the strumming of guitars envelop him.

As it got later and colder, those who remained moved in closer to the fire. Abe had a sense that, like him, these last dozen or so people didn't want the night to end.

"Clay convinced me we were gonna change the world," a mostly-bald man in a thick alpaca sweater said—Jim something or other; he'd been a counselor for a couple of summers, back in the early seventies. Earlier, when he'd embraced Abe, Abe had done a fairly convincing job, he thought, of pretending to remember who he was.

"He made me believe that right here, in this place," Jim gestured up at the pines, "we were creating a generation of citizens who would change the world. Who'd carry on the work our generation had started."

"Yeah, so much for that," a woman somewhere said, to laughter.

"Oh, come on," said Jim. "Some things are better. There hasn't been another Vietnam."

"No," the woman countered. "Just Granada and Nicaragua and the Persian Gulf..."

"Hey, at least there's free love," another man said. "Right in the Oval Office."

Everyone laughed again.

"Well," said Jim, "we did our best, right? It was really something for a while."

There was a quiet murmur of agreement, then silence, except for the snap and hiss of the fire.

Abe spoke up. "Do you think it could happen again?"

"Could what happen?" Jim asked.

"I mean, do you think we could bring some of the old values back? Get kids to start thinking about community and social change and the environment again?"

"It was like that, for a little while," said one of the neo-hippies, a skinny kid in dreadlocks. "In ninety, ninety-one, when we were here. Desert Storm was happening and Earth Day was a big deal. The economy was bad, and people were pissed, you know. They started waking up."

"Clay helped us start a recycling program at the camp," the girl next to him, longhaired and big-eyed, said.

"Yeah, right, but now," the dreadlock kid continued, "we got a Democrat in the White House and guys my age making millions off dot-com stocks, and nobody gives a crap about anything except about what kind of SUV they should buy. And kids—man, kids aren't interested in anything except surfing the web and playing X-Box. I mean, it sucks that Clay had to fancy up this place, but what else could he do, right? Kids don't want to spend their summer learning about community and becoming better people. They just want to be entertained."

There were grumbles of agreement all around.

"Here we are now, entertain us," a middle-aged woman warbled, annoyingly, sounding more Judi Collins than Kurt Cobain.

"They're not all like that," a voice said. Everyone squinted to see who it was: Eric. He was sitting back a few rows, out of range of the firelight. Abe hadn't even known he was here. "I've been here every summer of my life. It's not like it used to be, I guess, but it's not totally changed either. There are still a lot of good kids. And the counselors are great, most of them. My dad was—" His voice faltered. "He loved this place. He gave it everything he had."

Nobody said anything. Eric stood and zipped up his jacket. "Sorry," he said. "There's water in that can to pour on the embers when you leave." He walked away, moving briefly through the glow cast by the fire, and disappeared up into darkness.

"Of course Clay loved this place," Jim said quietly. "He did his best. It's the times that changed."

"Materialism is the opiate of the masses," the warbling woman said.

People started nodding and hmm-ing and Abe had a feeling the conversation was about to devolve further into one of those masturbatory liberal whine-fests—everyone pontificating about what was wrong with the world, trying to one-up each other in their indignation, congratulating themselves on how enlightened they all were. He did it himself sometimes; it could be comforting. But not tonight.

"Hey guys, I'm gonna turn in," he announced, getting to

his feet. "It's been a long day."

They wished him goodnight and the warbler added, "God bless," making Abe feel a pinch of guilt for being annoyed at her.

He caught up with Eric at the garden. "Hey," he said. "Hey, I'm sorry, buddy. I shouldn't have opened that can of worms."

Eric shrugged and kept walking. "It was a fair question. I just didn't like where things were going."

"Me either. You wanna go up the meadow?"

"Sure," said Eric. "Yeah."

"Hold on two minutes. I'll get us some beers."

He retrieved one of the six packs he'd stashed in the walk-in fridge in the dining hall kitchen, and he and Eric moved in silence past the tents at the base of the meadow, up the gentle slope of the hill, along the wide swath mowed through the taller grass—grass that would be thigh-high and singing with crickets by August.

At the top of the hill, near the edge of the woods, there was a small fire pit encircled by blackened rocks and, a few yards away, a pair of boulders—one about three feet high, and the other closer to four. The top of the larger boulder was flat, the perfect size for two people and a six-pack of beer. Abe had sat on its cold surface many times before—as a kid, with a pair of binoculars, watching for foxes and deer; as a CIT, with contraband booze and hopes of getting laid; and on visits in more recent years, with various girlfriends, when he thought the relationship was about to get more serious.

More often than not, those visits turned out to be the relationship's swan song. There was something about this place that seemed to magnify the flaws of the women he dated and underline his lack of connection with them. He'd never had the chance to bring Jess here, but he had a feeling she might have passed the test—a feeling he ushered quickly from his mind.

He twisted a can of beer off from the pack and handed it to Eric, then opened one for himself. In spite of the beer he'd already drunk and the pot he'd smoked, he still felt almost sober. But he couldn't have been. Because looking down at the flicker of lights in the tents below, feeling the cool breeze on his face, he felt a sense of something almost like contentment—a sense that everything was going to be all right. That he was where he belonged. And what besides intoxication could explain that?

"Today was good," he said. "I think Dad would have liked it."

"And Gail," said Eric.

"And Gail."

They were quiet for a few minutes, both of them, slurping thoughtfully from their cans, and then Eric said, "Did you see that biker guy? The one who looked like Hulk Hogan?"

"Sure," said Abe. He'd noticed his mother talking with him after the service.

"He was cool. We talked about tractors. He's got a place in upstate New York with a hayfield. He told me he knew mom back in the seventies, so I thought maybe you'd remember him. Dane Walden is his name."

"No," said Abe. "But there are a lot of people here today that I don't remember."

Eric was quiet for a moment. "After dinner, when I went to bring some garbage out back, I saw him and Mom, walking toward the lake together, alone. And he had his arm around her."

"Oh yeah?" said Abe. "Well, they're old friends, right? He

was probably just trying to be comforting."

"But she had her arm around him, too. Doesn't that seem kind of, I don't know, intimate?"

Abe smiled in the dark at his brother's innocence. The kid really needed to get laid. "Eric, buddy, just because a man and a woman are walking with their arms around each other, it doesn't mean they're romantically involved. You know how Mom is. She's all touchy feely with everyone."

"Yeah, I'm aware of that," Eric said. "Buddy."

"Sorry. I just think you're making something out of nothing. It's not that big a deal."

"I know what I saw," said Eric.

Supplement to the Eden Lake brochure, 1975

What parents have said about Eden Lake

"We just wanted to say thank you for giving Jennifer one of the most rewarding summers of her life. She made good friends and especially loved the arts and crafts options. She feels like she really found herself, and continues to be interested in creative projects. She's already looking forward to next summer." —Madge and Jonathan Baker, Chappaqua, NY

"Just walking onto the Eden Lake property when we dropped our son off, I felt a sense of calm and peace. Clay and Carol have created a wonderfully nurturing environment for children in a beautiful setting."—Heidi Rader, Westport, Conn.

"Julie truly blossomed this summer, and made huge strides in her self-esteem. She even learned to enjoy swimming, which she hated at her last camp, because they forced her to take lessons. The gentle, child-centered approach of Eden Lake was much better for her learning style." — Barbara Schapiro, Weston, Mass.

"Steven loved everything about Eden Lake: the activities, the counselors, the lake, the trips, even the food. Our only complaint: how come WE can't come, too?" - Phil and Judy Cole, Elizabeth, NJ

Abe

UNRELENTING. THAT WAS THE only word to describe the parents of the campers-to-be, whose phone calls and emails Abe spent hours fielding each day over the next two weeks. They were unrelenting in their need for reassurance, unrelenting in their demands and unrelenting in their insistence that they speak to the director. Not the assistant director, but the director: Clay's son. Abe was amazed at how important this was to people, how reassuring they found it. Most of the time it was the first thing people asked: Are you Clay's son? Then they'd tell him how sorry they were. Most of them, that is. Others jumped right into the reason for their call:

"How many miles is it from the camp to the nearest hospital?"

"When Becky's flight gets in, will someone meet her right at the gate, or at the baggage claim area, or at the curb?"

"It's just that Ashley—that's Ashley Wise Bliman, no hyphen—is concerned that she might get put into the cabin with the twelve-year-old girls instead of the thirteen-year-olds, because she is twelve, of course, but she's going into eighth grade, not seventh, because she skipped first grade, so she's used to being with kids a year older than her, and feels more comfortable with that peer group. And when I spoke with Clay back when we enrolled he said it would be no problem for her to be with the girls going into eighth, but we just wanted to double check in case that message didn't get passed along."

"Yes," Abe had to restrain himself from saying in response to this one, which came at the end of a particularly long and aggravating day. "In fact, my father's last words, as he lay dying in the wreckage of his plane were, 'Make sure Ashley Wise Bliman gets put in a bunk with the thirteen year olds. And that's Wise Bliman with no hyphen.'"

And then there were the emails. Dozens of them every day, sometimes three or four from the same few parents, who seemed compelled to shoot off a note every time a thought came into their heads: How many pairs of underwear should I pack for Joshua/Jeffrey/Dylan? Does Caitlin/Emily/Molly need to bring dress shoes for any reason? He wondered if they even expected responses or if writing the emails was some kind of release in itself.

It couldn't have been like this back in the old days. Sure, there were always one or two high-maintenance mothers—he remembered his father rolling his eyes when he talked to them on the phone as he did his charming, persistent best to reassure them. But this wasn't just one or two. This was ridiculous.

It was ironic: one of the major disadvantages for a lot of the kids who participated in AfterStart's programs was their parents' lack of involvement in their lives. Whether they were in jail or on drugs or just too busy working to try to make ends meet, they were parents who couldn't or wouldn't give their kids the attention they deserved. A month earlier, Abe wouldn't have believed there was such a thing as a parent being too in-volved in their child's life. But now, given the two extremes, he wasn't sure which was worse.

But of course he knew which was worse. The kids who came to Eden Lake would never want for anything.

When Abe started working at AfterStart the idea of trying to get some of their students up to the camp on scholarship had occurred to him, but the everyday demands of his job proved so consuming that he never found the time or energy to pur-sue it. Besides, he was too new on the job to be initiating new projects. But after the Ashley Wise Bliman call, Abe realized that he had to do something to inject a little social conscious-ness back into this place. For his own sanity, if nothing else.

That's when he remembered the rap sessions: Back in the seventies and early eighties, every day during afternoon free time, anyone who wanted could sit under a tree with Clay and talk about a given topic: feminism, racism, marriage and divorce, drugs, nukes. It was amazingly popular; Clay some-times had to turn kids away to keep the groups small enough. He was always able to get them talking, sharing their questions and feelings and thinking about how the issues related to their own lives.

Abe wasn't sure when the rap sessions had fizzled out. Maybe around '84 or '85. That was when enrollment started to skyrocket and the feel of the place began to change. New camper cabins were built. Tennis and horseback riding were added as activities and community chores were eliminated. Kids started bringing Walkmans to camp. Girls started wearing more makeup.

It was time, Abe decided, to bring the rap sessions back.

There was plenty to talk about—the Lewinsky scandal, the Balkans, AIDS, drugs, gay rights, racism, third world poverty, prayer in school. These were smart kids, with educated parents. He was sure that if he approached things the right way he could get them talking. He'd have to come up with a new name, though. Talk Time? Chew the Fat? Shoot the Shit? He'd figure it out later. As soon as things quieted down.

≈

Strickland Strawner, returning for a second year as Program Director, arrived on Friday afternoon. He was an eager twenty-six-year-old from Portland with a prominent Adam's apple, a prematurely receding hairline and a jaw rippled with acne scars. The five of them—Eric, Sergei, Aura, Abe, and Strickland—went out for pizza that night, and while they ate, Strickland told them, with great, gesticulating enthusiasm, about the system he'd thought up for making activity sign-ups less chaotic, and his plan to create an online version of the camp newspaper, so parents could read about what was going on from home. Abe went to bed that night charged up and hopeful, excited to meet the rest of the staff and get things rolling.

Staff week had been one of Abe's favorite parts of the summer when he was a kid. During those six days, he and Jude and Eric had the nearly undivided attention of twenty or thirty young adults full of energy and laughter and jokes—jokes that frequently went over their heads, but who cared? They got to sit next to them at meals and help them set up their activity areas and toss Frisbees with them on the main lawn. Every year, Abe would identify a favorite, usually one of the sports counselors, often from England or Australia, who'd call him "man" or "mate" and was always willing to kick a soccer ball around with him. There were invariably one or two duds, too—an uptight riding instructor or a humorless lifeguard. But all of the counselors, whether "fun" or not, held Abe in their thrall. He couldn't wait to be like them. Of course, that time had seemed ages away. Twenty-one? Twenty-two? They might as well have been a hundred.

But on Saturday morning, as the counselors began to arrive, Abe couldn't believe how young they seemed. Seeing the blank smoothness of their faces and the dullness of their eyes, watching them shuffle into the rec. hall in their flip-flops and college sweatshirts for the first meeting, grumbling about the drizzle outside, it was inconceivable to him that these—these *adolescents*—were the same age as the people he'd idolized and trusted summer after summer when he was growing up.

The plan had been for everyone to sit in a circle on the floor, which was still glossy and redolent with the fresh coat of polyurethane Eric and Sergei had applied the week before. But the mud and clumps of wet pine needles dragged in on the soles of shoes made that an unpleasant prospect, so Eric pulled out the racks of folding chairs.

While everyone was getting settled and the last stragglers arrived, Abe took the opportunity to note the names on each counselor's "Hello my name is" sticker and match them against the Excel spreadsheet Aura had done up with each counselor's name, cabin assignment and activities. He made brief notes to help him start connecting names with faces: Ted Regis (martial arts, waterfront): surfer-dude hair. Jen Carroll (dance and yoga): pixie haircut, hot. Bart Lopate (ropes course, outdoor adventure): big beard, giant calves. Henry Mataway (soccer):

Black. Michelle Schmidt (photography, creative writing): dark hair, pale, freckles and moles. Tamara McDonough (waterfront, sailing): pierced eyebrow, nice rack. And on and on.

At four twenty-five, Aura told Abe it was time to get started and raised her hand—the camp signal for "quiet." Abe raised his too, making a point of keeping his elbow slightly bent. Strickland and a few of the other returning counselors raised their hands, and soon the room was quiet, but for the pounding of the rain on the roof.

"Well," Abe began, "I know this isn't what any of you expected. Me running the camp, I mean."

Next to him, Aura shifted in her folded chair.

"Us, that is. But it's what my dad wanted, and we want to make this summer as good as it can be, in spite of the circumstances." Yee-haw, Abe thought to himself. Way to inspire them. If his father had a grave, he'd be rolling in it right about now.

He laughed and put his fist to his forehead. "I'm sorry, that was a terrible way to open. Let me start over. I'm Abe Perryweiss, this is Aura Mackinnon, and we're really glad you're here, and we're looking forward to a great fucking summer. Better?"

"Much better!" cried Strickland Strawner, with an awkward but heartfelt pump of his fist in the air.

Aura forced a laugh. "Of course we try not to use that kind of language around the campers."

Eric

ERIC WAS UP LONG before anyone else on the third day of staff week.

He'd only had two beers at Jolly Roger's the night before, as opposed to the three, four, seven most people had. And lately, it seemed, no matter what time he went to bed, he couldn't get himself to sleep past six a.m. He awoke with the first full light, each time with the sensation of moving forward at full speed, then stopping himself just before plunging over the edge of a cliff into the sudden void that sprang up before him: his father and Gail's absence. For the first few minutes, it was unbearable. And then, the ground would begin to level out again; he stopped seeing the emptiness. Instead, he saw his bathrobe, his toothbrush, his yin-yang face in the mirror: white skin, brown beard.

The lake was still in the mornings, flat and glossy. There was a place on the shore, a little inlet between two gnarled oaks whose exposed roots clawed the sand, where he liked to stand and do the little bit of t'ai chi he knew. He'd learned it the summer he was thirteen, from a counselor from California named Paul Koepke who was a radio DJ and a coke addict until martial arts changed his life. Paul was a good friend to him that summer, which was a memorably lonely one. His two best friends from the previous few years had decided not to come back, and all the boys his age were suddenly obsessed with girls, sneaking away to fool around with them in the woods and bragging about how far they'd gotten. Eric had crushes on a few girls himself, but was terrified to act on them.

He liked the cool dampness of the sand under his bare feet this morning; it made it easier for him to stay present, focused on the physicality of his body and breath, instead of distracted by thought. He did his brief practice, then picked up a stone from the shore and threw it into the lake. He stood watching until the last rings had faded and the surfaced of the water re-gelled and it was if he'd never thrown the stone at all.

He still had a few minutes before it was time to ring the wake-up bell, so he went and sat on the wooden bench swing at the edge of the main lawn. He pushed against the bare dirt with the balls of his feet and rocked, enjoying the familiar, plaintive creak of metal against metal overhead. Instinctively he looked up and checked the loops that connected the swing and the frame. They ate gradually through each other over time with the friction of movement, and had to be replaced periodically. Currently, there was a solid quarter-inch of metal at the intersection of the rings; Eric probably wouldn't have to replace them until next summer. Assuming there would be one.

Nobody had bothered asking him how he felt about the fact that their father had left the business to Abe. At first the arrangement hadn't bothered him. He wasn't cut out for running Eden Lake; he knew that. But the more he thought about it, the more it gnawed at him. He didn't see how his father could have thought it was a good idea to separate the property from the business of the camp itself. Or even possible. How could you separate the body from the soul?

"The permanent structures are considered part of the property," Dumont had explained. "All moveable assets, supplies, and equipment, as well the intangibles of reputation, contacts, and the perceived value of the Camp Eden Lake experience itself, are considered part of the business."

It was the "perceived value" part that especially bothered him. For example, horseback riding was a big reason a lot of campers came to Eden Lake, but the corral and stables were permanent structures, so they were part of the property, not the business. And the swing Eric sat on now: it was a quintessential part of the Eden Lake experience, featured on all of the camp brochures and the homepage of the web site. Rarely during the summer did it go unoccupied for more than a few minutes at a time. It was moveable, but not really. So whose was it?

It would only really matter, Eric supposed, if Abe decided to sell. He couldn't imagine anyone wanting to buy the business but not the land, and Jude would probably pounce on the chance to sell her share. Eric would have no choice. He would have to sell his share and leave Eden Lake. Just the thought of it made his spine clench. He didn't have the first clue where he'd go or what he'd do.

But maybe Abe wouldn't sell. He claimed to be exasperated by the work so far—the parents, the personnel issues, the million little things that needed to be done—but he didn't really seem that unhappy. There was energy in his movements, a sense of purpose when he walked the property. And late in the evening, when he and Eric and Sergei sat in the farmhouse drinking beers and listening to music, Abe seemed content, his bare feet up on the coffee table, his arm slung over the back of the couch, smiling at Sergei's stories. Maybe he would decide, as their father had for him long ago, that this was where he belonged.

Eric hoped with all his heart that he would.

At seven-thirty, he rang the wake-up bell, and at a few minutes after eight, the counselors began to shuffle in and make their way along the buffet, spooning up eggs and home fries, filling their cups with coffee. Most were red-eyed and greasy-haired, still reeking faintly of alcohol and smoke. Abe and Sergei arrived looking equally haggard. The only person who didn't show at all was Mike Voorhees, the pre-veterinary student who was going to run the animal care program, and who was supposed to go with Eric to Tuckerman's to pick up the animals that day. "I don't think you'll be seeing him until at least noon," his co-counselor, Josh, said with a grin and glances at the others at his table, who laughed. "He was fucking wrecked last night, remember?"

So Eric took Sergei instead. It took them about twenty minutes to get to Tuckerman's, but half an hour to get back; Eric drove more slowly when the trailer hitched to the truck was filled with animals.

Back at the camp, Sergei opened the broad, wooden gate of the animal care area, and Eric drove over the grass to the little barn. He got the rabbits settled first, placing them one at a time on the straw in the hutch. The baby rabbits were especially young this year, the size of guinea pigs. He'd chosen brown and black ones, and a few that were white with black spots, but none of the albinos. They reminded him of the first litter of rabbits he'd been responsible for, back when they kept animals at the camp year-round: six little albinos, just a few weeks old, that died when he transferred them to the outdoor hutch too soon.

It was mid-April, and the cold snap took everyone by surprise, but he should have known better. When he went out in morning to feed them, they were frozen solid in a heap, hard as stones. He'd run back inside and crawled into bed next to his warm, still-sleeping mother—into the space his father had vacated only two months before. When he told her what had happened, she put her arms around him and soon they were both crying. Eric remembered thinking he couldn't possibly be any sadder.

This hutch he'd built himself, half inside the barn, half out, with a rubber flap in between. When it was cold or rainy the rabbits could huddle on the inside, warmed by the bodies and breath of the other animals.

He was placing the last of the rabbits on the straw when he heard a clatter, a cry, and then what sounded like a small stampede. He ran outside to find Sergei running after the nanny goat, who was making a break for the gate—which Sergei had failed to close. Meanwhile, the rest of the bigger animals—two sheep, a pair of kids, three piglets and a donkey—were trotting nonchalantly down the ramp of the trailer and starting to fan out in the general direction of the gate. Inside the trailer, the chickens and geese squawked and honked, beating their wings against their cages.

"Let her go, just close the gate!" Eric yelled to Sergei, who was following the goat out of the pen and onto the gravel road, screaming in Russian what could be loosely translated as "fuck you, you fucking goat-fucker."

The piglets and one of the other kids were now almost to the gate, and Sergei was still following the goat, so Eric made a break for it. He managed to pull the gate shut in time, then jogged back to the barn for a lead to hook to the goat's collar.

"This goat is really a bitch!" Sergei yelled. "Look what she is doing!" The nanny had made it up to the farmhouse, and was now chomping on the tiger lilies beneath the living room windows. Sergei stood a few yards away, hands on his hips, shaking his head.

"Hold on," Eric shouted. "I'm coming."

He scaled the fence, swung his legs over, and was about to hop down to the ground when three things happened simultaneously: a piglet squealed beneath him, he remembered the piglet-sized hole in the chicken wire of the fence that he'd forgotten to fix, and a girl with strawberry blond hair appeared from behind the corner of the farmhouse, giggling, a tiny, alabaster hand over her mouth.

It was too late for Eric to arrest his descent, and as he dropped to the ground he stumbled over the piglet's back and pitched forward into the rain-filled ditch alongside the road, soaking the entire right side of his body up to his neck.

As he sat up, he saw the girl running toward him. "Are you OK?" she said, in a Russian accent with British intonation—the end of the question inflected down, not up.

She came to a halt with a little hop at the edge of the road and reached her hand down to help Eric up. She was so slight he feared he'd pull her down into the ditch with him if he took her hand. Which, it occurred to him, might be sort of nice. She was, quite possibly, the most beautiful, delicate girl he'd ever seen outside the pages of a fantasy comic. All she needed was a pair of gossamer wings.

"Yes, I'm OK," Eric said, and clambered to his feet on his own. "Thanks."

The girl stifled a smile, and then a high, exquisite giggle, merry as sleigh bells, rang from her mouth. "You fell over a pig!"

Eric grinned. "Yes, evidently I did."

They stood there for a moment, smiling at each other, until Sergei, still up by the side of the farmhouse, bellowed, "What the hell are you doing? Help me! This goat is going to eat the whole house!"

Indeed, the nanny had abandoned the tiger lilies, and was now up on her hind legs, chewing on a windowsill. Eric fished the lead out of the water and headed up toward the house.

"I'll help," the girl said, following. "My grandfather had goats at his farm and I was always taking care of them when I was very young. May I?" she took the lead from Eric, and as she did the side of her hand, cool and smooth as marble, skimmed his knuckles.

Both Sergei and Eric watched, transfixed, as the girl walked toward the goat, one hand outstretched, then began stroking the goat's back as it continued to nibble on the windowsill. After about a minute of this, she soundlessly hooked the lead onto the goat's collar and gave it a tug. The goat bleated in protest, but she continued to tug rhythmically until it relented and followed her onto the lawn.

"That was incredible," Sergei said, in English. "You are genius."

The girl replied in Russian. "Thank you. It's not so incredible, though. You just need to keep them calm."

"Her grandfather had goats at his farm," Eric said, also in Russian.

The girl looked at him in surprise. "*Gavareesh parusky?*"

"*Da, nemnogo,*" Eric said with a shurg. *A little.*

"He is being modest," Sergei said. "He speaks more than a little. Of course, not as much as me." He gave a little bow. "Sergei Dimov, at your service."

"Mariya Antipova," she said. "Masha. Translator for the Russian children. And you, the boy who falls on pigs, what is your name?" She cocked her head and smiled through pursed lips.

"Eric Perryweiss," he said, and added, to his own surprise, "I'm one of the owners."

"Ah, then you are my boss?" she said, in English, the same little smile still on her mouth. And in her eyes, too.

She was flirting with him. He could hardly believe it, but she was. He knew he had to think of something witty to say in reply, and think of it fast. All he could think of was "not really." Fortunately, before he got it out, Sergei laughed and whacked him on the back. "No, he is not your boss, only my boss. And boss of the animals. Your boss is his brother, Abe. Didn't you meet him?"

Masha shook her head. "I met the woman, your sister?" She looked at Eric. "She brought me from the airport this morning. What is her name?"

"Aura," Eric said. Something finally occurred to him—something clever he could say: "Like the cruiser."

"The cruiser?" said Masha, frowning. "Oh! You mean the Aurora. Yes."

"Right, yeah, the Aurora," Eric said, his heart sinking. How

could he be such an idiot? He'd done a whole report on the
ship for his advanced Russian seminar. There was a whole *song*
about it, for God's sake. This was what happened whenever he
tried to talk to a girl he liked. It was probably why the only
two sort-of girlfriends he'd ever had were girls who never shut
up. He didn't have to say a thing; they just yapped and yapped,
pausing only to tell him what a good listener he was; how
much sweeter than any other guy. Both had dumped him after
a few weeks with "let's just be friends."

"I suppose I should meet your brother," Masha said. "Do
you know where he is?"

"He is up at the rec. hall, I think," Sergei said, pointing.

"OK, yes. Your goat, Eric." She handed him the lead. "I'll
see you later, yes?"

"Yes," Eric said. As she started to turn away, he felt a lurch
of panic: she was going to see Abe. Any attraction she had to
Eric—and he was almost positive there was something there—
would instantly be vaporized when she met Abe.

"Wait. I'll go with you. I have to talk to him about some
things. Some maintenance issues."

"But what about the animals?" Masha asked.

"Sergei will take care of them." He offered the goat's lead to
Sergei. "Here. Take her back inside. And go get the piglet." He
gestured toward the other side of the pen, where the escaped
piglet was snuffling along the edge of the fence.

"I'll get the pig," Sergei said, "But I'm not going to touch
that goat. She hates me."

"OK, fine. We'll bring the goat with us." Eric gave her a tug.

"But why don't you just put her back into the pen?" asked
Masha. "I can wait, you know."

Eric felt his face warming, his heart thrumming. Of course she could wait. He just didn't think she'd *want* to. And now he was bringing a goat to the rec. hall? It was ridiculous. Masha knew it was ridiculous. The only thing he could think to do was take a breath and squint one eye, the way his father used to when he disagreed with someone and was about to make a firm rebuttal. "No," he said, "she's been cooped up in the truck. She could use the exercise."

And so the three of them trudged and stumbled and yanked their way past the farmhouse and the garden, across the lawn and into the rec. hall. Tim, the musical director, and one of the skinniest men Eric had ever seen, was at the upright piano on stage, playing "It's a Hard Knock Life," peering over his wire-rimmed glasses at the sheet music, while Jen, the dance teacher, shuffled and turned a few feet away, not quite dancing. Choreographing, Eric supposed.

Abe was up on a stepladder in front of the stage, fiddling with the lights. He had on jeans and an old green t-shirt with holes along the shoulder seams where it was wearing thin. He hadn't shaved for a couple of days and his hair was tousled and moist with sweat. Eric was glad he hadn't let Masha come up here alone.

"What the hell are you doing?" Abe said when he saw the goat.

"She needed the exercise," Masha said, and Eric could have kissed her right then and there.

The goat promptly deposited a small pile of turds on the floor.

Abe looked at Eric.

"I'll clean that up," he said. "This is Masha." He gestured

103

toward her. "The interpreter for the Russian campers."

Abe seemed to notice Masha for the first time. He descended the ladder, a smile spreading over his face, and came toward her with an outstretched hand. "Masha, hey, welcome. Nice to meet you."

Eric didn't like the way he was looking at her—intimate and twinkling, as if someone had set them up on a blind date, and this was their first meeting. Then again, Abe looked at most women that way.

Masha took his hand. "It's very nice to meet you," she said. She cocked her head at him and said, "You look so different. I would not think you were brothers."

"Yeah, well, Eric got our mom's good looks," Abe said, and glanced at Eric, who smiled at him with appreciation. Abe gave him an almost imperceptible wink. "And her brains. I don't know what the hell I'm doing with these lights, Eric. Can you take a look?"

"What's the problem?"

"Well, according to Valerie—"

There came a sudden, high-pitched squeal, which caused the goat to start, and then Valerie, the drama counselor, who'd emerged from the wings of the stage, was coming toward them, her arms outstretched. "A goat!" she cried. She seemed to forget that the stage was two feet up from the rest of the floor, and stumbled but recovered as she charged forward. She fell to her knees in front of the goat. "This is perfect!" she said. "Sandy the goat! Of course Sandy's supposed to be a dog, he's always a dog, but that doesn't mean we have to stick to the script, right? I think it would really *say* something if we used a goat instead. Or we could dress the goat up as a dog. Holy crap, think of the symbolism of *that*, right?" She looked up at them, smiling, expectant.

Masha looked at Eric, clearly hoping for some kind of explanation, but he had no idea what Valerie was talking about. She'd been like this the night before at Jolly Roger's, too, talking a mile a minute and not making a whole lot of sense. Eric—and everyone else—had just assumed she was drunk. Maybe she was now.

She scrambled to her feet and put her hand on the goat's back. "Tim!" she said. Tim stopped playing the piano and turned around. "Tim, what do you think? Sandy the goat! It's brilliant, yes? Forget about a kid in a dog suit, who needs it, right? We can use this goat and dress her up like a dog. Think of the symbolism!"

"Um, what symbolism, Val?" said Tim.

Abe gave Eric a furtive, questioning look. Eric shrugged in reply.

"A goat," Valerie said, gasping with giggles, "represents the devil. Or, that is…" she furrowed her brow and bunched up her lips, "according to scholars, the devil is represented by a goat. So…" She rolled her hands in front of her and flung them out at in front of her, waiting for someone else to fill in the punch line, which she seemed to think was obvious.

Nobody said anything. Abe wore a stiff, bewildered smile.

Valerie rolled her eyes. "Oh my god, you guys. Don't you get it? A *devil dog*!" She clapped her hands. "We have a Twinkie and a cupcake," she pointed to Tim and Jen, "A Yodel," she pointed at Eric, "A Snowball," she pointed at Masha, "A Drake's Cake"—Abe—"And…" she motioned with both outstretched arms at the goat, who seemed just as stunned as everyone else,

"A Devil Dog!" She started laughing again—bent over with her hands on her knees, laughing so hard that she didn't even appear to hear Tim, who came over and rubbed her back and started asking her if she was OK. She just laughed and laughed and laughed. And then, suddenly, she was curled up on the floor, sobbing.

Tim looked at Abe. "I think we'd better call a doctor."

Abe

ABE'S FATHER HAD CIRCLED the date, Saturday, June 27, in bright red, dry-erase pen, on the big whiteboard calendar on the wall of the office. In the box, he'd written "Arrival Day!!"

Several times during staff week, when had Abe felt particularly besieged by complaints and requests, stressed out by the amount of work he had to do, or dispirited by his grief, he'd looked up at that day on the calendar and felt buoyed by his father's enthusiasm for it—right there in red ink, alive and well, exclamation points and all.

But when the day actually arrived, all Abe felt was overwhelmed.

The campers started coming at ten in the morning and didn't stop until ten at night.

They came in SUVs and minivans and Volvos and Subarus, accompanied by crying mothers and stoic fathers and sulking siblings. They came by plane from San Francisco, Houston, DC, London, Paris, Rio de Janeiro, Moscow, and Tokyo, picked up by van at the Bangor and Portland airports and shuttled back to camp with their luggage strapped to the roof. And they came in chartered motor coaches—two that started in Cherry

Hill, New Jersey, and made stops in Manhattan, New Rochelle, Greenwich, and Westport, and another that collected campers in Wellesley, Newton, Cambridge, and Andover. One camper, a thirteen-year-old named Oak Wallace, came by bicycle. He and his father rode up together from Brattleboro, Vermont, camping along the way, as they apparently had every summer for the past three years.

They came bearing overstuffed duffels and enormous wheeled suitcases, tennis rackets and riding helmets, fishing rods and yoga mats. Some carried milk crates and laundry baskets full of miscellaneous gear—electric fans, CD players, stuffed animals. One girl got off the New York bus carrying a bright pink inflatable chair, which, according to the counselor who'd chaperoned the trip, had been inflated by being passed around the bus, each kid blowing into the thing until they got dizzy. Though Eric and Sergei and the CITs worked steadily, loading up the back of the pick-up and shuttling back and forth from the cabin villages, the luggage accumulated faster than they could haul it away. Abe recalled a time when all anyone brought was a sleeping bag and a single suitcase or army surplus duffel. But that was ancient history.

He circulated on the lawn in front of the farmhouse, doing his best to greet every camper personally as they arrived, as his father had always done. At first he offered kids his hand for a shake, then realized that it seemed to confuse some of the younger ones and the girls. He switched to a wave, but that seemed sort of clown-like and forced, so from then on out he just kept his hands on his hips and grinned.

He'd studied the binder full of enrollment forms and pictures the night before, and several times he was actually able to connect a kid's name with a relevant fact: *Hey, aren't you Emily Martin? Emily Martin from Mamaroneck who's going into fifth grade?* Or: *Jeff Silver – hey, Jeff, man, we're saving a space on the soccer team for you.* The parents were impressed, but only a handful of kids seemed surprised at being "known." And why not? They were accustomed to being the center of the universe. Why wouldn't the director of the camp know everything about them?

Abe spotted Chuck Niedermeier of Cambridge, Massachu-setts the second he got out of his mother's car: a helmet of unkempt brown hair, an MIT t-shirt tucked into knee-length denim shorts, and black Reeboks the approximate shape and size of submarines. Around his neck hung a pair of binoculars, which he immediately aimed up at the foliage of the oaks along the drive. *He's a very sweet, exceptionally gifted boy,* his mother had written on the "Special notes and considerations" portion of his enrollment form, *but he has some social adjustment issues, and sometimes struggles to fit in with his peers.*

Abe went over to him. "Let me guess. Chuck Niedermeier, right?"

The boy lowered his binoculars, looking stunned. "Hi," he said. Abe watched the boy's lips twitch over his clear plastic braces and heard a few quick intakes of breath; he was trying to figure out what he was going to say next. Abe waited.

"My reputation precedes me, I see," he finally said. "I'm probably the only kid here who's into birding."

"Oh, I don't know," said Abe. "There may be a few others. You never know."

Niedermeier nodded appreciatively. "That's a good point. Sometimes I'm a bit of a pessimist, I'm afraid."

"Well, we'll see if we can cure you of that." Abe smiled

at Mrs. Niedermeier, who'd approached and now stood with a hand on her son's shoulder. She was a sweet-faced, pink-cheeked woman with hair in a long braid, wearing a shapeless linen sundress and Birkenstocks. The kind of woman his parents might have been friends with way back when.

While Niedermeier wandered off with his binoculars, Peggy Niedermeier talked with Abe about her son's "social challenges."

"It's the other children I worry more about," she confided. "Children can be so cruel to each other."

"They can," Abe agreed. Especially twelve and thirteen-year-olds. If there were a flagpole at the camp, Abe would fully expect to find Chuck Niedermeier's underwear flying from it some morning.

"But apparently this place is pretty special. The non-competitive atmosphere, the emphasis on community and creativity and self-expression. Your father was very passionate about it when he met with us. What did he call this place?" She looked up, searching for the words. "A vision of what the world might be. We liked the sound of that."

So, thought Abe, his father had still been bandying that old phrase about. There was a time when it was on all the camp materials: *We like to think of Eden Lake as a vision of what the world might be if everyone lived in harmony with each other and with the land.* Now, of course, that vision included tennis courts, a climbing wall, and the unspoken right to bitch and moan if your kid didn't get to take horseback riding. But it was reassuring to know that there were still people who appreciated the original spirit of the place. And surely Peggy Niedermeier wasn't the only one.

"It is a special place," Abe said. "At least, we try."

Peggy chuckled to herself. "I went to this awful girls' camp when I was a kid. Camp Mohegan. We had to wear uniforms and salute the flag every morning. And we had these mean counselors. I mean, really mean. We all had to take swimming lessons, and if it was cold and you didn't want to go in the lake they'd throw you in. Literally, they'd pick you up and throw you in." She mimed a two-armed toss. "We had a camp song all about loyalty and sisterhood and the fondest days of our lives, and every time we sang it, I just wanted to scream, what a load of bullshit!"

"Yeah, no camp song here," Abe said. "Actually, for a while, 'Blowin' in the Wind' was sort of the unofficial Eden Lake anthem. I don't know if it gets sung much anymore, though."

"Oh, Chuck loves Bob Dylan. And Arlo Guthrie, Peter, Paul and Mary. All the old folkies. He was born too late."

"I can relate," Abe said.

Aura approached then, clipboard in hand, and told Abe he had a phone call in the office.

"Can't it wait?" he asked.

Aura shook her head with grave finality. Reluctantly, Abe shook Peggy Niedermeier's hand goodbye.

≈

Waiting for Abe on the line was the first irate parent of the day, a father whose nine-year-old daughter had called him on her cell phone from the bus in tears to say that a boy and a girl in the seats across the aisle were making out and had their hands up under each other's shirts. Abe spent the next twenty minutes apologizing and reassuring the father that the camp did not, in fact, "encourage reckless sexual promiscuity," and that he'd speak to the counselors who were on the bus to find out why nothing had been done. The counselors in question were Tamara and Ted, the lifeguards. Toward the end of staff week the two of them had been spending a lot of time together, and Abe wouldn't have been surprised to find out they were at the front of the bus playing their own game of tonsil hockey.

Seconds after he hung up the phone, it rang again. It was Michelle (photography; moles), who'd driven the van down to Boston with Masha to pick up the Russian campers. The campers had arrived, but their luggage had somehow ended up in Atlanta, and wouldn't be delivered for at least 48 hours. Now they were at a Wal-Mart so the kids could buy essentials for the next few days with the fifty-dollar cash compensation the airline had given each of them. "But," Michelle wailed, "the boys are buying Discmans and Swiss army knives, and the girls are buying sunglasses and trashy shoes and—"

"Well, let them," Abe said. "If they want to wear the same clothes for the next three days it's their choice." He lifted a hand in greeting to Nadine, the camp nurse, who had just come in. She whispered something to Abe that he couldn't make out, then started rifling through the drawer of camper files.

"OK, but how do I put this," Michelle said. "They reek. They just spent nine hours on a plane, and I don't think deodorant is a very popular product in Russia. Or mouthwash for that matter."

The screen door of the office croaked open again, and in walked Jen (dance teacher, hot) along with a small, sobbing, red-faced girl. "Homesick," she mouthed to Abe.

"Abe?" Michelle was saying on the phone. "What do you want us to do?"

"Just buy a bunch of deodorant and toothbrushes and toothpaste. No, forget the toothpaste, they can borrow other kids'. Have Masha tell them they have to each buy a pair of underwear. We'll give them all a camp T-shirt, and we've got towels from last year's lost and found."

Jen's camper had covered her eyes with her hands and her shoulders shook as she cried. Meanwhile, Nadine the nurse had taken a seat on one of the folding chairs in the corner, a pile of camper folders on her lap, and now blinked expectantly in Abe's direction.

"But how am I supposed to pay for the toothbrushes?" Michelle was asking. "We used the petty cash for gas and lunch."

"Use your own money. We'll reimburse you."

"I have, like, two dollars. And my credit cards are maxed out."

At that exact moment, a man and woman in matching green golf shirts walked into the office, flanked by a slump-shouldered, pimple-chinned boy in calf-length black shorts and a Korn T-shirt. The parents grinned at Abe, all white teeth and eagerness, while the boy positioned himself in the doorway and kicked the screen door back open each time it was about to swing shut.

"OK, forget it," Abe said into the phone, holding up a just-one-minute finger to the parents, to everyone. "I'll have some-one here run out and get stuff. Listen, I have to go. Someone's calling on the other line."

Right after Abe committed this white lie, the call-waiting tone beeped as if on cue.

"Wait, one more thing?" Michelle said. "I sort of got a speeding ticket on the way down. The camp will pay for that right?"

"Yes. No. We'll talk about it later." He switched over to the other line.

"Hey, yeah, hi, is this Abe?" Abe didn't recognize the voice; a young man's, maybe someone his own age. "This is Brendan Baker. You probably don't remember me, but I was a camper from eighty-four to eighty-seven."

Abe did, in fact, remember Brendan. But it was almost impossible to reconcile his memory of him—a quiet, bookish boy with glasses and headgear—with the jaunty, salesman-like confidence of the voice he heard now. "Brendan, hey, great to hear from you, man. I'm sorry, but could I—"

"It's the first day of camp, isn't it," Brendan said. "Damn. I am so sorry. You know it occurred to me, but then I thought… well, I won't keep you. I know how crazy things must be. I just wanted to send my condolences about your dad and Gail. When I heard about the accident—God, what a shock. Your dad was the coolest guy. I really looked up to him when I was a camper. All my life, in fact, he's been a role model to me."

"Thanks, I appreciate it." Abe tried not to sound too impatient, but everyone was staring at him. Meanwhile, Aura was slamming the panels of the copy machine open and shut, trying to fix a jam, while Strickland Strawner's nasal voice, amplified through a megaphone as he led relay races on the main lawn, leaked in from outside.

"I'm sorry again for calling on the first day," Brendan said. "My bad. I just wanted to pass along my sympathies. And there was something else I wanted to ask you about, but some other time. You can give me a call back when things settle down, or whenever."

"Sure, I'll do that." Abe said. He was about to sign off, but his curiosity got the better of him. "What is it you wanted to talk about?"

Brendan cleared his throat. "Well, I'm curious about your future plans for the camp. More specifically, I'm wondering if you're thinking about selling it."

Abe felt a flash of anger. Vulture, he thought. Ambulance chaser, opportunist, asshole. How dare he call and ask about this, so soon—his father hadn't even been dead a month—and on the first day of camp, no less? "No," Abe said, "I'm not."

"Sure, I figured. Keeping it in the family and all that. I completely understand. I just thought I'd ask. It's always been sort of a pipe dream of mine to run a summer camp, and now I've actually got some money to burn. This little company I started, LifeMonkey.com, just went public, and—"

"Brendan, I'm sorry, I've really got to run."

"Sure, sure," Brendan said. "If you ever change your mind…"

"Thanks." Abe hung up the phone.

Everyone in the office started talking at once.

≈

By five o'clock, the steady stream of arriving campers had slowed to a trickle, the phone had stopped ringing, and Abe was able to sneak out of the office. He sat on the steps of the dining hall deck and watched campers and counselors play "knots" on the lawn in groups of nine or ten. The idea was for each group to untangle itself from a jumble of joined hands into a single-file circle without letting go. It had been played at Eden Lake since the early days as a get-to-know-you, team-building game. But Abe remembered it primarily as an opportunity to hold hands with girls.

It was good finally to see the counselors in action, laughing and interacting with the kids. He'd had his doubts about them during the previous week. They'd generally seemed more enthusiastic about getting drunk than getting ready for the campers' arrival. As recently as Thursday, the waterfront buddy system tags still hadn't been made up, the fabric arts studio was in disarray, and the zip-line platform of the ropes course still wasn't repaired. That evening at dinner, when Abe reminded everyone that the campers would be coming in less than forty-eight hours, there were groans.

And, of course, there was the Jude factor.

Abe had been surprised—and thrilled—when she agreed to come up to replace Valerie (who, as it turned out, was severely bipolar and had stopped taking her medication in a misguided attempt to "go natural" for the summer and treat her condition with nothing but fish oil supplements). But now that she was here, she wasn't making much of an effort to assimilate with the rest of the staff, choosing to stay close to Abe or keep to herself instead. The only person on staff whose efforts at friendship she appeared to be returning was Tim, the music guy. ("I can't help it," she told Abe, "I'm a natural fag hag.") And she still insisted on dressing like she was in Manhattan, not Maine. He wondered if she even owned a pair of shorts, let alone a bathing suit.

But today, somehow, the whole staff, even Jude, had managed to rally. To see them now, he'd never guess these were the same people who, the morning before, were trudging into breakfast hung-over and sullen, smelling of cigarette smoke. Today, they seemed fresh-scrubbed and bright-eyed, exuding confidence and authority. Almost like the counselors he remembered from years ago.

In fact, watching the blur of bright-colored t-shirts and white arms and legs on the lawn, listening to the laughter and squeals, catching the occasional whiff of dinner wafting from the kitchen (starch, onions, the sweet tang of tomato; lasagna, maybe?) Abe could almost imagine he was ten years old again. He could almost feel the magic that this hour had always held for him here: the slanting, golden light that made the tops of the pine trees glow. The satisfying fatigue of a hard day's play— dirty hands and a face tight and salted with dried sweat. The gnawing hunger you knew would soon be satisfied. The anticipation of dusk, fireflies and the evening program.

For a few perfect seconds he felt it; he was there. Rather, it was here with him, now, that old sweetness. But trying to hold onto it was like trying to hold a handful of water. He glanced at the garden fence, where his father should have been leaning, smiling at the scene before him.

Abe got up and went into the dining hall. He hadn't checked in with Dave, the cook, all day, and the first dinner was the most important meal of the session. One burnt lasagna, one wilted lettuce leaf, and Abe would spend the entire next day on the phone with parents, defending the camp brochure's promise of "wholesome, delicious meals, expertly prepared using only the freshest ingredients"—another promotional phrase that had survived from the early days. Eden Lake had always been known for its food, and while it wasn't quite as "wholesome" as it was in the seventies, when sunflower seeds, sprouts and bulgur wheat seemed to make it into just about every item on the menu, it was still better than your average camp fare.

Abe approached the service window between the dining

hall and kitchen where Dave the cook, stout and ruddy, fore-arms splotched with faded tattoos, was smearing butter from a tub onto loaves of Italian bread. Behind him at a stainless steel table in the middle of the kitchen, his staff—Ed, a local kid, and two Polish brothers whose names Abe could never keep straight—chopped vegetables for the salad bar, while Tammy, the assistant cook, six months pregnant, sat on a stool nearby reading *People.*

When Dave saw Abe, he stuck his spatula into the tub of butter and held up his hands, in latex gloves. "Happy, boss?" he said.

"What?" said Abe.

Dave pulled at the wrist of his right glove and let it snap against his skin. "The latex. Just like you ordered."

"Sorry, Dave, I'm lost…"

"You don't know? Figures. What's her name, the blonde, comes in here a couple hours ago."

"Aura?"

"Right, *are*-uh. And she says we gotta wear gloves during food prep. Not just when we're handling stuff," he gave the end of a loaf of bread a quick, rough squeeze, "but all the time. Which is nuts. I been doing this for twenty-two years, and I never wore gloves. Not even up at the V.A. hospital." With the "sp" in "hospital" a fan of Dave's saliva arced gracefully out over the bread.

"Did she say why?"

"Health and safety guidelines. Wants us to follow 'em down to the letter."

Now Abe understood. Aura had recently started obsessing about the health and safety inspection, poring over the binder of regulations. Officially, the inspectors showed up unannounced, though according to Eric, they almost always came during the fourth week of the session. But Aura wanted to be ready from the get-go.

"Listen, guy." Dave took a more conciliatory tone. "I don't mind the hat, right?"—He pulled on the brim of his Red Sox cap—"And I always wear my shoes. That's just common sense. But gloves? Come on. We all know it's in the books, but that don't mean anybody actually does it."

"I do it," Tammy said. "I hate touching food."

"Yeah, I know it," Dave said, glancing back at her. "You haven't touched a thing all day. Go check on the lasagnas already."

Tammy made a face and climbed down from her stool.

"As far as I'm concerned you don't have to wear the gloves," Abe said. "Just keep the boxes around, and if the inspector shows up you can throw 'em on."

"Yeah? And what about blondie?"

"She talks a tough game, but she's harmless," Abe said with a wink.

Dave snorted. "If you say so." For the first time, Abe saw the trace of a smile in his eyes. "You know," Dave said. "You probably get this all the time, but you remind me a lot of your dad."

"Yeah, I do get that." Several parents had said it to him that morning when they dropped their kids off, and he'd found it awkward. How did they expect him to respond? Was he supposed to thank them? Deny it? Were they just saying it because they didn't know what else to say? Coming from Dave, though, it seemed more genuine.

"Yeah, you know," he was saying, gesturing at Abe with the

back of his hand, "your facial expressions, and how you talk, and—" He stopped. Suddenly, he was looking over Abe's head into the dining hall, his massive body rising up like a wave about to crest.

"WHAT THE HELL ARE YOU DOING IN HERE?"

Abe whirled around to find the victim of Dave's fury: a pudgy preteen girl in a Mets T-shirt standing just inside the main doors, her face frozen, open-mouthed. She didn't look so much scared as pissed off.

"Dining hall's closed!" Dave yelled, with only slightly less vigor. "Off-limits!"

Abe held up a hand to shush him. "Everything OK?" he called to the girl.

"I got stung by a bee," she replied, lifting her arm. "My counselor said I should come ask for some ice."

"You go to the infirmary for that," Dave said. "Who the hell is your counselor anyway? What kind of idiot sends a kid—"

"OK, OK, let me handle this," said Abe. Though he was wondering the same thing: where was the counselor? What had she been thinking?

Dave shook his head. "Jesus H. Christ, doesn't anyone give a fuck for rules around here? Tammy, get me some ice in a bag!"

Abe brought the ice to the girl and walked her outside, re-assuring her that she hadn't done anything wrong.

"My dad owns three restaurants," the girl said. "I know how cooks are."

The games on the lawn had ended, and now campers were scattered about, some on the swings, others by the tetherball poles, some sitting and talking in small circles on the lawn. Abe glanced at his watch; it was just about five-thirty. Any minute,

Strickland would ring the bell for the first camp meeting.

"What's your counselor's name, by the way?" Abe asked the girl.

"I forget," she said. "But she's got black nail polish. And she's not wearing a camp T-shirt like everyone else."

"Ah. Jude," said Abe. Now it made more sense; when they were kids, there was no ice machine or freezer in the infirmary. The dining hall was the source for bee-sting, burn and bump treatments. And the rules about going into camp buildings un-supervised weren't strictly enforced.

"Yeah, that's it, Jude," the camper said. "She's kind of weird. Can I switch cabins?"

"No, you can't. But you know what you can do? See Strick-land over there? With the clipboard? Go and tell him that I said you can ring the bell for camp meeting."

The girl beamed and ran down the steps. Moments later, while Abe sat at a picnic table on the deck, thinking about what he planned to say at the start of the meeting, the bell started to peal. It went on for longer than necessary, and Abe was about to get up and tell the girl to lay off, when there was a muffled clank and then silence.

A few seconds later, Aura was marching up the steps of the deck. "Did you tell that kid she could ring the bell?"

"Yes Ma'am." Aura was wearing surprisingly short, white shorts, and Abe couldn't help noticing how they set off the tan smoothness of her thighs. She might be a royal pain in the ass, but she did have some damned fine legs.

"Brilliant," she said. "The first bell of the session. Now ev-ery kid in the camp is going to expect to get to ring it."

"So? We always used to let campers ring the bell."

"The bell is off-limits, except to counselors," Aura said. "There's no way to be fair otherwise. What do we do, go down the list and make sure every kid gets a turn? And then there's a chance kids'll start ringing it as a prank, and the whole schedule will get thrown off and people won't know where they're supposed to be when."

Abe clutched his chest in mock agony. "The horror!"

Aura permitted herself a small smile, then turned and looked out over the main lawn. Abe rose and stood beside her. Campers and counselors had started to gather, clumped together by cabin group. Everyone was still standing up, milling and talking, nobody wanting to be the first to sit down.

"You ready?" Aura asked.

"Ready as I'll ever be."

"You'll do fine," she said, sounding more annoyed than encouraging.

Gradually, people began to sit, urged on by Strickland, who ran around making big, goofy flapping gestures with his arms. A couple of other counselors joined in, and soon everyone was seated. The older kids in the back were still talking, twisting around and standing up on their knees to shout out to their friends from previous years. A few counselors raised their hands, some campers did the same, and the chatter dissolved. Abe and Aura raised their hands, too.

"First and most important rule of Camp Eden Lake," Strickland said through the megaphone. "When the hand goes up, the mouth goes shut. See my hand? It's up. That means quiet."

"So how come you're still talking?" a boy in the back shouted.

The kids giggled, then hushed.

Strickland introduced himself and announced the agenda for the evening and the next day. Next, he did a brief survey of the crowd—a "contest" he called it—to see where everyone was from, and who had come from farthest away. A brother and sister from Tokyo were declared the winners and were each given a pair of plastic Groucho disguise glasses as a prize.

"And now," said Strickland, sweeping a hand toward the deck, "it is my great pleasure to introduce your director, Mr. Abe Perryweiss. Let's give it up for Abe!"

There was muted applause as Abe stepped down onto the grass. Then everyone was quiet—fidgeting, but quiet—waiting to hear what he would say. More than four hundred eyes fixed upon him. A wind riffled the trees beyond the lawn, and a flock of mallards launched suddenly from the lake in a cacophony of squawks and quacks. Abe felt as if a fault was opening in the middle of his body; a searing, cracking emptiness that threatened to split him in two. He could not do this; he could not be this. It wasn't where he belonged. It wasn't right.

He began to hear his pulse in his own ears, and felt the tension in the crowd mounting, the fidgeting turning into a hum. Desperate, he scanned the crowd. It was his father, he realized, he was looking for.

He was about to turn to Strickland and tell him to take over for him, when Jude, on the right-hand edge of the crowd, just a few rows back, shifted up onto her knees and back down again. The movement was a completely natural one—an adjustment anyone might make for comfort, maybe taking the pressure off of a limb on its way to sleep—but when his eyes found hers, and she smiled, he knew that she had done it on purpose. To help him find her. To rescue him.

He took a deep breath, and the chasm closed a few fractions of an inch. "Hi everybody," he said, as loud as he could manage—maybe not quite loud enough. He let himself pause, breathe again. "It is so great to have you all here. I'm Abe, and I'll be your director this summer."

Jude

THE FIRST SMALL CRISIS in Shangri-la, Jude's cabin, occurred during the half hour between the end of dinner and the beginning of the opening campfire. At dinner, Lizzie Polk, a pug-nosed, freckled brunette from the Upper East Side, announced her intention to paint her nails for the campfire. "They're just terrible," she'd said, and extended them for her bunkmates' inspection. She then proceeded to examine the nails of each girl at the table and proclaim them either "good," "*comme-ci, comme-ça*," (she'd just started taking French) or "poor."

Jude's co-counselor, Katie Magnus, tried to nip the whole thing in the bud. "My nails are disgusting," she'd said, wiggling her stubby fingers. "But who cares? It's camp. You're allowed to be a mess."

"Not if you want any boys to notice you," Lizzie had replied.

That did it. After dinner, all fourteen girls in the cabin—none of whom had brought nail polish of their own—begged Lizzie to let them borrow hers. Lizzie generously assented to let them use two of her five colors, Watermelon Sorbet and Firy Fuchsia. Jude suggested that it would be nice of her to share all the colors, so that everyone could do their nails in time for the campfire, but Lizzie refused. "The other ones are Mac—they're really expensive. My mom would kill me." That was when Jude dug into her own makeup bag and pulled out her bottle of Bruise. It was blackish purple and she could only convince two girls to use it—Tanya, from Moscow, who didn't seem to care one way or another if her nails got done, and Dahna Schwartz, who was slightly overweight, with a half-dollar sized grease stain on her t-shirt, right between the pointy knobs of her prematurely developing breasts.

When the bell for the campfire rang at seven-twenty, a panicked whimper went up from the girls; four were still waiting to use Lizzie's polish. The others started blowing frantically on their fingertips. With Jude's help, two more girls' nails got painted, but at seven twenty-six, there was no choice; they had to leave for the campfire or they'd be late. One of the unpolished girls was, unfortunately, Corey Marks, the same fragile kid Jude had taken to the office earlier because she was hysterical over the fact that she'd forgotten to pack a book she was supposed to read for her school's summer reading list. When Jude told Corey she'd have to skip getting her nails done, the girl's eyes filled with tears.

Meanwhile Lizzie and another camper were trying to come up with an alternative name for the bunk. "The Rainbow Ladies!" Lizzie was saying. "No, the Fabulous Fingers!" the other girl said.

"Yeah!" said Lizzie. "OK, everyone, from now on, we're the Fabulous Fingers!"

Corey started to sob.

Jude had no idea what to do. Katie would have, but she'd

left early for the campfire, to rehearse a skit with the other outdoor adventure counselors. Jude sat down next to Corey on her bunk and gave her a gentle punch in the arm. "Hey, don't sweat it, Corey. Bring the polish with you. You can do your nails at the campfire."

"But everyone will see!" Corey wailed.

"OK, Fabulous Fingers," Lizzie shouted, clapping her hands. "Let's go! Follow me!"

"Does everyone have a flashlight?" Jude said as the girls made for the door. "And a sweatshirt? It can get cold. And bug repellent. You should all wear bug repellent." She was sure half the girls didn't have any of the three—she should have been telling them this fifteen minutes ago. Corey was still blubbering, and Jude felt like shaking her.

Instead, she put her hand to Corey's back and pushed her up onto her feet. "Go get a sweatshirt and a flashlight and let's go."

Once they were down the cabin steps, she grabbed Corey's hand and they ran to catch up with Lizzie and the others. At the campfire ring, Jude gave Corey another little shove. "Go sit next to Tiffany, OK? She doesn't have nail polish either. Strength in numbers, right?"

Corey wiped her eyes with the back of her hand and nodded.

"Good girl," Jude said.

"You're not supposed to push the campers."

Jude turned to see Sergei grinning at her, his eyes obscured by twin reflections of campfire flames on the lenses of his glasses. Since her arrival, he'd made numerous attempts to talk to her, most of which she'd rebuffed. Even when she'd first met him, years ago, she could tell he was a little sleazy—the kind of man who liked women in a universal sort of way, and enjoyed sampling every type: fat, thin, black, white, pretty, not so pretty. As a teenager, she'd had the sense that he was attracted to her as the daughter-of-his-friends type. Maybe he still was. Or maybe she fit some new criteria now: the grieving daughter type? Artsy New York type? Sister of his boss type?

"She needed a push," Jude said. "Literally and figuratively."

Sergei gave her an arch look. "Maybe I will report you to the director."

"Maybe I give a shit."

"Fifty cents!" a boy behind her shouted.

Jude whirled around to see a boy of eleven or twelve with spiky blond hair and a tiny, pig-like nose, holding out his palm. "Fifty cents for swearing. Camp rule. Come on pay up." He looked over his shoulder at his counselor. "Right Mike?"

"There's no such rule," Jude said.

"There is, actually. It's new this year," Mike said, with a wink. Mike Voorhees, the animal care and basketball guy— tall and gangly, with pouty, almost girlish lips. So goddamned good-natured it made Jude want to puke. His constant winking seemed almost involuntary, a happy little punctuation mark at the end of every sentence.

"And," he added, "the fine is double for counselors. So, one dollar, please. Cash or check?" He winked again.

"Oh, eat me," Jude said, and turned back to Sergei. "You too."

"Eat you?" she heard Sergei say as she walked away.

She took a seat on the farthest back tier of benches, a few rows behind the girls in her bunk, out of the glow cast by the campfire. The only other counselors up this high were staff not assigned to cabins—the nurse, the stained glass teacher, the kitchen staff. Jude didn't care. Katie had their bunk covered. She was showing the various beaded and woven bracelets on her wrists to Corey and Tiffany. Jude could just imagine her explaining them one by one: *This one, I got at my first Dead concert, when I was fourteen. This one, I got at a Phish show in Platts-burgh. And this one, I made myself when I was shrooming—I thought the colors of the thread represented my soul.*

Of course, Katie would never say anything so inappropriate to campers. This was her third summer in a row, and she seemed to have counseloring down to a science. When Jude first arrived at the camp went to her cabin, Katie was hanging up big construction cut-outs of each camper's name, painted with multi-colored swirls and sprinkled with glitter. Jude had felt simultaneously relieved (at least one of them knew what they were doing) and apprehensive: was Katie going to expect her to be some kind of touchy-feely, gung-ho super counselor? Her apprehension deepened when Katie showed her the "Talking Stick"—one of those hollowed out branches from South America with seeds inside that sounded like rain when you turned it upside down. The Talking Stick, Katie explained, was for their nightly meeting. After evening program they'd all sit in a circle on the floor in their pajamas and whoever wanted to could share something from their day. It could be positive, negative, whatever, as long as it wasn't disrespectful of any camper or counselor. Whoever had the Talking Stick had the floor, then flipped it over and passed it to the next person who wanted to speak.

Since every other night one of them was off, this meant

that Jude was going to have to lead these meetings on her own half the time—something she dreaded. She wasn't much for "sharing," and, furthermore, had never mastered the kind of empathetic nodding that people like Katie were good at. The kind of nodding that made people feel like she was really listening; and not just listening—*hearing*. Katie was doing it right now, in fact, nodding with intense concentration at Corey. As if anything a ten-year-old girl would say could possibly be, in any way, interesting.

Strickland started the campfire off with a call and response nonsense song that got progressively more complicated and impossible for the campers to echo. By the end, everyone was laughing, even the older kids. Then Sergei played some weird Russian song on his accordion, explaining before he began that the words of the refrain meant, "Little bear, little bear, come eat your supper, little bear, it's getting cold now, and I won't re-heat it for you." A pocket of girls started cracking up at this, and throughout the song they erupted in snorts and bursts of laughter, which they tried to disguise as coughs.

Fifteen years ago, Jude thought, she might have been one of them. To laugh that uncontrollably, that spastically—it was the greatest thing in the world. She couldn't remember the last time she'd done it.

Next, Abe distributed copies of the camp songbook and played a couple of oldies on the guitar—"The Times They Are a Changin'" and "Yellow Submarine"—then handed it over to Michelle, the bitchy photography counselor, who sang "Isn't it Ironic?" in a fairly passable imitation of Alanis Morisette.

Finally, the counselors did their skits to advertise their activity areas. These hadn't changed much over the years, and Jude wondered if maybe they were outlined in the counselor hand-book (she hadn't bothered cracking hers open yet): Waterfront staff, do a skit about pirates whose plot is foiled because they don't know how to paddle a canoe or swim. (And the message here was what, exactly? Learn swimming and boating for a more fruitful life of crime?) Outdoor adventure teachers: two of you pretend you're lost and hungry and cold in the middle of the woods, and then one of you dressed as "Super Outdoor Man" (or some variation thereof) appears, laden with outdoor equipment, and shows the others how to use a compass and set up a tent. (The outdoor adventure skit was always kind of boring.) Arts and crafts teachers, do a mock art auction where clay pinch pots and decorative pillows are auctioned off for millions.

The drama staff's skit was the only one that tended to vary. Tim had composed a medley of songs from *Annie*, changing the words to advertise the camp show. Wearing a giant, curly red wig, he played on a portable electric keyboard and sang:

Sign up for the play, tomorrow!
Bet you'll want to come on down, tomorrow
To the rec. hall…
We'll teach you some songs, tomorrow
And we'll do some dancing, too, tomorrow
Come what may
Tomorrow, Tomorrow, we'll see you tomorrow
It's only a day away…

When he was finished, after the applause had died, Jude stepped forward, also wearing a red wig. "As you've probably already figured out, this session we're doing *Annie*," she said, doing her best to project. Tim played "NYC" softly in the background. "If you're interested, come to the rec. hall tomorrow at two for auditions. Everybody gets in, so you don't have to be nervous. If you don't get a big part, you'll get a smaller one, or be in the chorus. Or if you want, you can work on stage crew and help with sets and costumes and props. It's a pretty good show, I guess, if you like musicals."

From the corner of her eye, she saw Tim turn his head to look at her. In fact, it suddenly seemed like everyone was looking at her. Glaring.

"Anyway," she continued, "it's going to be a shitload of fun, so we'll see you tomorrow."

Tim burst back in singing, ("Tomorrow! Tomorrow! We'll see you, tomorrow!") almost succeeding in drowning out the cries of "oooh!" and "fifty cents!" coming from the campers.

Jude stalked back through the darkness to her seat, tears threatening in the back of her throat.

Why the fuck had she come here? She'd panicked, that's why. It was the fastest, easiest way to escape the mess she'd made of things in New York. She'd told herself that it was fate or some kind of sign that the drama teacher had flaked at the last minute. And maybe she thought that by coming here she'd magically revert to the happy, naïve kid she used to be, long before the divorce: the princess of Eden Lake, in denim overalls and flip-flops.

Instead, she felt unwanted and irrelevant. By the time she'd arrived, the staff had already bonded, found their rhythm. They didn't need her in the mix. She looked wrong, she spoke wrong, she felt wrong.

It was her father's fault. He was the one who drove her away from this place, who forced her to leave it behind and become someone new. Not that she minded who she was now. It wasn't like there was anything *wrong* with her. She just wasn't Jude of Eden Lake anymore. (So if there wasn't anything wrong with who she was now, why did articulating this fact to herself—the fact that she'd changed—make her so goddamned sad?)

She stood and slipped away from the campfire, moving softly through the trees. The grass on the main lawn was already starting to dampen with dew. She cut through the office and went into the farmhouse, which was completely dark. It still smelled the same after all these years: that dusty sweet, slightly fetid farmhouse smell of old paint and dry wood, mouse droppings, soap and damp. Jude breathed it in deep, wishing her own clothes didn't smell like cigarette smoke.

She went upstairs to her old bedroom, where Aura was staying now. A while back, Gail had made it over into a guest room in her own new-agey style. Crystals dangled in both of the windows, framed by opalescent green drapes. A giant Native American dream catcher hung over Jude's old twin bed, which was heaped with throw pillows in a variety of jewel-colored hues. On every surface—the bookshelf, Jude's old desk, the bureau—stood small forests of pillar candles in varying colors and sizes. But the old white rocking chair was still there, and some of Jude's old books were still on the shelves. She pulled a *Choose your own Adventure* called *Shipwrecked!* from the shelf, sat in the rocker, and began to read: *It is 1685, and you are a sailor on the Spanish galleon 'Esperanza.'*

Downstairs, a door opened, the upstairs hall flooded with light, and someone was creaking up the stairs. "Hello?" Jude called.

"Who's there?" a voice replied—spit-sharp, with a hint of

a Boston accent.

"Oh, hey, Aura," Jude called. "It's me. Jesus, you scared the shit out of me."

A few seconds later, Aura appeared in the doorway. "What are you doing in here?"

"Just looking at some of my old stuff. Sorry."

"No, I mean, why aren't you at the campfire?"

"Why aren't you?"

"I came to get some Advil. I've got a stress headache." She walked past Jude to the bureau. Jude watched her toss the tablets back into her throat and swallow them dry. "You know, you're gonna need to watch your mouth while you're here. You can't be cursing around the campers. We're cracking down this year."

"I know. I was just nervous."

"Yeah, but it's a big deal. You really need to be careful. If kids start thinking it's OK to talk like that—"

"I got it, Aura," Jude said. "I'll watch my big, stupid mouth, all right?"

Aura's face seemed to contract. "All right," she said, and Jude felt a little guilty for having snapped at her. But only a little.

Aura gave sudden, a nervous laugh and jerked her head toward the bed. "Can you believe we used to both sleep in that thing sometimes? It's so small."

Jude was shocked. This was the first time Aura had ever, *ever* made reference to that era of their lives—that year when she and Gail had first lived here. When she and Jude were inseparable. When the affair first began.

"Yeah," Jude said. "Of course, we were pretty small too, I guess."

"Yeah. But we sure could talk, right? We used to stay up half the night."

"I know," Jude said. "I used to hang on your every word. I thought you knew, like, everything."

Aura sat down on the bed. "Are you kidding me? I was a mess back then. I got kicked out of school for smoking in sixth grade. Lost my virginity when I was barely thirteen. Did all kinds of drugs when I was in high school. If your dad hadn't paid for tutors, I never would have gotten into college. You should thank your lucky stars you weren't as cool as me. All I ever wanted was to be like you and your brothers: Smart. Rich. With normal parents."

"Normal?" said Jude. "Ha."

"Compared to a single mom who had a new boyfriend every six months—most of them complete assholes—and got stoned and danced around naked with her friends in the kitchen? Yeah. Normal."

Jude couldn't help laughing. "Gail danced around naked in the kitchen?"

"Well," Aura said, "I guess it was only once. She was hanging out with these weird Wiccan dancer people for a while." She shook her head. "Freakin' Salem."

"But look at you now," Jude said. "You've got a good job, you're engaged. You always look—" Aura was wearing jeans and a cable-knit cotton sweater; her skin was impossibly bronze, her hair absurdly straight and flat, "—all put-together and neat. I'm the fuck-up."

"You've got your own style," Aura said.

"No, I don't mean that." God knows she dressed better than Aura. "I mean my life. Do you know why I agreed to come up here when Abe asked me?"

"No," said Aura. "I was pretty surprised when I heard you were coming."

"Yeah, well. It's because I screwed my boss, who's married, and everyone I work with found out."

"Wow," Aura said, smiling. "I guess that is sort of bad."

"Uh huh."

Aura pulled at the fringe on a chenille-covered throw pillow, twisting strands together. "My life isn't so great either. Matt and I have been fighting a lot. He doesn't like that I'm up here for the whole summer. He's thinks I'm, like, abandoning him or something."

"That's pretty lame," said Jude. "Your mother just died. He can deal for a couple of months."

Aura sat up straighter and smoothed the blanket she'd been fidgeting with. Jude had the sense that the wall of tension and mistrust between the two of them that had come down for these past few minutes was about to spring back up into place. "He likes having me around," she said. "That's not such a bad thing."

"No, it's not. But if he's bullying you..."

And up came the wall—Jude might as well have smacked into it face-first. "What," said Aura, "you think I'm some kind of doormat? That I'd stay with someone who was abusive?"

"I didn't say he was abusive. He just sounds kind of controlling."

"Well he's not. He's fine. Your married boss on the other hand—he sounds like a real winner." She brought her fingers to her temples and began to rub them. "This headache isn't going away. I'm going to stay here and lie down. You should get back to the campfire."

"Yeah, fine. OK if I take this?" Jude raised the book still in her hand. She wanted to see if the adventures were as tricky to get through now as they had been when she was eight, nine years old. Maybe now all the right choices would be obvious.

Aura shrugged. "It's yours, right?"

≈

The campfire ran late, so there was no cabin meeting afterward, to Jude's relief, though Katie did have everyone stand in a circle and join hands. She said something about it being a circle of trust and friendship, and then they did "pass the squeeze." Jude remembered doing this game when she was a little bit older than the girls in Shangri-la, and the joke was to squeeze people's hands as hard as you possibly could, trying to get them to make a noise and break the silence, disrupt the chain. But these girls didn't seem to know that trick. They all squeezed gently, guileless smiles on their faces, then started in with smothered giggles as the pulse moved faster and faster around the circle. Finally, everyone was squeezing at once, laughing and squirming, squeezing harder, but not with any intent to hurt. And then, the camp bell sounded, sonorous and solemn, announcing lights out. The girls climbed into their bunks and quickly fell silent. There was no whispering, no crying.

As absurd as it was for her to be playing the role of camp counselor, Jude thought as she lay in the darkness, it was probably good for her to be steeping in these girls' innocence, purging the sordidness of the Mitch affair from her system.

He hadn't emailed her since their last exchange, the day after it had happened. She knew that on one level this was a good thing. At the same time there was a small, stupid, ten-year-old part of her that longed for some small gesture. And an even stupider part that wished for a big one. She wondered if she'd ever actually told him the name of the camp in all their conversations. If she had, then that meant he could find her; he could drive up and get her and carry her off into the sunset with him. (Did he have a car? He could rent one.)

She knew she had to stop thinking like this. Aura was right. He was a jerk. Any man who would cheat on his wife was. She needed to exorcise Mitch from her mind, her heart, her libido—wherever it was that he lived.

Before she went to sleep, Jude read *Shipwrecked!* under her sleeping bag with her flashlight, getting eaten by sharks once and starving to death twice before finally managing to find the buried treasure and signal the rescue ship.

Eric

"IF YOU COULD BE any animal," Sergei said, "what would you be?"

Eric and Sergei sat on the larger boulder at the top of the meadow, passing a bottle of vodka between them. It was the third night of camp, and the evening program was "Name that Tune," which Eric was terrible at. The only bands whose music he knew well were Led Zeppelin, Rush and Pink Floyd, because that was what his friends in high school and college liked. He owned less than a dozen CDs, and rarely listened to them. So when Sergei suggested that they go up the meadow and "have some drinks," Eric accepted.

Now he was wishing he'd stayed down below and gone to the program anyway. Even though he wouldn't have been able to participate, at least it was a chance to be in the same place as Masha. Because she was always moving from activity to activity, translating for different Russian-speaking campers at different times, there was no predicting her schedule. Eric had managed to speak with her a few times, during and after meals, but these were the kind of quick, high-pressure exchanges he wasn't any good at. What he wanted was to have a real conversation with her, just the two of them.

The night before had been her night off, so theoretically, he could have asked her if she wanted to have dinner or a drink with him in Waterville. But people didn't do that kind of thing on nights off; they didn't go on dates. They went into town as a group and got pizza or bad Chinese food, then went to the bowling alley or Jolly Roger's for pool and pitchers of beer.

When Eric saw Masha piling into a car with other counselors, wearing a purple top he'd never seen before and more makeup than usual, he felt slightly betrayed. They invited him to come along, but he declined. Just the thought of it made him anxious: trying to sit near her at dinner and get in the same lane with her if they bowled afterward, feeling jealous and frustrated with himself if he didn't. And then there was the possibility that he'd have to watch her flirting with other guys and realize that he ought to give up on the idea of her entirely—something he wasn't ready to do just yet. He wanted to delude himself a little longer.

"I think I would be tiger," Sergei said, answering his own question. "The most powerful cat in the world. Or, no, maybe horse. Except I wouldn't let anyone ride on me. I would be a wild horse. Anyone comes near me, I trample them." He reared back and whinnied, holding the vodka bottle high.

Eric laughed. "I can see you as a horse."

"What about you?"

"An ape I guess. A gorilla or a chimpanzee. I'd want the ability to use tools."

"Monkeys don't use tools," Sergei said, and passed Eric the bottle.

"Yes, they do. They use sticks to poke in the ground for ants, for example."

"No," said Sergei. "Stick is not a tool. It's just a stick."

"When you use it to—hey," Eric stopped and squinted into the dusk. About fifty yards down, he saw what looked like someone sitting up, shifting a bit, then sinking back down into the tall grass. Something about the quickness of the movement suggested it was a child. Whoever it was, they had an unusually large head. "I think there's someone down there," Eric said.

Sergei laughed. "If there is one, there are probably two." He cupped his hands to his mouth and sang, "yoo hoo! Lovers! We are watching you!"

"Leave them alone," Eric whispered. The last thing he wanted to do was confront a couple of campers making out, or worse. He knew he was supposed to—it was something that had always been taken seriously at the camp, especially in the past couple of years: the danger of a pregnancy, or a rape or molestation accusation. A psychological trauma lawsuit. But what would he say to them? What would he do? Better just to pretend he hadn't seen anything.

"Yoo hoo!" Sergei sang again.

This time, the large head rose from the grass, and kept on rising, until the person—a boy, it seemed—was on his feet. He turned, extended an arm and waved, and now Eric recognized him: it was Niedermeier (Eric wasn't sure if that was his first name or last), the kid who brought his binoculars with him everywhere.

Eric handed the bottle back to Sergei and jumped down from the boulder. "It's a camper," he said. "I'll go see what he's doing here."

"Poke him with a stick!" Sergei said with a drunken giggle.

Niedermeier stood still, his hands at his sides, while Eric

waded through the grass toward him.

"Greetings," Niedermeier said. "I was just doing some star gazing. Of course, it's not quite dark enough yet, but Venus is visible."

Eric scanned the sky. Niedermeier was right: Venus, burning blue-white, blinked over the tops of the trees on the eastern horizon. "You need to go back to evening program," Eric said. "You're not supposed to be up here without a counselor."

The boy's smile fell, then bounced back up into place. "I'm not. You're here. And him, too." He pointed toward Sergei.

"We're not counselors, we're maintenance. And anyway, you're not with us. We're off duty."

"Have you been drinking alcohol?"

Eric's hand went to his mouth. Vodka was supposed to be odorless—that's what everyone said, didn't they? But maybe the smell of it was somehow clinging to his beard. Alcohol wasn't technically allowed on the property, except in private living quarters or at the staff cabin. But Eric didn't get the sense that Niedermeier was the tattling type.

"A little," Eric admitted.

"My father let me have a small glass of wine last Thanksgiving," Niedermeier said. "I believe it was a Bordeaux. I apparently got a little intoxicated. I didn't notice, but my mother said I was talking even more than usual." He chuckled. And then his brows crinkled with concern. "Are you Abe's brother?"

"Yes."

"I'm very sorry for your loss."

"Thank you."

"My grandmother died last year, and that's what everyone said to my grandfather. I don't think it made him feel any better."

"No, I guess it doesn't," Eric said. "But it's still a nice thing to say."

Niedermeier nodded. "Have you ever kissed a girl?"

"What?"

"I was just wondering if you've ever kissed a girl."

"Um, yeah," said Eric, flustered by this turn in the conversation. He hoped the boy wouldn't press for details. He'd only kissed four girls in his life, one of them during a drinking game his freshman year in college.

"I don't think any girl is ever going to want to kiss me," Niedermeier said.

"Why not?" Eric asked after a pause. He realized, now, that Niedermeier was after some kind of advice or reassurance. The boy couldn't have picked a worse person.

"Because I'm not like most kids my age," Niedermeier said. "I don't like sports, or rock music—that's why I left the evening program—or video games. Well, I like some video games, but they tend to be more role-playing and strategy types of games. Not combat games or driving games or that sort of thing. And I don't really like television, except for *Third Rock from the Sun*. It has an interesting premise."

Eric wasn't sure what to say. Niedermeier was right: he was going to have a hard time getting girls. Like Eric, he faced a future full of unrequited love. But Eric cleared his throat and said, "You don't have to like the same things as everyone else for girls to like you."

"I suppose not. But you do have to be handsome. I don't think I'm very handsome yet."

"How old are you?" Eric asked.

"Twelve and a half."

143

"Well, you've got plenty of time. Girls may not want to kiss you now, but I bet in a few years they will."

Niedermeier looked like he might cry.

"Or maybe even this summer," Eric said. "I don't know."

This seemed to cheer him up. "There's a girl here that I think I like."

"That's good. Have you talked to her?"

"Not yet. But he-e-e-y!" He stuck a finger in the air. He'd been working up to this. "Maybe you could help me. We could talk to her together, and then I wouldn't feel as shy. And you can give me advice, like on my outfits."

"I'm sorry," Eric said. "I don't think I'm the right person for the job."

"But you've kissed girls. You know what they like."

"I haven't kissed that many girls," Eric said. He looked back over his shoulder. Sergei had stopped singing to himself a few minutes back. Now he appeared to be lying down, the bottle balanced on his chest. Eric wondered if he should go check on him; make sure he was OK. He really should send Niedermeier back down to the rec. hall, and was about to tell him this when Niedermeier said, "I don't want to kiss that many girls either. Just Svetlana."

Eric whipped his head back around. "Svetlana? She's one of the Russian kids?"

"Da," said Niedermeier.

"Yeah, OK," said Eric. "Maybe I can help.

≈

The next morning, instead of a t-shirt, Eric put on his navy blue Polo golf shirt—a gift from Aura a couple of Christmases back. He didn't really like it—it made him feel like he was trying to be somebody he wasn't—but the summer before, an Australian counselor named Maggie had told him he looked sexy in it. At the time, the comment had annoyed him. He could tell she was patronizing him. But there must have been at least a grain of truth in it, he decided now, or she wouldn't have said anything at all.

He took special care with his beard, snipping away errant hairs, shaving his neck with a razor and cream instead of his electric shaver, and gathered his hair, freshly washed, into a neat ponytail in back. It was getting a little long—he could feel the end of it between his shoulder blades—and he picked up a pair of scissors from his desk, considering for a moment lopping it off, but decided it was too risky. It looked fine the way it was. And to cut his hair now, as he was about to embark upon a quest, would be like a samurai cutting off his topknot before a battle. He ran his fist down over the ponytail a few times, imagining that he was soaking up potency, courage.

Masha was sitting at the end of one of the corner tables, eating her breakfast with two Russian boys, Sasha and Vlad, plus Morgan, a counselor from Ireland, and a few female American campers. Eric got himself a bowl of Cheerios and sat down two tables over with some other counselors. He was hoping Masha would get up and refill her cup with tea or get a second helping of something so he could speak to her alone, but she didn't. She just took tiny bites of her eggs and bacon, chewing so slowly that her jaw barely moved.

Suddenly, Abe was straddling the bench next to Eric.

"Cold War's over," he said, punching Eric in the shoulder. "Stop spying on the Russians."

"I wasn't," Eric said, the back of his neck warming.

"Listen," said Abe, "I need to be back by ten for a parent visit, so we should leave for Jack's soon. Meet you out front in five minutes?"

It took Eric a few seconds to register what his brother was talking about: Jack, the mechanic. Half an hour away in Union. He'd put a new transmission in one of the camp buses, and today was the day they were supposed to go pick it up.

"Yeah, OK, five minutes."

Abe gave him a clap against the back and was gone.

Eric wasn't sure if the sensation he was experiencing, his whole body seeming to deflate, was disappointment or relief. He would talk to Masha later, at lunchtime. Maybe that was better anyway; maybe she was grumpy in the mornings. He stole another look at the side of her face—the slow, miniscule movements of her jaw—and just as he was about to look away, she turned and smiled at him.

"*Dobri dien*, Eric," she called in her bell-like voice. "How are you?"

A question: she'd asked him a question, and now he had to respond.

Instead of letting himself ponder his reply, Eric simply stood up. An unseen force seemed to be propelling him, or maybe it was simply that for once he wasn't exerting equal and opposite force to keep himself quiet and where he was. The effect was a looseness that caused him to practically stumble over to her table.

"I'm doing fine," he said. "And you?"

She nodded once. "Very well. You look very nice this morning. Is there a special occasion?" Her eyes dropped briefly to the place on his chest where his shirt V-ed open, and he felt it as keenly as if she'd pressed a finger there.

"No. Well, Abe and I are going to pick up the bus, but I wouldn't call that a special occasion." God, he hoped she wasn't thinking that he'd dressed up for her. Then, she was the one who'd started talking to him, not the other way around. There was no way she could know that he'd planned to talk to her, and therefore no way that she could know that the shirt was...

"Eric?"

"What?"

She laughed. "Nothing. You were just looking like a statue."

"Oh," he said. "Sorry. Um, actually, you know, I wanted to talk to you about something."

"Yes?" She took a sip of her tea, blinking at him over the rim.

"Well, one of the campers—" The bench in front of him suddenly shuddered, and he jumped back.

Masha laughed and pushed the bench out farther with her foot. "Sit down."

Eric sat. He hadn't been this close to her since that first day, when she'd helped him up out of the puddle. He could smell her shampoo, or maybe some lotion she was wearing—it was sweet and acrid at once, like goldenrod or Queen Ann's lace.

Eric cleared his throat. "It seems that a certain young male camper has a crush on Svetlana," he said, exactly the way he had planned.

"I'm sure there are many boys with crush on Svetlana," said Masha. "She is very pretty, don't you think?" She'd tipped her chin down, and looked at him with a little twist of a smile on her mouth. He felt his words—his carefully planned words—

jumbling up inside his mouth. Why did it feel like she was asking him if he thought she, Masha, was pretty, instead of Svetlana?

"I don't actually know who she is," he said.

"Well, who is the boy?"

Eric bit his lip. Stupidly, he hadn't anticipated this. Now, he realized, the whole thing could fall apart. If Masha knew anything about Niedermeier, that is.

He told her his name. Masha frowned. "I don't know who this is. What does he look like?"

"Brown hair, on the tall side for his age—maybe five-five." If he'd mentioned the binoculars, she would have known right away. "But he's really shy. So, I was thinking maybe at lunchtime, today or tomorrow, if you could sit with Svetlana I could come over with him and all four of us could talk together, so he'd feel more comfortable. And then maybe you and I could leave at the same time, so they'd have some time to talk alone."

"I understand," Masha said, a smile sliding onto her face. "A double date."

"No!" said Eric, "I mean, not really."

"Who's going on a date?" One of the girls at the table said, planting her palms on the table and turning toward Eric. "Oooh! Masha and…What's your name?"

"Eric," he replied with a sigh.

"Masha and Eric up in a tree," the girl sang. Her friend joined in. "K-i-s-s-i-n-g"

Sasha and Vlad started clapping along.

"That's enough," Masha snapped. Eric was startled by the harshness of it, and grateful. "Go clear your dishes, you'll be late for your first period class." She repeated this in Russian for the boys, even more forcefully, and they gathered their dishes up and left. Morgan had slipped away at some earlier point in their conversation; Eric hadn't noticed. Now the two of them were truly alone. And Masha thought he had just asked her on a date. To make matters worse, any second now, Abe, who was probably already out front in the pickup, the engine running, was going to start leaning on the horn.

"Anyway, maybe it's a stupid plan," Eric said. "I don't know."

Masha shrugged one shoulder. "I think maybe it's a good plan. But I thought we were not supposed to let the children be in couples."

"Well, we're not supposed to let them…you know."

Her eyebrows rose. They were peaked in the middle, like little circumflexes, and he wondered what it would feel like to run his thumbs over them; whether they'd be downy and soft, or a little bit prickly.

"You know, *do* things," he said. "But I think this would be pretty innocent."

"Ah," Masha said, leaning a few inches closer. "So, just some kissing, maybe?" She brushed a strand of hair away from her face and tucked it behind her small, pale ear.

Eric, to his dismay, felt himself getting hard. Damn her, he thought. Was she doing this on purpose, trying to torture him? Did she talk to everyone like this? "Yeah, maybe," he managed to croak.

And then it came: the low, grumpy chord of the pick-up truck's horn outside. Two long blasts, two short, then one long one that seemed to grow louder and more insistent.

"That's Abe," Eric said. "He's waiting for me. I'd better go." He didn't move.

"OK," said Masha. "So I will see you at lunch, then."

"If it isn't any trouble, that is."

She pouted and shrugged, in a way that Eric thought of as distinctly foreign—looking annoyed but apparently meaning to express just the opposite. "It's no trouble at all."

"Great," said Eric. "Thanks."

The horn sounded again.

"Shouldn't you go?"

"Yes," said Eric. "But, um, ladies first." He gestured toward her with an open hand. If she would just get up and clear her dishes, he could escape without risking her seeing the bulge in his pants. His jeans were old ones, faded and worn thin.

"But I'm not finished yet," Masha said, motioning at her plate, where a small clump of scrambled eggs and a strip of bacon remained.

"Oh, right," said Eric. "OK, then. See you later." He waited a few seconds more, then sprang up and turned away from her at the same time, nearly knocking the bench over in the process, and made a beeline for the back door.

Abe

ABE HELD THE FIRST rap session—"Free Speech" as he'd decided to call it—on the fourth day of camp, during afternoon free time. He'd announced it at camp meeting the day before, and at dinner a few counselors—Bart Lopate, Strickland, Stacy the riding instructor—made a point of coming over to tell him that they thought it was a great idea; they'd encourage their campers to go. The next morning before breakfast, Abe found a piece of damp, curling poster board in the program office, wrote on it in thick black marker, "FREE SPEECH: Join the revolution! Meet here today at 4:00," and tacked it up on the railing of the gazebo. He wasn't sure people would see it—the gazebo was tucked at the edge of the lawn between the rec. hall and the dance studio, not quite directly en route to anything. So he was pleasantly surprised at breakfast when Josh Ruben, a five-year veteran Eden Lake camper who wore his jeans halfway down his ass and was never without one or two fawning girls nearby, bumped his elbow against Abe's by the cereal dispensers. "Join the revolution, huh? What's that all about, dawg?"

Abe replied with a shrug. "Come to Free Speech and find out, man." Josh nodded and said maybe he'd do that, he was down with revolution, and Abe felt buoyed.

At quarter to four, he stood at the rail of the gazebo and scanned the lawn, waiting for the crowd to descend. But almost every time he was certain someone was heading his way, it turned out that his or her destination was, in fact, the waterfront or the camp store or somewhere else. He watched Josh Ruben saunter past at the other end of the lawn, his arm over the shoulder of a chesty girl in a baby doll t-shirt.

In the end, only five kids showed. One of them, no surprise, was Niedermeier. There were two other boys: a squirmy eleven-year-old named Jeremy in oversized jeans and a t-shirt that said "Skate or Die," and Oak Wallace, the one who'd ridden his bike to camp with his father. Then there was Dahna Schwartz, from Jude's cabin (who really needed to start wearing a bra) and a dark-haired thirteen-year-old named Willow, who obviously had a major crush on Oak. She sat next to him smiling down at the floor of the gazebo the whole time and blushed every time he spoke.

"I want this to be a place where you can feel free to talk about anything, ask any questions you want," Abe said, once they'd all introduced themselves. "All of us will listen and respect each other's different views and ideas. While you're in here," he pointed up at the roof of the gazebo, "you can't say the wrong thing. There is no wrong thing. OK?"

The campers nodded obediently.

"Are we going to talk about the first amendment?" Niedermeier asked. "I just thought, given the name and all."

"Yeah, we can. That's a great idea, Chuck. Free speech." Abe looked from face to face. "What does it mean?" The last time he'd been in front of a group of children like this was back in the Peace Corps, and he'd forgotten how much he liked it; the sense of gentle, benevolent power.

"It means you can't yell 'fire' in the movie theater," Dahna said.

"Right…" Abe said. "That's one part of it. Not abusing free speech. But what does free speech protect?"

"This is like school," Jeremy said, and bounced a red super ball, hard, against the gazebo floor. "I thought we were going to talk about fun stuff."

Abe started to say, testily, "You don't have to stay," at the same time that Oak said, "free speech means Jeremy can state his opinion and not get in trouble for it."

"I get in trouble for it all the time," Jeremy said, crawling forward on his knees to retrieve his ball and shoving it back into his pocket. "I told my teacher Mrs. Pratt my opinion that she's fat and she sent me to the principal's office."

Abe smiled in spite of himself. "OK, well you bring up a good point, Jeremy. How come sometimes we get in trouble for saying what we think?"

"I don't know." Jeremy slumped back against the railing.

"Because people have feelings," Willow said. "You shouldn't say mean things to people, especially adults. It's disrespectful."

Oak nodded at this, and Willow beamed at the floor with renewed fervor.

"All right," said Abe, "So, what if I say that President Clinton is stupid?"

"My dad says that all the time," Jeremy said. "He says he has a cock for a head, and he's got it stuck up his own ass." He snickered, and the other kids—even Chuck Niedermeier—laughed.

"OK, let's watch the mouth, Jeremy," said Abe.

"You said we could say anything we want here," Jeremy said. "You lied."

"You can say anything you want, but camp rules still apply. No swearing."

"I didn't swear. A cock is a rooster and an ass is a donkey." He slammed his ball down against the floor so hard that it hit the peaked ceiling on the rebound, bounced down and almost reached the ceiling again a second time. "I can do it even harder than that," he said, and hoisted his arm to slam the ball down again, but Abe caught his wrist in the air.

"Put it away, Jeremy. Or if you want to play with it, go do it somewhere else. We're trying to have a conversation here."

"But you won't let us *say* anything," Jeremy said, with surprising vehemence. He tore his wrist from Abe's grasp.

"You can say what you want. I'm just asking you to say it with respect. And without swearing, which you know perfectly well you did."

"How come counselors get to swear, then?"

"They don't"

"That lady at opening campfire said 'shitload.'"

"Yeah, and she got in trouble for it."

"Yeah, right," Jeremy said. "I heard she's your sister. I bet you didn't even say anything."

"You bet I did," Abe lied. He assumed Jude had felt bad about it; there wasn't any need to rub her face in it.

Jeremy stood up and stomped down the gazebo steps. "This camp sucks. I wasn't even allowed to bring my skateboard."

"Jeremy," Abe said, "come on back."

At the bottom of the steps, Jeremy spread his arms wide.

"It's *free* time. So I'm *free* to do whatever I want. See you suck-ahs later."

Abe watched him strut away, trying to think of something to say that would bring him back, but the only words that came to mind were: *get back here, you little shit.* He turned and sat back down. The other campers stared into their laps.

"Sorry about that. I think he just needs to cool off."

Nobody spoke for a few moments, then Dahna said, "Can I ask a question?"

"Absolutely," said Abe.

"I won't get in trouble?"

"No, of course not." God, he was doing a lousy job of this.

Dahna bit her lip. "What's a blowjob?"

The conversation went swimmingly after that. Abe provided the most euphemistic definition of a blowjob he could manage while the kids smirked and blushed, then he asked them what they thought about the Monica Lewinsky scandal—which, he assumed, was where Dahna's question had come from. With all the coverage on the news, all the jokes going around, it was impossible that kids couldn't have caught pieces here and there. And they were probably confused. The information they had, was, as it turned out, spotty ("Didn't the president buy her a blue dress, and his wife found out?" Willow asked). Abe filled them in, in broad strokes, and they went on to have a discussion about fidelity in marriage, and whether or not it mattered if the president of the United States cheated on his wife. The kids were talkative and thoughtful, endearing in their earnestness: "I want to have the kind of marriage where if one of us was considering being unfaithful, we'd tell the other person and talk about it," Oak proclaimed, causing Willow to blush furiously.

"Is it cheating if your mom talks to men in the grocery store?" Dahna asked.

The hour went well. Better than Abe had expected. But it still wasn't enough to outweigh the ugliness of the incident with Jeremy. He kept replaying it in his mind, trying to think of what he could have done differently, but he couldn't get past his own anger: the entitled little brat, with his super-ball and his Republican father.

There were plenty of difficult kids enrolled in AfterStart's programs—kids with behavioral issues far more severe than Jeremy's. On a visit to a program site during his first week, Abe had seen a twelve-year-old kid not much bigger than Jeremy hurl a chair at a wall in the midst of a violent outburst, missing another kid's head by mere inches. Later, Abe learned about the boy's situation: his father was in jail, his mother was an addict. The kid had been in and out of foster homes since he was five. Not that this made his behavior acceptable. But at least he had good reasons to be pissed off at the world. Unlike Jeremy Dyer of Darien, Connecticut.

When Free Speech was over, Abe went into the office and found Jeremy's enrollment form in the thick binder on Aura's desk. Clipped to it was a school portrait that must have been a year or two old: a younger, shorter-haired Jeremy, wearing a striped, collared shirt and a sweeter, more childlike smile than he had now. Under the interests and hobbies section was written, in a slanting, masculine hand: skateboarding, snowboarding, electric guitar (just started lessons), soccer. Abe remembered all this from several days before, when he'd scanned the enrollment forms to familiarize himself with the campers. What he hadn't looked at then was the other side of the page. Two separate phone numbers were listed under "parent information," one with a Connecticut area code and another with a code he didn't know. Written next to the father's address was an arrow and a note that said, "Send all correspondence here."

Abe felt something like a small jolt of electricity, which ran through his fingers and halfway up his arms, when he saw another note at the bottom of the page written in pencil, in his father's familiar, looping hand. It was almost like hearing his voice.

The note read: *Parents recently separated. Mother moved to Colorado, took Jeremy's 4-yr. old sister. Divorce/custody hearings this summer. Bad situation.*

≈

Abe found Jeremy that night after dinner by the tetherball pole, sitting in the grass, waiting his turn. He squatted down beside him. "Hey, Jer. I guess we got off on the wrong foot today at Free Speech."

Jeremy shrugged. "I guess." The ball whizzed several times fast and high around the pole. "I play winner!" Jeremy said.

"You know, I think if you'd stuck around you might have liked it. We actually talked about what a jerk Bill Clinton's been lately." Abe wasn't proud of himself for pandering to the boy's father's political views, but it seemed like the right way to connect.

But Jeremy just shrugged again.

Abe watched the boys at the pole wham the ball back and forth at each other, each punch harder than the last. The taller boy was ahead, as was almost always the case when there was a height difference. But the shorter boy was playing a fierce defensive game, and he could jump. Each time the ball sped toward him, he shot upward with a spastic, squirming motion of his hips, and hammered his fist against the ball.

"I was thinking," Abe said, "maybe tomorrow we could talk about divorce. You know, Willow's parents are divorced. And so were mine. I was a little older than you when it happened, but it's a crappy thing no matter what."

Jeremy stood up. The taller boy had finally managed to prevail: the tetherball leaned tight against the pole, inches from the top.

"It might feel good to talk about what's going on with your parents," Abe said.

Jeremy looked down at him for a moment, his face slack, and then walked out onto the sand.

Bad situation. The words, in his father's hand, flashed through Abe's mind again. How strange it would have been, he thought, if his parents' divorce had turned Eric—who'd been about Jeremy's age at the time—into a little terror. In fact, Eric had come through it remarkably well, probably the best of the three of them. Jude seemed bent on staying angry with their father, even now. For Abe, the anger had long since faded, but the sorrow, the sense of loss, never completely had.

He was eighteen, a senior at the Agnes Harris School, when their marriage fell apart. His father had called him the morning he left home, from a gas station pay phone, on his way down to Gail's. Abe was taking the AP biology exam later that day, and although it wasn't like his father to remember something like that, Abe's first thought was that he was calling to wish him good luck.

When Clay said that he was leaving, Abe felt as if someone

had whacked him in the knees with a two-by-four. How was it possible that his parents could split up? They were Clay and Carol. Carol and Clay. They'd built a kingdom together and reigned over it side by side. They'd been married for almost twenty years, had three children together. How could they just walk away from all that?

"You don't mean you're leaving for good, do you?" Abe had asked him.

"Yes, for good," his father had said, his voice breaking.

And for Gail? Gail had always been like a little sister to his parents. Not only that, she was the butt of jokes and fond eye rolling between the five of them when she wasn't around: flighty, goofy Gail, who was always locking her keys in her car or getting lost on the back roads between Talbotts Corner and Augusta; Gail who believed fervently in astrology and the curative power of crystals. Sure, she was physically attractive, and sure, maybe his father was flirtatious with her sometimes, but he was that way around lots of women.

How could he have actually fallen in love with her? Fallen so far that he would choose her over their mother?

He said it wasn't just the affair; that he and Carol had been having problems of their own. Abe knew that they'd been arguing more frequently, with regard to the camp at least. His father wanted to build new facilities and expand enrollment, while his mother wanted to keep things more or less the way they were, and focus on starting her US–Soviet peace exchange program.

"We just don't share the same vision for our lives anymore," Clay said.

At the time, Abe chose to believe him. It made it easier,

thinking that there was some larger logic or meaning behind it all; that this was inevitable.

But now he didn't see it that way. He no longer bought the "infidelity as symptom of something that's wrong with the relationship," theory. Sometimes, people just made bad choices.

He'd done it himself. There had been nothing wrong with his relationship with Jess when he cheated on her. In fact, things had recently turned a corner. They'd started saying "I love you" and keeping toothbrushes at each other's apartments. They spent whole weekends together, walking around the city with Jess's dog, Oscar, or day tripping out of the city to go hiking or mountain biking. For the first time, Abe was starting to be able to imagine their relationship turning into something permanent.

So why, then, had he been so attracted to that woman, Lucy King, that he couldn't resist her? He'd had a few drinks at the party, granted, but he wasn't drunk enough that he couldn't have stopped himself. He did, in fact, walk away from her earlier in the evening when he started to feel the electricity between them; when she put her hand on his to emphasize a point and left it there a beat too long. But an hour later, there they were in the darkened study, necking like teenagers.

Worse, he made plans to see her again. He admitted that he was involved with someone, but played it off as if it was something casual and new. When word got back to Jess a couple of days later—Lucy's roommate, as it turned out, worked with Jess at the World Wildlife Fund—that was the part she said hurt her the most. She might have been able to forgive a one-time, drunken make-out, she said. But for him to lie outright about the meaning of their relationship—that, she couldn't.

"What is it you're looking for?" she kept asking him during the final, tearful argument. "What is it that's missing from us that you're trying to find?"

Abe had no answer. All he could keep saying was that he'd been weak and impulsive. He'd given in to temptation, and he was deeply, deeply sorry. But it had nothing to do with any deficit on her part. The two things were completely independent.

"No," Jess said, "they're not. Because if you really loved me, you wouldn't have done something that you knew would hurt me."

What Abe didn't say to her in response, but what he knew to be true, was that people who really loved each other did hurt each other, all the time.

≈

Jeremy didn't show up at Free Speech the next day. But the others did, along with three new campers, all of whom had divorced parents—Abe had announced at camp meeting what the topic would be. The discussion went well, and at the end, when Abe asked for suggestions for future topics, the kids were full of ideas: Dating. Drugs. Racism. Chat rooms. AIDS and "how gay people make love" (Dahna's sheepish suggestion). Global warming (Oak's). Hobbies (Chuck Niedermeier's).

The evening program that night was a performance by an ensemble called The Ipso Facto Traveling Circus, which did acrobatics and juggling and other circus-type stunts, all with a wry, comedic twist. Abe sat on the benches along the side of the rec. hall with the rest of the staff, next to Jude. He'd barely had a chance to talk to her in the past few days.

"Did you book these guys?" she asked him after they

watched a man ride a unicycle on a miniature tightrope while playing a medley of pop songs on a kazoo.

"No, Dad did. I guess they've been coming for the past few years."

"They're really good. A little corny, obviously. But good."

"Camp is supposed to be a little corny," Abe whispered. The next act, involving folding chairs and three women in bright green leotards, was starting. "Hey, you know that girl Dahna in your cabin?"

"Yeah."

"Yesterday afternoon, I told her what a blowjob is. And tomorrow I'm going to tell her about anal sex."

"What are you talking about, you sicko?"

Abe told her about what had happened at Free Speech.

"Oh, well, that explains it," Jude said.

"Explains what?"

"Why this morning at breakfast all the girls in my bunk started giggling when I ate a banana."

Abe laughed, then abruptly stopped. A prickling coldness spread through him. "You mean you think she told everyone in the cabin?"

"Of course," said Jude. "I mean I'm sure some of them already knew what it was. But Dahna's, you know, kind of a loser. Knowing that kind of thing would have scored her major cool points. Jesus, Abe." She shook her head. "You better hope none of them write home to mom and dad about this: 'Today I did pottery and learned how to paddle a canoe, and then the camp director taught us what a blowjob is.'"

When Abe said nothing—he'd been thinking exactly the same thing, with a growing sense of dread—she patted his knee and whispered, "Don't worry. It's not like any of their parents are lawyers or anything."

On stage, the women in the green leotards were doing handstands on the folding chairs, their feet linked at the ankles. Joined in that precarious way, they suddenly, all at once, flipped over backward in synch and landed on their feet. The kids went wild.

≈ J A N E   R O P E R

From the original Eden Lake Counselor Handbook, 1969

What it means to be a counselor at Eden Lake

From a legal point-of-view, we, the staff of Eden
Lake, act "in loco parentis" to the campers while
they are here. Our primary responsibility is to make
sure the children in our charge stay healthy and
safe. Mostly, this is a matter of common sense: Make
sure campers take showers or swim regularly, brush
their teeth, and wear clean clothes. Encourage them
to eat well, and try a variety of foods. If they are
ill or injured, take them to the camp nurse. Inter-
vene if you see campers engaging in risky activities
(e.g. rough horseplay at the waterfront, being care-
less during kitchen duty, playing on the tractors or
other camp vehicles / equipment). If you feel that
a camper has emotional, physical or other problems
that you aren't comfortable addressing, please tell
Clay or Carol.

But our responsibility as counselors goes well beyond simply seeing to the campers' day-to-day wellbeing. As a counselor at Camp Eden Lake, you also
have the opportunity to be a MENTOR, TEACHER and
FRIEND to the campers. It is a unique type of adult-
child relationship that most children (and adults!)
don't experience except in an intentional community
setting like ours.

As a MENTOR, you serve as a role model to children
– a young adult whose values, attitudes, and tal-
ents children can emulate. Remember that while kids

have their own distinct personalities, they are also
very impressionable. Be mindful of your words and
actions, knowing that they carry more weight with
children than they might with adults.

You have the opportunity to be a special kind of
TEACHER while here at Eden Lake - not the kind kids
have in the classroom, doling out grades and punishments. Being a teacher here means helping kids ac-
quire new skills — from making crafts to learning how
to garden and cook — via hands-on experience. There
are no grades, no homework, and no wrong answers. At
summer camp, children find the joy in learning, dis-
covery and curiosity - a joy that we hope they will
carry with them for the rest of their lives.

One of the most rewarding parts of being a camp
counselor at Eden Lake is the chance to be a FRIEND
to the campers. You can laugh and play and do things
together, in the spirit of fun and community. You can
listen to campers' thoughts and concerns, and share
your advice and experience with them. Is it possible
to be both a friend and an authority figure? In our
experience, the answer is yes. When trust is estab-
lished between counselors and campers, campers are
MORE likely to respect their counselors' authority.
Counselors, in turn, are less like to over-use their
authority. The result is a community where kindness,
respect and understanding - not anger, hang-ups, and
power struggles - win the day.

Jude

THE NIGHTLY CABIN MEETINGS weren't as bad as Jude feared. The things that the girls wanted to share were benign and generally superficial: they missed their dogs / cats / parents / TVs. They made something really good in pottery / jewelry making / fabric arts that day. They cantered on a horse for the first time, and it was scary, but fun. They made it to the high platform on the ropes course. Sometimes they talked about boys they had crushes on, at camp or back home. One night, they all decided to have their stuffed animals introduce themselves in high, squeaky stuffed animal voices. (That was somewhat nauseating.)

All Jude had to do was nod and say, cool, great, fantabulous, swell. The occasional, sympathetic "oh, that's too bad," thrown in as needed. And the kids seemed perfectly satisfied with her performance, though she wondered if things were different when it was Katie's night on. Maybe on those nights, they opened up and told her their secrets, asked her their most pressing, "are you there, God?" questions. Better her than me, Jude thought. She didn't mind being the less beloved counselor, if that's what she was.

She'd never been close with her counselors as a kid, because there'd never been a need. She had her parents. When she was at the younger end of the camper spectrum—eight, nine—it was her mother she would go to when she felt "homesick." Even living right there, on the camp property, just yards away from her own house, she sometimes got to missing family dinners and her own bedroom.

It got more complicated when she was older, and began to feel more acutely the differences between herself and the other girls her age. They shared a common vocabulary of pop-culture references and "naughty" schoolyard songs (*Miss Suzy had a steamboat, the steamboat had a bell...*) that were completely foreign to Jude. They wore and talked about brands of clothing Jude had never heard of—most of her clothes came from yard sales, thrift stores and the LL Bean catalog—and decorated their bunks with pictures of movie actors and rock bands Jude had only vaguely heard of: Rob Lowe and Kevin Bacon. Def Leppard and Duran Duran.

She was a quick study. She learned how to roll her eyes and say "duh!" the way they did, and joined in when they ranked boys on their cuteness and kissability. She started shaving her legs and wearing makeup to evening programs. On trip days, when they went to Camden or Boothbay Harbor, she bought rubber bracelets and *Tiger Beat* magazines and did whatever else seemed like the normal, acceptable twelve and thirteen-year-old girl things to do. (*Not* going into the galleries and looking at the paintings by local artists; *not* browsing in the bookstores or sitting by the harbor looking out at the boats, imagining what it would be like to sail around the world in one.)

But there were times when she thought she might implode

from trying so hard; times when she longed for everyone to just go away and leave her alone. Sometimes, she'd go up to the loft of the boathouse and hide there with a book or her sketch-pad, or even sneak into the farmhouse and nap in her own bed, though she wasn't supposed to. Her parents, especially her mother, were adamant that she and her brothers act just like all the other campers during the session. No special privileges.

More and more often, though, she would go to her father. They'd walk around the lake, or sit up on the boulders at the top of the meadow and talk. Not just about Jude's feelings that she didn't quite belong, but about everything: What was happening in the world, what things were like when Clay was a kid, where the family would go on their big Fall trip. They talked about camp issues, too. He told her which counselors were involved with each other, why certain members of the staff from past years hadn't been asked back, which campers' parents were the biggest pains in the ass. Jude loved being entrusted with this adult knowledge. It felt like a locket around her neck—a special, secret thing that she carried with her.

It never once occurred to her that maybe her father shouldn't be telling her quite so much. Why would it? He was her father. He was perfect.

Little girls loved their daddies. And her campers weren't any different.

One afternoon during free time while Jude lay on her bed reading—she was supposed to be outside patrolling the cabin village, but close enough—she overheard a few of her campers out on the porch talking about what they were homesick for. A ten-minute discussion of food and television shows ensued, followed by a bunch of excruciatingly boring stories about pets. When they finally got around to people, they all agreed that they missed their fathers more than their mothers. Their fathers were more fun. They bought them stuff and coached their soccer teams and let them have their way.

They will disappoint you, Jude wanted to tell them. So they'd know, so they could steel themselves. *It's only a matter of time.* But of course she said nothing.

≈

By the start of the second week of camp, Jude was starting to seriously worry about the state of *Annie.* Casting had been easy. Rachel Greenberg, a fourteen-year-old with double D cups and a voice like Ethel Merman's, was the only contender for Miss Hannigan, the nasty orphanage mother. Tess Shields, pretty when she took off her glasses, with a sweet, slightly churchy soprano, got the part of Grace, Warbucks' secretary. Daddy Warbucks went to a stocky fourteen-year-old from Falmouth named Bobby Denzig, the only boy whose voice was deep enough to play the part convincingly. The smaller parts—Orphans, Lilly, Rooster, Burt Healy, the Warbucks mansion staff—were easily doled out to the runners up.

As for the starring role, Little Orphan Annie, there was no question. Though Jude wasn't thrilled about it, the part had to go to Lizzie Polk. There were lots of girls who could belt out "Tomorrow" with impressive force, and get through the lines without sounding completely wooden, but Lizzie was a professional. Literally. At the audition, she'd handed Jude an 8x10 glossy with a resume on the back. She had been in fourteen national TV commercials, a dozen radio spots, endless print ads, a sitcom pilot, an episode of *Blossom,* an off-Broadway musical, and was the understudy for the young Cosette in *Les Miserables* for a year. After her audition, she said, "Thank you very much for the opportunity," punctuated by a sugary, Shirley Temple smile, and Jude felt like kicking her in the teeth. But when she and Tim were making the final cast list and they came to the part of Annie, all they had to do was look at each other and shrug. Who else?

To Jude's relief, the posting of the cast list was uneventful. Several of the girls in her cabin had been hoping for Annie, but they were all cheerfully congratulatory to Lizzie and Lizzie was uncharacteristically (or perhaps just theatrically) gracious. The only seriously disappointed camper was the kid who'd gotten the part of Rooster, Miss Hannigan's conniving brother: an effeminate thirteen-year-old named David Kazzi, who'd been hoping for Daddy Warbucks. "I've studied tap and jazz for two years," he whined to Jude. "I guess it was all for nothing."

"But Rooster is supposed to steal the show," she told him. "That's why I gave you the part. He sings, he dances, he makes evil plans. Daddy Warbucks is just a rich, bald asshole." This won from David a small smile.

But actually getting the play off the ground was proving to be significantly more challenging. The only real directing Jude had ever done was of one-act plays, back in college. This was completely different. And she wouldn't have cared that much—it was just camp; the show didn't have to be great—except that, according to Tim, a lot of the parents came up to see it, and had high expectations.

Eden Lake had apparently acquired a reputation for the quality of its performing arts. A few years back, Clay had put a professional sound and lighting system in the rec. hall and added rigging for scrims and backdrops to the stage. Most camps comparable to Eden Lake had three- or four-week sessions, which didn't leave enough time for a polished production. But since Eden Lake was six weeks, as it had always been, there was time to mount something more impressive. Supposedly.

Ten hours of rehearsal a week for six weeks sounded like a lot, but it wasn't, really, given the time wasted every day trying to get the kids to settle down and shut up. Plus there was the fact that they were completely flaky. They forgot to bring their scripts to rehearsal. They couldn't keep left and right straight when Jude gave stage directions. Anything they learned one day—a song, a dance combination, the blocking for a scene—was completely forgotten the next. When Lizzie came to Jude after a rehearsal and said, "I'm getting really fed up with the lack of professionalism around here," Jude was actually able to muster some sympathy. "Hang in there," she said. "It'll get better. Maybe."

Maybe, sung in plaintive, orphan-y tones, to the melody of the song, became Tim, Jen and Jude's joking refrain. Do you think we're ready to start choreographing the big ensemble numbers? *Maybe!* Is the backdrop Jude and the CITs are painting going to resemble, even faintly, the inside of a mansion? *Maybe!* Is this play going to completely suck? All together now: *Maybe!*

By the end of the first week of camp (Saturday and Sunday were "trip days" where half the camp each day would go on a day-trip and the other half would stay back and swim, play games, or do "one-shot" activities), Jude was exhausted. And not feeling particularly optimistic. Already, they were a day behind the schedule she and Tim had roughed out, and to make matters worse, Tess, who played Grace, had come down with strep throat.

She spent the first trip day—her day off—in Camden. Her mother was still out on a garden consultation when Jude arrived, but she retrieved the hidden key from under the stone Buddha in the garden and let herself in. In the kitchen, she made herself a cup of tea and sliced a piece from the fresh baked loaf of bread on the counter. When she opened the refrigerator for butter, she saw a twelve-pack of Millers on the bottom shelf. This was strange; her mother almost never drank beer. Then, on the way to the living room, she nearly tripped over a pair of very large flip-flops—much too large to be her mother's. Had Abe visited recently, she wondered? The beer could be his, too, she supposed, though he usually drank fancy microbrew stuff.

A quick peek inside her mother's bedroom solved the mystery. On the dresser lay a stick of men's deodorant while the armchair by the window was draped with men's clothing—a pair of jeans, a couple of t-shirts. On the seat cushion sat a neat stack of tighty-whities, and a few balled pairs of socks.

Someone was shacking up with her mother. But who? And since when?

Jude went into the living room with her tea and bread, kicked off her shoes, and thumbed through the magazines on the coffee table—*The Utne Reader, Mother Jones, Downeast*—for a few minutes before noticing that on the floor beside the table were a couple of old photo albums. She hefted the top one up onto her lap, then hesitated: it probably wasn't a good idea to get bogged down in memories. It would only depress her. But even as she paused, she knew she wouldn't be able to resist.

She remembered this album well; she'd looked through it countless times as a child and teenager. The photos started in 1976: Her mother in a hospital bed with a tiny Eric bundled in her arms. He was the only one of the three Perryweiss kids who hadn't been delivered at home by a midwife; he was breech, delivered via C-section at the hospital in Augusta. The next photo showed Abe and Jude, six and three years old, respectively, sitting next to their mother on the hospital bed, her arms tight around their shoulders. In another photo, their father sat in a corner in a molded plastic hospital chair with Eric in his arms.

The photos on the next pages spanned the following two or three years: Eric in his crib and baby swing. Herself and Abe in snowsuits, helping their father carry firewood. Various groups of hairy adults with wineglasses in the farmhouse dining room. A tender close-up of her mother, in profile, a blue bandana on her head, working in the garden. Another, taken probably minutes later, of her wearing a silly grimace and holding up a giant radish by its leaves, as if it were a severed head. Shot after shot of campers and counselors, doing all the same things campers and counselors did now—feeding goats, playing games on the lawn behind the dining hall, playing guitars, making pottery—except all in goofy seventies clothes, with bad haircuts.

Jude didn't recognize the other album. It was much thinner, with black pages instead of manila, and no captions written underneath the photos, a number of which had come loose and fallen into the creases of the binding, having been glued to the pages instead of carefully affixed with photo corners as in the other album. These weren't family pictures; they were pictures from her mother's trip to India.

Jude didn't know exactly when her mother had gone—

sometime after Jude was born, but before Eric. She had never said much about the trip, though Jude had always been aware of the fact that she'd taken it. The colors of the photographs were so different from the foggy greens and blues of Maine: red, saffron, ochre, sapphire and black. Crowded streets and market-places, women in bright saris, salmon-colored rooftops and arid yellow riverbanks.

Then came a series of photographs of Americans or Europeans, mostly in groups, sitting on the ground on blankets, preparing food over a fire, posing with their arms around each other. They were tanned and young, in their twenties and thirties, wearing combinations of Indian and western clothing— long, flowing blouses over bellbottom jeans; t-shirts over loose, wide cotton trousers or wrapped skirts. Most of the men were bearded, mustachioed or mutton-chopped, with long hair. The women's hair was long, too, worn in braids or pulled back into buns. There was a picture of Carol, in a blue sari, her hair loose on her shoulders, holding a wide-eyed Indian boy of two or three. He was light-skinned and she was deeply tanned. If not for her curly hair, she could almost have been mistaken for his mother.

Jude heard the back door open and her mother's merry, "hello, hello, hello!" She came over to the back sofa and kissed Jude on the crown of her head. "Ah, look what you found."

"I didn't find it exactly, it was right here," Jude said, turning to look at her. "How come I've never seen these before?"

Carol leaned her elbows on the back of the couch. "I always sort of kept them to myself."

"Why?"

"I suppose because it was such an intense, personal time

in my life." She came around the couch and sat next to Jude, pawed her fingers gently through her hair. "Start back at the beginning, and I'll tell you what's what."

Carol remembered in impressive detail where each photo was taken, and why she'd taken it, what she was trying to capture. Pointing to a picture of a legless young man, begging, she said, "I talked with this man for a long time. He only spoke a few words of English, but we communicated. I felt almost a kinship with him at the time, him being crippled." She laughed. "Of course now that seems awfully naïve of me. But, you know, I was scared, and feeling sorry for myself. I'd gotten my diagnosis just a few months before I left. I mean, the diagnosis was the whole reason I went to India. But I've told you about this before, haven't I?"

"No," said Jude. She knew she hadn't. Why would she pretend she had?

"I thought I had," Carol said evenly, and took her hand away from Jude's hair. "I had always wanted to go to India. I had friends who'd been, and friends who were still there, and it had changed their lives. You know, these spiritual quests we were all on back then. Anyway, when I got my diagnosis, I was afraid I'd never make it there. My first doctor was horrible. He told me I could expect to be wheelchair-bound within five years."

"How long did you stay there?"

"A little over three months."

Jude had thought it was much shorter—a month or six weeks, at the most. "So, you just left Dad alone with me and Abe?"

"It wasn't easy, believe me. I missed you guys like crazy. But it was important to me. And your dad was completely supportive."

Jude snorted. "Yeah, because he was probably was screwing someone while you were gone."

"Jude," her mother scolded. "Your father may have done some awful things, but he was not the monster you make him out to be."

Jude was stunned. Her mother had never defended her father before, or chastised her for hating him. "Whatever," she said. She turned to the next page of the album. "Who are all these other Americans?"

"That was at the ashram. It was almost all Americans and Europeans, an Australian or two, some Canadians. That's my friend Diana from Wellesley, who told me about it." She pointed to a picture of a plump woman with sunburned cheeks and John Lennon glasses, carrying a bucket of water.

"Was it some kind of cult?"

"No, no. It was just—well, we did a lot of meditating and yoga. And a lot of work. God, there was a lot of work! Cooking and gardening and washing clothes and cleaning out latrines. I had no idea what I was in for." She laughed, and then her voice softened. "But it was wonderful. Really magical."

"Magical how?"

She was quiet for a moment. "I didn't end up in a wheelchair, did I?"

"You actually think the meditating and stuff helped?"

"Maybe."

"Or maybe it was the interferon therapy you started when you got back."

"Ah, my little skeptic." She gave Jude's forearm a squeeze before working her way up from the couch and moving toward the kitchen. "I see you found the bread. Good?"

"Yes. Hey, isn't there something you'd like to tell me?"

Carol stopped and turned back toward Jude. Something like panic flickered over her face. "What do you mean?"

"Who is he?"

"He?"

"The guy who's staying here. Or have you started drinking Miller Lite and wearing size ten flip flops?"

Carol's face relaxed into a smile. "Oh you mean Dane. You remember him. From the memorial service."

"The biker dude?"

"Yes. I guess you could say we've become sort of involved."

"What? I thought you hadn't seen this guy in years. And now you're living together?"

It wasn't like her mother to rush into a relationship. In the ten-plus years since the divorce, she'd only dated three or four men, and only one of them, a soft-spoken boat builder named Michael, for any significant amount of time. Even after she and Michael been together for more than two years, Carol didn't call him a "boyfriend" or "significant other." Just "my friend." Once, when he and Jude and were doing the dishes after a Thanksgiving dinner, he'd asked her where the plates went. At first Jude thought he was joking, and laughed. She was embarrassed to find out that he truly didn't know.

"Well, it's not like we haven't been in touch," Carol said. "We've written letters and things. And we saw each other once about a year ago."

"How do you know him again?"

"Oh, we go way back," she said, with a toss of her hand. Exactly what he had said—in the same vague words.

"Way back to when?"

"College. He dated a friend of mine during college. Anyway, he's not living here. He's just visiting for a while. And today he's down in New Hampshire with his daughter and grandkids. We're just, I don't know…" She made a bobbling motion with her head that looked vaguely Indian. "Exploring things."

Jude wrinkled her nose. Carol laughed. "Come on, get up off your *tuchus* and let's go sit outside for awhile, before it starts raining. I want to hear how things are going for you at camp."

Jude was startled by the sudden change of subject. It wasn't like her mother to be so cagey.

"Oh, and do me one favor." Carol put her hand on Jude's knee. "Don't mention anything about Dane to your brothers. Not yet, all right? I feel a little awkward about it. You know, so soon after…"

"What's the difference?" Jude said, a bit more harshly than she meant to. She softened her tone. "I mean, you and Dad split up years ago."

Carol closed her eyes for longer than a blink. "Still."

Eric

THE DOUBLE DATE WITH Masha and Svetlana hadn't been a success—not for Niedermeier, anyway. Svetlana's English was minimal, so Masha had to do a lot of translating. And neither Niedermeier nor Svetlana were exactly scintillating conversationalists. "What are your hobbies?" Niedermeier would ask, through Masha, and Svetlana would reply, "Ballet, swimming, computer, and movies." End of exchange, until Niedermeier thought of something else to ask. After ten minutes or so, Niedermeier had learned how many siblings and pets Svetlana had, along with their names, what her favorite band was (The Spice Girls), that she wanted to be a surgeon when she grew up, and that her favorite kind of ice cream was chocolate. Masha asked Svetlana, in Russian, if maybe she'd like to ask Niedermeier some questions about himself, but Svetlana just shrugged.

"Why don't you let her try your binoculars," Eric suggested. She had been eyeing them.

"I don't know," said Niedermeier. "They're very fragile."

"She'll be very careful," Masha said. "She's going to be a surgeon, remember?"

Svetlana said, "Please," and held out her hands, pouting. So

Niedermeier took them off and looped the strap over Svetlana's head while she giggled. Things seemed to be going well for a little while after that. Niedermeier helped her focus and adjust the binoculars, and found things for her to look at—a bird on the garden fence, the weathervane on top of the barn. But then one of the other Russian boys, Sasha, came over and asked Svetlana if she wanted to play ping-pong. She handed the binoculars back to a crestfallen Niedermeier and started to leave.

Masha told Svetlana, with that sudden, unexpected sternness Eric found so sexy, that she was being very rude, and should invite Niedermeier to come with them. Svetlana looked at Niedermeier and jerked her head in the direction of the covered pavilion at the edge of the lawn where the ping-pong and foosball tables were. "You can play," she said.

Niedermeier looked at Eric. "What about our lunch plates?"

"I'll take care of them. Just go."

When they'd left, Eric said, "I don't think that went so well."

"No. But perhaps he is very good at table tennis?"

"I seriously doubt that."

"So, tell me, Eric," Masha said, in a stiff, nasal voice which, Eric gathered, was meant to be an imitation of Niedermeier, "what are your hobbies?"

The next twenty minutes were perfect. The two of them talked and laughed and Eric didn't feel tongue tied or flustered for a minute. Masha was not as overtly flirtatious as she'd been other times, and for this, Eric was grateful. Instead of feeling like she was testing him, baiting him, he felt as if she truly wanted to hear what he had to say. And he felt quite sure that this was not the last time they would talk like this. They were becoming friends.

So, he didn't mind when Niedermeier reappeared and sat down between them, a wrinkle of consternation between his eyes. Sasha had beaten him at ping-pong twenty-one to six. And when Svetlana booed, Sasha had picked her up and pretended he was going to throw her in the garbage can. "I think it was a form of flirting," Niedermeier said. "She seemed to actually be enjoying it. Which is weird. Who wants to get thrown in a garbage can?"

"Mm, well, don't give up," Masha said.

Niedermeier stood up a little taller. "I was thinking I could make something for her in pottery class."

Eric was about to tell him that maybe he should wait; he didn't want to look desperate and scare her off. But Masha clapped her hands and said, "that's a perfect idea," so Eric nodded in agreement. Who knew; maybe it would work. She knew what Russian girls liked better than he did.

Over the next week, he frequently sat with Masha at lunch. Usually there were other counselors with them, and sometimes some of the Russian campers. A couple of times Niedermeier joined them, too. But it would always eventually be just the two of them, lingering with their empty plates and drained cups of bug juice.

On trip day, when half the camp went to the Skowhegan Fair, Eric arranged it so that he would be the one to drive the bus Masha was on. He liked the idea of her seeing him in a position of authority, with people's lives in his hands. At the fairgrounds, he, Sergei, Masha, Morgan, and Strickland walked around together, looking at the livestock, playing the impossible-to-win ball and ring toss games, eating fried dough. Masha was afraid of the Midway rides, but Morgan convinced her to go on the Tilt-a-Whirl. Though spinning rides always made Eric slightly sick, he couldn't pass up the chance to sit so close to Masha. The ticklish lurch he felt in his stomach each time the car caught a spin was far outweighed by the pleasure of Masha's body pressed against his, pinning him to the hot metal side of the car.

Afterward, Masha felt sick herself. They sat her down on a bench, and Eric bought her a Coke. "It will settle your stomach," he said, handing it to her.

"That's an old wives' tale," Strickland said. "It's better if she doesn't eat or drink anything for a while."

Masha glanced first at Strickland, then Eric, then put her pale lips to the straw and drank.

≈

Half way through the second week of camp, Aura announced to Abe and Eric that the health inspector was coming on Friday. She was almost positive. She gave no reason, only that she "could just sense it." Abe asked her if it was something she read in her horoscope, and she picked up a pad of Post-it notes and hurled it at his head, growling, "For the millionth time, I don't read the fucking horoscopes!" Abe laughed and flung the pad back at her like a Frisbee, hitting the side of her hip.

Eric spent all of Thursday morning with her, combing the property, looking for potential red flags: a rotting step, a precariously dangling broken branch, an exposed rusty nail. The counselors were supposed to clean their own cabin bathrooms on a weekly basis, with the campers' help, but Aura insisted on going through and inspecting each one, spot cleaning as needed. Together, they scrubbed toilets, sinks, and showers that looked perfectly clean to Eric. He didn't like being in the bathrooms of the girls' cabins, seeing their razors and little zippered pouches of makeup or who knows what in the wooden cubbies next to the shower stalls.

He didn't like spending this much time alone with Aura, either. It wasn't that he felt uncomfortable with her, exactly. There was just something about her that made him tense, and always had. She seemed to be working hard all the time just to be. Everything she did, everything she said, seemed unnaturally intentional.

And she talked to herself. While she was scrubbing a toilet or sweeping a floor, Eric would hear little pieces of words or half-laughs from her, and when he looked, her lips would be moving, or her face flickering through different expressions—anger, indignation, amusement, surprise. She seemed to be rehearsing whole dialogues inside her mind.

And then, suddenly, she'd start speaking aloud, as if in mid-conversation. "I'm just not sure your brother really understands how important this is," she said to Eric at one point, while they were cleaning the bathroom of Oz, the twelve-year-old girls' cabin. Her voice, inside the shower stall, was hollow and metallic. "They'll be paying extra close attention this year."

Eric ran a sponge over the already clean bowl of the sink. "I'd think they would be easy on us this year. Or even not come at all. They know what happened."

"Your father wasn't exactly cozy with the board of health and safety, as you probably know," said Aura.

Eric did; his father had made no secret of his disdain for the bureaucrats in Augusta with their codes and rulebooks and inspections: "I'm all for government regulation, believe me," he would say. "But these guys are fucking fascists. Why don't they go bother the paper mills dumping chemicals into the rivers or the shipbuilders mucking up the ports instead of harassing summer camp directors? Bunch of damned anti-Semites is what they are." The fact that Clay was not Jewish himself was, as far as he was concerned, irrelevant. "They know where our income comes from," he said.

A few years back he'd gotten into an altercation with a particularly meticulous inspector who found numerous small violations throughout the property, and then, at the very end of the inspection, threatened to shut the camp down that day on account of the temperature of the walk-in freezer being three degrees too high. Eric was there, and saw the whole thing: his father taking boxes of frozen vegetables and bags full of hamburger patties and jugs full of tomato sauce and dropping them down onto the floor of the freezer to show that they were frozen solid. He was making a joke of it at first, smiling, trying to get a laugh from the inspector. But she just watched, her face impassive, her arms folded around her clipboard. Finally she said, "I'll consider letting you stay open if you get rid of all this food, which I have to consider contaminated, regardless of its consistency. I'll be back in five days to see that the thermostat has been repaired, and the other violations have been addressed."

That was when Clay started slamming the food down in earnest. "Fine," he said. "You want me to get rid of this food? All this frozen food? That's just fine."

She stuck a big yellow "Violation" notice on the freezer door, and left Clay there, hurling food onto the floor. Eric brought in a box of garbage bags from the kitchen, and was about to start filling them with the "contaminated" food, but his father told him to stop. "There's about a grand worth of perfectly good food in here. No way am I throwing it out."

They loaded it all into the back of the pickup truck, threw some bags of ice and a tarp over it all, and drove to the food bank in Augusta. Clay was careful to get a receipt for the full value of his donation, which he planned to write off from his taxes. "My little 'fuck you' to the man," he said to Eric as he folded the receipt into the back pocket of his jeans.

It was a different inspector who returned five days later for the follow-up, and gave the camp a pass. They hadn't seen the woman inspector since.

Eric asked Aura if she knew about the freezer incident.

"Yeah, my mother told me all about it. She thought it was hilarious. 'Just Clay being Clay,' she said." She stepped out of the shower stall and turned the faucet on to give it a last rinse. "She was probably laughing while he was doing loop-de-loops in his airplane, too."

Eric stopped what he was doing. "What?"

Aura pulled the shower curtain closed and busied herself arranging the hooks so they were evenly spaced across the rod. "I just have my suspicions about what happened up there, that's all."

Eric balled the sponge in his hand. "You think it was—" He couldn't bring himself to say the word "fault." "You think it was pilot error?"

"If that's what it's called when the pilot is messing around, doing tricks, and then loses control, then yes, I think it could have been pilot error. Don't you?"

"No," said Eric. His father might have taken risks, but not deadly ones. The so-called tricks Aura was talking about were nothing, really—the kind of exercises he'd probably done countless times in flight school, to get comfortable with the controls, to know he could pull the plane out of a dive if he needed to. If anything, he'd probably almost saved them. He would have done everything right, everything possible to hold onto control of the plane and land it.

"It was a mechanical failure," said Eric. "That's what the report said."

"Sure, to make us all feel better. What are they supposed to say? You flew with him. You know he did those dips and dives and things. He did it the one time I went up there. That's why I never got in that plane again. I told my Mom she shouldn't either."

Eric picked up his bucket of cleaning supplies. "This bathroom is clean," he said. "They're all clean. And the bell's about to ring for lunch." He started to go.

"Wait," Aura said. "Don't leave."

Eric stopped.

Aura was blinking strangely. "I'm sorry," she said. "I shouldn't talk about him that way. He was our father."

Eric nodded. He'd never heard her refer to Clay as her father before.

"I'm just a little stressed out, that's all." She started to pull at the shower curtain, then, arranging its folds. "You know, I never asked him about it or anything, but I was hoping Clay would walk me down the aisle when I Matt and I got married."

Eric felt the need to cough and swallowed it back. God, he hoped she wasn't going to ask him to do it. "One of your uncles could do it," he said. Gail had two sisters, both married. "Or Abe."

"Abe," Aura said disdainfully. "No, one of my uncles will do it. You're right. That probably makes more sense than Clay anyway. Someone I'm actually related to."

Eric thought for a moment. "You're no more related to your mom's sister's husbands than you were to"—it felt strange to say it—"our dad."

Aura let the curtain drop from her fingers and turned to him. "That's true." She seemed to be waiting for him to say something else.

"I'll bet he would have really liked to do it," Eric said at last. "Walk you down the aisle."

The lunch bell started to peal. And into Eric's mind sprang an image of Masha in a shimmering wedding gown the color of the moon, her red hair spilling down her back like flame.

Aura rubbed her forehead with the back of her wrist and smiled. "Thanks," she said.

≈

Eric was eager to find Masha and sit with her, but Jude intercepted him at the salad bar: The riser platform the CITs had built for the show had collapsed during third period while the kids were in the middle of rehearsing the choreography for one of the big dance numbers, and she needed Eric's help fixing it—immediately. He asked if it could wait—he'd really like to eat his lunch—but Jude put on a pleading grimace. "Couldn't you please come do it now? And that way we can finish the choreography today during fourth period and maybe the show actually won't completely, totally suck?"

So Eric spent the next hour and a half shuttling back and forth between the rec. hall stage and the maintenance shed, attempting to salvage the busted riser platform. It was amazing the thing had been able to stand up at all; it had been built completely wrong, perfectly engineered to collapse in on itself. Once he'd finished, just before the end of rest period, he and Jude slid it into position and jumped on it a few times to test its sturdiness.

"Thank you," Jude said. "At least that problem's solved. On to the next ten."

"What other problems are there?" Eric asked.

She puffed out her bottom lip and blew air up into her bangs. "Well, our Daddy Warbucks is tone deaf, the orphans won't learn their lines, the kid playing Rooster has a serious case of ADD, or maybe he's acting out in some kind of subconscious reaction to his latent homosexuality. That's what Tim thinks, anyway. And I just have a hard time believing it's all going to come together in the next four weeks. Most of the kids don't seem to give a shit. I'm not exactly the world's most inspiring drama teacher."

"I'm sure you're doing great," Eric said.

Jude extended her arm and knocked the side of her fist against his shoulder. "Thanks, little brother. How are you doing anyway? How are things with Masha?"

Eric's face blazed with sudden heat. "What do you mean?" He'd never said anything to her about Masha. Was it that obvious?

"You've got a thing for her, don't you? I always see you two hanging out together."

"We're friends."

"Why stop there?"

Eric looked down at the toes of his work boots. "I don't know. I guess...well, yeah, maybe something will happen." The last time he'd had a conversation with Jude about this kind of thing was last Christmas, at their mother's house. They'd both had a lot of wine, and had sat up in front of the dying fire for a while after everyone else had gone to bed. Jude had asked him how many people he'd slept with, and he'd been drunk enough to tell her the truth: none. But he wasn't drunk now, and didn't like talking to her about this kind of thing. It felt vaguely incestuous.

"*Make* something happen," Jude said. "There's a dance coming up, right? You could dance with her during a slow song. Not too close, you know, because all the kids will give you shit. Just a nice, friendly dance." She lifted her arms up into a dancing posture. "Then ask her if she wants to go get some dinner in town on her next night out."

"She'll probably just laugh. Not in a bad way, I mean. She just laughs a lot. It's hard to get her to be serious about stuff."

Jude let her arms flop to her sides. "She won't laugh. And if she does, then forget her. She's a bitch and doesn't deserve you."

"She's not a bitch."

Jude put her hands on Eric's shoulders and bowed her forehead close to his. "Then she won't laugh. Do it, OK?"

"OK, OK," he said, backing away from her touch. "Fine."

"Cool," she said. She folded her arms over her chest, and Eric felt a little guilty for having rejected what she'd meant as an affectionately bossy, big sisterly gesture.

"Remember when we were kids," he said, "and you used to pull me around in that red wagon with the wooden slats that came out?" Fast, she'd pull him. Crazy fast, zigzagging up and down the gravel roads and over the bumpy grass, more than once turning so sharply that the wagon had overturned and he'd fallen out. Still, he kept letting her do it. She called them "thrill rides." "Do you want a regular ride or a thrill ride?" she'd ask him. And he always said "thrill" because he knew she wanted him to, and because he didn't want her to think he was chicken. And maybe because he sort of liked it. At least, he liked feeling afterward that he'd been brave.

"Yeah, I remember," Jude said, smiling. "Sorry about that."

Abe

ON THE SECOND SATURDAY of the session, on his way back to the farmhouse to change for dinner after a swim, Abe stopped into the office with plans to rib Aura about the inspector's failure to appear. He had played along with her hunch, double-checking safety equipment and signage at the "high risk" areas she enumerated for him—waterfront, ropes course, climbing wall, riding area—but only in a half-assed way. Everything was fine, and if there was a minor infraction he was confident he could talk his way out of it. They wouldn't shut the place down. But "they" never showed.

Aura was just ending a phone call when Abe came in. After hanging up, she stared at him evenly for a moment, then shook her head. "You are unbelievable. Do you know that?"

"Well, yeah," he said, flexing a bicep. He was wearing nothing but his swim trunks, his towel slung around his neck. "You're actually not the first woman to say so."

At some point—Abe wasn't sure quite when—their banter had taken on this slightly flirtatious tone. He'd started it, he supposed. And it wasn't like he meant anything by it; she was practically his sister. It just seemed to be the most effective way to defuse the tension between them. It flustered (maybe flattered?) her enough that she'd relax a little about whatever it was that she was annoyed at him for at the moment—not writing it down when he took petty cash, not returning a phone call fast enough, leaving half-full mugs of coffee on the collating table next to the copy machine. And then he would feel guilty (there was something unsavory about deploying flirtation so strategically) and relent a little, and they'd find something resembling a middle ground.

This time Aura just glared. "That was Dahna Schwartz's mother."

"Oh?" Dahna from Free Speech. Blowjob Dahna. Shit, Abe thought. Shit, shit, shit.

"She just wanted to thank us," Aura said, her voice suddenly bright with sarcastic cheer, "for talking so openly and frankly with her daughter about such important contemporary issues."

In spite of the relief flooding through him, Abe played it cool. "Yeah, great. She's a regular at Free Speech. Good kid. That's nice of her mom to call. I'm glad she appreciated it."

"You explained to campers what oral sex is?" Aura whisper-shouted. "Are you crazy?"

"I explained it in very innocuous terms. Most of them already knew what it was anyway, I'm sure. How could they not? It's all over the news."

"Abe, you cannot talk about stuff like that with campers! What else did you tell them? How to roll a joint?"

"That was the only day we talked about anything controversial. And afterward, I realized it probably wasn't the best idea. But the girl's mother is happy, so what's the big deal?"

"Her mother sounds like a nut job," Aura said, sitting back

in her chair. "Let's just hope none of the more normal parents get wind of this and sue us for psychological damage."

"Let them try. If I'm going to run this place, I'm not going to run it tiptoeing around a bunch of hysterical, overprotective parents. If they want to control every little thing their kid hears or sees or does, they shouldn't send them to camp in the first place. Not this camp, anyway."

"You don't think your dad tiptoed around parents?"

"He didn't use to. He didn't have to. The parents were on board."

Aura rolled her eyes. "Wake up and smell the expresso, Abe. This isn't nineteen seventy anymore."

"Espresso," Abe said, but immediately wished he hadn't.

"Whatever. Anyway, even back then it wasn't all peace and love and flowers. And your dad would not have been talking with campers about oral sex. Even if it was in the news."

Abe tugged up and down on the ends of his towel, the back of his neck warming under the friction. She was probably right, not that he'd admit this to her. "Imagine the headlines," he said. "LBJ gets BJ. Dick Nixon gets his—"

"Yeah, yeah. Real funny."

"Listen," said Abe. "I know times have changed. But I have to believe there's a way we can run this place as a business and still do some good for these kids. Get them to open their minds and grow as people."

Aura was looking at him with a mix of amusement and disdain. "Yeah, that's great, Gandhi. But in the meantime, could you just be a little more careful with this Free Speech business?"

"I'll be more careful," Abe said. "We'll keep it PG-13, all the way."

"PG would be better. Or G. Seeing as there aren't actually any parents around."

"We're *in loco parentis*."

"Yeah, you're loco all right."

Abe grinned. "Loco like a fox."

Aura rolled her eyes again, snapped off her computer, and stood up from her desk. "I've got to get out of here," she said, pawing around in her purse for her keys. "We've got a seven o'clock dinner reservation supposedly. Not that he'll get there on time."

It took Abe a moment to remember what she was talking about: Matt was driving up from Boston and they were going to spend two nights in Boothbay Harbor. He'd overheard her on the phone talking with him about it a few times—testy exchanges that often ended in her saying she'd call him back later.

"You excited?" he asked.

"Yeah, of course. Why wouldn't I be?"

"I don't know. Why wouldn't you be?"

She hoisted her bag up onto her shoulder and shook her head. "You are so freakin' weird."

Abe snapped his towel at the back of her legs as she walked out the door.

≈

On Sunday, instead of staying in the office to cover while Aura was in Boothbay with Matt, Abe left Strickland and a couple of CITs in charge and went up to Acadia National Park with the older half of the camp. He was apprehensive; not only had the area been one of his father's favorite places on earth, it was where he and Gail had been headed in the plane. But it turned out to be immensely satisfying to spend a day in the landscape his father had loved so much: the crashing surf, the sandy paths, the beach roses.

He took a small group of campers on a hike up the Precipice—a short but exhilarating climb involving precarious scrambles up rock faces using steel pegs and ladders. Several of the hikers were Free Speech regulars, but some were kids Abe hadn't talked to before, and wouldn't have expected to be interested in hiking. Like Jodi from Cherry Hill, who was thirteen but had the body of a 24-year-old, and her sidekick, Ashley, who looked like she'd just stepped out of a J. Crew catalog. The two of them regularly sauntered around camp in their bikini tops with towels around their hips and headphones around their necks, looking bored and slightly disgusted by their fellow campers. But that day they were charmingly self-deprecating, entertained by the notion of themselves doing something as uncharacteristic as hiking. "We're not going to break our nails doing this, are we?" Jodi had asked as they started up the trail. Abe started to reply, with a "well…." But Jodi laughed and said, "I'm *kidding!*" and Ashley added, giggling, "I'm probably going to break, like, my neck, knowing what a klutz I am. You'll catch us if we fall, right Abe?"

At the end of the climb the kids built a small, squat cairn on the summit, and planted in it a flag made out of a stick and Ashley's pink paisley bandana. They posed for pictures in front of it, hands linked triumphantly overhead, as if they'd just scaled Everest. After the hike, back down at Sand Beach, Abe led them on a screeching sprint into the icy Atlantic. Only a couple of people actually managed to submerge themselves. The rest—including Abe—stayed in the shallows and mounted a massive splash fight. Campers who had been sunbathing on the beach joined in, and at its height, the splashing war was twenty campers and counselors strong.

On the long bus ride home, Abe tried to lead some songs—classics from the Eden Lake songbook, like "This Camp is Your Camp," and "Leavin' on a Jet Plane," but the campers were much more enthusiastic about singing the "Brady Bunch" theme and "Summer Nights" from *Grease*. Some of the girls who were in the camp show started in with tunes from *Annie*, including a screaming rendition (was there any other kind?) of "It's a Hard Knock Life" while a rival contingent of boys shouted "Ninety-nine bottles of beer on the wall." Abe joined them, imagining, with a certain pleasure, how he'd dress down any parent who called up to complain that her child was singing a song about alcohol.

They lost steam at around sixty bottles, and then a lovely quiet settled over the bus. For the last half hour of the trip there was little sound but rumble of the engine and the occasional pop of a stone up against the undercarriage. Kids next to the windows leaned their heads against the glass and slept, open-mouthed. Others opened up their copies of *Harry Potter* or pulled on headphones and retreated into the private world of their music. A few talked quietly.

Abe, sitting in the back of the bus next to a softly snoring Chuck Niedermeier, watching ramshackle farms, patches of dense forest and ranch houses with yards full of lawn ornaments glide past, felt a great fondness for everyone and everything.

He was happy. Was it possible that he was happy?

The grief hadn't faded completely. It still caught up with

him first thing in the morning sometimes, when he lay on hazy border between waking and sleeping. But the rest of the time it was kept at bay by the constant activity of his days; the ceaseless march of meals and meetings and things to do. Even the pestering phone calls and emails from parents didn't bother him so much anymore. He dealt with them the way he used to deal with drunks at Madam's Organ, staying detached as he replied to them, letting a voice more genial and conciliatory than his own do the talking. It worked with the campers, too. When they complained to him that they hated the food or wanted to be able to stay up later or desperately wanted to call their parents (phone calls were only allowed in emergencies), he could unclip himself from his aggravation—float up over it and handle the situation with humor and aplomb. Nothing could touch him.

This must have been how his father felt when he was running the camp: powerful. Free.

And loved—that part of it, Abe had to admit, was nice, too. Or maybe loved wasn't quite the right word; it was more like how he imagined celebrities felt: acknowledged. Known. He'd been flattered when, at brown bag skit night, more than half of the skits the kids came up with using their random assortment of ridiculous props and costumes featured a portrayal of him. Of course, it was a natural to spoof the camp director; but still, it seemed to him there was real affection in it.

And why wouldn't there be? Two weeks into the session, and he knew most of them by name. He made a point of getting out of the office and checking in on the day-to-day activities of the camp, the way his father had. Campers loved it when he showed up at their classes and stumbled over themselves to show him the pottery knickknacks they'd made or show him how they could back dive off the dock.

Even Jeremy Dyer seemed to be coming around. He was less disruptive at Free Speech and other camp activities. His attitude wasn't quite as sourly defiant. And although Abe hadn't actually succeeded in getting him to open up about his feelings around his family situation, at least on some level, maybe, it was getting through to the kid that someone cared. And maybe it would make a real difference.

As soon as the bus turned off the pavement to rumble and bounce down the dirt road leading to Eden Lake, the sleepy silence they'd traveled in for the last hour was broken. The campers awakened one by one (except for Niedermeier, who remained sound asleep) filling the bus with their animated chatter.

"Hey, Abe?" a girl of eleven or so (Rachel something-or-other; he could never remember) called from two rows ahead, up on her knees, backward in her seat to face him. "What's for dinner tonight?"

Dahna Schwartz popped up next to her. "Is it pizza night?"

"Umm…actually," said Abe, putting a finger to his chin, "I think we're having worm burgers and fried daddy long-legs, and caterpillar ice cream for dessert."

"No, really," Rachel said.

"I'm serious!" said Abe. "You know, when I lived in Africa, I ate fried termites once. With a little salt." He rubbed his belly. "Delectable."

"I hear that in some parts of the Amazon rainforest they eat grubs," said Niedermeier, who had woken up at some point.

The insect eating gross-out banter expanded to include

three or four other campers, and continued even as everyone filed out of the bus and onto the lawn in front of the farmhouse. *Frog lasagna! Yellow jacket casserole! Chipmunk milkshakes!*

Once all the campers had dispersed, heading back to their cabins to shower and clean up before dinner (whatever that might be), Abe took a seat on the granite step at the front door and leaned back on his elbows to let the day's last warm rays of sunlight bathe his face.

And although he didn't quite believe in an afterlife, he felt like his father was with him somehow—watching, participating, approving.

He let himself settle into the comfort of that feeling.

Jude

LIZZIE WAS PLANNING TO wear makeup to the dance, which meant that all the other girls in the cabin had to wear it, too. After dinner, Jude found herself applying her own mascara and blush to the eyelashes and cheeks of twelve ten-year-old girls. Not the most hygienic thing in the world, no doubt, but better the whole cabin catch conjunctivitis than throw a collective hissy-fit because Lizzie got to doll herself up like a little Jonbenet Ramsey and they didn't.

After escorting the girls to the dance, Jude went down to the camp office to shoot the shit with Abe and check her email. Yesterday, Courtney had written to give her the latest work gossip—Anamaria, the wardrobe mistress, had gotten arrested for cocaine possession—and Jude had, perhaps stupidly, written back. It was her night off; a bunch of the staff had gone out to see *Batman and Robin* which she had no interest in subjecting herself to, and Tim had a cold, so she was at loose ends, alone in the media loft with a bottle of wine. She told Courtney what she was up to, asked her how she was doing, and by the way, was everyone still talking about what a slut she was, or had the whole thing blown over? The second after she sent the email she regretted asking, but now she was eager for Courtney's reply.

As she approached the office, she heard Abe and Aura yelling, and thought that maybe, finally, their bickering had exploded into a knock down, drag-out fight. But when she got to the door, she saw that this wasn't the case; in fact, Abe sat at his computer and Aura stood behind him, her arms folded across her chest, smirking. He pounded furiously at the keyboard while she watched, yelling, "You suck, Perryweiss! You totally suck!"

Disappointed—and slightly confused—Jude tried to edge away, but Abe saw her.

"Hey, Jude," he called, glancing briefly at her. "We're having a Tetris tournament. You want in? Aura's amazing. This is all she does all day at her job back in Boston."

"Oh, shut up," said Aura.

Jude stayed on the other side of the screen door. "No, that's OK," she said. "I'm on duty, actually. I was just going to check my email real quick."

"You can use my computer," Aura said.

Jude hesitated. She didn't particularly want to sit there checking her email while the two of them yukked it up a few feet away. (When had they gotten so buddy-buddy, anyway?) But her eagerness to see if Courtney had written back won out. She sat down at Aura's computer, and angled the screen so the two of them wouldn't see, though she needn't have bothered; they were oblivious to her presence.

Courtney had, in fact, written: a lengthy, rambling note, mostly about her latest roommate crisis and the guy she'd just started dating, plus more about Anamaria and the cocaine bust.

But nothing in response to the question Jude had asked. Which either meant that Courtney had forgotten to address it, or that she'd chosen not to because, in fact, everyone was still talking. It was hard not to assume the worst.

Jude angrily hit delete, and then, on an impulse, hit "compose" and typed Mitch's email in the address line. In the subject line, she wrote, "Hi," then erased it and wrote, "Checking in" instead.

She stopped. This was idiotic. She absolutely should not be writing to Mitch. Nothing good could come of it. She was about to click the window closed when Abe, in the heat of his game, screamed "No!" Jude's arm jumped, and, suddenly the "send" button was illuminated. She watched in dumb horror as the screen flickered and a message appeared to inform her that her message had been successfully sent.

"Fuck!"

"What happened?" said Abe.

"Nothing." Jude stared at the screen, the back of her mouth filling with a sick, metallic taste. Should she write Mitch another email, telling him that the previous one was an accident? No. She shouldn't do anything. It would just make things worse. If by some chance Mitch wrote back, she'd just say it was a mistake; she was trying to write to someone else.

"Fuck," she muttered again. She signed out of her email and headed for the door.

Abe and Aura were too absorbed in their game to say goodbye.

≈

The music at the dance was for the most part god-awful—Backstreet Boys and Hanson and Madonna gone electronica.

Jude sat on the wooden bench that ran the length of the rec. hall, debating whether or not to go back to the office and write to Mitch. Maybe just a quick "sorry about that, please disregard," would be the best thing. She didn't *want* him to write back. (Damn Abe and Aura and their Tetris-fest.) She felt so restless and jittery that she actually got up and danced with some of the girls from her cabin to "Get Jiggy With it," hoping to burn off some excess energy. They seemed to find the fact that she was dancing hilarious, as did some of the other counselors, who pointed and smiled, feigning shock.

Humiliation aside, she did feel a little better after that. It was just a blank email, she reasoned to herself; an obvious mistake. It wasn't like she'd poured her heart out to him. She stayed on the floor for the next few songs. As long as she was moving, she found, she didn't think too much.

The first slow song of the night was, predictably, "My Heart Will Go On" from *Titanic*. This prompted a collective "ohhh!" from the girl campers and sent the younger boys scurrying outside to the water fountain. The older ones stayed and partnered up.

Jude remembered suddenly that this was the night Eric was planning to make his move with Masha, and scanned the floor, hoping to see them dancing together. But instead, she found the two of them standing side by side at the back of the hall, talking but not looking at each other. Eric shifted from foot to foot, his arms tightly clasped across his chest. *Ask her,* Jude whispered under her breath, *ask her, ask her!* Then, Strickland Strawner approached. *No! Go away!* Jude thought and watched, her heart breaking for Eric, as Strickland led Masha out onto the dance floor.

She was about to go to Eric, when Sergei appeared in front of her, bowing low.

"May I have the honor to dance with you?" he said, extending a hand.

"I don't know," she said. "I don't really—"

"It's OK, I'll lead," he said, and grabbed her hand. His grip was firmer than she'd expected, and when they got out into the crowd of swaying couples, he pulled her so close that her nose practically touched his Adam's apple.

"Easy there, cowboy," she said, and pulled back a few inches.

"It's slow song."

"Yeah, but I still need to breathe. And we're surrounded by young, impressionable children."

"Yes, well that child has his hand on that child's backside," Sergei said, nodding over Jude's shoulder.

Jude craned her head to look: Bobby Denzig, her Daddy Warbucks, and a red-headed girl in tiny denim cutoffs were grinding in slow motion, pelvis to pelvis.

"Little perverts," Jude said, turning back to Sergei.

"I think it was those two that I saw kissing in the woods last night," Sergei said as he swayed Jude side to side. "I think the girl had her hand inside the boy's pants."

"Gross. What'd you do?"

The corners of his mouth pulled downward in indifference. "I did nothing. I was not working, just walking. I was, you know…"

"You were plastered, weren't you?"

He smiled. "Yes. Shit faced." He said it like it was two words.

"What a fine asset you are to this camp. What exactly is it you do here again?"

"Jude," said Sergei, looking suddenly serious, "tell me, do you have boyfriend?"

Oh great, thought Jude. "Yeah, kind of," she said.

"What is his 'kind of' name?"

"Mitch," she said, and immediately felt like stomping on her own foot. If she was going to lie about having a boyfriend, why not make up a fake name, too? Alexander. Mustafa. Pablo. She was trying not to think about Mitch, for Christ's sake.

"Is it serious relationship?" Sergei asked.

"I don't know. Why?"

He gave a laconic shrug. "For example, will he be angry if you have sex with other man?"

Jude swiveled her head around to see if any of the kids had heard, but fortunately they all appeared to be caught up in their vertical humping. "Yes," she said, lowering her voice to a near-whisper. "He will be angry if I have sex with other man. Sergei, this is a really weird and inappropriate conversation. Can we change the subject, please?" She scanned the hall for Eric but didn't see him anywhere.

"OK," Sergei said. "New subject. You have many earring holes. Do you have the body piercings, too?"

Jude let go of Sergei and took a step backward. "It's been fun, but I'm going to go find Eric."

"I'll come with you."

"No, listen, I have to talk to him. Sister to brother. Why don't you go ask Tamara to dance? I hear she's got a pierced clit."

Sergei reached out and grabbed Jude's hand, with a desperation that was almost sweet, albeit in a pitiful sort of way. "Listen, please, you will dance with me again later?"

"Yeah, fine," Jude said, "but no more personal questions, OK?"

"OK," Sergei said, and pumped her hand. "Deal."

≈

Jude found Eric sitting on the picnic table behind the rec. hall, chin in hands, looking out at the lake. She sat down next to him on the creaky tabletop. It was one of the few surviving tables on the property from the old days, painted the same deep green as the oldest buildings: the dining hall, the pottery and candle making studios, the first cabins. The new picnic tables, like the newer buildings, were left unpainted, in their natural wood state, coated with clear stain and left to weather slowly from blond to gray.

Jude picked at a bubble of paint, revealing damp, dirt-colored wood underneath. "What happened?" she said. "How come you let that dork Strickland ask her?"

"I don't know," said Eric. "I just couldn't make myself do it."

"She was waiting for you to ask her. I could tell."

"You couldn't tell anything." He sounded uncharacteristically annoyed.

"Trust me, she was. Anyway, you'll have plenty more chances. That was only the first slow song."

"Yeah, I guess I can give it another try," Eric said. He stroked his beard between his thumb and forefinger. "Do you think I'd look better without this? Or this?" He tugged on his ponytail.

"Look at me," Jude said. Eric obeyed, gazing just past her left ear. It was hard to objectively assess his attractiveness—he'd always just been her little brother, quiet and awkward, almost asexual. Since he was old enough to grow a beard, he'd had one, and it was hard to imagine him without it. She put her fingertips to his cheek and gave his head a little push so she could see the line of his jaw better.

"I'm not sure," she said. "Maybe stick with the beard but lose the ponytail. You'd look a little more, you know, up-to-date." *Less like a cloak-wearer*, she thought. It was what she and her college friends called people who were into role-playing games and Renaissance festivals.

"Yeah, OK," Eric said, a little sadly. He ran his hand down over his ponytail.

"But not if you don't want to."

"I don't know. If she really liked me it wouldn't make a difference, right?"

"Maybe not. But forget your hair. You should go back in there and ask her to dance, before Strickland does it again."

Eric let out a long breath, then slapped his palms against his thighs. "OK. I'll do it."

As he was starting to stand, there came the sound of twigs crunching underfoot, and a high, birdish giggle, followed by a goofy chuckle. Both Eric and Jude turned around: Masha and Strickland were walking past, about ten yards away, heading into the darkness of the trees, in the direction of the campfire ring. They were holding hands.

Eric turned quickly back around.

"Eric…" Jude began.

"Forget it," he said. He sprang to the ground, the planks of the table creaking beneath him. "I'm going to bed. Goodnight."

She watched him stalk off into the darkness, his hands stuffed into the pockets of his jeans, his head bent forward, and knew there was nothing she could do or say to make him feel better.

She sat for a few minutes longer, watching the lake ripple in tall black stripes between the trees, breathing in the sweet-sharp smell of pine needles. Damn the smells here, she thought, so distinct and powerful: the smoke of the campfire, the polyurethane on the floors, the softly rank, mildewed smell of the bathrooms. When they caught her in quiet moments like this they set a whirl of fondness and sorrow and longing spinning inside her—a useless, frustrating blend of emotions. They made her miss her father. Not the father she hadn't spoken to in four years, but the one from her childhood, whom she didn't despise.

She wished she could just mourn that man. But every time she tried, her thoughts were drawn forward to the last time she'd seen him, when he showed up at her college graduation after she'd told him not to. And to the phone conversation two weeks before that.

It was the first real argument they'd ever had. Until that point, she'd been simply, slowly, edging him out of her life. Not visiting Eden Lake over holidays. Saying she was busy when he came to New York on camp business and proposed meeting for dinner or lunch. Keeping their conversations terse and polite. He'd never protested or asked why. But that day, when she told him, feeling numbly powerful as she did, that she'd rather he didn't come to the graduation ceremony, he said, "What did I do, Jude?"

"What did you do?" she had said, and laughed, incredulous. "What do you mean, 'what did I do'? You cheated on Mom for almost four years. You made me take your side. You fucked up our family. That's what."

Now he laughed, but gently, fondly. "Sweetheart, where is

this anger coming from all of a sudden? This is all water under the bridge."

"No, it's not. And the fact that you think it is—that's why I'm so angry. You blinded me. You made me think it was all OK, all meant to be, and I forgave you. No, you know what?" She hadn't realized it herself until just then. "I *didn't* even forgive you. I didn't think there was anything *to* forgive. I didn't see what an asshole you were, to Mom, to me, to all of us. But I see it now. And I don't want you at my graduation. I don't want you in my life." Everything was shaking. Her voice, her hands, her lower lip. She hadn't planned to say so much. She hadn't planned to unleash the anger, but she couldn't help herself. "Not now, and maybe not ever."

He'd shown up at her graduation anyway, holding a cheap, cellophane-wrapped bouquet that he'd probably gotten from a gas station bucket on his way to campus—an afterthought. He wasn't coming for her; he was coming for himself. To win back her favor and doting. At least, that's what she thought at the time.

No, she still thought it; but she wished she hadn't been quite so cold to him. She wished that she hadn't handed the bouquet back to him and turned away.

≈

There were no major dramas at the dance for the girls in Shangri-la. A few of them had slow-danced with boys, and some were disappointed not to have been asked, but nobody was heartbroken. There were no tears, and everyone fell asleep quickly, except for Jude. Her mind flickered with thoughts of Mitch, the email fiasco, the camp show, her father—everything stirred up and muddy. At midnight, she was still awake. The cabin was filled with the sound of the girls' whistling breath and surprisingly loud, wet snores. The air smelled like damp towels and dirty socks. After a mosquito whined in her ear for the third time in five minutes, causing her for a third time to flail helplessly at her head with open hands, Jude had had enough. She pulled a cardigan on over her t-shirt, stepped into her sandals, and went outside. Katie wasn't back yet, and she wasn't supposed to leave the girls alone, but whatever. They were all sound asleep.

At first, her plan was to go to the office or the media loft to see if Mitch had written back, but she realized, with some relief, that they would both be locked at this hour. Good. She'd just go down to the lake and get a little air. It always felt a few degrees cooler there.

There was a moon, but not a particularly attractive one; it was three quarters full and misshapen, like a hard candy someone had bitten and sucked on for a while, then spit out. When Jude walked out onto the dock, she was puzzled to see what appeared to be an empty canoe, floating just outside the buoy line that marked the boundary of the swimming area. One of the lifeguards must have forgotten to put it back into the boathouse and it had slid into the water from the shore. Or maybe it was some kind of practical joke? There could be someone lying down inside, kidnapped sleeping bag and all, and set afloat. Pranks had always been strongly discouraged at Eden Lake, but every once in a while, something happened: sugar in the salt shakers. Shaving cream on the toilet seats. Never something as major as setting someone adrift in the middle of the lake, but who knew? Maybe the ante had been upped since she was a kid.

Jude cupped her hands to her mouth and whisper-yelled at the canoe, "Hello?" Nobody answered, though the canoe might have rocked a little bit. "Is someone in the canoe?" she said, louder.

She nearly jumped when someone suddenly sat upright in the boat. Sergei. The moonlight glinted off his glasses. "What time is it?" he yelled, too loudly.

"After midnight," Jude said. "What are you doing?"

"I was—oh shit. Where's my paddle? Shit to hell!"

"Shut up, Sergei. You'll wake up the whole freaking camp. Are you sure you had one?"

"Had what?"

"A paddle."

"No," said Sergei. "But probably. It must be floating away." He leaned forward and started paddling with his hands. When the canoe was finally in reach, Jude helped pull it in close to the dock and held it while Sergei stumbled out, barefoot, a bottle of Smirnoff in his hand.

"At least you held onto the important thing," Jude said.

Once they'd pulled the canoe up onto the dock, Sergei sat down and dangled his feet in the water. "Come have a drink," he said. Jude kicked off her sandals and sat down next to him. He offered her the bottle and she took a healthy gulp.

"What were you doing out there?" she asked.

"I was just lying down for a minute. It's very nice to lie in canoe and rock on the water. Did you ever try it?"

"No."

"It's like you're baby again. In a cradle." He rocked an imaginary baby in his arms. "Google google."

Jude laughed. "Google google?"

"You know, like a baby."

"It's goo goo. Not that babies say that either. I don't think."

"Goo goo," Sergei repeated thoughtfully. He looked at Jude and frowned. "Why aren't you in your cabin? Is not your night off, is it? You were at the dance, as we both know. And, by the way, I am still angry that you did not dance with me again."

"You didn't ask me again, stupid." She'd seen him dancing with at least three other female staff members over the course of the night, including Tamara. Absurdly, she'd been a little jealous. "It's so fucking hot out. Give me another sip of that. Maybe it'll help me sleep."

Sergei handed her the bottle. "Why can't you sleep?"

"I don't know. Just thinking about things." She took another gulp from the bottle and felt it almost immediately—a warm tingling in her calves.

"Good things or bad things?"

"Bad mostly." She took another long draw, but swallowed wrong, and the liquid seared her windpipe. Sergei thumped his palm between her shoulders as she coughed, then held it there. "Are you all right?"

Jude nodded, her eyes squeezed shut. "I'm fine," she croaked. She lifted the bottle for another sip, thinking it would help stop the coughing, but Sergei gently took it from her just as she touched it to her lips.

"No more," he said. "It's not good idea to drink too much when you are unhappy. Only when you're happy."

"You must be one happy guy," said Jude. His hand was still on her back, and, strangely, she didn't mind. For once, he didn't seem like a complete goofball; he seemed kind, and strong. She let herself lean a few fractions of an inch closer to him, and after a moment, he moved his arm around her shoulder.

"Now I am happy, yes," he said. "Maybe I'll have another drink."

Jude laughed.

"You have had a difficult several months, yes? With the accident, of course. And with this boyfriend in New York, this Mitch. I think you would not have come here for the summer if things were so good with him."

"No," said Jude. "Things were not so good."

"Maybe you should forget about him," Sergei said.

"Right. Like it's that easy."

"No, of course, I understand." He took off his glasses and set them on the dock at his side. "But do you think it would be possible to forget him for, perhaps, ten minutes?"

Jude lifted her head—which had at some point, without her realizing it, come to rest on Sergei's shoulder—and looked up at him. Without his glasses he looked at once wiser and more vulnerable. Forty-some years of living to his credit, and it was as if he'd refused to let any of it scar or harden him.

"Ten minutes?" Jude said. He was looking at her mouth.

"Or maybe just five."

"Yeah, all right," she said, and let her face move toward his, "I could probably manage five."

Eric

EACH TIME ERIC THOUGHT of Masha's hand in Strickland's, he felt as if he'd drunk bad milk. He could taste it, sour and thin, coating his tongue. At one point on his way to Camden, he stopped the truck and bent over the grass on the side of the road, thinking that if he could vomit it would give him some relief—purge the image and the feeling that went with it. He even tried sticking his fingers down his throat, but it only made him cough.

It wasn't as if he hadn't been rejected by girls before. He'd more or less come to take it for granted that anyone he was interested in wouldn't feel the same. But this time he'd felt like he actually had a chance. And this time it wasn't just any girl. He suspected he might be in love with Masha. It was why he'd proceeded with such caution. He wanted to get it exactly right, and until tonight, he thought he was doing just that.

What he hadn't told Jude was that when that first slow song had come on, Masha had wrinkled her nose and said it depressed her. She'd seen *Titanic*, and whenever she heard the song, all she could think of was all those dead bodies, floating frozen in the ocean. That was why he hadn't asked her. Not because he was too scared to do it. Of course, now he realized he should have anyway. He should have made some kind of joke or flirtatious comment. He should have said, "Maybe if we dance together to it, you won't think it's depressing anymore."

But she still probably would have said no. Because, as Strickland proved, it wasn't that Masha didn't want to dance to that particular song. It was that she didn't want to dance with Eric.

It was almost ten when he got to his mother's. As he turned into the driveway he had, for an instant, the strange sensation that he'd come to the wrong house: there was a motorcycle parked in the driveway. A brand new Harley.

Dane from the memorial service, he thought, once he registered that he was, in fact, in the right place. It had to be Dane. How many people with motorcycles could his mother possibly know?

Warm yellow light poured from the windows of the house, casting gridded shadows on the perennial garden and stone walkway, and as Eric approached the front door, he felt almost as if he was coming home—which was strange, since he'd never actually lived in this house.

His mother answered wearing a long, silk robe painted with suns and moons, the crepey skin of the top of her breasts and the deep cleft between them exposed. She held a glass of red wine in her hand, half empty, and her cheeks were flushed. Eric felt suddenly, acutely embarrassed; he shouldn't have just shown up like this.

But his mother smiled, then laughed, as if at some sort of inside joke she had with herself, and embraced him tightly. "My baby boy. I'm so glad you're here." Over her shoulder, Eric saw Dane standing up from the couch, pulling on a t-shirt.

"I'm sorry," Eric said, pulling away from her, "I should have called first." His hand went to his belt, where he normally clipped his cell phone, and he realized that in his hurry to get off the property he'd forgotten it. All he had was a fresh t-shirt, a pair of underwear and his toothbrush, thrown hastily into a plastic shopping bag.

"Nonsense," his mother said and laughed—higher and a bit wobblier than usual. She was clearly tipsy, which was rare for her. These days she almost never drank.

She took his bag and hung it on the coat rack by the door, then guided him forward with a firm hand to his back. "Eric, you remember Dane. I think you two spoke at the memorial service."

"Yes, hi," Eric said.

Dane looked as embarrassed as Eric felt. He gave him a small wave. "Hi."

"Well sit, sit," his mother said, and directed him to the big wicker rocker catty-corner to the couch. It was a chair that used to be in the farmhouse at Eden Lake, and Eric had always been afraid of it. When you rocked back, it went just a little farther than a rocker ought to go, and you felt certain it was going to dump you backward onto the floor, even though you knew it wouldn't. He perched on the edge, and accepted the glass of red wine his mother handed him.

"You look upset," she said. "What's wrong?" She settled down onto the couch, very close to Dane.

"Nothing serious," Eric replied. "I just needed to get out of there for a little while."

Dane nodded twice, slowly, as if he understood completely; nothing more needed to be said.

His mother pressed on. "Did you and Abe have a fight? I've been wondering if it's been hard for you, with the outcome of the will and all."

"No. It's nothing like that."

His mother dipped her chin. "A matter of the heart, perhaps?"

"Carol, babe, leave the man alone," said Dane. "He doesn't want to talk about it."

Dane's eyes met his, and Eric felt his "thank you," and Dane's "you're welcome" pass silently between them. He liked that Dane had called him a man.

"So," Eric said, focusing on the rim of his wineglass. "Are you guys, like, living together?"

"We're trying it out," his mother said. "Does that upset you?"

He shrugged. "No. I'm happy for you guys. I guess it seems a little fast, but it's none of my business."

"Your mom and I have known each other a real long time," Dane said. "Since before you were born. So I guess it doesn't feel so fast to us."

"How did you meet again?" Eric asked.

Dane seemed to falter. "Well, I worked at the camp for a couple of summers. You were real little."

"I thought you said it was before I was born."

"Right," said Dane. "That's right."

Carol closed her eyes and began shaking her head. "No. No, honey, the truth is, we met when I was traveling in India, in seventy-five. When—"

"Carol," said Dane, a note of warning in his voice.

"It's all right, Dane. He's here, we're all here. It's as good a time as any."

"Carol," Dane said again, more sharply. "Stop."

Eric wished she would. He had the feeling that something awful was about to happen.

But his mother was already reaching forward, pulling a photo album out from beneath the coffee table. "Here," she said, and handed it to Eric, splayed open to a page in the middle. He took the book onto his lap and she bent over him, pointing to a picture of eight or so people standing on some kind of deck or terrace, some of them wearing Indian clothes, others in jeans and T-shirts.

"Right there on the left," she said. Indeed, it was Dane; he had the same full handlebar mustache—reddish brown instead of white—plus sideburns and long hair pulled back into a ponytail.

"Look like anyone you know?" Carol asked.

Eric was about to reply, when Dane spoke, his voice gruff: "Carol, don't. This isn't what we talked about. You've had too much to drink."

"I know what I'm doing," she said. She sat down on the edge of the coffee table and pressed her hands to her knees. "Baby, look again. Do you see?"

Eric stared at the picture a while longer, and then, all at once, he saw.

He could have been looking at a picture of himself.

At some point, while he was staring, his legs had lifted from the rug and the rocking chair had started to tilt slowly back, back, back toward that place of no return, where it felt like it would throw him mercilessly onto the floor. He quickly leaned forward, planting his feet on the ground again, letting the catch of terror in his solar plexus subside.

"I don't understand," he said.

But he did. And yet, it was impossible. How could Dane be his father? For a moment, he wondered if he'd somehow forgotten the chronology of his own life. Had his parents divorced before he was born? Of course not. No.

He felt his mother's hand on his knee. "Your dad—Clay—knew. But he never thought of you as anything but his own son. He loved you fiercely, Eric. Just as much as he loved Abe and Judie."

On the couch, Dane sat with his legs wide, his elbows planted on his knees, frowning down into the glass of wine in his hands.

"Are you OK?" Carol said. "Talk to us."

Eric's lips and the hollows of his cheeks felt cool. His fingertips, still gripping the black pages of the album, were cold, too. "What do you expect me to say?" he finally said.

"Eric, sweetheart, don't you see? You still have a father." She was smiling at him as if she'd just given him a gift.

"My father's dead," said Eric. He slammed the photo album shut, tossed it to the floor and stood, the chair springing backward as he did.

"Wait," his mother said. "Please don't. There's so much that needs to be said. Dane?"

As Eric was pulling the door shut behind him, he heard Dane say "let him go."

≈

There was an old motel on Route 17 that Eric had passed a million times, never catching the name until tonight: The Blue Sky. Out front was a peanut-shaped pool with a slide and beside the door to each room, an orange plastic chair resembling a laundry basket. Eric paid at the front desk and asked the clerk—a woman with a crooked gray beehive hairdo and glasses on a chain around her neck—if they had a razor he could use.

"Why, gonna kill yourself?" she asked, chin in hand.

"No, just shave," Eric said.

"We're not the Ritz, you know," she said, and disappeared through a door behind the desk, returning a few minutes later with an orange disposable. "My husband's. Looks like he used it a couple of times." She ran her thumb down the blade a few times to clear it of hairs, and handed it to Eric. "No charge."

He turned to go, then stopped. "Sorry, but do you have a pair of scissors I could use, too?"

The woman narrowed her eyes at him. "Somebody looking for you or something? I don't want any trouble."

The lie came to him with surprising ease. "I've got a job interview tomorrow morning, and just want to neaten up a little."

The woman didn't seem convinced, but handed him a pair of scissors from a drawer in her desk, the black paint almost completely chipped away from the handles.

When he got to the room, Eric remembered that he didn't have any shaving cream. He soaked a washcloth in the hottest water he could stand, and lay on the bed with it draped over his mouth and chin while he watched the end of an old episode of *Cheers*. Then he stripped off his shirt and jeans and went into the bathroom, where he cut off as much of his beard and mustache as he could with the scissors. The shampoo in the little bottle on the sink vanity worked up into a good lather, and he did his best to build a thick layer of it over the patchy bristle that remained on his chin and upper lip. The razor wasn't completely dull, but still burned against his skin. He took the mustache off first. Left with just it and no beard, he was afraid he'd look even more like the picture of Dane he'd seen.

He shaved his beard next, and when he was finished he stood staring at his reflection. The skin was pale, almost bluish, where it had been covered with whiskers, and tingled beneath his fingertips when he touched it. He had expected to look younger this way, but in fact, it was just the opposite: not having the beard and mustache emphasized the angularity of his face, and the straight, serious line of his lips.

He loosed his hair from the elastic that held it and began to cut, starting on one side, working his way around the back to the other. It ended up ragged and uneven, so he just kept cutting until no strand of hair was longer than an inch. He looked ravaged and sickly, like a cancer patient whose hair had just started growing out. He didn't care.

He took a shower to rinse the clinging, itching strands from his neck and back, put his underwear back on and crawled into bed. For what felt like hours, he lay with his eyes open in the dark, trying to absorb what he had just learned, trying to understand the ramifications: his father was not his father. His mother was an adulterer and a liar—maybe at greater fault than his father ever was. Jude and Abe were his half siblings, his father's real children. Eric was an interloper. His father's ward. His mother's shame. These realizations rolled fast into his mind, one after another, but each time he tried to hold onto one, to internalize it and make it his own, it would slip from his grasp like water.

When he finally slept, it was fitful, and he was wide awake by six a.m. as usual. The sight of his shorn head in the bathroom mirror was at first jarring, then satisfying. He liked the starkness of his new appearance. He looked as exposed as he felt. If no one else in the world was honest, at least he would be. No more hiding behind his hair.

There was nobody in the office when he went in, so he put his key, the razor, and the scissors on the counter and left. He got an egg sandwich and a cup of coffee from a gas station convenience store a few miles down the road, and then turned onto a northbound route he'd never taken before, but which he knew would lead him neither back to the camp nor to his mother's house.

Nobody knew where he was. He could just keep driving if he wanted, to the north woods of Maine where there were no towns, just tracts of land, numbered and laid out in grids. On to New Brunswick, Quebec, Newfoundland. The roads would grow more desolate, the sky clearer, the days longer. He might, it seemed, be able to launch himself off the very edge of the earth.

Maybe he was meant to be on the plane with Clay and Gail that day after all.

But then, he was never really meant to exist in the first place.

It was almost ten o'clock when he saw a sign for Route 100, which would take him back toward Talbotts Corner. He'd grown increasingly sleepy over the past few miles, and was at the point where he knew he ought to stop and rest. There was a pull-off on the road just after the sign, and he stopped there, locked the doors, and lay down across the seat of the cab. When he woke up, about forty minutes later, his urge to keep driving had vaporized, and he was filled with the dull, matter-of-fact certainty that it was time for him to go back to the camp.

It was lunchtime when he arrived, but he wasn't ready to be seen yet. He went into the farmhouse and heated up a can of tomato soup. As he stood at the stove, watching the bubbles on the surface of the soup grow larger, his anger grew inside him: anger at his parents—make that his mother and Clay—for lying to him. Anger at himself for not having figured it out on his own. Anger at having built his entire life on a foundation now crumbling beneath him.

He ate his soup quickly, standing at the kitchen counter, and let the screen door slam behind him on his way out. He spent the next two hours on the John Deere, his old UMass hat pulled low on his head. Nobody waved to him as he passed, and although he liked being left alone, he wondered why everyone was acting like he was invisible, until he remembered his shorn face and hair. They probably thought he was a stranger—some local who'd been hired to mow. Even Sergei sauntered by him in an oblivious daze, twirling a dandelion between his fingers.

Abe was the first to recognize him. He jogged up to the tractor as Eric was heading back to the barn, jumped up onto the running board and pulled Eric's hat off.

"Holy crap!" he yelled. "What did you do?"

Eric braked and set the engine on idle. "I needed a change," he said.

Abe eyed the top of Eric's head. "What did you do it with, a butter knife?"

Eric swiped his hat from Abe's hands and put it back on his head.

"Sorry, it looks good," Abe said. "Hey, you should come by Free Speech today. We're going to talk about appearance and self-expression. You could be our guest speaker."

"I'm not trying to express myself," Eric said, "I just wanted to cut my fucking hair." He started the engine again, full throttle. The tractor lurched forward and Abe half-jumped, half-stumbled onto the road.

Abe

IN THE SUMMER OF seventy-nine, when Abe was ten years old, a freak storm—a tornado, some said—ripped a jagged path through Talbotts Corner and the surrounding towns and villages, taking the roofs off of houses, felling trees and flipping pick-up trucks into ditches. At the storm's peak, around midnight, Clay and a couple of counselors ran from cabin to cabin with flashlights, closing the shutters and instructing everyone to get onto the bottom bunks. Abe—who himself had to climb down from his top bunk and squeeze in next to fat Noah Weisman below—immediately understood why: if a tree came down through the roof of a cabin, the steel frames of the upper bunks might offer some protection.

Luckily, there was no significant damage to the camp or anyone in it; a few downed tree limbs and a couple of shutters ripped off the farmhouse, nothing more. The following morning, Clay loaded the CITs, a few counselors and all of the thirteen- and fourteen-year-old campers onto one of the school buses and drove them out to Podge Road, a densely populated stretch by Talbotts Corner standards, which had suffered a direct hit. Abe showed up at the bus with a pair of hedge clippers and asked if he could come, too. "Don't tell your mother," his father had said and nodded him aboard.

Clay and Pierre Rouleau, a big, bearded giant of a man from Quebec who was in charge of maintenance at the camp that summer, went at downed trees with chainsaws while the others rolled and carried the pieces off to the side of the road. At lunchtime a van from the camp kitchen arrived and a huge bologna sandwich-making assembly line was formed. Campers went from house to house, farm to farm, delivering sandwiches, cookies and cups of lemonade, and offered to help residents clean up their debris-littered yards. Some curtly refused—there had long been rumors in town that the camp was a commune, a nudist colony, a communist breeding ground—but most were friendly and grateful. At one of the houses Abe visited, the wife led the campers around back to the edge of the woods, to a wall of raspberry bushes at least thirty feet long. She gave them old mason jars and let them gather up the berries that had been flung to the ground by the storm, and pluck the slightly firmer ones that still clung to the bushes. They thought they were doing it for her, and dutifully returned to her when they were done, offering up the brimming jars with red-stained finger-tips. The woman had laughed. "Give them to your camp cook, and tell him to make pancake syrup," she said, as if it were the obvious thing to do.

Abe had always harbored fond memories of that day, and that summer in general. There was a special sense of connection between the campers and counselors who had been a part of the clean-up, and that spirit seemed to infuse the whole camp.

Nothing like that could happen now. The whole thing

would be considered a minefield of potential lawsuits: allowing children within close proximity of chainsaws without protective eye gear; letting them walk amidst downed power lines and trees onto privately-owned properties where storm-damaged houses and barns teetered close to collapse.

But his father had been lucky. Nothing had gone wrong that day. And in the almost thirty years he'd run the camp, there had never been an injury more serious than a broken bone or a crisis serious enough to bring a lawsuit. Once, just a few years earlier, according to Aura, a counselor had smacked a kid across the face, hard, and the parents had threatened to sue, but somehow Clay was able to talk them out if it. The counselor was fired and the child's tuition was refunded in full. He even ended up coming back to camp the following year.

Having dodged the free speech blow job bullet and successfully gotten halfway through his first summer as director without a single incident more serious than a missed Ritalin dose (very quickly spotted and resolved) Abe was starting to feel confident that he was in the clear. Maybe he'd inherited his father's good luck. Or maybe the place itself was just charmed. Whatever it was, he decided he'd better not give it too much thought, lest he jinx himself.

But by then it was too late.

On the third Friday of the session, he was leaning on the rail of the garden fence with a cup of coffee after breakfast, chatting with Bart Lopate about potential improvements they could make to the ropes course for next year, when Mike Voorhees walked by with Jeremy. Jeremy's hand was cupped up to his left ear, and his normally sluggish shuffle was even slower than usual.

"Hey Jeremy," Abe called. "Where's the fire, buddy?"

Jeremy didn't look up—he seemed intent, in fact, on looking at the ground—but Mike said, "We're on our way to the
infirmary. Little earring problem going on."

"Earring?" said Abe. "What earring?" He went to Jeremy
and reached toward his ear.

Jeremy twisted his head away. "It's fine."

"Come on, show him," Mike said. Then, to Abe, "His ear was
pierced, but I guess he hadn't worn anything in it for awhile.
Some girl gave him a stud to put in a couple days ago, and now
it's infected."

"Come on, man, let me see," Abe said, and with a sigh,
Jeremy let his hand drop. His earlobe was bright red, and the
skin around the small, silver square stuck through it was crusted
with blackish, brownish blood. "That looks nasty, buddy. Does
it hurt?"

Jeremy shrugged. "It's not that bad." He looked up at Mike.
"Can we go? I'm gonna be late for soccer."

"Hang on," Abe said. "I never noticed before that your ear
was pierced. Did you, Mike?"

Mike paled. "No, I guess I never really noticed, but he's usually got a hat on. And he didn't have an earring in, so…"

"Can we please go?" Jeremy said, still refusing to look in
Abe's direction.

"Bring him by the office when you're done. I want to make
sure he's OK."

A half hour later, Jeremy trudged in. The earring was gone
and his earlobe had been cleaned, though it was still an angry
red. Abe took him outside, down to the duck pond, and they
sat side by side on the wooden bench at its edge. A lone female

mallard bobbed in place on the oily surface of the water.

"This pond reeks," said Jeremy.

He was right; the air around it stank of mud and frogs and rotting reeds. But it was a smell Abe had never minded—the smell of life, in the most biological sense of the word.

"You want to tell me what happened?"

"The nurse took the earring out and now I have to go to the infirmary twice a day for the rest of the week so she can wash it off and put some kind of goo on it."

"No, I mean, you want to tell me how that hole got there in the first place? Because you and I both know it wasn't there before."

Jeremy kicked at the packed mud under his feet. "Yeah it was," he said, without conviction.

"Jeremy, cut the crap."

Over the next ten minutes, Abe was able to coax the story from him: The day before, during free time, Jeremy and his bunkmate, Brian O'Hara, had snuck into the fabric arts studio. They numbed Jeremy's earlobe with a popsicle purchased at the camp store, then Brian used a sewing needle to pierce Jeremy's ear. They put in a silver stud that Jeremy had gotten from a girl in Narnia cabin, whose name he wouldn't reveal. The boys hadn't bothered to wash either the needle or the stud, let alone their hands before they performed the operation, and Jeremy didn't wash his ear afterward because Brian told him he had to build "scab tissue" around the hole so it would stay open.

"What would your dad think about you piercing your ear?" Abe asked.

Jeremy made a face that was half smile, half sneer. "He'd hate it."

"Yeah, I'll bet he would."

It didn't surprise Abe that Jeremy would have pierced his ear in part to piss off his father. What he feared was that he may have planted the idea in Jeremy's head at Free Speech on Wednesday.

The topic was appearance and self-expression. It had been a good discussion, with better than usual attendance. The campers had brainstormed all the different ways people changed and shaped their own appearance, from the shoes they wore to the color of their hair, and why people dressed and looked the way they did.

It was Niedermeier who brought up the idea of rebellion: "A lot of young people will do something their parents disapprove of, like getting a tattoo or a body piercing or dyeing their hair an inappropriate color, to try to make them angry," he said.

After this, the kids felt compelled to describe every tattoo or piercing or bizarre hairstyle they'd ever encountered in their short lives.

Dahna Schwartz, true to form, asked if it was true that some people pierced their "privates," and didn't it hurt a lot? Another girl reported that her mother was going to let her get a tattoo of a heart with wings on her ankle for her sixteenth birthday, as long as it wasn't too big. This led to each camper saying what he or she would want as a tattoo if they were to get one. For Oak, a Chinese symbol meaning "life" or "peace." For Jeremy, a skeleton on a skateboard. For Niedermeier, a blue jay.

To get things back on track, Abe asked the kids why they thought most parents disapproved of their kids getting things like tattoos and piercings.

"Because of society."

"Because you might regret it later."

"Because you can get an infection or a disease, like AIDS."

"Because it makes it look like you're not responsible, and you probably do drugs."

"Because it makes them sad that you're growing up."

"Because they're stupid."

This last gem of insight, naturally, came from Jeremy. He went on to say that when he was eighteen and moved out, he was going to get his tongue, eyebrow and chin pierced.

So, Abe thought, it could have been worse. And maybe Jeremy would have done something like this regardless. It wasn't as if Abe had actually *encouraged* anyone to get a piercing or a tattoo. He just said that kids had the right to express who they were through their appearance, as long as—and he was careful to add this—their parents were OK with it.

"Did you do this because you're angry at your dad?" he asked Jeremy now.

"I don't know. Maybe I was just trying to express who I am. Like we talked about in Free Speech."

Abe felt a withering in his chest. "And who, exactly, are you?" he asked.

"A little shit."

"What?" said Abe. For a panicked moment he wondered if he'd said it aloud at some point, and Jeremy had overheard.

"Brian said he heard Ted the lifeguard say it. And the cook did, too, when we went into the kitchen to try to get ice for my ear. He said, 'get out of here you little you-know-whats.' So we got a popsicle instead."

"I highly doubt that Ted said that," Abe said, though he didn't doubt it all. The guy seemed to genuinely dislike children, and Abe wondered why his father had asked him back for a second summer. "As for Dave, the cook, well...he's kind of nutty. He was just angry that you were in the dining hall between meals. You know you're not supposed to go in there."

Jeremy shrugged.

"You're not a little you-know-what. You're a great kid." Abe dared to gently knock his elbow against Jeremy's. He didn't flinch or protest. "But there are still going to be consequences for this. And you're going to have to call your dad and tell him what happened."

Jeremy turned his face up to Abe's, his forehead pleated with worry. "But the nurse said the hole would close up. Probably by the time I go home you won't even be able to see it."

"Sorry, buddy, that's the deal. Listen, I understand that you've got a lot of tough stuff going on in your life right now. But that doesn't mean it's OK to do something like this without permission. You're lucky you didn't really hurt yourself."

"You mean like blood poisoning?" He sounded almost excited by the idea.

"Yeah. Or a bad infection. Or even just a really bad piercing. You're lucky Brian had decent aim."

Jeremy actually smiled.

"Ready?" said Abe.

"Could you tell him first and then I'll talk to him?" He looked frightened. From what Abe had gleaned so far, Jeremy's father wasn't a particularly thoughtful or understanding guy. But what if he was actually abusive? Abe felt a surge of almost primal protectiveness. "I'll be right there with you," he said.

≈

Abe reached Bill Dyer at work—a company in Stamford, Connecticut called Avix.

"I'm really sorry to disturb you at work, Bill. I hope this isn't a bad time," Abe began. He was conscious of trying to sound exactly the way he would on the phone at work with a teacher or volunteer: professional but affable, on the unspoken knowledge that they were in this together; it was all about the kids. "But unfortunately, there's been a slight—"

"What'd he do?"

Abe chuckled, hoping Dyer would do the same. He didn't. "I think he'd like to tell you himself." Abe handed the receiver to Jeremy with a nod that was meant to be both stern and reassuring.

Jeremy took the phone. "What?" He rolled his eyes at whatever his father said in response, and began tearing at the edge of a file folder on the desk. Abe slid it out of his reach. Jeremy eventually told his story, interspersed with the occasional whine ("But it looked good," "But Lucas has his ear pierced," "Mom would have let me,") and Abe was relieved that Bill Dyer seemed to be taking it calmly. His voice wasn't audible through the receiver, anyway.

Jeremy handed the phone to Abe. "He wants to talk to you. Can I go now?"

"No," said Abe. "Bill, hi. I'm very sorry about all of this. We're certainly planning to take some kind of disciplinary action. And the hole should close up completely, seeing as we caught it early enough. Hello?"

There was a terrible silence on the other end of the line.

"Let me see if I understand the situation, Abe," Bill Dyer said with chilling calm. "My son was completely unsupervised.

He waltzed into an unlocked building full of dangerous equipment and had his friend poke a hole through his ear with a rusty needle. And nobody noticed this until forty-eight hours later. Is that correct?"

"Well," Abe began, "Apparently he—"

"Is that correct?"

Abe's right heel began drumming the floor, and he couldn't keep an edge from creeping into his voice. "Like I said, we're extremely sorry. But as I'm sure you can imagine, it's impossible for our staff to keep an eye on every single camper at every single moment of the day."

Bill Dyer gave a dry, humorless laugh. "Isn't that their fucking job? To keep the campers entertained and make sure they don't sneak off and disfigure themselves? Christ, I mean, what kind of operation are you running up there? I pay five grand and this is what I get?"

"I'd be glad to discuss a partial refund, if that would help," Abe said, then added, grudgingly, "Or a complete refund." Ridiculous, but perhaps a small price to pay to placate the man.

But he wasn't one to be easily placated. "I'm about to get into a fucking custody battle. And I'm supposed to look like the fitter parent after I send my son to a summer camp where kids go around impaling each other with the arts and crafts equipment?"

"The hole should close up completely within a few weeks," Abe said. "It'll barely be noticeable." Impaling themselves. What an asshole.

"I am going to make two phone calls when I hang up with you," Bill Dyer said. "The first one, to Muffy or Buffy or whatever the hell her name is. The referral agent. I want her to find me another camp—a reputable one—that'll let Jeremy transfer in as soon as possible. And you know who I'm going to call next? Take a guess."

Abe's teeth gripped the inside of his lip. Maybe he couldn't fight back, but he'd be damned if he was going to dignify this bully with a reply.

"I'll be calling my lawyer."

"Mr. Dyer," Abe said, "I really don't think it's necessary to get lawyers involved in this."

"No? Well I do." The line went abruptly dead.

Abe slammed the receiver down onto the cradle.

Jeremy fished his super ball out of his pocket and slammed it down onto the floor. "He's gonna make me go to another camp, isn't he."

Abe reached forward and caught the ball. "He's going to try." He placed the ball in Jeremy's outstretched hand. "But maybe I can convince him not to. If you want me to."

Jeremy snorted. "Good luck."

"Jer, do you want me to see if I can work something out so you can stay?"

Jeremy glanced at Abe, then away. "Yeah."

≈

After Jeremy had left, Abe dove immediately into his father's Rolodex for Mitzy (not Muffy, Not Buffy) Gable's number. Though Abe had heard his father talk about Mitzy for years, he hadn't actually met her until the memorial service. A slight woman with white hair in a voluminous up-do and what looked like a very expensive navy blue suit, she'd clasped his hands in hers and told him that if there was ever anything

she could do to help him through this first, difficult summer—
"any little thing at all"—to please call her. She gave him an
engraved card with all of her numbers on it: Her Manhattan
apartment, her vacation house in the Hamptons, her lake cottage in New Hampshire, her mobile phone, her office phone.

Her business was matching children with summer programs.
She received a ten percent kickback from each camp or program she sent a camper to, which, while not an inconsequential
amount of money, wasn't nearly enough to finance the three
swank addresses on her card. Clay had explained it once, in a
spot-on imitation of Mitzy's affected, vaguely British accent:
"She married extremely well, but she divorced even better."

Abe reached her at her house in the Hamptons. After he'd
explained the situation in detail, right up to the part about Jeremy wanting to stay, Mitzy said, "Oh, dear."

"Is it that bad?" Abe asked.

"No, no it's not *that* bad. Lord knows I've heard of much
worse. I'm just so sorry it had to happen this summer. With all
that must be on your mind. You poor thing."

"Thanks," Abe said, trying not to sound too impatient. He
wanted her help, not her pity. "I was hoping that when he contacts you maybe you could try to talk him out of it. You know,
put things in perspective for him. Remind him that sometimes
these things just happen."

"Oh, no, dear," Mitzy said after a pause. "I couldn't do that.
As much as I love Eden Lake, and as much as I adored your
father and will surely come to adore you, too, I can never take
the program's side in these situations. If word gets out that I'm
defending this sort of mishap my reputation will be…I won't
be able to…well, you must understand. My job and yours is to

keep the parents happy, so they'll tell other parents about us and so on and so forth and everybody's happy."

"Right," said Abe. "But it's also our job to look out for the kids' best interest, isn't it?"

"Well yes, of course." Mitzy sounded flustered and mildly offended. Good, thought Abe.

"So, I just thought maybe you could help convince Dyer that it's not a good idea to move Jeremy somewhere else. He's going through enough as it is."

"Ah, yes," said Mitzy. "The parents are divorcing, aren't they? I'm remembering now. In fact, yes, of course. That was why I thought Eden Lake would be a good match for the boy. It's such a nurturing place."

"I think it's been really good for him," Abe said.

Mitzy was silent for a moment, and Abe heard a clicking sound. He imagined French-manicured nails rapping against a glass-topped desk. "Well, I'll do what I can. But I can't promise anything."

"Thank you," said Abe. "I really appreciate it.

"And in the meantime, you'll send him a full refund, yes? With a nice note. Full of apologies. And another thing?"

"Yeah?"

"Never mind. I was going to say you should take measures to make sure that this sort of thing doesn't happen again, but of course you'll do that.

"Sure, of course, absolutely," he lied. What was he supposed to do? Put ankle monitors on all the kids?

"You know," Mitzy said with a wistful sigh, "you really do remind me so much of your father. I'm sure you're sick to death of hearing it, but it's true. I'm so looking forward to seeing you when you come down to the city this fall. I already have some wonderful families lined up for you to meet, and we'll have to be sure we do dinner at least once. Do you like Tuscan, like your father? Or French?" She laughed fondly. "How your father loved dusting off his old boarding school French to speak to the waiters at *Daniel*. He was terrible, of course, but always insisted on doing it."

"Pizza," Abe cut in. "I like pizza."

≈

Jude had already told Abe that Dane was essentially living with their mother. And when he called to ask if he could come out to Camden for dinner, his mother did tell him that she was "exploring a relationship" with an old friend of hers. But he didn't quite believe it until he saw the motorcycle leaning in the driveway, looking like some strange, predatory insect. Though his parents had divorced years ago, this evidence that another man was living here somehow emphasized the stark fact of his father's absence. He had to sit for a moment in the car, shudder through a few brief, tearless sobs—wrenching, unsatisfying—before he could go to the door.

It was Dane who answered, wearing Carol's blue checked apron over his black t-shirt and jeans, a large spatula in his hand. "Your mom's out back," he said. "I'm just making us some burgers. You want one or two?"

"Two," said Abe, confused. His mother was a vegetarian.

She rose from her chair to hug him when he came outside and he was grateful for the strength of her embrace. As he sat, he noticed the brand new charcoal grill down on the grass, black and bulbous and shining. It could have been the motorcycle's arachnid cousin.

"A grill?" Abe said. "And burgers? You're eating meat now?"

"Don't be ridiculous," she said. "I'm having a veggie burger."

"Good. At least something is the same as it always was."

His mother, looking suddenly concerned, leaned in close. "Did Eric say something to you?"

"Eric? About what?"

"Nothing, nothing." She shook her head quickly. "He just...he was here the other day and...well, I think..." She sat back and laid her hand on Abe's arm. "I know it must be a little strange for you kids to see me with someone like this, now. Even though Dad and I hadn't been together for so long. It's a little weird, right?"

"I guess. But as long as you're happy..."

She smiled then and said, with girlish, almost breathless exuberance, "You know, I am, Abie. I really am."

Abe wanted to be as happy for her as she obviously was for herself, but couldn't quite manage it. He needed some sound advice, and here she was all giddy and distracted. As he told her about the earring situation and the conversations with Dyer and Mitzy Gable, she appeared to be listening and concerned, but he knew he didn't have her full attention.

"It's the way parents are these days, Mom," he said. "They think about sending a kid to camp the way they think about buying a new car or a piece of furniture or a grill." He motioned toward Dane, who was positioning skewers of vegetables. "Like it's a *thing*, not an experience. It has to be perfect. Exactly what they ordered."

"I know," Carol said, shaking her head. "Everything's a product. Everyone wants a money-back guarantee."

239

"And I'll give the guy his money back. Fine. But there's no way in hell I'm going to pay him on top of that. I mean, for what? What's a few thousand bucks to this guy?"

"True enough, but, then, what's it to you?" his mother countered. "That's what liability insurance is for. If it gets him to go away and leave you alone, then it's money well spent, isn't it?"

"It's the principle," Abe said. "I don't want to let this asshole win."

"Of course you don't. But you may not have a choice. If he does sue, the insurance company may insist that you settle."

"Settle," Abe repeated, hating the soft, cowardly sound of the word. "You and Dad wouldn't have settled for this shit. Not back in the old days."

"The old days, the old days," she sighed. "You've got to let go of the old days, Abe. Live in the now. And choose your battles wisely."

"Thanks for the platitudes, Mom. Those are always real helpful."

She shrugged this off with one of her knowing, above-it-all smiles. "I mean it, Abie. If you fight every battle that comes up, you'll burn yourself out in no time."

Abe tried to think what, in the context of Eden Lake—Eden Lake now, the way he envisioned it—would be a battle that *was* worth fighting, if not something like this. He wasn't so naïve as to think he could wind the clock back to 1968 and try to change the whole world from a sheep farm in Maine. But couldn't he at least draw some lines when it came to people like Bill Dyer?

"But maybe you're getting ahead of yourself," his mother continued. "Maybe it will all just blow over once he cools off a bit."

"I doubt it." Bill Dyer didn't strike Abe as the kind of man who cooled off quickly.

"You tried active listening with him?"

Active listening was one of the conflict resolution techniques his mother used to teach during staff week. Even as a kid, Abe thought it seemed like an absurd way to have an argument. You were supposed to say things like, "I hear you saying that you feel hurt by what I said, and I acknowledge and validate those feelings. Let me tell you how I feel…" And somehow, once everyone's feelings were out in the open, the issue would magically resolve itself. Or it wouldn't, but at least everyone felt validated.

"Bill Dyer is not the active listening type," Abe said. "He's more the go fuck yourself type."

"The world really has gotten uglier, hasn't it?" his mother mused, not sounding terribly upset about it. She got up from her chair, stood behind Abe and began kneading his shoulders. "You're all tensed up."

Abe exhaled and closed his eyes, trying to relax. Just as he was starting to feel the knot between his shoulders loosen, his mother's hands stopped moving. "Baby, careful you don't let the tomatoes get overcooked, or they'll slip right off," she called to Dane. "Do you need anything from inside?"

Dane shook his head. "All good."

"All good," she echoed with a happy sigh. She gave Abe's shoulders one last squeeze. "You want a glass of iced tea? I'm going to get one for myself."

"No, I'm fine," Abe said. "I actually should get back to the camp."

"What? What about dinner?"

"I'm too stressed out to eat," he said. "You guys enjoy your-selves."

"I'm sorry, Abe, was it something I—?"

"No, it's nothing you said, Mom." Abe bent down and started putting on his Tevas. He wasn't quite sure what he needed right now, but he knew it wasn't this.

≈

The next day at Free Speech, Abe discovered that news of Jeremy's piercing had spread and metastasized into something much larger and uglier than it was. He was in the middle of trying to explain the Israeli-Palestinian conflict to the kids when Dahna raised her hand and asked, "Is it true that Jeremy's going to have to have his ear amputated?"

"He's not getting it amputated," another camper said with disdain.

"Then how come he's not here?" Dahna countered.

Abe hushed them and explained the situation: no, Jeremy's ear wasn't going to be amputated; it was barely even infected. And the reason he wasn't here was that he and Brian were on trash detail with Sergei as part of their punishment.

"I didn't know we had punishments here," said Jodi.

"When something like this happens, we definitely do."

"Hey Abe," said Oak, his chin resting thoughtfully on his knee, "do you think he was inspired by our discussion about self-expression last week?"

"Maybe," Abe said. (Damned Oak. What right did a thir-teen-year-old kid have to be so perceptive?) "But he knows perfectly well—as all of you do, I hope—that altering your appearance in a permanent and potentially dangerous way, like a piercing, is not something you do without your parents' permission."

"Sure," said Oak. "We talked about that."

A wave of relief broke over Abe. "That's right, we did."

"But maybe that's why he did it," Oak continued. "Maybe he wanted to get in trouble. He wanted the attention."

"If that's the case, he's getting what he wanted. But I don't think he's too happy about it. His father is pretty angry."

He almost added that Jeremy might be leaving the camp, but stopped himself; there was still hope. With the refund check he'd sent that morning, he'd written what he thought was a gracious note—it wasn't rude, anyway—apologizing for what happened and expressing his hope that Dyer would reconsider taking Jeremy out of camp. ("He's really blossoming here," he'd written.) And maybe Mitzy would grow a spine and say something, too.

Niedermeier raised his hand. "Would the medical term for the amputation of an ear be an aurectomy?"

"I have no idea." Abe said. "And he's not getting his ear amputated,"

"Not even the infected part?" asked Dahna.

"No. And if you hear anyone saying that, please let them know it's not true." He wondered if Dahna had already gone and blabbed to her mother that a kid was getting his ear amputated. And it occurred to him that he'd better do a little preemptive damage control. He just hoped it wasn't too late.

That night, while everyone was in the rec. hall playing "Triple Dare," a knockoff of a kids' game show on TV, Abe sat in the office with a beer and composed an email about the earring situation to send to all of the campers' parents. He explained what had happened, glossing deftly over the details, and assured them that "appropriate disciplinary action" had been taken. It sounded firm, official, a touch ominous. Not very Eden Lake at all. But probably exactly what the parents would want to hear.

He read the email aloud to Aura before sending it. She was being surprisingly level-headed about the whole situation, and he was grateful. In fact, she was the one who'd reminded Abe about the camper contract that every kid had signed at the beginning of the session, stating that they would not break camp rules—which included going into activity areas without a counselor.

"So," he asked, "what do you think? Good letter?"

"It's OK," said Aura. "But you never actually apologize."

Abe scanned the letter again. She was right. "But apologizing isn't in fashion these days, don't you know? The leader of the free world can cheat on his wife, get caught, and not apologize."

"Yeah, and a lot of people are pretty pissed off about it."

Abe sighed, added another sentence to the end of the note, and read it aloud. "We're very sorry this happened, and will do everything we can to ensure that it doesn't happen again."

"Everything in our power," Aura said, now clacking away at her own computer.

"Fine. Everything in our power. Should I add something about if they'd like me to bend over so they can whack me on the ass, I'd be happy to oblige?"

"Whatever turns you on," Aura said dryly. She stopped typing and eyed the beer in Abe's hand. "I'm going to go get one of those. You want another?"

"Yeah, what the hell." He could stand to get a bit of a buzz on. It had been a hell of a day. On top of the Jeremy mess, Rob

the boating instructor had found an empty vodka bottle in a
canoe, a toilet had overflowed quite gruesomely in Neverland,
the oldest boys' cabin, and when Abe spoke to Dave the cook
about having called Brian and Jeremy little shits, he'd threatened to quit unless Abe put locks on the dining hall doors so
people couldn't come in between mealtimes. When Abe told
Eric about this, he said he'd add the locks to his to-do list but
only after snapping that maybe Abe ought to learn how to do
a few things around here himself, seeing as he was the owner.

While Aura was getting their beers, Abe read the email over
a final time, then hit send. When she returned, he shut down
his computer, stood up and stretched his arms overhead. "What
do you say we call it a day? Hang out inside and watch TV or
something?"

"I've still got invoices to pay."

"They can wait. Come on. You look beat."

Her hand went to her cheek. "Do I? Yeah, I guess I didn't
get much sleep last night."

"Another late-night chat with Matty?" A few nights earlier
Abe had woken up at around one-thirty and couldn't fall back
to sleep. When he started down the stairs to the kitchen for
something to eat, he heard Aura talking on the phone, hushed
and defensive, saying, "No, of course not. Of course not. No.
No." Abe had stopped and crept back up to his room, hoping
she hadn't heard him.

"Yeah," Aura said, "Not that it's any of your business."

"No. But if you want to talk about it—"

"No," she said. "Thanks. So, fine, we can hang out inside,
but you're not making me watch that PBS crap."

"We can watch the home shopping network," Abe said, following her inside. "Would that be better?"

"Oh, screw you," she shot back over her shoulder.

In fact, they didn't watch anything at all. Abe lay on the couch and Aura sat in the leather armchair with her bare feet on the coffee table and they drank their beers and talked. Mostly about the counselors: which ones they liked, which ones drove them nuts. Aura was fed up with Ted and Tamara's indiscrete displays of affection: "I went down to the waterfront during free time yesterday to see if they were going to shut down, because it looked like it was gonna storm, and Tamara's lying face down on the dock and Ted's massaging her thighs, right up near her butt. I said 'what are you doing?' and he says, 'just putting on some sunblock.' And Tamara's like, 'I burn really easily.' And I'm like, hello, it's practically *rain*ing."

They laughed and loosened up, let the time amble by. For as much time as they spent together in the office, this was the first time they'd ever really hung out and talked shop, just the two of them. No Eric or Sergei. No Tetris or TV.

It was surprising, how comforting it was just to hang out here with her; how refreshingly easy.

They eventually got around to talking about the old days. 1982, specifically—the year Aura and Gail lived at Eden Lake, when the affair between Clay and Gail began. Abe had been fourteen at the time, in his last year of homeschooling before he left for Agnes Harris. Aura was eleven, though she'd seemed older.

"Do you remember that fake fur jacket you wore all the time?" Abe asked her. "You always had it sagging off of one shoulder." He recalled thinking that there was something vaguely sexy about it. Even though she was just a kid.

Aura smiled. "That wasn't fake. That was genuine rabbit fur.

At least that's what Uncle Bobby said when he gave it to me. Of course, Uncle Bobby was a pathological liar."

"Uncle Bobby?"

"My mom's ex-boyfriend. The guy we were running away from." She stared into middle space for a moment, then shook her head. "What a bastard."

"Yeah?"

Aura gave a snort of a laugh, but said nothing more. Abe had the feeling he shouldn't press.

"And so up we came to Eden Lake, to stay with the sunshine family. Sweet little Eric and smart little Jude and dreamy big brother Abe." She batted her eyelids.

"Oh, I was dreamy?"

Aura laughed and bent her forehead to touch the mouth of her beer bottle—a strangely girlish gesture for her. "I had such a crush on you. You didn't know?"

"No idea," said Abe, flattered. "I figured you thought we were a bunch of hicks."

"Oh, sure, I did." She put her beer down and straightened a little in her chair, and Abe sensed she was embarrassed at having confessed her crush. "Well, not hicks. But weird. Up here in your bubble, the happy little family. I didn't know such perfect people existed."

"We don't," said Abe. "My father was boffing your mom, remember?"

Aura smirked. "Did you just say 'boffing'?"

"Yeah, what's wrong with 'boffing'? It's a great word. Boff you."

"Go boff yourself."

"Motherboffer." They laughed—stupid, tired laughter. Like

a couple of wired kids in the back seat on a long car trip. "Boff the magic dragon boffed by the sea."

Aura was laughing harder than Abe had had ever seen her laugh before. And then, suddenly, there were tears on her cheeks. "Oh, God," she said, wiping them away. "Look at me. I am such a fucking mess."

"A boffing mess," said Abe.

"Right," she said, smiling, sliding a finger beneath her eye to fix a smudge of mascara.

"You OK?"

She pressed her lips together and nodded.

"Hey," he said, and stood. "Come here." He held out his arms, and she stepped into them.

He only meant to give her a hug. A comforting, brotherly hug. But before he knew what was happening, her mouth was on his, her lips nudging his open with surprising—and surprisingly arousing—tenderness. And he was kissing her back.

And then his hands were sliding down along her waist to her hips, cupping her buttocks, pulling her closer to him.

He tried to tell himself that he had to stop; that this was Aura. This wasn't right.

But his body wouldn't let him listen. It had been far too long since he'd been with a woman, and this felt far too good. By the time she was straddling him on the sofa, tugging at his belt, the knowledge of who she was and how wrong this was only fueled his desire even more.

And she, clearly, wanted it as much as he did. It wasn't until he was inside her that she murmured, close to his ear, "Jesus, Abe, what are we doing?"

But by then it was too late.

The Eden Lake Times
July 9, 1976

An Interview with Clay Perry, Director of the camp
By Jesse Winehouse and Theresa T. Kinney

We recently interviewed Eden Lake's director Clay
Perry. Read on to see what we learned! (Key: ELT =
Eden Lake Times. CP = Clay Perry.)

ELT: How long have you been the director of Camp
Eden Lake?

CP: Carol and I bought the camp just after we got
married. It used to be a farm, and we had to do a
lot of work to get it ready for campers. We built
cabins and turned what used to be a chicken coop
into the dining hall. Our first session was summer
1969. There were about 40 campers. This summer we
have almost 100.

ELT: Is it true that Eden Lake is really just a
pond?

CP: Yes, on the state map it's called Stout Pond.
We decided to rename it Eden Lake because we thought
it looked too big to be a pond. Even a stout one.
Get it?

ELT: Did you always want to be a camp director?

CP: No. When I was a kid, I wanted to be an ar-
chaeologist, a cowboy, a space explorer, a spy, and
a movie star. When I was older, I wanted to work
in the government, and then I changed my mind and

wanted to work in schools as a teacher or a principal. I didn't think about running a camp until I met
my wife. She had experience with camps. Now I feel
like it's the perfect job for me.

ELT: What's your favorite part about being a camp
director?

CP: All the great kids and staff I get to meet and
spend time with every summer. The people make this
place special.

ELT: If you could change one thing about Eden
Lake, what would it be.

CP: I would make it 8 weeks instead of 6!
(Laughs.) I would also like to have more campers
from other countries and from different backgrounds.
And I would make sure it never rained.

ELT: When did you learn how to ride a unicycle?

CP: I taught myself during college. I found a unicycle in an old junk shop, and practiced riding it
in the halls of my dormitory.

ELT: What's your favorite camp food?

CP: All the food's great! But I guess if I had to
choose, it would be the vegetable lasagna and the
anadama bread.

ELT: Thank you for agreeing to be interviewed.

CP: You're welcome. I'm a big fan of the Eden Lake
Times. Keep up the good work.

ELT: We will.

Eric

HIS MOTHER HAD TRIED repeatedly to reach him on his cell phone the day after he learned of his bastard-ness, but Eric ignored the calls and didn't listen to the voicemails she left either. For the next several days he didn't hear anything from her. At first it was a relief, and then he began to feel like he'd been abandoned. A few phone calls and that was it? He went back and listened to her messages, but they didn't contain anything of substance, just her repeated plea to call her so they could "begin to heal." On Monday morning, he tried calling her at home, but got no answer. And then, that same afternoon, she and Dane appeared at Eden Lake, on the back of Dane's motorcycle.

Eric was repairing the animal pen gate, which had torn from its hinges when three campers at once had attempted to swing on it. There had been plenty of chores to keep him busy the past few days, for which he was grateful. Everywhere he went on the property, he was able to find things that needed his attention: busted screens in cabin windows, weeds pushing up through cracks in the tennis courts, light bulbs and toilet brushes and soap dispenser bags that needed replacing. The night before, after the younger campers got back from a trip to the beach, he single-handedly scrubbed down every vinyl seat in the two school buses, wiping away three field trips' worth of sweat and spilled soda and ice cream smears. Meanwhile, a few hundred yards away on the main lawn, the campers had lain in their sleeping bags watching *The Princess Bride* on a huge white cloth tacked to the side of the dining hall. It was one of Eric's favorite movies, and Masha's, too. When he quoted lines from it she always laughed. He couldn't have stood to watch it now.

He'd exchanged only a few words with her since he'd been back: hello, how are you, fine, nothing more. The first time she saw him she'd smiled coquettishly and told him how "stern and handsome" he looked with his short hair and shaven face. He responded with a curt nod of thanks, and watched the smile vanish from her eyes and mouth. She was hurt, and he was glad.

As Dane's motorcycle rumbled up the drive, a group of younger campers ran up from the duck pond to see. They stood a few careful yards away from the bike, shyly toeing the gravel. From the gate, Eric watched his mother dismount and pull the helmet from her head. Her hair tumbled out and swung around her shoulders, glinting with auburn in the late afternoon sunlight. She looked like a much younger woman—the one she might have been twenty-some years ago—and Eric felt a fresh stab of pain at her betrayal.

She spotted him immediately, and walked toward him. Dane stayed where he was and talked to the campers, who edged closer to his bike.

Carol stopped a few feet in front of Eric, her hands clasped in front of her, at the level of her groin. This gesture of hers was so familiar, and yet the rest of her looked so different. She looked like a biker's girlfriend: jeans, black boots, a black leather jacket with fringe along the sleeves.

"I haven't seen you without a beard since you were seventeen," she said to Eric, smiling. "It's nice to see your face. You look handsome."

"Thanks. You look ridiculous."

She laughed and spread her hands at her sides, looking down at herself. "I know, it's silly, isn't it? It just makes sense for riding. Dane bought me leather chaps, too, but I was afraid you kids would have a heart attack if I showed up in those."

"You should have called before you came," Eric said. "I'm busy today. I don't have time to talk. If that's what you came here for."

Her face fell, much in the same way Masha's had when he'd given her the brush-off. He rather liked it, this new power of his to hurt women.

"Sweetheart." She took a step forward and reached for his cheek. He ducked away. "I'm sorry about the way things came out the other night. I didn't mean for it—well, I'd had a little too much to drink. I hadn't intended to drop it on you out of the blue like that. But I wanted you to know."

Eric turned back to the fence and tightened the screws on the new hinges. "Why? What's the difference? I didn't know for twenty-one years. I could have gone on not knowing and I would have been fine."

"You have the right to know who your biological father is." She said this slowly, with whispery incredulity in her voice. Like she felt sorry for him.

"Fine, so now I know. What do you expect me to do?"

"You don't have to do anything. It doesn't change anything, really."

Eric laughed and glanced over his shoulder at her. "Are you joking?"

"It doesn't change how much Clay loved you or you loved him. It doesn't change anything between you and your brother and sister."

He turned to her. "Half brother. Half sister."

And didn't Dane have two kids of his own? At the same time he was losing family, he was gaining it. Lose a father, gain a father. Lose two full siblings, gain four half ones—four halves equal two. Mathematically, nothing had changed. Otherwise, everything had.

"I just thought you had the right to know," she said slowly, her eyes closed. "And since it seems like Dane's going to be a part of my life now—our family's life—I didn't want there to be any secrets. I'm too tired for secrets. I want everything out in the open. And Dane does, too."

"When are you going to tell Abe and Jude?"

"I don't know when exactly. You can tell them yourself, if that's what you prefer."

Eric considered for a moment. While part of him wanted her to have to face their anger on her own, another part of him wanted to own this new information; to control it. "Yeah, I think that's what I'd prefer."

"All right." She seemed surprised.

"I've got to finish fixing this gate."

"I'll go say hello to Abe." She started to go, then stopped, and gestured toward the gate. "You know, Dane could give you a hand with this if you like. He's very handy. In fact, that's probably where—" She stopped herself.

"I can do it myself," Eric said. He turned back to the gate and put all of his weight behind the screwdriver to make sure that the top hinge was as tight as it could be.

≈

It took him another ten minutes to finish the job, and he was swinging the gate in its new fittings when he heard foot-steps coming over the gravel toward him. He turned around to see Dane standing a few yards away, backlit by the sun.

Eric put his hand over his eyes and squinted at him. "I told my mom I don't need any help."

"I wasn't coming to help," Dane said. Eric couldn't make out the features of his face; only the shape of his silhouette, outlined in bright light.

"Well, I don't feel like talking, either, if that's what you had in mind."

Dane took a step forward, into the shadow cast by the pines at the south edge of the fence, and suddenly all his features were clear. He hooked his thumbs in his pockets and looked down at the ground. "Yeah, that's what your mom was thinking I should do. But I don't really want to either. Some stuff there's just no point talking about." He jerked his shoulder back toward his bike. "Do you—" He stopped and held his chin between his thumb and index finger. "Do you want to take a ride?"

Eric hadn't expected this. "I don't know," he said, truthfully.

Dane put his hands behind his back, elbows bent. "You just have to hold onto the back. The little bar over the seat." He seemed to know what Eric was thinking: that he didn't want to have to put his arms around Dane, the way his mother had been doing when they rode in. Maybe Dane wasn't comfortable with the idea himself.

"Yeah, OK," Eric said. This was more than a little bit strange. But he'd never ridden a motorcycle before, and had always been curious. And somehow, in spite of everything, he had a hard time conjuring any anger or resentment toward Dane. The idea of it seemed as pointless as being angry at a rock or a tree.

Eric gathered up his tools and brought them to the barn. Dane handed Eric his helmet. "Your mom's would be too small on you."

"What'll you wear?"

"I'll be fine," he said.

The campers who'd been gawking at the bike before, now back down at the duck pond chucking stale bread into the brown water, turned and waved as the two of them rumbled down the driveway and onto the main road. Eric held onto the back of his seat like Dane had instructed, and watched Dane's white ponytail twitch over the black leather of his jacket. He had an urge to reach out and touch it, to see if it felt the same as his own hair had.

They built up speed as they headed up the dirt road, through the tunnel of trees, past occasional houses and farms. As they turned out onto the paved road, into the slanted, golden sunlight, Eric wished he could pull off his helmet and toss it onto the side of the road. He wished he could stand up and spread out his arms and lean into the wind. He wanted Dane to drive faster and faster—so fast that the bike and their bodies would break apart and scatter, in a glorious explosion of metal and blood.

What had his father done when he knew the plane was going down? Eric wondered. Did he scream? Did he attempt to shield Gail from the impact, or did he cover his own head with his arms? Did he really die instantly, painlessly, or was that just something people said to make everyone feel better?

Eric squeezed his eyes shut and opened them again in an attempt to erase the violent images in his mind. They were passing the abandoned barn on the corner of Pyram Road—the one that tilted perilously leftward, as if being blown by a strong wind. Swallows dove in and out of the places where the roof had disintegrated.

His father would have wanted to die suddenly, Eric decided. Not break down slowly over time, suffering for everyone to see. Dying was no way to live. Not for Clay Perry. Eric hoped that when his time came, he'd go the same way: fast and unexpected. Right in the midst of living.

When they got back to the camp and Eric climbed off the bike, his whole body felt like it was vibrating. His legs were warm where they'd been close to the heat of the engine, while his arms and face were pleasantly cool. He hoped that the feeling would last.

He extended his hand, and after a brief pause, Dane, still straddling the bike, shook it. "Thanks," Eric said. "I liked that."

Dane nodded once. "Nothing else like it."

Eric scanned the yard, the duck pond, the barn. Suddenly, nobody else was around. "Can I ask you one thing?"

"Sure," said Dane.

"In India. When you and my mom got together. Did you know she was married?" Eric had a feeling he already knew the answer.

"No. Not until just before she left."

"But you forgave her? Even though she lied to you?"

"She didn't lie. She just didn't say."

"I'd call that a lie," said Eric.

Dane smiled. "I guess you're right. It was just sort of like that there, though. People didn't talk about where they came from or what they left."

"You lived in the moment," Eric said, not sure whether he wanted it to sound disdainful or not.

"That was the idea," Dane said. "But sure, I was disappointed when I found out. And maybe a little angry. I forgave her, though."

"So you kept in touch the whole time, while she was with my dad?"

Dane frowned. "No, no. She wrote to tell me she was pregnant. But we both agreed after that that there shouldn't be any contact. I got back in touch after I got divorced, a couple years ago. We wrote letters. Saw each other now and then. But she didn't want any kind of relationship until now."

"Now that my dad's gone." Eric considered correcting his use of the word "dad," but decided against it.

"I guess so," said Dane. "Your mom felt awful bad about what happened between us. She always did. Not about having you, of course," he quickly added.

Eric nodded. He swept away an arc of gravel with the toe of his sneaker, revealing a crescent of dry, putty-colored earth below.

"So, I guess we talked after all, huh?" Dane said, a smile in his voice.

"I guess so."

"Listen, man, just so you know. I don't expect you to start thinking of me as your father or anything. Clay's your dad. Like you said. If we could just be friends, though, that would be nice."

Eric nodded again, and, with his instep, spread the gravel back over the bare spot he'd made. It didn't look quite the same as before; the tiny, angular stones looked like they'd been sprinkled there on purpose. They didn't fully cover the ground.

He looked up at Dane. "Thanks again for the ride."

Jude

JUDE TOLD HERSELF—AND SERGEI—THAT what happened between them on the dock that night after the dance was not going to become a habit. But the very next night, after getting back from Waterville with the rest of the B shift, tipsy on dollar drafts, they ended up fooling around again, and on Sunday night, after hanging out at the staff cabin for awhile, they had sex in the boathouse loft.

Jude was surprised by how aroused she was during the whole thing. Sergei was a surprisingly tender lover, not oblivious to her needs the way she might have expected him to be. He pleasured her for a long time, with his hands and then his mouth, gently but firmly holding her in position each time she attempted to move away, thinking he'd probably had enough. "Not yet, please," he would say.

This was what she had always imagined it would be like to sleep with Mitch—something slow and sure, not the drunken, adolescently frantic tumble they'd shared. Though she knew it was stupid, she couldn't help hoping that she and Mitch might have another chance, to do it right.

Lying in the dark with Sergei afterward, Jude shone her

flashlight over the counselors' names carved into the roof planks overhead and told Sergei stories about the ones she remembered. Sergei suggested they carve their names, too: "How about, 'Jude and Sergei forever,' but with the number 4 and 'ever,' like that one over there." He guided Jude's hand so the flashlight shone on a heart with the names Pamela and Jeff thus inscribed.

"How about 'Jude and Sergei for three nights, and that's it,'" Jude said.

"If you prefer," he said. "But why do you keep saying we can't do this? What is problem?"

"The problem is it doesn't make any sense. We have nothing in common. We barely know anything about each other. And you're, like, fifteen years older than me. At least."

"Your sort-of boyfriend Mitch, he is same age as you?"

Jude sat up and groped in the dark for her jeans, which she wriggled into, and her bra. Her shirt was nowhere to be found. "No, he's a little older, I guess."

"So, you like old men," Sergei laughed, patting her back in a friendly, avuncular sort of way that made her cringe. She lay back down, threw her thigh over his and put her hand to his chest under his t-shirt. "I'm freezing," she said.

≈

At breakfast the next morning, Sergei presented her with a bouquet of wild daises and goldenrod, tied together with a piece of yarn. Megan and Lindsey, from Jude's cabin, broke into "Jude and Sergei up in a tree," which Jude successfully silenced by chucking a handful of dry cheerios from the top of her bowl at them. "We're just friends," she said, then wondered why she was bothering explaining herself to a bunch of ten-year-olds.

Megan wrinkled up her nose. "Good. Because that would be gross. He's, like, old, isn't he?"

"Yes. Ancient."

"Yeah," said Lindsey. "He's old enough to be your dad."

"He's not *that* old," Jude said. But for the rest of the day, the girls' comments, in their needling, nasal voices, echoed in Jude's mind. And she couldn't escape the creeping realization that maybe it really was as banal and obvious as it seemed: since her falling out with her father, she'd been drawn to older men.

Mitch and Sergei weren't the only ones. There had also been Michael Goode, an English professor whose twentieth century American literature class she took her senior year at Vassar. He was only in his late thirties but his hair was flecked with gray, he wore tweed sport coats, and he was divorced. Nothing ever happened between them, though Jude had wanted it to. She went to his office hours regularly and arranged to meet over coffee to discuss class work. She flirted, timidly, curious to see what might happen, and was amazed when she realized that he was flirting back—a half smile here, a teasing rebuke there. Once, a lingering tap of his pen against her wrist. When, mid-way through the semester, she proposed meeting over a drink, he drew the line, but in such a way that it confirmed his attraction to her, leaving her feeling victorious rather than embarrassed: "I'd love to," he wrote in his email reply, "but I don't think it's a good idea, do you?"

She went to his office hours a few times after that, enjoying the sensation of knowing she was a temptation to him. In his comments on her final paper of the year, he'd signed off with

"Don't break too many hearts out there."

Girl feels betrayed and disappointed by her father as adolescent; as young woman, seeks to seduce and win affection of older men. It was just so Psych 101. Jude was repulsed by her predictability; her needy textbook heart.

And still, when she saw Sergei later that afternoon, on her way to the rec. hall for play rehearsal, she pulled him behind the dance studio for a clandestine kiss, starving for the chivey, sweaty smell of him and the feel of his stubble against her face.

"I thought you said this would not happen anymore," he said.

"It won't," said Jude. "I just needed a little something to get me through rehearsal. We're choreographing 'I think I'm Gonna Like it Here.' It's going to be hell."

"It is going to be excellent."

"No, it's really not."

"I mean the show will be excellent. You are very talented director."

Jude smiled. "How would you know?"

"I know," he said, with a nod.

She kissed him on the cheek. "Thank you."

≈

On Tuesday morning during first period classes, when she wasn't strictly required to be anywhere in particular, Jude went up into the media loft to check her email. When she saw Mitch's name in her inbox (Re: Checking in), her heart leapt. She clicked on the message and cursed as the computer churned and clicked, the blue bar at the bottom of the screen creeping forward with excruciating slowness.

When the message finally appeared she scanned it wildly, searching for a word or a sentence that would sum up its entire tone or meaning, dreading and anticipating what that might be. She had to force herself to stop and read line by line from the beginning.

> *Hey. How are things at Sunnybrook Farm? I'm not sure if you meant to email me or not, but I was really glad to see your name in my inbox when I got home tonight. (I've been in New Jersey the past few days. My mother had what they think was a mild stroke, and was in the hospital. She seems to be doing OK.)*
>
> *So I've been thinking about you a lot. I know it's crazy and I know I shouldn't, but there you go. Like we've both said, what happened that night was stupid. We were drunk and should have known better. As the supposedly older and wiser one, I'll accept 60% of the blame. I know we promised it would never happen again, but the thing is, I want it to. But next time, I want us to do it sober, with our judgment intact. (The sex would be a whole lot better, too. Not that I'm complaining.)*

Jude's mouth went dry and she felt herself getting wet. Was there anything better in the world than to be wanted?

> *I know it's wrong to want this. We should probably forget it happened and never see each other again. I'm confused, Jude. I don't know what's going on with my marriage, or where it's headed. I can't see leaving Anika, but I can't see staying either. I don't know exactly what I'm trying to say. I guess I'm just*

hoping that when you come back to New York, we can talk.

I hope you'll write back. Even if it's just to tell me to go to hell.

Mitch.

She looked at the time in the heading of the email: 1:32 am. It was nine-thirty now; he was probably just getting to work. She shouldn't write back yet, shouldn't appear too eager. On the other hand, why not? He'd probably be checking his email every five minutes, waiting for her response, hoping he hadn't made a mistake. The tentativeness in his sign-off made her wish she could run to him, put her arms around him, tell him yes, yes, I want this, too.

Mitch, she began, and then stopped. Her hands, poised over the keyboard, seemed to vibrate from within. Her mind was a tangle of words and feelings, but she couldn't find the end of a thread to pull on, a place to begin. Then, footsteps on the stairs. She quickly collapsed the window she was typing in.

It was Eric—the new Eric, shorn and angular. It still took her a second to connect this new person with the softer Eric she was used to. She'd barely seen him over the past few days, and hadn't had the chance to ask him about his haircut yet. He'd done it for Masha, of course. She hadn't realized just how infatuated he was with her.

"Checking email?" he asked, and sat down at the computer next to her.

"Yeah." He didn't even know about the Mitch situation, and yet she had the feeling he knew he'd caught her at something.

He nodded, then fell silent as his computer chortled and

beeped to life. Jude re-opened her window and saved a draft of the email. It was good that Eric had come in, actually. She was better off waiting to reply until she'd thought about things a little more.

"I like your new look," she told him.

"Thanks."

"So, I guess Strickland and Masha are together, huh?"

"Looks that way."

"It probably won't last."

Eric gave half a shrug. After what seemed like a considered pause he said, "Are you and Sergei together?"

"What?" She said it a bit too sharply, her anger at Sergei seeping through. He'd promised he wasn't going to say anything to anybody.

The trace of a smile bent Eric's mouth. "I saw you guys behind the dance studio yesterday."

"Oh." Jude sighed. "Well, yeah. We've sort of, you know, gotten together a couple of times. It's nothing serious."

Eric looked at her. "That's good," he said. "He's kind of a womanizer, I think. I mean, he's probably just looking for…you know. I just wouldn't want you to get hurt."

It was all Jude could do to keep from tilting her head and smiling at Eric's innocence. "Thanks. I'll be careful."

He turned back to his computer and punched a few keys. "Did you see Mom and Dane when they were here yesterday?"

"Yeah. The three of us hung out with Abe for a while, trying to talk him down from the ledge. He's totally stressed out."

Jude still couldn't believe that Aura had taken off the way she had, especially now, in the thick of this ridiculous earring crisis. The official story—the one Abe had given the staff—was that she'd had a family emergency. But something about the way he said it made her suspect there was more to the story. She wondered if it had something to do with Matt. She wanted to ask Abe about it, but it seemed unlikely that they'd ever have a minute alone together. Since Aura had left, he'd been basically chained to his desk.

"It's nice that Mom offered to come help out, I guess," Jude said to Eric. "I'm kind of surprised, actually. But it'll be good for Abe."

"What?" said Eric. "Mom's going to work here?"

"Abe didn't tell you? She's going to help out in the office a few times a week for the rest of the session, as long as she's feeling up to it. Answer phones and deal with the bookkeeping. The kind of stuff she used to do."

"Great," Eric said. "Perfect."

"What's the big deal?"

Eric turned back to his computer screen. His palms were on his thighs, braced. "They had an affair," he said quietly. "Her and Dane. Back in the seventies, in India. That's where she knows him from."

Jude laughed; it just rolled right up out of her. "What the hell are you talking about?"

"She told me herself, the other night."

Jude jiggled her mouse to wake up the screen of her computer, which had gone dark and was filling with images of slow-moving tropical fish. "No way. I don't believe it."

Eric stood suddenly, his chair shooting out from under him and rolling back into the opposite bank of computers. "You think I'm lying?"

Jude stared at him. She'd never seen him this worked up

before. "No, I don't think you're lying. But…"

But it wasn't possible that her mother had had an affair while she was in India. Things with their father were good then. He hadn't turned into an asshole yet. Besides, she would never do such a thing and keep it secret all these years—through the whole divorce, the aftermath, the billion conversations the two of them had had about love and marriage and fidelity. She couldn't possibly be that hypocritical. "I just don't understand how—"

"You need to get over this belief of yours that our mother is a saint and our father was the fucking antichrist." Eric looked briefly taken aback by the force of his own words. "It's a lot more complicated than that."

"I don't think our mother is a saint," Jude said. "Dad didn't know about this, did he?"

"Yeah, he knew." Eric riffled a hand through his cropped hair.

Again, it didn't seem possible: How could her father not have told her something like this in all their long, confidential talks? He'd told her about the arguments he and her mother had, the things he used to feel for her that he didn't any more, even their sex life, for God's sake—the fact that they didn't have much of one, anyway. Why on earth would he have withheld something like this?

She couldn't help feeling stung. And then ashamed for feeling that way.

"Well, at least she didn't try to hide it from him," she said. "At least she didn't have an affair for four years behind his back, with one of their good friends. She slept with a guy while she was ten thousand miles away from home. So what? She'd just gotten her diagnosis, she was on this life changing trip…"

Eric had begun nodding. The kind of nod that said he was fed up with her, fed up with the conversation. "Go ahead and defend her. That's fine. I figured you would. Just don't say anything to Abe, OK? I'll tell him when I'm ready."

"When *you're* ready?" she said. "Eric, why are you taking this so personally? What do you care if she had a one-night stand twenty years ago?"

As she spoke the words, a shocking possibility occurred to her. In the same instant, Eric bowed his head and closed his eyes. Jude's hands went to her mouth. She almost gasped. "Oh my God…She didn't…You're not…"

Eric looked at her, then away. "Yeah," he said. He spread his arms at his sides. "Meet your half brother."

His face seemed to transform itself in front of Jude's eyes, and suddenly it was obvious: the eyes, the cheekbones, the shape of his jaw. Looking at him, all she could see was Dane.

"Holy shit," she finally managed to say. "Eric, you—" She wondered if she should stand up, embrace him, do something, but it was as if she was in a dream—the kind where she wanted to move but couldn't. "You're still my little brother, you know," she said at last. "This doesn't change how I feel about you." It sounded so puny and trite beside the enormity of this new truth.

"Yeah, thanks," said Eric. "But this isn't really about you."

Jude's lips parted. She felt like she'd been slapped.

"Sorry," Eric said. He took a breath to speak, then stopped, turned as if to go, then stopped again. "Just don't say anything to Abe, OK?"

Jude nodded.

269

"Thanks." He turned and strode quickly toward the door.

If she saw him only from the back, Jude thought, she wouldn't recognize him anymore.

Once his footsteps in the stairwell had faded to silence, she turned back to her computer and sat staring at the fish on the screen—pairs of fat yellow and black striped ones, schools of tiny blue ones, a seahorse bobbing hypnotically up and down—trying to fathom the meaning of what she'd just learned. *Her mother had had another man's child.*

It didn't excuse what her father had done. Not in the least. But it did mean that her mother wasn't the innocent victim Jude had always made her out to be. And all her talk about openness and emotional honesty—was all that bullshit, too? What else was she hiding? Was every family this fucked up?

It was too much to think about. Too much to take in at once.

She scattered the fish with a flick of her mouse and re-opened her email to Mitch.

Hi, she wrote. *Of course I'm writing you back, and of course it's not to tell you to go to hell. Don't be ridiculous. I think about you a lot, too.*

Outside, the bell for second period began to ring. Jude should have been at the rec. hall already, getting things ready for rehearsal. They were planning to block the last big musical number today, the finale. She started to click on the "save" button—she could finish writing to Mitch later—then stopped. "Fuck it," she said aloud. Why fight what was obviously some kind of genetic disposition toward irresponsible sexual behavior?

I'll write more later, when I have more time. But yes—when I come back to New York, we'll talk. We'll definitely talk. And who knows what else.

Yrs trly,

Rebecca of Sunnybrook Farm

Abe

ABE AND JEREMY SAT side by side on the granite slab in front of the farmhouse door, Jeremy's lumpy duffel bags and camouflage knapsack at their feet. They'd been talking about skateboarding. That is, Jeremy had, describing in detail every trick he could do or sort of do or hoped to learn how to do eventually. Abe had never heard the kid talk so much in his life. He tried his best to pay attention, but every few minutes his mind would veer off and he'd find himself imagining what he was going to say to Bill Dyer when he arrived. Face to face, he hoped, they'd be able to talk about things in a reasonable manner, one human being to another. It was too late, obviously, to convince him to let Jeremy stay. His note hadn't worked, and neither had Mitzy (if she'd even tried). But maybe at least he could get him to drop the lawyer bullshit.

A big legal entanglement was the last thing he needed on top of the mess with Aura.

He'd done everything he could to convince her to stay. He told her he was sorry—as if he'd been the one who'd initiated things, not her. (Then again, hadn't he been the one who had pushed their relationship in a flirtatious direction? Hadn't some part of him—even if it was just the one in his shorts, that had gotten him into trouble so many times before—wanted her all along?) He told her the place would fall apart without her. He told her that everyone was counting on her. He even told her, as she'd wanted so badly to hear in the past, that she was part of the family. That hadn't gone over well. She'd squeezed her eyes shut and said, "Stop it! We're not related! We're not!"

But she'd made up her mind. "I never should have come back here," she'd said as she tucked in her t-shirt and buttoned up her jeans. "I belong in Boston, with Matt."

On one level, Abe was relieved. To have to see Aura every day, and be reminded of yet another stupid sexual mistake he'd made would have been less than pleasant. But having her around would certainly have made running the camp a lot easier. Since she'd left, emails and phone calls from parents and prospects and vendors had begun piling up. Bills needed paying. Brochures needed sending. He was beginning to realize just how indispensable she'd been.

Having his mother in the office was helpful to an extent, and he had appreciated her volunteering to help out. But, of course, she didn't know any of the names of staff or campers or their parents. And her computer skills had left off somewhere around 1987. Hiring a temp would have been just as practical, or more.

He glanced at his watch. Bill Dyer's email had said he'd be there by one o'clock, but it was past one-thirty now. Abe had hoped that Jeremy could leave before rest period ended. It would be easier on him, he thought, to slip away during this quiet time, when everyone was napping or reading in their cabins. He also would have preferred Bill Dyer to see the camp in its calmest, most contained hour.

On the other hand maybe it would be better if Dyer saw
all the campers happily—and safely—involved in their fourth-
period classes: feeding the animals, kicking balls around the
soccer field. Or, even better, maybe Dyer would come right as
the two o'clock bell was ringing. He'd see campers passing on
their way to their classes, waving hello and saying goodbye to
his son, who they'd come to know and like. He'd see that he
was ripping Jeremy away from a community.

Maybe Eden Lake hadn't exactly transformed Jeremy. He
was still a wise-ass, and still had a mean streak. It's not as if
three-and-a-half weeks at a summer camp—any summer
camp— could take away the pain of having a prick for a father
and being abandoned by one's mother. But at least Jeremy had
become engaged in the place. He came to Free Speech frequently. He'd stopped declaring everything at the camp stupid
or sucky. Two nights earlier, when a magician had performed,
he had volunteered to go up on stage to be the "victim" in the
sword trick, and each time the magician thrust a sword into the
box Jeremy lay in, Jeremy let out a more gruesomely agonized
and ridiculous yell than the last. By the fourth sword, the whole
place was in hysterics, and even the magician couldn't keep a
straight face. After the trick, a beaming Jeremy bowed with
the magician, to thunderous applause, and did a backscratcher
jump off the stage.

Abe knew the camp Dyer was transferring Jeremy to: Camp
Micmac, an hour and a half north. It was all boys, all sports
and outdoor survival skills, including riflery. One summer, back
in the eighties, when Eden Lake had a particularly good soccer counselor—an Australian who'd played semi-pro—they'd

invited Micmac down for a friendly match: Eden Lake's rag-tag, co-ed team, which included Abe himself, versus Micmac's crisply uniformed, humorless death squad. It was, predictably, a slaughter, ending seven to one. But nobody on the Eden Lake side cared. At the end of the game Clay got the whole camp chanting "We're number two! We're number two!" And that one goal—scored by a girl, no less: tiny Julie Nickerson—was talked about for the rest of the summer.

Micmac was the last camp on earth Jeremy Dyer belonged at.

At quarter to two, Bill Dyer's car—not a BMW or a Lexus, as Abe as expected, but a late model Camry—rolled up the driveway.

"Ready, pal?" said Abe, and laid a hand on Jeremy's shoulder.

"I guess," he said, slowly standing. "I wish I hadn't pierced my stupid ear. Ear piercing's for fags anyway."

"Whoa, hey, Jer, what did we say about that word?"

He sighed, annoyed. "Sorry. I mean it's for gays."

Abe suppressed a smile. "Not that there's anything wrong with being gay."

"I know, I know," he said, heaving his knapsack up onto his shoulder.

Bill Dyer rolled down the passenger-side window. "Come on Jer," he yelled. "Throw your stuff in the back and let's go." The trunk popped open.

The bastard wasn't even going to get out of the car. Abe picked up one of Jeremy's duffels and helped him lift the other one into the immaculate, carpeted trunk, then went around to the driver's side of the car.

The level of Bill Dyer's head was a good six inches lower

275

than Abe had expected it to be: he was short. Very short. And he wasn't the Gordon Gekko-esque villain Abe had pictured either, all slicked back hair, gold cufflinks, and aquiline nose. His light brown hair was thinning and his nose was small and upturned, like Jeremy's, making him look younger than he probably was. His blue dress shirt, with its stiff white collar and French cuffs, had a second-rate sheen to it and didn't sit quite right on his shoulders. Definitely not custom tailored.

Abe felt a warming toward him. He thrust his hand through the open window. "Hi Bill, Abe Perryweiss. It's good to finally meet you. I'm really sorry again about all this."

Bill Dyer stared straight ahead. "Yeah, I got your note."

"Listen, Mr. Dyer—" Abe began.

Dyer craned his neck around and shouted as if Abe wasn't there. "Jeremy, quit fucking around back there and get in the car."

Abe couldn't help himself. "Hey, easy with the language, OK?"

Dyer cocked his head to the side and laughed, still refusing to make eye contact. "First you try to tell me where I should or shouldn't send my kid to camp. And now you're going to tell me what I can and can't say to him? You got kids of your own? No, you don't. So don't tell me how to raise mine." He cocked his head once more. "Fucking unbelievable."

"No, I don't have kids," Abe said, "but I think I know a thing or two about—

"One dollar," said Jeremy, who'd slid into the passenger seat next to his father.

"One dollar what?" said Dyer.

"Nothing," said Jeremy. He folded his arms and kicked the

knapsack at his feet. "Let's go."

"Let me see that ear," Dyer said, and swiped Jeremy's hat from his head. "Jesus Christ. What did you use, a knitting needle?"

One dollar. Abe realized what Jeremy was talking about, and felt a surge of triumph. "A dollar for swearing," Abe said. "It's a camp rule. Fifty-cent penalty every time you curse."

"Is that so?" said Dyer. He looked at Abe now. His eyes were small and rimmed with red. Like an opossum's, Abe thought. "Well given how much money you're going to owe me, I'm not too fucking worried. Fuck, fuck, fuck. There, I owe you another buck fifty."

"Two," said Abe. "But who's counting?"

Bill Dyer's last word, before he peeled out on the gravel and roared down the drive, was "asshole." Abe thought he heard Jeremy, at the same time, say, "Bye, Abe."

≈

The next morning, a fax arrived from Bill Dyer's lawyer, stating intent to sue for negligence, bodily harm and psychological trauma, to the tune of ten thousand dollars.

"Psychological trauma to whom?" Abe's mother asked, after Abe had read the document aloud. "The boy or his father?"

Abe tossed it on top of the growing stack of papers in his "to be processed" pile and drained the last of his lukewarm coffee. Dyer might have been planning to sue anyway, but Abe had a feeling their interaction the day before had sealed the deal. And probably made things worse than they might have been otherwise.

"Ten thousand bucks," he said. "You know what ten thousand bucks would do for AfterStart? We could use it to buy computers for the kids, or pay part of a teacher's salary. Hell, it's almost a third of my pathetic salary."

His mother gave him a sympathetic smile. "You were starting to really like that job, weren't you?"

"I was." He felt like it had been years, not weeks, since he'd left his life in Washington behind. And almost as long since he'd even thought about it. He felt a sharp, sudden longing for his colleagues, with all their energy and idealism; the patient-as-saints teachers; the kids in the programs, who needed so much and asked for so little.

"You know, if you wanted, you could try to bring some of those kids up here next year," his mother said. "I don't know if you remember, but when we started out, we always had some inner city kids, poor kids, in the mix. It's something I still regret we didn't do more of."

"I've thought about trying to do something like that," Abe said. But would the satisfaction of providing an enriching summer experience for disadvantaged kids outweigh the unpleasantness of dealing with people like Bill Dyer?

"Of course, it has its own challenges," his mother continued. "I remember one camper we had up here in seventy-four or seventy-five, a little African American boy from Roxbury named Dennis. He was miserable here. Just so homesick, hated everyone, didn't want to do anything, acted out. He started stealing things from his bunkmates, and we ended up having to send him home. We just weren't equipped to deal with a kid like that in this environment."

"Integration's no walk in the park," Abe said distractedly. He'd started scanning the names and subject lines of the messages in his inbox, while simultaneously thinking about all the things he needed to do: call Charles Dumont, call the insurance company, find a time to meet with Strickland before the staff meeting, mail a rent check to Ben. He picked up a legal pad and was about to compose a list when someone thumped on the frame of the screen door. "This the main office?"

Abe squinted to see who it was—a portly middle-aged man in a short-sleeved shirt and tie, bushy gray mustache, aviator sunglasses. No one he knew.

"Welcome to Eden Lake," Carol said. "How can we help you?"

The man stepped inside. He was carrying a faded blue, canvas attaché case, which he hoisted briefly. "Don Levesque, Department of Health and Human Services, health inspection program. Hope I didn't catch you at a bad time."

≈

Abe and Eric spent the better part of the morning with Don Levesque. He was a genial fellow, chipper and polite. Several times, he expressed his sympathies for Clay and Gail's "demise" and complimented Abe and Eric on how well they seemed to be doing. His admiration and sympathy, however, didn't stop him from noting violation after violation on the checklist he carried with him: a camper in a kayak without a life jacket. A burnt-out taillight on one of the buses. Dave and his staff, hatless and gloveless in the kitchen. In one of the cabins, the bunks and cubbies were arranged in such a way that they constituted a fire hazard. In another, the wastebasket from the bathroom was missing. In the infirmary, a medicine cabinet was unlocked.

Abe pointed out that the only medicines it contained were Neosporin ointment and Pepto-Bismol, so was it really a problem?

"I know it may seem a little over-cautious on our part," Levesque replied, cheerful and matter of fact, as he had been on everything. "But you know, a kid overdosed on Pepto once over at Camp Pine Brook. Made him deaf in one ear. At least, they think that's what did it. Can't take any chances these days, what with lawsuits and all."

"Right," said Abe. "Lawsuits."

As they toured the property, Abe kept trying to catch Eric's eye, hoping for some kind of reassurance. Was it normal to have this many things cited? Was Levesque going to shut them down, or were minor infractions like these par for the course? The two of them finally had a moment alone when Levesque went to take samples of the lake water. It occurred to Abe that his father's and Gail's ashes were dispersed throughout that water. Did that constitute a code violation too?

"How do you think things are going?" he asked Eric. "I can't get a read on this guy."

Eric shrugged. "I don't know. It's a different guy from the last few years. They always mark some stuff down, but whether or not they do anything about it depends on the person, I think."

"Am I doing OK? I mean, should I be trying to kiss up more? How did Dad do it?" At the water's edge, Levesque was holding up his test tube of lake water, swirling it like it was a glass of Cabernet.

Eric turned to Abe with an expression almost hostile in its neutrality. "Dad's dead."

"I'm aware. Thanks."

"So, do it your way. You're in charge."

Abe shook his head, baffled. "What the hell is with you lately, man? You want to tell me what's going on?"

"Nothing's going on."

"Is this about the will? About running the business?"

"No," said Eric. "I don't want to run this place."

"But you're angry that Dad didn't leave it up to us to de-cide."

"No, it makes perfect sense that he left it to you. You're his son."

"Yeah, but so are—"

"Sh," said Eric, with an upward nod in the direction of the lake. Levesque was making his way up the small sandy beach, toward the needle-carpeted clearing in the pines where Eric and Abe stood. "Here he comes."

There were fourteen infractions in all, most of them minor. The results of the lake and well water tests would be back from the lab in one to two weeks. Levesque or another inspector would be back, too, in three to five days, to make sure that all of the problems had been addressed.

"So does this mean we're on probation or something?" Abe asked him.

Levesque chuckled. "Sure, if you like."

"But is this a normal number of infractions? A lot? A little?"

Levesque shrugged. "Some places get more, some less. I'm not shutting you down, obviously. But make sure everything's taken care of by the time I come back, or you're looking at some fines." He held out his hand to Abe, gave him a hearty handshake, and then did the same to Eric. "Take care now, boys," he said, and climbed into his state-issued sedan.

≈

That afternoon, when his mother had left and he was alone in the office, Abe called Aura. Although most of the problems Levesque pointed out would have been there regardless of whether or not Aura had jumped ship, he was aware that had she not been so obsessed with doing everything by the book, there might have been many more. And it had been almost a week now since she'd left. The least he could do was check in on her.

As he'd hoped and expected, she didn't answer. It was the middle of the afternoon, a weekday. She would be at work.

"Hi, it's me," he said to the machine. Then, fearing that sounded a touch too intimate, added "Abe, that is. I hope you're doing all right. I guess you're at work. I just wanted to check in. You know, the health inspector was here today, and we had a few infractions, but nothing major, and I just wanted to say thanks for helping make sure everything was up to code. I know I gave you a hard time about it, but it turns out you were right. So, thanks. For everything. I mean, you should see the office. It's a mess without you here."

He meant every word of what he was saying, and yet he feared it sounded glib. He was avoiding what he really ought to be talking about.

"What happened between us," he began after a pause. "I don't know, Aur. I guess we both know it was a mistake. We'd had a few beers, and we just got caught up in…we both needed…Shit." He sighed. "Listen, we're both going through a hell of a lot right now. We just lost our parents, for Chrissake."

His voice caught in his throat and he had to pause. "I'm just saying, I don't think we should be too hard on ourselves. That's all. Go easy on yourself, OK? And I'll try to do the same."

He hung up the phone feeling good about what he'd said to her, hopeful that it was what she would need and want to hear. At the same time, he was left with a guilty, unsettled feeling—a sense that he'd tried to get away with something he shouldn't have. Later that afternoon, as he stood watching the campers emerging from rest period in their cabins for their fourth period classes, waving back at the ones who waved to him first, he realized what it was:

He didn't want to go easy on himself. He didn't want to be the kind of person who took the easy road, capitulating to the vainer and baser parts of his nature, and let himself off the hook for it every time. Whether it was sex or money or admiration—the fact that it came easy didn't mean it was his destiny. He didn't want to keep letting it in just because it kept knocking at his door.

His father had. But he didn't have to.

Jude

IN THE SUMMER OF 1986, on a bright, warm morning two thirds of the way through the session, Jude went up to the woods at the top of the meadow to wait for Nate Meyer. The two of them had started going out two days before, but hadn't yet managed to get in anything beyond a couple of quick, closed-mouth kisses. It was Nate's idea that they skip their second period classes and "go somewhere," as he put it. The plan was for Jude to arrive first and him fifteen minutes later, so no one would suspect.

Jude suggested the clearing. She thought nobody but she and her brothers knew about it. It was about a hundred yards back into the thick woods at the upper right-hand corner of the meadow: an incongruous circle of bright green grass and springy moss, about fifteen feet across. To one side of it was a tree that, in late spring, blossomed white and snowed petals everywhere. She and Abe discovered it not long after they'd gotten a book about gnomes that they'd both spent hours reading, and decided that if gnomes existed (they both knew that probably they didn't, but there was always an outside chance) they would definitely frequent a place like this. Once, they cut doors and windows into a couple of shoeboxes, set them in the clearing, lightly camouflaged with leaves and branches and waited, a few yards back in the woods, hoping for gnomes to come inhabit them. They didn't, of course. But even just the waiting, the hoping, had been exciting.

As Jude walked up the meadow that day to meet Nate Meyer, keeping close to the edge of the woods so she wouldn't be spotted, she considered whether or not to tell him about the gnomes. Either he would find it cute or he'd think she was a complete dork. She didn't know him well enough to be sure. What she did know, or was reasonably sure of, was that he was going to try to get to second base with her. Danica Woods, who'd gone out with him the summer before had warned her. "He likes you the same reason he liked me," she'd grinned, pointing at her own prematurely developed chest and then at Jude's. Jude wasn't as big as Danica, who, at thirteen, had bona fide cleavage when she wore a bathing suit, but she had recently gone from a B to a C cup.

Jude didn't quite know how she felt about the idea of losing her second base virginity. She'd only ever French kissed once, sort of, during a spin the bottle game, so it felt like a big jump. Still, Nate was one of the cutest boys at camp—too cute for her, she'd thought—so she figured if he wanted to feel her up, she'd probably better let him. She wore her nicest, least favorite bra—the purple lace one that itched like crazy.

But Nate Meyer's hungry hands and her itching breasts were not destined to meet that day. As she approached the clearing, Jude heard something strange—a rhythmic, rustling sound, punctuated by a high-pitched wincing sound. She froze where she was. Her first thought, absurdly, was *gnomes!*

She took a slow, minuscule step sidewise, careful not to make even the slightest sound. When she did, she could see, between the branches of a fir tree ahead, the flashing of pink flesh—a thigh, a calf, a buttock. And when she took a half a step more, she could see everything much more clearly, including the faces: Gail's was upturned, dappled with sunlight, mouth open, eyes closed. Her father's jaw was clenched but his eyes were open and he looked down at Gail as he moved over her.

Jude had to stifle the urge to scream.

She turned and walked as quickly and quietly as she could back out to the meadow, a sickening ache in small of her back, radiating down through the backs of her legs. She hurried down the hill to Nate, who was just starting his ascent, and by the time she reached him she was hyperventilating, sucking in big, wheezing breaths. She told him she'd stepped on a bee's nest and pointed to a couple of mosquito bites on her legs, claiming they were stings.

They were the first of many lies she would tell on her father's behalf.

After dinner, she found him and told him she needed to talk. They sat on an overturned canoe at the lake's edge while the last of the day's light bronzed the trees and tinted the sky and water the blues of an old Technicolor movie.

"Boy stuff?" he asked. It was what a lot of their talks had been about recently.

Jude shook her head. Her heart felt like a trapped housefly, bouncing around inside her. "I saw you with Gail today in the woods," she blurted. As she said it, she realized that the fact that he'd been keeping a secret from her almost made her angrier than the cheating part. She thought he told her everything.

"You mean you saw us—"

Jude felt the blood rush to her cheeks. "I didn't watch. I mean, I turned around as soon as I saw."

"Oh my God, I'm sorry," her father said. He sat for a long time with his elbows on his knees and his head in his hands, not speaking, only sighing every few seconds. Then he said, "I could tell you it only happened once. But I think you're grown up enough to hear the truth."

"I think so, too," said Jude.

So he told her. That he and Gail had been lovers for more than three years. That it had started in the summer of '82, when Gail and Aura were living at the camp, and had continued on and off since then.

"Are you and Mom going to get divorced?"

"I don't know," he said. "I don't know what to do. I've tried to stop it so many times, but I just can't, Judie. I can't."

That was when her father started to cry. His face crumpled, his shoulders hunched up close to his ears and his body rocked. Jude had never seen him like this before, so broken and so weak. It frightened her.

"Do you still love Mom?" she asked.

He lifted his head, to her relief.

"I'll always love your mom. But I don't know that I'm *in* love with her anymore. It's hard to explain."

"I think I understand," Jude said. She was glad he'd stopped crying, but she didn't want him to stop talking. She didn't want him to tell her this was adult stuff that she wouldn't understand.

"We've been fighting a lot about the camp," he continued. "I want to ride the momentum, keep it moving forward, build it. But she's fighting me on it every step of the way.

She doesn't want to build new facilities. She doesn't want to expand enrollment. She's so focused on the social awareness stuff that she refuses to step back and think about what we need to do to succeed as a business."

"Yeah," said Jude. "It's like she's stuck in the sixties or something."

"Exactly. I mean, this whole Russian peace exchange kick she's on. I respect the sentiment behind it. Of course I do. But the logistics and the paperwork and the expense…not to mention that we don't even know if it's something that would appeal to kids. Or their parents. I just said to her the other day: 'Carol, sixty percent of our campers are Jewish. Do you really think their parents are going to be excited about them spending the summer with kids from a country that's notoriously anti-Semitic?' And she said, 'well, that's part of the point.'" He let his hands fly up and slap back down on his knees. "Sometimes it's like she's just checked out of reality."

"I know," Jude said. "She gave me a *speech* the other night at evening program just because I was wearing a tiny bit of lipstick about how women her age had worked hard so their daughters wouldn't have to conform to conventional standards of beauty. And I'm like, God, Mom, it's just a little lip gloss."

Her father gave a brief laugh, then folded his arms across his chest, tight and high. "But I know things have been tough for her," he said. "Her exacerbations have gotten worse."

Jude nodded. Again, she had the sense he was about to cut the conversation short. "But you've always been really supportive of her." He did all the cooking and cleaning (with Jude and Abe's help) the times when their mother was so tired she could barely walk. And he kept her laughing when things were bad, like the time the year before when her leg went numb and dragged and he called her "Igor."

"But still," he said. "I feel like something's missing."

"Have you talked with her about it?"

"Some, yes. But—" he closed his eyes and shook his head, then put his hand on Jude's back. "I'm sorry, sweetheart. I shouldn't be burdening you with this stuff."

"I don't mind."

"I know you don't. You're great. But this is…shit. I'm sorry." He pumped his clasped hands between his knees. "I'm so very sorry about what you saw today."

Jude shrugged and dug the toe of her sneaker into the damp sand.

From behind them, on the lawn, came the arrhythmic slap of hands against a tetherball, the shouts and laughter of campers.

"Hey Jude," her father said, "What exactly were you doing up there?"

In spite of everything, she couldn't suppress a smile.

"Ah," he said. "Well. I won't tell if you won't."

"I won't."

"Not even Abe, OK? I'll tell Mom eventually, when the time is right, but that time isn't now. Hey, look at me." He put his hand to her cheek. "You promise?"

"I promise," said Jude.

≈

She kept her promise, and then some.

In thirteen years, she had never told anyone about the fact that she'd discovered her father and Gail *in flagrante delicto*. Not

Abe or Eric or any of her closest friends. Certainly not her mother. She didn't even tell the whole story to Leona M. Sawicki, the therapist she saw in college.

Jude was assigned to counseling by the dean of students after ending up in the emergency room with alcohol poisoning after a masquerade party, in February of her freshman year. Jude knew she didn't have a drinking problem—she'd never so much as thrown up before as a result of alcohol; she just hadn't eaten dinner that night, and couldn't taste the vodka in the punch they were serving, so had no idea how drunk she was getting until it was too late. But she hadn't felt like herself since the semester had begun and figured it couldn't hurt to talk to someone.

Leona, who had spiky, salt and pepper hair and a tendency toward sudden, dramatic hand gestures, was outraged when Jude told her that her father had confided in her about his affair. A parent, she said, should never ask his or her child to keep a secret from the other parent, and should certainly never ask for their child's advice in marital matters.

"But it wasn't like he forced me or anything," Jude had said. "I could have told him I didn't want to talk about it. I could have told my mother what was going on. It was my decision."

"Was it, though?" Leona asked, hands shooting up from her lap. "Was it really? You were a child. You wanted his love and his approval and his friendship, and you thought you would lose that if you betrayed him."

"So I betrayed my mother instead," Jude said.

Leona's mouth became very small. "No, no, no, dear, you didn't do anything wrong. Not one thing, you understand?"

Jude had said yes, she understood. And the more she met

with Leona and the more she thought about it, the angrier she became at her father. Not just for confiding in her, but for the deception, the selfishness, the mere fact that he'd cheated so calculatingly, for so long, on his wife who had been nothing but (Jude thought at the time) faithful. And who was dealing with a serious illness, for God's sake.

But Jude also came to realize that she, too, was at fault. Because the truth was—and she could never bring herself to tell Leona this—she had encouraged her father to leave her mother.

She even once said (the thought of it made her very bones contract with shame) "I don't blame you for cheating on her."

She couldn't remember why, exactly; if it was because she and her mother hadn't been getting along, or because she knew it was what her father wanted to hear. But it didn't matter. What she had done was weak and hateful. Her mother hadn't deserved it.

At least she didn't used to think so.

Jude had more or less avoided her ever since Eric had dropped his paternity bombshell. It wasn't difficult. Play practice took up most of the morning, and lately she'd been bringing her lunch to the rec. hall and working on the set straight through until afternoon rehearsal, adding shading and detail to the backdrop for the Warbucks mansion, playing around with drapery and tarps to make their "Hooverville" shacks look more authentically desolate. She'd found an antique desk chair at a yard sale on one of her days off, and once she'd fixed it up it was perfect for Miss Hannigan's office.

But it was getting harder to come up with excuses for slighting her mother. And she was tired of pretending. On Thursday at lunch, she went straight up to the table where Carol sat with Abe and a few other staff members and stood there, arms akimbo. "Mom," she said, "after lunch, do you have time to take a walk or something? Alone? I was hoping we could talk."

Carol's expression suggested that she'd been expecting this. "Of course, Judie," she said.

They started at the waterfront and followed the path around the lake for a few hundred yards until they came to what Jude and Abe used to call Turtle Rock—a craggy slab sloping down into the water where they had never actually seen turtles sunning themselves, but had always hoped they might.

Jude helped her mother maneuver up onto the rock and sit down. The surface of the lake shone with endless, tiny diamonds of bright flashing light. Over at the waterfront area, unseen but audible, campers were playing some kind of game. Periodically a lifeguard's whistle would sound, followed by an eruption of giddy screams and the thrashing of limbs through water.

"Let me guess," Carol said. "You want to talk about something that Eric told you."

"Bingo."

"I figured that was why you've been avoiding me." She raised her hand to her forehead to shield her eyes from the glare of the lake. "Bright here."

"Do you want to go somewhere else?"

"No, this is fine." She reached over and pressed her palm to Jude's knee. "I'm sorry," she said, and paused. "I don't know what else to say. I don't have any excuse or justification. Only that it was a strange time for me, in India. Like I was telling you. I'd just gotten my diagnosis. I was scared. And here was this place where suddenly I felt so totally alive, so totally present. And with Dane—it was really more of a spiritual connection than a sexual one. At the time, it felt very…I don't know… pure. I know that probably sounds like a load of bull to you, but it's true."

"Yeah, well, Dad bought it, apparently," said Jude.

She withdrew her hand. "It wasn't an easy time, but yes, we got through it."

"Not for long."

Carol bobbed her head from side to side in that Indian way again. "We had a few more good years before he started up with Gail. And to answer your next question, no, I don't think my affair was the reason he had his."

"It had to be part of it, though," Jude said. How could it not be?

"Maybe. It's all so complicated. What's cause, what's effect. He'd made his own little mistakes before—nothing major, kisses, you know—which I'd forgiven. Or maybe I didn't. Who knows. But it doesn't matter now. Dad's gone, Dane and I are together, and we wanted to get everything out in the open."

A trio of red canoes slid into view, and the campers paddling them waved when they spotted Jude and Carol on the rock. Carol waved back and called, "hello!" with what sounded almost like desperation.

Jude lifted a hand in half-hearted greeting, then let it fall back to the sun-warmed surface of the rock. "He never told me," she said.

"What?"

"Dad never told me about not being Eric's father. Or even about the fact that you'd slept with another man."

"Of course not," her mother said. "Why on earth would he?"

Jude gave a short, bitter laugh. She had never told her mother about her confidential chats with her father. Mostly because she knew it would only hurt her to learn that Jude had known about the affair before she had. But also because in spite of the fact that she knew—she really did know—that it wasn't her fault, a part of her was still deeply ashamed.

There was no reason to tell her now. Like her mother had said, none of it mattered anymore. But on some level it must have, because suddenly Jude's lower lip was trembling and her eyes were filling with tears and before she could swallow them back she said, "Because he told me everything else. I knew about the affair for months. I saw them together in the woods. And I talked with Dad about it. We talked about it a lot. He confided in me. You know, asked for my advice." She wiped her eyes with the back of her hand, which came away smeared black with mascara. "I'm sorry, Mom."

She put her arms around Jude. "Oh, baby," she said, "Honey, it's OK. You don't have to apologize."

"I should have told you about the affair," Jude said through her tears. Her mouth drew down at the corners and her breath shuddered. She hadn't cried like this since she was a kid.

"No." Her mother pulled away and shook her head, slowly at first, then with more force. "No. That was your father's responsibility. You didn't do anything wrong. You understand?"

Jude nodded, her mouth clamped tight. She hated this. She hated feeling this raw. She was grateful when her mother put her arm around her again. She dropped her head to her mother's shoulder and shut her eyes.

"Now at least I understand a little better why you stayed angry at him for so long," Carol said. "And here I thought it was all on my behalf." She gave a little laugh.

"It was that, too," Jude said. "He was an asshole to you."

Jude felt her mother's lips, nestled against the top of her head, flex briefly into a smile. "Well, you won't get an argument from me there." She was quiet for a moment. "I'm really sorry, Jude. I'm sorry he put you in that position. It was completely unfair to you and totally inappropriate. Lord knows the man had boundary issues."

"Just a few."

"But he really didn't say anything to you about me and Dane?" It was more a statement than a question.

"No, not a word," Jude said. He'd been true to her mother on that, at least.

"Well," said Carol, "that's one thing you can give him some credit for anyway, isn't it?"

"Yeah," said Jude, "I guess it is."

≈

That night was the Mr. and Ms Eden Lake pageant, a tradition dating back to the early eighties that was always one of the most popular evening programs. The boys' and girls' cabins were paired off by age group and each one picked a camper to send over to their counterpart cabin to be dressed up as the opposite sex. The categories were the usual pageant fare: talent, an interview, formal wear and swimwear. This last one was always tricky for the girls-dressed-as-boys, given the issue of breasts, budding or in full bloom. The brave girls went shirtless with only a towel around the neck, held strategically in place.

It was Jude's night off, technically, and she could have gone into town, but she didn't want to miss the pageant. She was a contestant herself once, back when she was around eleven. Instead of trying to hide her voluminous hair under a hat, the boys who dressed her decided to use it to their advantage, and had fashioned her into a hippie-dude with a headband and a flower painted on her cheek. She'd been too scared to do the towel trick for the swimsuit contest—or, more accurately, too embarrassed to do it in front of her parents—so she wore a life jacket over a tank top and carried a canoe oar—her idea. She hadn't hammed up her performance enough to earn the crown, but was a runner-up. More importantly, she discovered that she liked being in a show. Not so much the performing itself, but the excitement of the whole thing: the way the rec. hall was transformed with streamers and balloons and signs, the picnic tables set end to end to form a runway; the brightness of the lights on the stage and the contrasting shadow on the faces of the audience; the nervous, backstage anticipation.

Lizzie Polk was, of course, chosen to represent Shangri-la, and was done up like a geek by the boys in Rivendell, with pants pulled up to her chest and a pair of glasses taped around the middle. For the swimsuit competition she wore swim trunks, black socks and an MIT t-shirt. She threw herself into the role, with goofy guffaws and slouching posture and got more laughs than any of the other girl contestants.

But the boys dolled up like girls, with tennis balls for boobs, were the real hit of the show, as always. This event had never been one of Eden Lake's more shining examples of wholesome, progressive fun. In fact, Carol had always hated it, and thought it was demeaning to women and girls. Jude agreed in principle, but couldn't help enjoying it.

At the end of the evening, Lizzie was crowned Mr. Eden Lake, and the honor of Ms Eden Lake went to Bobby Denzig, in a blue gingham Dorothy dress swiped from the costume shop. Afterward, as Jude and Katie were walking back to the cabin with the girls, all of them exuberant with victory and hopped up on lemonade, Abe jogged across the main lawn toward them. "Is Lizzie here?" he called.

"Present, sir," Lizzie said in her geek voice, launching her cabin-mates into giggling hysterics.

"Your mom just called," said Abe. "She wants you to call her back right away." He looked at Jude. "You should probably come along, too."

Jude's stomach clenched. Dear God, she thought, please don't let it be something bad: a dead grandmother, a dead pet, a dead anything. She would have no idea what to do or say. Katie might, but not her. (Why did Abe want her to come instead of Katie, anyway?)

"No, no," said Abe. "It's good news."

Lizzie clapped her hands. "Maybe I'm getting a baby brother! Come on!" She grabbed Jude's hand and tugged on it. Jude followed her to the office with a sinking feeling. Good news or not, the look Abe had given her hadn't boded well.

Jude stood leaning against the collating counter while Lizzie sat in the swivel chair at Aura's desk and made her call. Jude could hear Mrs. Polk's voice honking on the other line, but couldn't make out the words. All the while, Lizzie's face stretched into a gradually bigger and more gleeful smile. Then she sprang up from her chair and began jumping up and down. "Really?" she squealed. "Really, really, really?" Mrs. Polk's voice through the receiver chirped up and down in mad arpeggios. Lizzie held the phone against her chest. "I got a part in a movie! The girl who was going to do it got the chicken pox and had to quit and they want me to do it instead!" She sat back down.

Jude shot Abe a questioning glance: what was the big deal? But he just smiled tightly in return.

After she'd hung up the phone, Lizzie turned to Jude. "I'm really sorry, but I can't be in the show."

Jude glanced at Abe and back at Lizzie. "You mean they need you right away?"

Lizzie nodded cheerfully.

"Is it a big part? I mean, do you have to take it?"

"Jude," Abe warned.

Lizzie crossed one leg over the older and folded her hands around her knee. "It's one of the friends of the main girl. Not the best friend, but another friend. There aren't tons of lines, but I'll be in lots of scenes. And there may be one where we get to swim with dolphins."

"Sounds dangerous," Jude said.

"It *sounds* like a great opportunity," said Abe, giving her a pointed look. "And I'm sure we can find someone else to take over Lizzie's part in the play. That's really cool, Lizzie. Congrats."

"But the show's a week away. And you're the star," said Jude. "Without you, there *is* no show."

In a gesture so canned it looked like she'd practiced it in front of a mirror, Lizzie shrugged, hands up by her cheeks, and tilted her head to the side. "Sorry. That's showbiz."

≈

After she'd walked Lizzie to the cabin, Jude went back to the office. The screen door was covered with moths, and before she opened it, she gave the frame a kick, sending them flying. Inside, Abe was at his desk, bent over a stack of paper, the heels of his palms pressed to his temples. He looked up at her briefly as she entered. "It's a hard knock life, huh?"

"Yeah," said Jude. "Thanks for all your help, there."

"What was I supposed to do? Try to talk her out of it? Try to talk the *mother* out of it?"

"She made a commitment to the camp show," Jude said. "I thought you were all about making this place back into a community and shit. Not giving in to spoiled kids and their asshole parents." She slumped into one of the folding chairs by the door, feet splayed out in front of her.

"This isn't a case of a spoiled kid or an asshole parent," Abe said. "It's a case of priorities. The kid has a career. And as messed up as that may be, that's the way it is. She can't turn down something like this."

"How am I supposed to teach her part to someone else in less than a week? This isn't just some crappy, amateur production. It's supposed to be *good*."

And recently, Jude had been starting to get the feeling it would be. The sets were looking great, thanks in no small part to her contributions. Most of the actors were finally off book. They still had a ways to go, but things were definitely coming together.

"Isn't there something we can do? Talk to her agent? Reschedule the show? We could probably pull it together by this weekend if we really hustled."

"We can't do that. There are parents who come up to see

it. Listen, no offense, Jude, but I've got way more serious stuff to worry about right now." He tapped his pen against the stack of papers in front of him. "I don't know if you heard, but it's official. This Bill Dyer dick is suing us."

"Shit," said Jude. She'd heard rumors from other staff members, and everyone knew that Jeremy had left, but no one knew for sure whether an actual lawsuit had materialized. "Do you have to go to court?"

"Nope. You don't even get the satisfaction. You fill out reams of paperwork, lawyers talk to lawyers, the insurance company pays a settlement and that's pretty much it."

Jude walked over to Aura's desk chair and sat down in it, swiveling to face Abe. It had been a while since she'd seen him up close, and she was surprised at how tired he looked. There were crescents of gray beneath his eyes, and the lines around his mouth seemed deeper; less suggestive of laughter and more like signs of aging. "You look like hell," she said.

He granted her half a smile. "Thanks."

"You know, you don't have to do this."

"I don't have to do what?"

"Run the camp."

"Thanks for your permission."

"No, I mean it," she said. "I know you feel like you have to—it's what Dad wanted and blah blah blah—and I know you don't completely hate it either. You're good at it. But the fact is, it's never going to be the way you remember it. This place might have been a kinder, gentler camp way back when, but it never was and never will be"—she put on a mock dreamy tone and twirled her wrist—"a vision of what the world might be…"

"Yeah, yeah," said Abe, his voice rising to overtake hers. "I'm aware that it wasn't paradise on earth. But there was something special about it. You felt it, too, and you know it. Otherwise you wouldn't be so perpetually pissed about mom and dad splitting." He flung his pen aside, and it landed with a plastic clatter on his keyboard. "I just miss it. I was hoping maybe I could bring it back. But I obviously can't."

Jude bit the inside of her lip. She hoped to God that Eric wouldn't wait too much longer to break the news about Dane to Abe. It was all she could do not to blurt it out herself. He needed to know that there were snakes in the garden long before Gail or Reaganomics or Bill Dyer and his ilk. He needed to know, and he needed to move on. They all did.

"I think what you really miss is Dad," Jude finally said, standing and walking toward the door. A particularly large moth was thumping repeatedly against the screen in its light-induced frenzy. She reached over and flicked the switch to turn off the outside light. In the sudden darkness, the moth bounced against the screen once more, then fluttered away.

She looked back at Abe. He was sitting forward, elbows on the desk, head slumped between his shoulders. "Yeah, I miss him a lot," he said.

"I do, too."

Abe lifted his head. "That's the first time you've admitted that."

Jude shrugged. "It's not a matter of admitting. I just haven't missed him until now, that's all."

This wasn't quite true, she supposed. It was just that until now, what she'd felt was more complicated than simply "missing." It still *was* complicated. But it was as if there was a new wash over her feelings for her father now. Everything seemed softer and blurrier. Corners had become curves.

"Why the change of heart?" Abe asked.

"I don't know. The five stages of grief or something. I'm in the forgiveness stage, I guess. Anyway, speaking of stages, I should get to bed. Gotta get up tomorrow and find me a new Annie." She gave a sarcastic fist-pump.

"OK," said Abe. "But for the record, forgiveness isn't one of the five stages."

Jude grasped the door handle and gave the frame a gentle kick, scattering the last of the moths that clung to the screen. "Maybe it should be," she said.

Eric

THERE WERE STILL TIMES when all Eric wanted was to be alone. But it wasn't easy to avoid contact with other human beings at a summer camp in session. He could only spend so much of his time pent up in the maintenance barn (where Sergei always showed up, anyway) or his apartment, or taking solitary walks around the lake. And it wasn't as if he could just ignore campers who greeted him as he drove by on the tractor or in the pickup, or not acknowledge the people he sat with in the dining hall. He couldn't even bring himself to give his mother the complete silent treatment, though he tried his best to avoid her. It might have been easier, he supposed, if he'd left Eden Lake completely, like Aura so abruptly and mysteriously had. But where would he have gone?

What he hated even more was having to see Masha and Strickland together. They didn't hold hands or kiss or otherwise express their affection in front of campers; it would have been a violation of camp rules. But on a rainy-day trip to the Roll-o-Rama, Eric had been subjected to the sight of Strickland teaching Masha how to skate: her clinging to him, giggling and squealing as they clunked around the rink together under the spinning colored lights. To Eric, it was just as painful as if he'd seen them embrace. Maybe worse, because he could see from her face just how happy she was.

Sergei, to whom Eric had confessed his feelings for Masha, mostly to get him to stop asking him why he was in such a bad mood, thought Eric should just steal Masha out from under Strickland's nose: "All you must do is get her a little bit drunk when Strickland is not around, then kiss her, and"— he snapped his fingers—"she will realize what she has been missing. That Strickland, he is nice, but he has skin like pizza." Sergei touched his fingertips to his cheeks. "And he is only program director. You are the brother of the director of whole camp. You have money, and you own land. This is very exciting to a Russian girl."

Jude, meanwhile, thought that Eric ought to forget Masha and move on. "What about Jen?" she said, referring to the dance teacher and choreographer. "She said she thought you looked good with your new haircut." But Jen was not only several years older than Eric, she was entirely too good-looking for him. In fact, she terrified him, with her long neck and her nipples that always showed through her tight, thin t-shirts. If he hadn't had the guts to make a move with Masha, how on earth could he make a move with someone like Jen, even if he'd wanted to?

The person with the best advice, it turned out, was Niedermeier. On a cool afternoon during third class period, while Eric was repairing a loose plank on the boat dock, Niedermeier approached him, dripping wet in his swim trunks, his pale skin pimpled with gooseflesh. "Hi. L-l-long t-t-time n-n-o t-t-t-talk," he said through chattering teeth.

"Yeah, hi," Eric replied. "You're taking swimming this week?"

Niedermeier nodded. "I'm an ad-ad-vanced int-t-t-erme-diate."

"You're going to freeze to death," Eric said. He took off the flannel shirt over his t-shirt and tossed it to Niedermeier. "Here."

Niedermeier put it on. "I'm not as c-c-cold as I look. I just have an overactive shivering reflex," he said, then grinned. "D-d-did you hear the g-g-good news?"

"I haven't heard any good news in awhile."

Niedermeier looked concerned. "Yes-s-s, I've noticed you've seemed a little down in the dumps. But maybe this will cheer you up. I have a girlfriend."

"Oh yeah? Who?" It wasn't Svetlana, that was for sure; the other night at the staff cabin, Jude had told everyone that she'd caught Svetlana and Dimo making out in the loft over the boathouse.

"I'm involved with Dahna Schwartz," Niedermeier said. "I guess most kids say 'going out' but that doesn't make much sense seeing as we can't really go anywhere."

"That's great," said Eric. He had no idea who Dahna Schwartz was—he generally only knew campers by their faces—but even the name, solid and simple, seemed more Niedermeier's speed than Svetlana-something-ova. "I'm really happy for you."

"I haven't kissed her yet, except on the cheek. But she's never had a boyfriend before and I've never had a girlfriend, so we're taking it slow."

"That's good," Eric said distractedly. Over Niedermeier's

shoulder, he'd spotted Masha on the beach by the swimming area, pulling off her t-shirt and stepping gingerly out of her shorts. She stood on the dark sand in her green bikini, shielding her eyes from the sun with her hand. The concave swoop of the small of her back followed the gentle, convex curve of her pale belly, so that her torso seemed almost serpentine. He tried to tell himself he didn't like it.

Niedermeier turned to see what Eric was looking at. "It's too bad things didn't work out with you and Masha," he said.

"What?"

Niedermeier tapped a finger against his temple. "I may be a kid, but I'm pretty smart."

"Yeah, well, I guess I liked her a little," Eric said. "But she didn't like me back. Just like Svetlana didn't like you back. That's the way it goes sometimes." He felt immediately guilty for having mentioned Svetlana, but Niedermeier didn't flinch.

"How do you know for sure she didn't like you back?" he asked.

"She's going out with Strickland, isn't she?"

Niedermeier frowned. "Maybe she didn't know you liked her."

"She knew," said Eric. How could she not have? All the flirting, all the effort he made to spend time with her. She knew.

"So you told her you liked her?"

"Not in so many words, but I made it clear."

"I was so scared to tell Dahna I liked her," Niedermeier said with a goofy grin. "I was afraid she wouldn't like me back either, like Svetlana. But I decided what the heck. There are only two weeks left of camp, so what's the worst thing that can happen? And when I gave her the pottery candleholder I made with a note saying I wanted to be more than just friends, she told me she'd always liked me, she just thought I didn't like her. Which is partly true. I didn't, at first, because I liked Svetlana. But when I realized she wasn't going to like me back, I started liking Dahna. She's not as pretty, but she's much nicer. I didn't tell her that, though, because I thought it might hurt her feelings." He paused thoughtfully. "I can show you how to make a pottery candleholder if you want. It's really easy. And it doesn't have to be for a candle, since candles aren't allowed in the cabins anyway. You can use it to store little pieces of jewelry or coins. You can also roll the note up and put it in the candle place. That's what I did. I'll bet Masha would really like it."

"Thanks, but Strickland's my friend," Eric said. "I'm not going to try to steal his girlfriend." He was surprised, frankly, that Niedermeier would suggest such a thing. He seemed like a morally upstanding kid.

Niedermeier brought his hand to his chin and thought for a moment. "I don't think it's stealing," he finally said. "You can't really steal a person unless they're a slave. Which is illegal, of course."

Eric narrowed his eyes at the boy. He had a point.

≈

The following afternoon, Eric helped Strickland and a few other counselors get the rec. hall ready for casino night. They hung signs and decorations, set up tables for card games and bingo and rigged up the big, hand-painted wooden roulette wheel that had been used on this night for years. Instead of betting on numbers, campers bet on staff members, their names written on strips of thick masking tape stuck to the wedges of the wheel, peeled off and replaced each year. Last year's names were still in place when Eric pulled the wheel out of storage, including "Clay" in bigger, bolder letters than all the others, with little red and green magic marker lines radiating out around it like laser beams. Eric pulled the tape off carefully and stuck it to a piece of blank paper, which he folded and slipped into his back pocket. The rest of the names—except for those of the eight or so returning staff members, himself included—he ripped off quickly and crumpled into a big, sticky ball.

He felt guilty, working casually alongside Strickland, all the while thinking about what he was going to say to Masha. Tonight, he'd decided, would be the best possible opportunity: Strickland would be busy running things and Masha wouldn't need to do too much translating for the Russian campers. Gambling was fairly self-explanatory. It wouldn't be difficult for the two of them to duck away for a quick talk. He even had a natural, if somewhat corny way to segue into the conversation: something about how this was a good night for taking chances.

At one point, while Eric and Strickland were moving a table together, one of them at each end, Eric decided he should forget the whole thing. What if he were in Strickland's shoes? What if he found out that someone he trusted and liked had bared his heart to his girlfriend? It wasn't the kind of thing friends were supposed to do to each other.

But when he saw Masha that night, wearing the same purple, sleeveless dress she'd worn at the dance, pale green eye shadow over her eyes, her lips shimmering, he felt a swell of longing, followed by an almost physical urge to act. He had a brief vision of himself striding across the hall to her, putting his hand to the back of her neck and kissing her passionately, right there in front of everyone, like in a movie. He wouldn't, of course. But he held on to the feeling of it, the boldness. And when, finally, he saw her standing alone, he did stride across the hall to her. He strode and stood in front of her and said, "Masha, do you have a minute? I need to talk to you about something."

"Of course," she said. "What is it?"

He glanced around. He'd originally planned to ask her to go outside, where they could talk in private. But here, he realized, in this building full of campers and counselors and color and noise (Frank Sinatra playing over the sound system, the click-clack-click-clack of the roulette wheel, the rattle and churn of bingo balls) they would be less conspicuous than they might be sitting alone on the swing or standing by the garden.

"Masha," he said. He held his right fist against his left palm, like a martial artist about to take a bow. It made him feel strong. "Do you believe that it's important to know the truth about things, even if it makes things more complicated?"

The start of a smile twitched on Masha's lips.

"I'm serious," Eric said, a bit more sharply than he meant to.

Her smile vanished. "Yes," she said.

"Good. Me too. Because the truth is, Masha, I'm attracted to you. Powerfully attracted." This wasn't what he had planned to say at all. He didn't quite know where it was coming from, but he didn't care. Maybe this was what people meant when they talked about doing things from the gut. "And I hate that you're going out with Strickland. I understand it, of course. He's a good guy, and I see why you like him. He deserves you. But I wish it were me, and I just wanted you to know. That's all."

For a few seconds Masha said nothing and Eric felt as if the world was caving in around him. He couldn't breathe. He thought he heard laughter, directed at him. Then, he felt something cool against the back of his wrist: Masha's fingertips. They'd brushed his skin for just a second, but the sensation lingered and buzzed.

"Erichka," she said, her head tilting ever so slightly to one side. "Why didn't you tell me?"

"I'm telling you now."

She folded her bare arms across her chest. "Well, you are right. This truth makes things complicated. Because I am with Strickland."

"I know," said Eric. This was what he'd expected, what he'd prepared himself for. It didn't matter, he told himself. The important thing was that he'd said what he'd needed to say. Who cared anyway? His life was a conflagration of lies and tragedy and failure. What was one more stick added to the fire?

"But I would rather be with you."

He thought he'd misheard her over the noise in the hall. "What did you say?"

Her smile was sad and small, a rosebud beneath her nose. "I said that I would rather be with you. But it is too late now."

"But maybe it's not," Eric said, breaking his promise to himself that if this happened—if, by some insane chance she told him that she liked him back—he wouldn't try to persuade her to break up with Strickland. "We'd have time to be together. There's a whole week and a half left, plus the cultural tour after camp." The Russian kids would travel for two weeks before returning home: Boston, New York, Philadelphia, Washington and, finally, Orlando. "I could come along and help out, maybe."

A smile bloomed on Masha's face. "Yes. And Strickland would not even have to know. We could keep it our secret, yes?"

Eric's heart sank. "No," he said, "We can't do that."

"But Strickland will be so upset. He'll hate me."

"No he won't," Eric said. "Not if he—"

"Say, now, what's the big idea? Getting fresh with my girl?"

Eric turned to see Strickland behind him, grinning, fists raised. He was dressed as an old-time card dealer: green visor, pinstripe vest, garters on his shirtsleeves.

Eric glanced at Masha, who was smiling stiffly, then said to Strickland, clapping him on the shoulder as he took his leave, "Of course not, Strick. She's all yours."

≈

The night was dark and moonless, but Eric's feet knew the contours of the mowed path up the meadow so well that he didn't need a flashlight, and didn't once stumble. He was nearing the boulders at the top when it struck him that the shape of one of them had changed. As he drew closer, he realized that someone was lying on it, knees bent over the edge, feet dangling. He started to turn away—he'd find somewhere else to be alone, to try to process the infuriating blend of exhilaration and disappointment he felt—when the person on the boulder said his name. It was Abe.

"So," he asked, "what are *you* escaping from?"

"Everyone," said Eric.

"But you can't escape your family. Come on up."

Eric climbed up onto the smaller boulder and lay on his back. Usually when he stared up at the vastness of the universe, thinking about how far away and ancient and enormous each star was, it helped put his troubles into perspective. But tonight, the stars just looked like static, cluttering and obscuring the sky. He closed his eyes.

"I came here to escape being a camp director," Abe said after a moment, as if Eric had asked. "Get this. Apparently Dave snapped at some kid in the dining hall today at lunch because she was taking cucumbers off the salad bar with her hands. Made her cry. She called her mother, who called me, and wanted me to put Dave on the phone so she could tell him off herself."

"Did you?"

"No. I told her I'd talk to him, and have him apologize to the kid, and that seemed to satisfy her." The heels of his sneakers thunked quietly against his rock. "One more thing on my list of shit to do that I don't want to do."

Eric tried to think of something sympathetic to say, but the fact was, he was having a hard time conjuring much sympathy for Abe. Yeah, he had a lot of headaches to deal with at the moment, but they were just that; headaches. Not heartache.

"I don't know, little brother," Abe said. "I may not be cut out for this business." When Eric said nothing, he added, "I'm sorry. You probably hate it when I call you that."

"I don't mind it that much," Eric said. He took a breath and let it out slowly "You know, I've been thinking maybe I should go away for awhile," he said. "Maybe take next summer off."

There was a pause. "Really? Where would you go?"

"I don't know yet. I could travel, maybe. Tour around the country. Maybe I'll buy a bike."

"You have a bike, don't you?"

"I mean a motorcycle." Since his ride with Dane, the thought had crossed his mind a few times. He'd only imagined himself riding it around here, on the back roads of Maine. But why stop there?

"Dane's really made an impression on you, hasn't he?" said Abe with a mildly condescending laugh. "You gonna grow a handlebar mustache, too?"

"He's my father," Eric said.

Abe laughed. "What's that supposed to mean?"

Eric wasn't sure how to proceed; he hadn't planned on telling Abe until camp was over. He hadn't even planned to tell Jude the other day, but it had come out in a moment of emotion, the way this had. What was happening to him? It was as if he was suddenly full of cracks and fissures, unable to contain all the things he felt and thought and knew.

He swallowed hard. "I'm serious. He's my biological father. Mom had an affair with him when she traveled to India. Ten months before I was born."

For a long time, Abe said nothing. As Eric's ears adjusted to the silence, he noticed that it was, in fact, specked with the first tentative cricket songs of the summer, staccato and irregular. He also began to hear the gently thumping bass of the music down in the rec. hall, pulsing through the air. He wondered if Masha was still there.

"What are you saying?" Abe said at last.

Eric pushed up onto his elbows. "Mom told me a couple of weeks ago. Dad knew about it all along. They decided not to tell us. But now that he's gone, and mom's involved with Dane, she wanted me to know."

"Holy shit," said Abe. He sounded far away. Then quickly closer. "Holy fucking shit, are you kidding me? Please tell me this is a joke. Or some kind of delusion. Some kind of, I don't know, paternal substitution fantasy."

"I'm sorry," Eric said. "It's not."

"Who else knows? Does Jude know?"

"Yeah. I told her."

"And Aura?"

Strangely, the question hadn't even occurred to Eric. He'd assumed, perhaps naively, that Clay had never even told Gail. "I don't know," he said.

Abe made a clutching gesture at the sides of his head. "I can't process this. I can't get my head around it."

"Try being me," said Eric.

Abe turned to him. "I'm sorry. You're right. This has got to be nuts for you." He lay back down. "Shit," he said. "So she cheated first. She's the one who fucked things up. Not him."

"I don't know. Maybe Dad had cheated on her before. I didn't ask. I don't really care."

They lay in silence, side by side, for a few minutes. Then Eric began to climb down from his boulder. "It's getting cold. You want to go down to the farmhouse?"

"I think I'd rather stay up here a little longer," Abe said. "I think I need to be alone for a while."

"If you want to talk more, just let me know."

"Thanks," said Abe. "I will."

≈

Eric had gotten into bed and was at the edge of sleep when the knock came at his door. Thinking it was Sergei—he'd been known to show up in the middle of the night, drunk, looking for conversation or a game of chess—Eric ignored it. Then it came again, faster, sharper. As he made his way to the door, he heard Masha's voice. "Eric? Are you there?"

He opened the door and there she stood, an Eden Lake sweatshirt pulled over her purple dress. Her eyes were pink and swollen, with green smudges of makeup beneath them.

Before Eric could say anything, she stepped forward and put her arms around his neck. "I told him, Erichka," she said. "I told him I wanted to be with you."

Abe

ABE DIDN'T SLEEP MORE than a couple of hours the night after Eric's revelation. He felt like he needed to revisit all his memories—every moment starting from the day his mother came home from India (he remembered being at his grand-parents' big house in Concord, playing Tiddlywinks with his grandmother while his father drove to the airport)—and re-consider them with this new knowledge in mind. He thought of the photo of Eric at one, holding onto their father's hands, on the shore of Eden Lake, learning to walk. *His father had raised another man's son.* He thought of the summer after camp when the five of them drove cross-country in a VW bus to visit Yel-lowstone and Grand Teton, and Eric, then seven or eight and obsessed with American Indians, gave everyone in the family Indian names. Abe's was "Brother Coyote." *Half brother coyote.* He remembered the bleak, miserable spring vacation he spent at Eden Lake his senior year of high school, soon after his father had left, and the days when their mother was too depressed even to leave her bed. While Jude stayed in her room with the door closed and Eric lost himself in text adventure games on the computer, Abe was the one who would bring their

mother bowls of soup and cups of tea, and let her sob soundlessly against his shoulder. Now, those tears seemed more complicated. Had she been crying not just for their father's betrayal,
but also for her own?

Oddly, he couldn't quite find it in himself to be angry with
her—either for the fact of cheating on their father, or for keeping Eric's paternity a secret all these years. What he felt instead was a dull ache, like pressure on a bruise that was almost
healed. The only thing that made him angry was the timing of
her confession. Why tell Eric—and by extension, all of them—
now, when the pain of their father's death was so fresh?

In the morning, when she arrived to work, he asked her.
They sat together on the bench swing and watched the martial arts class on the main lawn: Ted and a half dozen campers,
throwing kicks and punches into the air.

"It was probably a mistake," she said. "I should have waited
until after camp was over. I guess I just thought it might make
things a little easier for him. To know that he still had a father."

Abe felt a stab of envy. Eric's father wasn't dead.

"If dad hadn't died, would you have told us?" he asked her.
"Ever?"

"I don't know. We left it up to your father. When he wanted
to say something, he would."

"So what if he never planned to say anything? Don't you
think you should have respected that?"

"He's gone," Carol said, and let her hand rest lightly on
Abe's. "We can't spend the rest of our lives trying to guess what
he would or wouldn't have wanted. The one thing we can be
reasonably sure of is that he would have wanted all of us to be
happy."

He slid his hand out from under hers. "It blows my mind sometimes that the two of you, you and Dad, could be such idealists—the way you created this place and wanted to change the world—and at the same time be so…"

"So human?"

"Yeah," Abe said. "Yeah, I guess that's right."

The campers in the martial arts class faced each other in pairs now, feet set wide, and practiced blocking each other's punches, laughing as they did.

"I'm sorry," his mother said. "I hope you can forgive us."

The sixth stage of grief, Abe thought. "I can," he said. "I mean, I will. Eventually."

≈

There was a new face at Free Speech that afternoon: a twelve-year-old girl named Chloe Mayer, red-haired, freckled and small for her age. She arrived early with Morgan, her counselor, who explained that Chloe had just heard from her parents that a classmate of hers had died, and she wondered if she could talk about it with the group. Abe said of course; he hadn't had a topic in mind anyway.

Lately, he hadn't been giving as much thought ahead of time to Free Speech. The conversations had become freeform, and more often than not deteriorated into trivialities—the kids listing all the foods and TV shows they missed, comparing how many states or countries they'd been to, talking about movies they liked. It was less meaningful discussion, more show and tell. But Abe didn't have the energy to steer them back on course.

Chloe was afraid if she told the group what had happened she'd start crying, so Morgan did it for her, in her gently lilting brogue. "This poor boy, Christopher, in Chloe's class, he drowned in a riptide at the beach last week. Chloe just found out about it and has been very sad, of course, so she was wondering if anyone had any advice for her."

There was a brief, reverent silence, and then Chloe said, "He's the first person I ever knew who died."

Niedermeier cleared his throat. He was sitting next to Dahna, as usual, though Abe had noticed that lately, sometimes, they sat so that their knees touched. "I'm very sorry for your loss," he said. "My grandmother died last year. Of course, that's not the same, because old people are supposed to die and kids aren't. So I don't know if this helps, but it made me feel better to think about good times I spent with her, playing Rack-o and making pudding and things. So if you have any good memories of Christopher, maybe you should concentrate on those."

"We were badminton partners in gym once," Chloe said. "I know nobody wanted to get me as their partner because I'm so short, but he was really nice about it, and we had fun."

A few other campers shared their death stories—pets and grandparents, mostly—and their suggestions for Chloe: remember the good times. Be glad you're still alive. Think of Christopher up in heaven, getting to do whatever he wants.

Abe listened with half an ear. He was thinking of the day he'd learned of his father's death, and how obliviously content he'd been in the hours and minutes before he knew. Suppose he'd just gone on not knowing? (If a plane crashes in a field, and you don't know about it, did it really happen?) He wondered why Chloe's parents had chosen to tell her about the boy's death while she was still at camp. Why not let her enjoy the last week?

Oak, who'd been unusually quiet, spoke, snapping Abe to attention. "Abe, I hope you don't mind me bringing it up," he said, "but I was pretty upset when I found out about Clay and Gail. A lot of us return campers were." A few other kids nodded in agreement. "Would it be OK if we talked about that a little bit?"

Abe felt the weight of the children's eyes on him, and felt suddenly ashamed for never having broached the subject at Free Speech before. Of course campers would be upset about the accident. How could he, or the camp at large, not have offered them some outlet for it?

"Of course we don't have to," Oak said. "It's a lot harder for you than any of us."

"No," said Abe, "It's OK. We can talk about it. It's a good idea. What do you want to know?"

"Do you think it hurt when they crashed?" Dahna Schwartz asked. "Like, did they get burned up?"

"Tsk, Dahna," Ashley scolded. "That's so rude."

"No, it's all right, she can ask," Abe said. "Free Speech, remember?"

Besides, it was the question they were all thinking—the same one he'd asked himself countless times. "I don't know for sure, but if it did hurt, it didn't hurt for long. The plane went down fast, and the impact of it hitting the ground probably broke their necks."

"Where are they buried?" asked Josh Ruben—Ashley's boyfriend that week.

"They weren't buried, they were cremated," Abe told him. "That's where they burn the bodies." He almost went on to say that the ashes were scattered in the lake, but thought better of it. It was strange enough for him, the few times he'd gone swimming, knowing that in with the sediment and microorganisms and whatever else was suspended in lake water, were tiny, charred particles of his own genetic material. The campers, if they knew, might never go in the lake again.

"Can we not talk about this anymore?" said Ashley, her fingertips pressed to her cheeks. "It's freaking me out."

"Sorry, babe, my bad," said Josh, and put his arm around Ashley, who leaned against his shoulder.

"It's just so sad." She sounded suddenly much more upset than she had a few seconds before.

"It is," said Abe. "But I think it's good to talk about this stuff. Death is a natural part of life. If we think of it that way, it's easier to accept. So they say."

"Do you have nightmares?" Chloe asked.

"I dream all the time that my father's still alive," Abe replied. "And when I wake up I remember he's not, and that feels like the nightmare instead." Nobody spoke, and Abe wondered if, now, he'd been too honest. Truth was such a tricky thing when it came to children. When was it good medicine and when was it poison?

Niedermeier came to the rescue. "I have a Semitics question," he said.

"I think you mean semantics."

"Oh, right. Semantics. Are you considered an orphan because your mom and dad died, even though you're an adult?"

"Gail wasn't his real mom," said Bryan—Jeremy's old piercing buddy. "His mom's that lady who's been working in the office. Her." He pointed, and everyone turned to look: there was Carol, across the lawn at the edge of the garden, pulling on a clump of vines that had coiled itself out through the garden fence and started to encircle a nearby birch sapling. In her gold cotton tunic and green pants, hair in a bun low on her neck, she looked like a sunflower that had jumped the fence. Abe had thought she'd already left; she usually had by this time. It was surreal to see her there, tending her garden again—as if time had gotten tangled up, and past and present were overlapping.

Carol seemed to sense that she was being watched. She stood up straight and waved in the direction of the gazebo. Everyone waved back.

"Yeah, I've still got a mother," Abe said, watching her return to her struggle with the vine. Too much work for her, he thought; she'll tire herself out. "But I don't think adults whose parents die are considered orphans anyway. That would make for a whole lot of orphans in the world."

"It would make me an orphan," said Morgan. "My dad died when I was thirteen, but Mum died just over a year ago." Her voice wavered and she paused for a moment. "I don't consider myself an orphan. But there are times when I feel like one. It's a lonely thing not to have your parents around to look out for you, even when you are a grown-up."

"So what do you do?" asked Chloe. "How do you not be sad all the time?"

"Well," she said, "I suppose you try to keep busy. That's part of it. You think about the person and remember them, like Niedermeier said. But you don't do it all the time. You have to put your mind to other things. And little by little, it gets easier."

"You have to just keep living your life," Abe said, "That's the most important thing."

But even as he dispensed this advice, he knew wasn't doing

a very good job of following it. This wasn't his life he was living. It was his father's.

≈

When free speech was over, he went over to the garden. His
mother was inside it now, kneeling before a cluster of irises,
pulling up what Abe assumed were weeds. In spite of all the
hours he'd spent working beside her here as a child, he'd never
gotten to be any good at distinguishing what should stay from
what should go.

When she saw him, she smiled and wiped the back of her
gloved hand across her forehead. "It's a jungle in here," she said,
"but not beyond hope. It just needs a good purge."

"You're not going to wear yourself out, are you? It's pretty
warm out today." The heat bothered her sometimes, a strange
symptom of her MS.

"No, I'm fine. But you're right; I probably should call it a
day. It's late." She gathered up her trowel, hand rake, and a pair
of clippers, tucking them into a handled basket, then lifted her
hand for Abe to help her up onto her feet.

"Listen, Mom," he said. "You've been an incredible help this
past week and a half. I really, really appreciate it."

She narrowed an eye at him. "Am I about to be fired?"

Abe slid his hands in the back pockets of his jeans. "I wasn't
going to call it that. I just think…" He looked away, toward
the gazebo, puzzling over how to explain what it was that he
needed.

"You're angry at me," she said. Her eyes, to Abe's surprise,
had started to fill. "I understand." She started to move past him,
but he stopped her with a hand to her shoulder.

"I'm not angry, Mom. I mean, a little, maybe. Yeah. But mainly I just—I think it would be better if you weren't here right now. I think I—well, we—need to get through the end of the summer on our own. Me and Eric and Jude."

"I understand," she said again, though she still looked hurt. "Are you sure you'll be all right? The end of the session is so chaotic…"

"We'll manage," Abe said.

"You're sure?"

"Yes."

He put his arm around her and they walked out of the garden together.

≈

It wasn't hard to track down Brendan Baker. Plugging his name into Yahoo turned up a few recent articles on his company, LifeMonkey.com, and its recent IPO. At the site, Abe clicked on the "Our story" page to see a photo of Brendan and his company co-founders, Yuri and Anish, sitting side by side in the sun on a low brick wall, posing as the "see no evil, hear no evil, speak no evil" monkeys. Brendan was the one with his hands over his mouth.

He arrived on Sunday morning in a brand new Saab, wearing a light blue, retro-style bowling shirt that didn't look quite right with his khaki pants, loafers, and short, well-gelled haircut. It was like he'd decided—or someone had told him—that he ought to start dressing the part of a dot-com hipster, but wasn't quite sure how to go about it.

When they shook hands, Brendan grinned, revealing a mouthful of preternaturally straight teeth—the headgear had paid off, it seemed—and told Abe how jealous he'd always been of him. "I thought it must have been the coolest thing in the world to be the directors' kid, and get to stay at camp year-round."

"It was a pretty cool way to grow up," Abe said.

As they set off to tour the property, Abe asked Brendan why he was interested in buying a camp. "It seems like things are really taking off for you with your business."

"They are," Brendan agreed. "They absolutely are. But for all my success, there's a part of me that's still searching. I want to step out of the mainstream, you know? Do something that's not virtual." He stopped and looked around, fists to his khaki hips. They stood by the tetherball poles, looking across the main lawn toward the fabric arts building. In front of it, kids stooped over white plaster buckets, tie-dyeing T-shirts and towels and pillowcases.

"Lazy day for half the camp?" Brendan asked.

"Yep," said Abe. "The other half is in Camden for the day. Then, tonight, there's a dance. Disco night, I think."

Brendan laughed. "This place hasn't changed a bit. I love it."

"It's a lot bigger now, actually. Capacity for over two hundred campers. A whole bunch of new buildings. A climbing wall, a computer lab, an expanded riding area…" Abe wasn't listing these things as selling points—just the opposite, in fact—but Brendan nodded with enthusiasm.

"Awesome. That's what you have to do, right? Keep things growing, keep up with demand."

Abe decided not to point out that seconds earlier Brendan was enraptured by the idea of stagnation. "I guess so. It certainly has done well. I mean, it's not money anywhere near the scale you're used to. But it's a decent living. It would keep you in Saab payments." He smiled, feeling slightly greasy as he did.

"I paid cash for the car," Brendan said, smiling greasily back. "But point taken."

They spent the next hour walking the property, and Abe described the highlights of each area: the light and sound equipment in the rec. hall, the cantilevered floor in the dance studio, the fleet of almost new, lightweight canoes by the boathouse. Then they joined the buffet line for lunch and ate at a picnic table at the edge of the lawn, away from everyone else. Abe hadn't told Eric or Jude that Brendan was coming, and felt slightly guilty about it. But he wanted to test these waters on his own. Hopefully, if either of them spotted him with Brendan they would just assume he was a friend, visiting.

"So, what's the set-up?" Brendan asked, his mouth half full of a chicken patty sandwich, "Do you and your siblings own everything jointly?"

Abe finished swallowing the bite he'd just taken. "Jude and Eric hold the deed to the land, actually. I own the business."

"Well, I'd definitely want the whole package. Land and business." Brendan swept his arm in arc over his head, a gesture that seemed to Abe just a touch too proprietary. "You think they'd be amenable to that?"

"To be honest, we haven't really discussed it at length. We've been so busy just trying to get through the session…"

"I understand. And I'm not in any hurry. I mean, yes, I'm looking at a couple other camps, but I'm not on any fast track. And of course, this place has special meaning to me, being the first camp I ever went to."

"Where else are you looking?"

He named a few other Maine camps, a couple of them similar to Eden Lake, including Moosehead, a teen program that many Eden Lake campers, including Brendan, had "graduated" to. But the others he named were nothing like Eden Lake: a sailing camp; a traditional boys' camp along the lines of Micmac; a place called Craggy Pines that Abe had never heard of.

"So," Abe said, "tell me a bit about your…you know, your vision for running a camp."

"My vision?"

"I mean, what kind of place would you want it to be? What kind of underlying principles or values?"

Brendan squinted at Abe for a moment, then frowned and nodded at his plate. "That's a great question. And I'd have to give it some more thought to give you a real answer, but off the top of my head…well, as you know, I'm a big believer in the entrepreneurial spirit. I think everyone should have their own dream and pursue it. So I'd want it to be a place where that kind of individual achievement is encouraged, you know? Where kids can try new things and build skills, gain confidence, learn that they can accomplish anything they set their minds to. Whether it's…I don't know…learning how to swim out to the far dock," he gestured toward the lake, "or throwing a perfect pot on the wheel, or starting their own company. It all comes from the same place. It's the same thing." He pressed his hand to his chest, between the zigzag stripes of his bowling shirt.

"The American dream," Abe said.

Brendan's eyes shone. "Exactly."

"This Camp is Your Camp"
By the Summer of '72 campers & staff
(Sung to the tune of "This Land is Your Land")

As I went walking
Up through the meadow
I saw above me the forest's shadow
I saw below me the children playing
This camp was made for you and me

Chorus:
This camp is your camp
This camp is my camp
From Carol's garden
To the lakeshore's warm sand
From the meadow hilltop
To the duck pond waters
This camp was made for you and me.

I've roamed and rambled
The streets of the city
The lights are bright and the people are pretty
But there's no green grass, no pine trees swaying
This camp was made for you and me.

(Chorus)

The sun comes shining
And the camp bell's ringing
Around the campfire, we all are singing
Of peace and justice, of love and freedom
This camp was made for you and me.

(Chorus)

Eric

ERIC DIDN'T MAKE LOVE to Masha that first night, when she knocked on his door. But they kissed for a long time, half-reclined on the futon couch. Eric discovered that Masha's lips were much smaller and thinner than his own, so that as they kissed, his mouth felt the soft, peach-fuzzed skin around hers. He'd never wanted someone so badly in his life. He didn't care that he was a virgin, didn't care if he made a fool of himself or came too soon, didn't even care that they had no protection. But as his hands began to slide up the backs of her legs, under her purple dress, she pulled away. "We should stop," she said. "I want to go to bed with you. But tonight, just to sleep. I would feel bad to do more just after telling Strickland we are break-ing up." In spite of his desire, he agreed. And liked Masha even more for saying it.

They slept in his small, single bed, Masha's head nestled in the crook of his arm, their legs woven together. For the first time since his father's death, Eric didn't wake up with the dawn but at seven o'clock, to the sound of his clock radio, which he always set just in case. At seven-thirty, as on every other morning, he rang the wake-up bell. But this time he knew that Masha, who still lay in the warm sheets of his bed, waiting until breakfast had begun to sneak back to her cabin, was listening, thinking of him. And although Eric knew perfectly well that sound traveled outward from its source in waves, that morning the pealing of the bell felt as if it emanated from two directions; it was a current that ran between him and Masha; Masha and him.

For the rest of the day the sensation continued—this sense that the two of them were tethered to each other, even when they were apart. Each time he saw her from afar, he felt as if a chord had just been strummed inside him, and the few brief times they were together, he couldn't stop smiling. The only blight on his happiness was the knowledge that Strickland was unhappy. Though Eric wasn't looking forward to it, he knew he had to talk with him as soon as possible. Maybe there was a chance they could remain friends.

He approached him after all-camp meeting that evening, as the campers rushed to the dining hall for dinner. Strickland had been all business: none of his usual corny jokes or "I can't hear you!" after he asked everyone how their day was.

"Can we talk?" Eric said.

Strickland made a few swift marks on the paper on his clipboard. "Not much to talk about, is there?"

"I guess not. I just wanted to say I'm sorry. I didn't try to convince her to break up with you, I swear. I just told her how I felt. It was driving me crazy, seeing you two together."

Strickland looked at him. Eric had forgotten just how bad his skin was—layer upon layer of acne scars, giving his jaw the texture of hardened oatmeal—and felt momentarily sorry for him.

"We're friends," Strickland said. "If you'd told me in the first place that you were so smitten, I would have stayed away."

"I'm sorry," said Eric. "I guess I didn't see the point. I didn't think she'd actually like me back."

Strickland shook his head. "You're an idiot, you know that? I could tell from the first day of camp that she was into you. I couldn't believe my luck that you didn't seem to like her back."

Eric couldn't think what else to say, so he said it again: "I'm sorry."

"It's not like it was serious or anything," Strickland said. "She's going back to Russia in a few weeks anyway. Neither of us will probably ever see her again."

Eric kept his eyes on the ground. Masha had already asked him, the night before, if he would come and visit her in Moscow after camp was over.

"Anyway, all's fair in love and war." Strickland held out his right hand. Eric took it, and as they shook, Strickland said, unsmiling, "Congratulations."

As they walked silently to the dining hall together, he thought to himself how much easier life would be if there were simply good guys and bad guys; the dark side of the force and the light.

More and more, it seemed, everyone, himself included, was a little bit of both.

≈

Over the next week, Eric and Masha stole as much time alone together as they could, taking walks around the lake or down the road, going into Waterville for pizza on Masha's nights off and sneaking to Eric's room during rest period to kiss and laugh and nap together in his bed. One of those times, he told her he was a virgin, and was both relieved and a little insulted when she told him that she wasn't surprised. It didn't matter, she said. She had only slept with one person herself, her longtime boyfriend Vlad. They'd broken up six months earlier, in part because he hadn't wanted her to come to America for the summer. They'd been together since they were fifteen years old, and had planned to marry one day. "But it wouldn't have been right," she said. "I am even surer of that now that I know you."

She told Eric there was no reason to rush into having sex. "And anyway," she said, laughing, squirming in the narrow bed in an attempt to get more comfortable, "I think it would be much nicer in a much bigger bed. And maybe in a room that doesn't smell like macaroni and cheese."

Eric would have been happy to make love to her standing up, in a vat full of macaroni and cheese—and told her this—but admitted that he also liked the idea of their first time being in a more romantic setting. Besides, as strong as his physical desire for her was, his desire simply to be with her was even stronger. In fact, it was overwhelming. After spending time with Masha, talking and listening so intently, Eric felt physically spent—almost as if they had made love (he supposed). It was the sweetest exhaustion imaginable.

And it was a relief. When Masha had been with Strickland, Eric had told himself that if he and Masha had ever gotten beyond flirtation and casual friendship, he would have been disappointed in her. What he thought he sensed behind her laughing, coquettish façade would prove to have been an illusion; a reflection of what he wished her to be and nothing more. He'd made the case to himself so convincingly that when they actually did get together a part of him was still braced for disappointment. But the more he got to know Masha, the more familiar she seemed to him; the more she was, in fact, the girl he'd hoped she would be.

He learned that her schoolmates used to make fun of her because she preferred to stay indoors reading and studying foreign languages than play outside. He learned about the university she was attending in Moscow, and the park across the street from her parents' apartment building where she liked to study, on a particular bench beneath a pine tree, whose needles she would brush from the seat before she sat down. He learned that her mother drank too much, that she had two nephews, and that she was very close with her grandmother, who lived in the same building as her family. "When she dies," Masha told Eric, "she'll be the first person I will lose that I will truly miss." She'd frowned then and let her hand rest lightly on his thigh. "But I suppose people do not always die in the order they should."

Eric, meanwhile, revealed his life to her as they strolled around the property. He showed her the stones in the woods behind the animal care area where the family pets were buried—barn cats and rabbits and a border collie-German shepherd mutt named Hubert. He sat with her on the boulders at the top of the meadow and told her about the cold February morning after his father had left their mother, when he and Jude built an igloo at the base of the meadow, by the brook, and Jude had tried to reassure him that everything was going to be fine—better, in fact, because their parents wouldn't fight anymore.

And then, one humid night at the beginning of the last

week of the session, he took Masha out on the lake in a row-boat and told her told her that the water was full of his father and Gail. He told her about the day they'd died: the state trooper. The morgue. The crushing task of telling his mother what had happened.

When he was finished, Masha came and sat next to him, the boat rocking precariously as she did. She put her arms around him and shushed him as if he were crying. It had the effect of bringing him close to actual tears.

"So I lost one father," he said, once he'd collected himself. "But I got another one."

"Sorry?" said Masha.

He told her about Dane, his mother, their secret.

"That's why I was so upset a couple weeks back. That and the fact that you were going out with Strickland."

Masha cupped Eric's face in her palms. "Poor Erichka," she whispered. "You must feel so confused."

He put his hands atop hers. Even in the sticky warmth of the night, they were cool. His Russian snow princess. "I am confused," he said. "I am, and on the other hand, I'm not."

"No?"

He peeled her hands from his face and held them on his lap. "Were you serious when you said you wanted me to come visit you in Russia?"

"Of course."

"Good," he said. He had an idea, the start of a plan. "I'm technically still a student at UMass," he began, thinking out loud. "And if I went back this fall, maybe I could apply to spend spring semester or next summer studying in Moscow."

Masha squeezed his hands. "Could you really?"

"I don't know," he said, and laughed. It was crazy, but already he was imagining himself in Moscow, walking down the pedestrian shopping street, the Arbat, holding Masha's hand. It seemed, suddenly, like the most obvious place in the world for him to go. He knew the language, he understood the culture, and now, he loved—or something close to it—a Russian woman. "I have no idea," he continued, "but I'll find out. There are exchange programs and fellowships. Internships. There's got to be a way. And if there's not, maybe I'll just come over anyway. I've got the money my dad left me. I could rent a room somewhere or live in a hotel. Maybe I could be an English tutor. You could help me get students, right?"

Masha nodded vigorously. "Of course, of course." Her brows knitted with sudden concern. "But what about your work here? Who will take care of this place? Abe can't do it alone, can he?"

"He'll have to hire someone, I guess," Eric said. "I don't know." He looked toward the shore. It was late, and only a few lights were still on—the floods mounted on the corners of the dining hall and the central lavatory; the dim yellow bulbs on the porches of the boys' cabins. They winked into view, then disappeared behind the trees, then winked again as the boat rocked. Farther beyond, he saw the windows of the farmhouse glowing with light and felt momentarily guilty. Not at the thought of Abe having to hire maintenance help—that wasn't so bad; the Crary brothers would probably be happy for the work—but at the thought of leaving him here alone.

Then again, lately Eric wasn't sure where Abe stood on the camp's future. Yesterday, he'd seen him walking around the property with a slick-looking guy in a bowling shirt, too young to be a parent and not the counselor type, either. But possibly the buyer type. When Eric asked Abe who it was, all he said was that it was a former camper who "happened to be in the neighborhood," and quickly changed the subject. A couple of weeks earlier, Eric might have been angered by his secretiveness. But now—now his own fate didn't seem so inextricably intertwined with Abe's decision.

"Abe will manage," he said. "And he'll understand." He had to. Wasn't he the one who was always telling Eric to leave Eden Lake?

"He loves you very much," Masha said. "I can tell. Your sister does, too."

"Half sister," Eric said.

Masha gave him a shove. The boat rocked beneath them. "Stop it," she said. "There is no half or whole. They are your family."

"I know," he said. It was strange, but he actually sort of liked the idea that his siblings were, in fact, his half siblings. There was something liberating about it.

"I think I need to take a break from my family for a while," he said. "Right now, I don't feel like being anybody's brother or anybody's son."

"How about somebody's boyfriend?" Masha said, leaning against him.

"Da," said Eric. He put his arm around her and drew her closer, breathing in the goldenrod smell of her hair. "That's exactly what I want to be.

Jude

THE FIRST COMPLETE RUN-THROUGH of the show was on Monday afternoon. And while it didn't go horribly—there were only a few missed entrances and fumbled lines, and only one mid-musical-number box-step collision—it didn't quite feel like a *show* yet. The sense of energy or flow or whatever it was that turned a sequence of scenes and musical numbers into something alive and whole wasn't there.

Only four girls had shown up to audition for the part of Annie after Lizzie had left, two of whom could barely carry a tune. Tanya, who'd been playing Pepper, one of the other orphans, was the only reasonable choice, and not an ideal one at that. Though her voice was powerful, her sense of pitch was not. And then there was fact that she was African American (one of only three black kids at the camp), which made the notion of putting her in a curly red wig somewhat absurd. Jude decided the best thing to do was to embrace the fact that Tanya was black and have her do it *sans* wig. It actually added an interesting socio-historical layer: sure, a white, Republican industrial tycoon in 1933 could feasibly fall for and adopt a white orphan. But imagine the social repercussions if he adopted a black child? Instantly, Daddy Warbucks became a much more complex character.

But Tanya would have none of it. "How will I look like Annie without the wig?"

"Annie's white," Jude told her. "You don't look like her anyway. This can be our own, modern interpretation."

Tanya pouted. "My Aunt Angie has red hair. And she's black."

"But she dyes it, right? A little black girl in the thirties, an orphan, wouldn't dye her hair. It just doesn't make sense."

"Daddy Warbucks would let her get it dyed. Just like he gets her the red dress."

"Tanya, please. Work with me here."

"Forget it," Tanya had said, and sat down on the edge of the stage. "If you won't let me wear the wig, I don't want to do it. It's discrimination."

"For Christ's sake, Tanya. Be reasonable."

Tanya had lifted her chin and folded her arms tight across her chest. She refused to move or speak until Jude relented.

Once the wig issue was settled, however, Tanya proved to be a hard worker and a fast learner. She sacrificed a trip to a Portland Seadogs game and an afternoon of tie dyeing to work with Jude and Tim in the rec. hall, reading through her lines and practicing her songs. But at Monday's run-through, she still had to carry the script around with her on stage, which didn't exactly stoke the confidence of the rest of the cast.

Jude gathered everyone together onstage after rehearsal. She'd always been up front with them about how they were doing—maybe too much so. If she'd stood there and told them that everything was hunky dory, they would have known she was full of it. But she knew she had to give them some kind of encouragement; something to feel good about.

"You're all doing a great job," she began. "You know your lines, you know your songs, you know your dance steps. But something's still missing. Anyone know what it is?"

Corey Marks from Jude's cabin, who played an unnamed orphan, shyly raised her hand. "Costumes?"

"Not exactly what I was thinking of," said Jude, "but yeah, you're right, costumes will definitely make things better. Because it's fun to wear costumes, right?"

"Not if you have to wear a bald cap," said Bobby Denzig.

Everyone laughed. "Thank you, Bobby," Jude said. "You just demonstrated the missing ingredient. It's *fun*, guys. You need to let yourselves have a little more fun. Because if you're not having fun, the audience won't either." Dear God, she sounded like a bad high school drama teacher. But Tim was nodding, as were a few of the kids.

And the next day's run-through—tech and full dress—was decidedly better. But it was also very, very silly. The pillow fight scene at the end of "It's a Hard Knock Life" got way out of hand, the boy playing Sandy at one point lifted up his hind leg and pretended to pee, and for some reason Jude couldn't fathom, Bobby Denzig had decided to say all his lines in a bad, vaguely Cockney accent. The more the other kids giggled in response, the more he played it up, until Jude actually had to stop the show and remind him that Daddy Warbucks was American, thanks.

That night, out at Jolly Roger's with Tim, Jen, Sergei and a few others, she drank a few more beers than she ought to have, and smoked too many Camels. But it was a much-needed release. When they were all good and drunk, they started singing: Will Tanya remember her entrances? *Maybe!* Will Sandy the dog come down with rabies? *Maybe!* By the end of the night, the bartender and a few locals were joining in, too: Will the Red Sox ever win the pennant? *Maybe!*

On the way back, in the darkness of the van, Sergei's hand found its way to Jude's leg. And although she'd sworn up and down to herself that she wasn't going to end the night fooling around with him, she let it rest there, and didn't protest as it traveled slowly, steadily upward over the course of the half-hour ride. By the time they rolled onto the property, she was horny as hell, and the next thing she knew, she and Sergei were in the boathouse, going at it in an inflatable raft.

"When you go back to New York," he asked as they lounged afterward, "will you tell Mitch that you have new boyfriend? Or am I your secret lover?" He said "secret lover" in a deep, breathy voice.

"Oh, Jesus, Sergei," Jude said. "We've been over this before. We're not boyfriend girlfriend. We're not lovers. We're friends who happen to screw sometimes. That's all."

Sergei sighed. "Yes, yes. I know." With considerable effort, and much squealing of rubber beneath him, he maneuvered onto his side. "Will we still be this kind of friends after camp?" he asked. "Because I was thinking maybe I will come to New York. I have a friend in Brooklyn. I could stay with him. Maybe look for job."

Jude gave him what she hoped was a kind smile. "I don't think so, Sergei."

"Because of Mitch?"

"Mitch," Jude repeated. Strange, how little thought she'd

given to him the past week.

Right after she'd replied to his email, she'd fantasized about what it would be like when she got back to New York: They would get a hotel room somewhere and spend a long afternoon and evening together, with take-out food and wine. They'd have sex and lie in bed laughing and talking. She wouldn't go back to her job, because it would be too difficult, too torturous for them to pretend all the time, so she'd take some time off and waitress while she looked for something else. Mitch would come to her apartment on his lunch breaks, and they'd have dinner at tiny restaurants in far, obscure corners of the city. Occasionally, he would call her late at night, desperate, whispering, "I have to see you. Can you meet me at…"

Now, all of that seemed like the self-indulgent fantasy of a teenager. Did she really want to be some man's mistress? And if, by chance, he actually did leave his wife for her, did she want everyone to forever think of her as the Other Woman?

"No, it's not because of Mitch," she told Sergei. "I don't think we're going to be getting back together. I just need to be alone for a while."

Sergei rolled onto his back, took a long drag from his cigarette, and shot the smoke straight upward. "Alone, alone, alone," he said. "I suppose I will stay here with Abe and Eric, then. Or perhaps I should find myself new girlfriend before camp ends, and she'll take me home with her." He laughed.

Jude laughed, too, though it irked her to think that his motivation with her all along might have been, in part, somewhere to go when camp ended. "Why don't you go home to Russia? You must have family and friends there who miss you. Women whose hearts you broke."

"Oh yes," said Sergei. "But I can't go back, of course. I left illegally, and I am here in U.S.A. illegally. I would be arrested if I tried to return."

"There's a new government, in case you hadn't heard."

He laughed, a puff of air through closed lips, and said, with a weariness in his voice that Jude had never heard before, "It does not matter. Russia is not my home anymore. I cannot go back. It's more complicated than you realize."

Jude moved closer to him and snuggled against his shoulder. "Try me."

"Ah, well, if you were my girlfriend, maybe I would," Sergei said. "But for two friends who may never see each other again, well…" He shrugged. "I think it is too long and sad a story to tell."

"Fair enough," Jude said. And though she felt the sting of rejection, she knew he was right. She couldn't have it both ways.

They lay together for a few more minutes, and then, almost simultaneously, they yawned and said it was getting late. Outside the boathouse, they hugged chastely, Jude even giving an "mm" of affection, the way her mother did whenever the two of them embraced. It felt right to hug Sergei this way; so right that it made everything else they'd done seem lewd and slightly ridiculous in retrospect.

As she watched him walk away, she considered going to him and telling him she was sorry for hurting him, if she had. Then again, the whole time, she'd been straight with him about her feelings and her intentions. Just because he'd wanted more from her didn't mean that she was obligated to give it to him.

He seemed to understand that.

≈

The day of the show—the second to last day of camp—was Carnival Day. There would be no rehearsal, just a quick "sing-through" of the major musical numbers before dinner. For the rest of the day, the kids were free to ruin their voices screaming at waterfront relay races, risk major injuries jumping on the inflatable moonwalk and set themselves up for a major blood-sugar crash by gorging themselves on ice cream, cotton candy and gummy-worms.

After doing her shift at the tattoo booth (whatever happened to face-painting?), inking hearts and roses and ersatz Celtic symbols onto countless sunburned limbs, Jude stopped by the dunking booth where Strickland was seated over the tank. At least a dozen campers waited in line for their chance to sink him, including Dahna Schwartz and Niedermeier, holding hands and not talking, like an old married couple. Meanwhile, nearby, Eric was helping a bunch of the Russian campers climb up onto the flatbed trailer behind the tractor for a hayride. Masha was among them, wearing Eric's old UMass cap. Jude didn't know exactly how he'd gone about winning her away from Strickland, but she was glad he had. She'd never seen him so happy.

Love was in the air. But not for her. And she was just fine with that.

"Hey Jude, did you go to the galley yet?"

Jude turned to see Corey Marks and Emily Stein, another girl from Shangri-la, their arms linked.

"Did I go to the what?"

Emily rolled her eyes. "The gallery. Whatever. In the dining hall. You have to come see our stuff!" They each grabbed one of Jude's hands, and yanked her down the lawn.

At the end of the session, the campers' arts and crafts projects were displayed on the walls, windows, and tables in the dining hall. The purpose of the "gallery" was two-fold: a chance for the kids to feel like their work was being celebrated, and a way to ensure that they took it all home with them. Anything that wasn't claimed by its creator by lunchtime the following day was up for grabs, and whatever was left after that was thrown away, in theory. In the old days, Jude and Abe sometimes took pity on particularly good or interesting abandoned works. Jude once rescued a little goggle-eyed pottery frog, glazed green and gold, and spackled it to a rock by the waterfront, where it remained for several summers.

Corey and Emily had both made pillows in fabric arts, Corey's covered with buttons (cute, but rather uncomfortable looking) and Emily's appliquéd with what looked like a pink light bulb with eyes and a tail. (A cat, supposedly.) Corey had also made a few impressive wheel-thrown pottery pieces, one of which she plucked up from the table and handed to Jude. It was a mug, vaguely hourglass-shaped, with a thick, curving handle. Most of it was glazed purple, but the inside was coated with thick black glaze that dripped out over the rim onto the outside, like some sort of viscous brew.

"This is really cool, Corey," Jude said, turning it in her hands.

"It's for you," Corey said. "I picked the colors because they reminded me of your nail polish."

"Really? You're sure you don't want to take it home?"

Corey shook her head. "Everything I made is a present for someone. They come out better that way."

She insisted that Jude try the mug out immediately, and Jude was at the water dispenser filling it when Abe suddenly appeared, looking concerned. "Hey," he said, "Some guy named Mitch is on the phone for you, and he says it's urgent."

Jude's stomach dropped: Had his wife found out? Had he lost his job?

She had a show to put on tonight. She didn't need this.

"This is the guy, isn't it? Your boss?" Abe's expression darkened from one of concern to one of anger. "You want me to tell him to fuck off? You shouldn't be mixed up with this dick, Jude."

Jude couldn't help smiling. She liked it when he got all big brotherly like this; it seemed like it had been a while since he had. "I know," she said. "Thanks."

But she took the call. More specifically, she told Mitch to call her back on the farmhouse line, so they could speak in private. The old black rotary phone that used to sit on the sideboard in the dining room had long since been replaced by a cordless, so she could have roamed while she talked, but she felt the need to stay firmly in one place. She sat at the dining room table, its every scratch and nick and bit of sticky residue clearly visible in the mid-afternoon sunlight filtering through the tall front windows.

"I miss you," was the first thing Mitch said.

"I miss you too," Jude said, then wished she hadn't. "What's going on?"

"I just needed someone to talk to. I'm—I don't know. I'm a mess. I think I'm going to leave Anika. Not because of us or anything. I mean, of course it's all related, but I'm not saying I want to…"

"I get it. You're not leaving her for me," Jude said. "That's good. I wouldn't want you to." She was about to say more—that she didn't think they should see each other when she got back—but he cut her off.

"I'm so confused, Jude. We had this nasty fight last night, and I realized that…well, let me back up a little. It really started last week, when I was supposed to pick Jack up from school, and…"

As he started speaking, the light in the room changed—a cloud must have moved over the sun—like a fast-motion film of daylight turning into dusk. The white of the walls went from warm to cool and the veneer of the dining room table went dull and it seemed like maybe everything would just keep getting darker and darker, until the whole world was the color of the inside of Jude's new mug, which sat before her, half-filled with water she couldn't even see. "Mitch," she said, "Stop."

"What?"

"I can't do this. I can't be the person you talk to about this stuff."

"But there isn't anyone else. All of Anika's and my friends are mutual."

"I'm sorry, but you have to find someone. It can't be me."

There was a brief pause, and Jude thought, good, he understood. He realized that she was right. And then: "What the hell, Jude? We were friends before we fucked, as I recall. Or was that all you were after? Hey, gee, maybe it would be fun to seduce an older man, just to see if I can…"

"Jesus, Mitch, you know that's not—"

"I thought you actually gave a damn about me."

"Of course I do," said Jude, "but that doesn't mean—"

"You know what, forget it. I don't know what I was think-ing calling you anyway. You're just a kid."

Jude took a deep breath in through her nose, and let it out. A "cleansing breath," her mother might have called it. "Yeah, that's right," she said. "A kid who's evidently a lot more mature than you."

She hung up the phone and walked out the front door of the farmhouse, sat down on the sun-warmed granite step, and hugged her knees close. She expected to start crying, but instead found herself smiling like a lunatic, the corners of her mouth trembling, feeling happier than she had in ages. What-ever it was she'd just done, it was exactly right.

She was still sitting there a few minutes later when she heard a car coming up the dirt road. It turned out to be a silver Saturn, and at first Jude thought it might be the parents of one of her cast members, up to see the show. She stood, planning to introduce herself, but as the driver emerged from the car, she saw that it wasn't parent at all. It was Aura.

Not the usual Aura, though. In her sunglasses, shorts, and baggy University of New Hampshire T-shirt, her hair in a messy ponytail, she looked like a celebrity out running an er-rand incognito. She seemed paler, and maybe a little thinner.

"Hey," Jude said, "welcome back." She ought to have been cooler toward her, she supposed, after the way she'd left Abe in the lurch, but it didn't seem worth the effort. Strangely, she was glad to see her.

Aura lowered her small, black carry-on case to the ground and pushed her sunglasses up onto her head. "Hey," she said, smiling warily. "You're in a good mood."

Jude realized that she was still grinning like an idiot. "Yeah, well, I just told my boss—the one I was stupid enough to screw—to go to hell."

Aura clapped her fingertips to the heel of her hand in polite applause. "Congratulations. Good call."

"Thank you," said Jude. It was unexpectedly gratifying to have Aura's approval. "What are you doing back here?"

"Your Mom called me," Aura said. "She said she thought you guys might need a hand, since she can't help out the next few days. And I've been feeling like sort of an asshole for taking off without saying goodbye to any of the staff, or the kids. So," she shrugged. "Here I am. But just for the weekend," she quickly added. "I have to be back at work on Monday."

"Did Abe know you were coming?"

"I left a message." She glanced away, then pulled her sunglasses back down over her eyes. "Did he tell you anything about why I left?"

"He said it was some kind of family emergency," Jude said. "But I wondered if maybe it had to do with Matt. I know you'd said you guys were having a hard time."

Aura nodded quickly. "Yeah, that's right."

"I take it things are better now?"

"Well, no," she said, her voice contracting. "They're over, actually."

"Oh, Aur, I'm really sorry." Jude was surprised at the depth of sympathy she felt, given how odious Matt had seemed the one time she'd met him. But Aura was clearly hurting.

"Thanks," she said. "It's a good thing in the long run, though, believe me. Like you and your boss." She tucked a curling tendril of hair that had escaped from her ponytail behind her ear, then smiled wearily. "You and me both deserve a hell of a lot better."

Bettah.

Jude smiled back.

≈

Before the show, the whole cast and crew gathered on the stage and stood in a circle. In their stage makeup—orangey foundation (except for Tanya), dark eyeliner, circles of rouge on their cheeks—the kids looked like images on a TV with the color turned up too high. To the audience, of course, they'd look more or less normal. The stage crew, in their black t-shirts and pants, looked appropriately inconspicuous and professional. Everyone was twitchy with energy and quick to laugh. The bell summoning people to the rec. hall had rung, and on the other side of the curtain, the sound of voices grew gradually from a murmur to a hum to a crackling buzz. Jen reminded the kids to smile while they danced, and not to look at their feet. Tim reminded them to sing out, annunciate, don't forget to breathe. Jude gave a few reminders about entrances and quick costume changes, told the main actors to say their lines even louder and more slowly than they felt like they should, then thanked everyone for all their hard work.

"It's going to cost me a buck to say this, but I'm going to say it anyway," she said. "This show is going to kick ass." The kids laughed and smiled, and seemed to grow a little bit taller and more confident in front of Jude's eyes. Such was the power of talking to children like they were adults. "Before we start, there's just one last thing I want to do. And actually, this was an idea I got from one of our cast members." She looked at Corey. "Do you remember what you said to me today about all the arts and crafts you make?"

Corey gave an uncertain grimace. "That they're presents?"

"Right," said Jude. "You said everything you make, you make as a present for someone. And that makes them come out better. So tonight, I want everyone to think of this performance as a present for someone. Your Mom and Dad or one of your friends in the audience. Or maybe someone who's not even here. Your grandmother, your next-door neighbor, your cat. Whoever. Just take a minute, and let's all close our eyes, and think about that person."

"Or animal," someone said.

Jude watched everyone close their eyes, then closed her own. Though she didn't say anything about joining hands, someone must have started it, because simultaneously, Tim, standing next to her, took her right hand, and Tanya, on the other side, took her left.

"While you're doing the show tonight," she continued, "think about your performance as your gift to them. If we all do it, the show will be great." She opened her eyes. Everyone was bobbing their heads, eyes still closed—some squeezed tight. "You can open your eyes now."

There was an awkward moment of silence. They all seemed to expect her to say something else, but she had nothing. She turned to Tim. "Anything you'd like to add?"

"Yes," he said. "Break a leg, people!" He started applauding, and everyone joined in, then Bobby Denzig got everyone to crowd together and put a hand into the middle of the circle for a big football-style huddle and whoop.

While the kids scattered to the wings and the stage crew checked to make sure everything was in place for the opening scene, Tim said to Jude, "That was really great."

"Yeah, everyone seems pumped."

"No, no, I mean the gift thing. That was a really nice idea."

"Thanks."

"And let me guess," he said, mischief edging into his voice. "You're doing it for Sergei?" Tim was the only person on staff besides Eric who knew about her liaisons with Sergei, and only because he'd guessed.

She smiled, and was about to quip, "of course, who else?" but stopped. "Actually, you know what?" she said. "I think this one's for me. Is that allowed?"

Tim shrugged. "It was your idea. You get to make up the rules."

"Yeah, all right then," Jude said. "This one's for me."

Abe

Dear Abe,

How are you. Micmac sucks. The counsilers here are really mean and all but 6 of the other kids are jerks and to competatave. The 6 kids I like are Shawn, Mike P, Mike R, Alberto, Nick and Jona. One of my counselors is OK to, his name is Martin and he's black. The other things I like here are the soccer field (better than yours), doing archery (you should get archery) and a pool instead of a lake. But the rest sucks. There's no staned glass. You have to take swimming and you have to finish all your food or you don't get desert and you have to say the plegde of allegance everyday at the flag pole before breakfast. If you don't say the pledge you get in trouble = NOT FREE SPEECH!! We had a dance with a girl's camp last night and the girls were all hot but snobs. Theres this anoying kid here named Harris and noone likes him and yesterday a kid I hate named Brent called him a fag and I told him he should not say that he should say homo-sexual. I thought you'd be glad to here that. So tell everyone at E.L. I say yo and stay cool.

Sincerly,
Jeremy Dyer
PS – Sorry I peerced my ear.

Jeremy's letter came on the last day of camp. During a brief, blessed pause in the onslaught of phone calls from parents calling to confirm or change or complain about their child's travel arrangements, Abe read it aloud to Aura.

Having her back in the office today, it was almost as if she'd never left; as if nothing had ever happened between them. She wasn't as nervous or awkward as he might have expected her to be, though when he'd hugged her the day before, when she first arrived, she made a point of keeping everything from her shoulders down a good two feet away. And that night at the staff cabin, where the B-shift, including Jude, Jen and Tim, toasted the success of the camp show with many a beer, she'd kept her distance from him.

He learned from Jude that she and Matt had broken up, but knew better than to mention it. He wondered if she'd confessed to Matt that she'd cheated on him, and if that was what led to the split. He'd probably never know for sure, and it was just something he'd have to live with—the guilt of knowing that he might have been part of the cause of the break-up of a serious relationship. Not a particularly healthy relationship, from what he'd gathered, but a relationship nonetheless.

"Cute," Aura said, in response to Jeremy's letter. She was at the collating counter, sorting through camper travel forms. "Let's hope he doesn't turn out like his dad."

"No kidding," Abe said. He scanned the boyishly crooked writing on the page again. Who knew; maybe Jeremy would turn out OK. Maybe he'd mature into a thoughtful and caring person, and maybe Eden Lake would have played some small part in it. It was gratifying on some level. But how much difference would it really make?

His father would have said that it had the potential to make a huge difference. That was the whole idea behind Eden Lake: that children would take what they'd learned here and pass it along to others and the ripple effect would, ultimately, change the world. The end of war, injustice, intolerance—it all began with teaching children about community, kindness, and respect for one another. On some level, Abe agreed.

But when his parents started Eden Lake, a whole generation was trying to save the world. They were singing songs and staging sit-ins, burning bras and draft cards, marching on Washington. In that kind of atmosphere, you could believe that even a bunch of privileged kids making pottery and canoeing in the middle of Maine were part of a larger and more important movement; a sea-change of consciousness in the world. You could believe almost anything.

Social change wasn't like that today. Today, people talked tactics and strategies and measurable results. Venture Philanthropy and ROI. Best practices. Benchmarks. The causes were still lofty—like the ones AfterStart was committed to. But the method was stripped down and pragmatic. It didn't inspire anthems or mass movements; didn't have a spokesperson or a zeitgeist to speak of, or fashion statements and pop culture phenomena associated with it.

In a way, Abe realized, it was much less about the helpers, and a lot more about the helpees. Which seemed like a pretty good thing.

The phone rang, and Aura darted over to her desk to answer it. After she'd asked who was calling, she held the receiver to her chest and said to Abe in a low voice, "Someone named Brendan Baker?"

"Tell him I'm not here," Abe whispered. "I'll call him back."

Aura politely disposed of the call. "Who was that?" she asked. "He sounded like a salesman."

Abe smiled. "He was a camper here back in the eighties. He was here the other day to check the place out. He's interested in buying it." This was the first time Abe had told anyone.

"Really?" said Aura, jerking her chin inward. "Since when did you decide to sell?"

Abe plucked up a paperclip from his desk and started to unbend it. "Well, it's become pretty clear to me over the past couple of weeks that being here, running this place, probably isn't the best thing for me right now. I'm not exactly thinking straight." He kept his eyes down on his paperclip to avoid Aura's—for her sake. He knew any reference to what they'd done, no matter how oblique, would embarrass her.

"So, you think you're going to sell to this Brendan person?" she asked, returning to the collating table. He could tell from the stiffness in her voice that she was embarrassed anyway.

"I don't know," Abe said. "I'm not really sure I like him."

But of course, he did know, and he was sure. He would never sell Eden Lake to Brendan Baker. Every time he thought about it—even in his coolest, most rational moments, when he could think of a dozen reasons why selling the camp would be an excellent idea—when he imagined actually sitting across a table from Brendan Baker, signing Eden Lake away to him, his whole being balked. He could almost taste the regret.

"I'm sure you could find someone else if you start spreading the word," Aura said. "What about Strickland? He'd be a pretty good director, right?"

"He would," said Abe. But it was unlikely that Strickland would be able to come up with the money. During the year, he worked as a sixth grade teacher in the Portland public schools, and was still saddled with college debt. He came from a blue-collar family; his father was a crane operator for a shipbuilding company.

Then again, who was to say that the director and the owner had to be the same person? There was no reason Abe couldn't hire someone to run the camp for a while. He could still serve in an advisory role, as needed. And if he ever did want to come back and run the camp someday, he could.

Someday when he could be sure he was doing it for the right reasons.

Aura held up a mint-green photocopied form. "Why is Ashley Wise Bliman listed for the van to Portland airport? She's supposed to be on the New York–New Jersey bus."

"Change of plans," Abe said. "She's flying to meet her parents on vacation in London instead."

"Oh, well la-di-da," said Aura. She replaced the form, then gathered up a stack of folders in one arm and started to go. "Well, I'm off to go track down the international campers."

"Sure. Hey, Aura?" said Abe. "Don't say anything to Eric or Jude about this selling the camp business, OK? Things have been kind of crazy the past couple of weeks, and I haven't actually had a chance to talk to them about it. Cool?"

Aura, at the door, drew pinched fingers across closed, smiling lips, twisted, and threw away the key.

≈

The last night of camp was a traditional Maine lobster dinner with steamers and drawn butter, corn on the cob, cole
slaw and fresh lemonade. There was lasagna for vegetarians and
campers who kept kosher or were grossed out by the idea of
eating an animal that actually looked like one. Although this
meal had been an Eden Lake tradition for as long as Abe could
remember—a tradition he'd always enjoyed—tonight, something about it seemed excessive. Maybe it was the white table-
cloths that the kitchen staff had put out. Or maybe it was the
fact that with the exception of Niedermeier in khaki pants and
a white collared shirt, and Abe himself, freshly showered and in
his least faded jeans, nobody had dressed up for the occasion,
even a little.

But by the time dusk had fallen and people started gath-
ering for the final campfire, some of the sense of weight and
ceremony Abe had always associated with the last night had
begun to descend. Notebooks, autograph books and T-shirts
were passed around for signing. Kids scrambled in and out of
groups for photographs. And once the program began, everyone was more sedate than usual: the boys didn't perform "light
shows" on the tree trunks with their flashlights, or beam them
into their bunkmates' eyes. The girls refrained from whispers
and giggles during skits and stories and even, miraculously, the
comically mispronounced, off-key, a capella rendition of "The
Rose" that one of the Russian girls sang. ("Soom say laf, it eez
a reevah…")

Toward the end of the evening, as was the tradition, Abe
invited campers and staff to express their thanks or appreciation
for someone or something that had made the last four weeks
memorable. There was no need to raise hands, and no need

for applause, Abe explained; anyone who wanted to should simply stand and speak. Strickland began, with a thank-you to all of the campers, for being enthusiastic and cooperative participants in camp activities. Bart, the ropes course instructor, thanked B.J. Soper, a diminutive, curly-headed nine-year-old boy, for reminding him that you could do anything you set your mind to. After repeated tries, B.J. had managed to make the leap from the high platform to the trapeze—something most full-sized campers never pulled off. A boy thanked the lifeguards for teaching him how to dive; a girl thanked Clover, the horse she'd ridden all summer, for being such a great horse. Oak thanked Abe for Free Speech. "It was really great to have a forum for discussing important stuff," he said.

Chuck Niedermeier was the next to stand. "I was going to also thank Abe for Free Speech, but Oak beat me to it," he said, then gave a clumsy, soundless "shucks" snap of fingers. A few counselors chuckled, causing him to beam. "Yeah," he said, and did the snap again, even less successfully. "And I also wanted to thank the kitchen staff—are any of them here?" Niedermeier tented his palm over his eyes and scanned the crowd. "For all the food they made for us, and especially the raisin bran, which I guess they didn't make, but which they ordered, I assume, and which was a really good variety. Oh, and thank you to everyone for being so careful with my binoculars when I let you borrow them."

As he sat back down, a boy, Abe wasn't sure who, said, in a nasal voice muffled behind a hand, "And I want to thank Niedermeier for finally shutting up."

There was laughter, but also a few disdainful "tsk"s. A girl on the other side of the campfire ring—Ashley, maybe?—said,

"You're such a jerk, Jeff," and seconds later the boy was being escorted away from the fire by his counselor.

Abe raised his hand to quiet the group, still murmuring and tittering, and after a few moments silence descended. Rather, what descended was the sacred non-silence of the campfire: the shifting of charred wood, the hissing of flame, the popping of sparks. Abe kept his hand aloft, as if in benediction.

This was when his father would have made his traditional closing speech. The one urging everyone to take the spirit of Eden Lake home with them; to spread it to their family and their friends and everyone they encountered so that it would, in turn, spread around the world. Abe could have recited it nearly word for word. He had planned to. But as he stood up and drew breath to speak, he felt suddenly weak with grief. Weak and bone weary, as if he'd been carrying a great weight for many, many miles. All he wanted to do was lie down somewhere dark and warm and sleep for days on end.

He scanned the crowd for his family. There was Jude, in the first row, flanked by her campers, firelight flickering on their faces. Eric was on the other side of the fire, next to Masha and the Russian campers. Aura sat just behind them, next to Sergei. His mother wasn't there, and Abe felt a pang of regret for having sent her away—it would have been nice to see her tonight. But it also might have made it harder for him to say good-bye to Eden Lake, which was what he was doing tonight, inwardly if not publicly.

He suspected that Jude and Aura, and maybe even Eric, were doing the same.

"As you all know," he said at last, "just before the summer started, my father and stepmother, Clay and Gail, the directors of the camp, died in a plane crash. For those of us who knew and loved them, including many of you, it's been a difficult time. But the one thing my dad and Gail would have wanted most was for things at Eden Lake to go on as usual. So wherever they are, if they're watching, I'd guess they'd be pretty happy right about now, seeing us all here around the campfire, singing and telling stories and expressing our appreciation for one another. They'd be glad to know that you all had a good time here this summer. Which I think you did. I hope you did." His voice began to break. "Thanks."

He sat back down to soft but persistent applause. Twice, just as he thought it was about to end, it strengthened and continued.

Strickland caught Abe's eye and gestured toward the milk crates at his feet, full of white candles and round paper drip shields. "Now?" he mouthed.

Abe nodded. "Now."

The CITs began distributing the candles and shields to the campers and Strickland explained how the candlelight farewell ceremony worked: Abe would light his candle from the campfire, then light the candles of all the other non-cabin staff members present, who would stand in line next to him. Then, one by one, cabin by cabin, as Strickland called their names, each camper and counselor would begin making their way down the line, saying goodbye to each person, then touch their candle to that of the last person in the line, and take their place at the end. They would keep going until the line stretched all the way down the path alongside the lake, and onto the main lawn. At the end, they'd form a giant circle of light.

"I know everyone wants a chance to say goodbye to everyone, but try to keep things moving so we don't have a big traf-fic jam," Strickland said, over the rising din of voices. Campers were starting to stand up, restless and eager, in spite of their counselors' efforts to keep them sitting down.

"And the idea, folks," Abe shouted, raising his hand over his head, "is to keep this quiet, please. Keep your voices low." He crouched and thrust a long stick from the kindling pile into the embers until it caught fire, used it to light his candle, then took his position at the entrance to the campfire ring.

Eric came and stood in front of him. "Are you OK?" he asked.

"No," said Abe. "But I will be. Thanks."

To Abe's surprise, Eric put his arms around him and gave him a brief but firm hug. "Thanks for understanding about my going on the trip with Masha," he said.

"I'm happy for you," said Abe. "We'll have a lot to talk about when you get back."

Eric nodded, then held out his candle for Abe to light.

The nurse, the kitchen staff, the stained glass teacher, and Sergei came next, followed by Aura. "Goodbye until five a.m. tomorrow," she said to Abe. They'd both have to be up at the crack of dawn to get the campers with early flights onto the first airport van. The first charter bus, destination Cherry Hill, New Jersey, would arrive at six and be on the road by seven. "Don't forget to set an alarm."

"Gee, thanks," said Abe. "I hadn't thought of that."

"You're welcome, dickweed," she said with a smile.

The campers began filing past, then, some uttering nothing more than a quick, obligatory, "have a good year," eyes trained on the ground, others—girls, mostly—throwing their arms

around Abe's neck and crying in artificially pinched voices that
this had been the best summer of their lives. Oak shook Abe's
hand and told him he really hoped to come back next year as a
CIT. "That is, if you're still running the place," he added.

"Why wouldn't I be?" Abe asked.

Oak smiled cryptically. "I don't know. You look like maybe
you could use a break."

Abe gave the top of Oak's head gentle swipe. "See you
'round, man."

As the string of flickering lights grew, stretching along the
path toward the lawn, the campers moved more quickly past
Abe and the others at the head of the line, eager to find their
friends and get their candles lit. Once everyone had made it
through the procession, Strickland herded them into a giant,
slightly lopsided circle on the main lawn and Katie Magnus
strummed on her guitar, leading the group in "Kumbaya." One
stanza into the song, some of the older campers began landing
hard on the first syllable, pronouncing it so it rhymed with
"drum" instead of "boom." The joke caught on, and soon it
sounded like the whole camp was singing "Cum-baya." Some
of the older girls were doubled over, snorting with hysterical
laughter. Strickland looked to Abe for instruction, but Abe just
shrugged and smiled wearily. There was nothing they could do.
And who knew what the hell "kumbaya" meant, anyway?

≈

It took Abe and Jude just under an hour to get to the field—
a pasture, actually, part of a dairy farm called Birch Hill. Jude
was quick to note that there were no birches in sight; fir trees,
mostly, and a few big oaks. A tire swing dangled from the lowest

branch of one of them, alongside the house. The dirt beneath it was littered with toys. Chickens strutted and pecked nearby.

As it turned out, Birch Hill was named not for its vegetation, but for the family that owned it. The man who answered when Abe knocked on the farmhouse door introduced himself as Hugo Birch. He was big and ruddy, his broad chin shaded by a few days' stubble. "I was wondering if you folks might show up sometime," he said. "Your brother here with you? Nice kid. I met him the day of."

Eric was the only one in the family who'd been here before, on the day after the accident, when they hauled the wreckage away.

"No," said Abe, "Just my sister." He nodded back toward the car where Jude waited, leaning against the hood. She lifted a hand in greeting.

It had taken some serious campaigning on Abe's part to convince her to come here with him today. She'd planned on getting a ride back down to New York with Tim yesterday, when most of the staff left. She finally caved when Abe promised to drive her back down himself at the end of the week. "And then I'll camp out in your apartment for a couple of nights and make sure you don't call that dick boss of yours." She'd liked that.

"You two want a glass of iced tea?" Hugo Birch asked Abe.

He kicked gently at the stoop. "Thanks, you're real nice to offer, but I think we'd rather just…" He let his voice trail off, hoping Hugo would jump in, but he just stared. "Well, sure," Abe said. "Why not. Jude, come on up here a sec."

Hugo retreated into the dimness of the farmhouse and returned a couple of minutes later with two tumblers full of muddy brown liquid. Abe's glass had Tweety Bird painted on it, and Jude's Yosemite Sam. "Sorry, they're the kids'. The only clean ones I could find," he explained with a sheepish smile. "My wife and them are up visiting her sister up in Dover for the week and I'm a little behind on dishes."

"It's no problem," Abe said. "I always liked Tweety Bird."

Hugo smiled, and seemed to soften, as if all this time he'd been holding his breath. "So, this camp that your father ran. You running it now?"

"I am," said Abe, for the sake of simplicity.

"My wife and I were thinking maybe our daughter Jenny would like something like that for a couple weeks next summer. Swimming and horseback riding and stuff. How much you charge?"

"Um," Abe rattled the ice in his glass. "You know, I'm not even sure exactly. I don't really handle—"

"It's a six-week program, and it's around four thousand bucks," said Jude. She glanced at Abe. "Right?"

"Right," he said. More like five thousand, actually.

The color drained from Hugo's face. "Oh. Well, what about for just a week?"

"Unfortunately, we don't usually offer that option," Abe said. "At least we haven't in the past. But it's possible that—"

Now Hugo did jump in. "Sure, sure. I understand." He held out his hands for their glasses. "You probably want to get on down to the site."

He led them silently across the road, to the dirt yard in front of the milking barn. Cicadas clicked in the tall grass by the roadside, and the Holsteins closest to the fence lowed softly. Abe expected at any moment to hear the sound of a plane's

engine come ripping through the pastoral quiet. The sky overhead was perfectly blue, with only a few, compact fair-weather
clouds, just like that day. If his father and Gail had come down
in hail and thunder and wind, or even a heavy fog, Abe wondered, would their deaths have seemed less cruel?

"I was right here tinkering with my Deere when it happened," Hugo said, and thumbed over his shoulder at the
mud-spattered tractor behind him. "The plane came in from
the southwest, over there,"—he pointed over the roof of the
barn—"at a real steep angle. He probably saw the pasture and
was trying to land, but I don't think he had much control at
that point." Hugo put his arms out to his sides and tilted back
and forth, indicating the motion of the wings. "Went down
right over there, just at the edge of the tree line." Now he
pointed over the heads of his cows, down the pasture toward
the woods. "You bring something you wanted to put up?" He
looked to Jude, who looked back at him, uncomprehending.

"You mean like a marker or something," Abe said. "No.
We didn't." He felt callous for not having brought anything; a
plaque, some flowers.

"My wife nailed a little cross up. I hope that's OK with you
folks. She was pretty shaken up by the whole thing."

"Of course," Abe said.

Hugo led them through the milking barn and out the back
door into the pasture. "Take your time," he said, then turned
and left.

The ground was knobby and uneven: hillocks of tamped-
down, muddy grass; hard-packed, damp dirt cut with hoof
marks; partially exposed boulders, most of their bulk still buried beneath the earth. Abe and Jude made their way slowly

down the gentle slope toward the woods at the far end of the pasture, stepping carefully to avoid cow pies and divots.

"Why did you tell him how much it cost?" Abe asked Jude.

"Why not?"

"It's embarrassing. Now he probably thinks were a couple of rich assholes."

She snorted. "Like he didn't already? Our father crashed his private plane into his farm. Anyway, I thought maybe you'd offer them a scholarship or something." She cursed as she teetered and almost fell over the rotting remains of a log, and Abe caught her by the elbow.

"It's not a bad idea," he said. "But it may not be up to me."

Jude stopped, turned, and looked at him questioningly.

He sighed and stuffed his hands into his pockets. He didn't particularly want to talk about this now, and regretted broaching the subject. He'd come here to think about his father, not the camp. He was determined—today, in this moment, if nothing more—to keep the two separate.

"I'm thinking about hiring someone else to run the place for a while. Until I—until we—decide what we want to do long-term."

"Who?"

"I don't know. Strickland, maybe, if he's interested. I haven't really thought through the details yet. But let's not talk about this now. I shouldn't have brought it up." He resumed walking, and Jude followed.

"I think it's a good idea," she said after a moment. "I thought maybe you were going to say you wanted to sell it. But I'm kind of glad you didn't. Believe it or not. Hey, look. We're here."

In front of them, over a swath of earth about forty feet long and twenty feet wide that stopped at the edge of the woods, the top layer of earth looked as if it had been scraped away, revealing rocky, almost sandy soil below. A few saplings at the edge of the woods had been snapped in half, folded over like broken toothpicks. A length of wire fencing right along the tree line, had been recently replaced, and tacked to one of the fence posts was the cross Hugo had mentioned. Except there was more than that. In addition to a white, plastic cross, Hugo's wife had put up a wreath of yellow and blue silk flowers, and a small picture frame containing Clay and Gail's obituaries from the *Kennebec Journal*. Moisture had found its way behind the glass, encircling the clipping in a fog of tiny condensation bubbles.

"I'm glad there's something here to mark the spot," said Abe. "And the broken trees, and these." He motioned to the remains of the heavy-duty tire tracks leading from the swath of scraped earth up toward the road. From the truck they used to haul the wreckage away, he assumed. "It would have been worse if it looked like nothing had happened."

"I guess we should have brought something," Jude said, straightening the frame on the post. "But it's not like it's a grave. We're not going to come back here again. I'm not, anyway."

Abe sat down on the dirt and hooked his arms around his knees. "I probably won't either. I just felt like I needed to see it once."

He had the idea that coming here would make the whole thing feel more real somehow. All he wanted in his life right now was what was real; things he could see and touch and feel. He was eager to return to the routine and certainty he'd left behind in Washington. Even the material accoutrements of his life would be a welcome sight, in their simple solidness: his books, his bed, the beat-up brown oxfords he wore to work most days.

"It's still kind of hard to believe they're gone, isn't it?" Jude said. She came and sat down on the dirt next to him. "Sometimes I still feel like maybe they're just on a trip or something, and they're coming back."

"Yeah," he said, "but it's starting to sink in."

"It is."

Abe closed his eyes and turned his face up to the sun. "That sun feels good," he said.

"Mmm," said Jude. "In L.A. it's gonna be sunshine all the time."

"L.A.?" said Abe. "Who's going to L.A.?"

"Me, maybe. I've been thinking maybe I'll try to go back to school. Get an MFA in scenic design. UCLA's got a good program."

"Wow," Abe said. This was good. He was proud of her, even for considering such a move. But she would know that. "Jude in L.A.," he said, and shook his head with mock pity. "You'll have to get a whole new wardrobe. Maybe dye your hair blonde. Start tanning."

Jude made a throaty, exasperated sound. "L.A.'s not all like that," she said. "It happens to have a kick-ass theater scene. I know a few people out there."

"You'll miss the seasons," Abe said. "The snow, the cold, the misery."

"I'll come back and visit."

"You'd better."

A soft breeze swept down over the pasture, carrying on it the clink of cowbells, ruffling the leaves of the trees, exposing their pale undersides. There was a touch of coolness in the air, and for a brief moment Abe thought, with resignation and a little relief, *fall is on its way.* Then he remembered that, in fact, it was only the second week of August.

There was still a lot of summer left.

Notes and Acknowledgements

THIS IS A WORK of fiction. The places and people depicted herein are the products of my imagination. Camp Eden Lake— I'm sorry to say, for those who are ready to sign up their kids or apply for a job—is not a real place. It is, however, inspired by some of the Maine summer camps I attended and that my parents worked at or ran during my childhood.

I offer my heartfelt thanks to the many people who helped and encouraged me throughout this project: Armand Inezian and Erika Dreifus, for bringing me into the Last Light Studio fold; Erin Almond, Jami Brandli, Rebecca Morgan Frank, Ellen Litman and Jessica Murphy Moo, talented writers all, who provided invaluable feedback and encouragement as I was writing this book; Steve Almond, for his wise counsel and good chocolate; Stephanie Cabot, who believed in this book and persevered valiantly on its behalf; Lori Salmeri for her design genius; Mara Brod for a truly fun photo shoot with marvelous results; Tom Simons and everyone at PARTNERS+simons for making generous accommodations to support my fiction writing jones; Grub Street Writers, the heart of my writing community; my *Baby Squared* readers, for their virtual friendship; my parents and in-laws, for their loving support; Elsa and Clio, for being good sleepers and the lights of my life; and most of all, Alastair, my best reader and best friend.